D0259763

Errors of Judgment

By Caro Fraser

THE CAPER COURT SERIES

The Pupil
Judicial Whispers
An Immoral Code
A Hallowed Place
A Perfect Obsession
A Calculating Heart
Breath of Corruption
Errors of Judgment

a&b

Errors of Judgment

CARO FRASER

Allison & Busby Limited
12 Fitzroy Mews
London W1T 6DW
www.allisonandbusby.com

First published in Great Britain by Allison & Busby in 2013.

A CIP catalogue record for this book is available from the British Library.

First Edition

ISBN 978-0-7490-1472-8

Typeset in 11/16 pt Sabon by
Allison & Busby Ltd.

The paper used for this Allison & Busby publication has been produced from trees that have been legally sourced from well-managed and credibly certified forests.

Printed and bound by
CPI Group (UK) Ltd, Croydon, CR0 4YY

For Geraldine and Joan, with love

CHAPTER ONE

Friday was one of those rare October days, a wistful reprise of summer, the sky a sharp, pellucid blue, the sun falling warm upon the cobbled courtyards of the Temple and gilding the autumn roses in Inner Temple Gardens. Its unexpected warmth had enticed the lawyers and clerks from their chambers and offices at lunchtime to bask on the benches with their sandwiches and stroll about the gravel walks, but now at four o'clock, as the shadows of the plane trees began to lengthen on the grass, a chill reminder of autumn was creeping into the air behind the fading sunshine.

In The Royal Courts of Justice in the Strand, Mr Justice Cable was delivering himself of his deliberations in the matter of *Kirkbride and Others v. Texmax Holdings Inc.*, an *inter partes* hearing of a motion whereby the plaintiffs sought an extension of an injunction previously granted against the defendants to prevent them from disposing of certain company shares, pending trial. The dusty fingers of afternoon light which played across the judge's pudgy features made him look like some bewigged cherub of advancing years.

Leo Davies QC, appearing for the plaintiffs, was pretty much certain of success, and sat slumped in his seat, only half-listening.

'—I come now to the balance of convenience,' intoned Mr Justice Cable. 'Miss Lightfoot stressed that the onus in this regard was upon Kirkbride, which is of course correct, but – and in my view again plainly rightly – she accepted that if the injunction were to be refused, there would be serious difficulties in Kirkbride enforcing any specific performance order it might obtain at the trial. In addition, if Kirkbride is left to its remedy in damages, the history of the matter indicates that Texmax has limited funds available and it is unlikely that any money judgment would be satisfied . . .'

Leo leant back, stifling a yawn, adjusting his barrister's wig slightly on the silver hair of his head. It was a peculiar feature, this silver-grey hair on a man still only in his forties, and contrasted strangely with his youthful features, his square-jawed good looks and sharp blue eyes. He made a couple of desultory notes and let his thoughts wander. Today's glorious spell of Indian summer had made him restless. He'd spent the last month slaving over a difficult joint venture dispute, which he'd settled on favourable terms just that morning, and he felt he deserved a break, to get away from the City before autumn turned to winter and the nights grew long. It had hardly been a satisfactory summer. He'd rented a fabulous château in the Lot, intending to spend July there with his on-off girlfriend Anthea and his six-year-old son Oliver, plus school chum of Oliver's choice, with assorted friends coming out at weekends. Oliver's mother, Rachel, had of course managed to scupper that plan, in her inimitable way, by taking issue with Leo's choice of friends, and making holiday arrangements of her own which limited Oliver's availability. The situation had put Leo's already fraught relationship with Anthea under considerable pressure, and after an enormous row Anthea had disappeared for the entire summer, leaving Leo and Oliver, plus his mate Tarquin, to spend just ten days together on their own at the house. In the end, Leo had made a gift of the remainder of the lease on the château to a couple of impecunious young barrister friends and their children.

Perhaps, Leo reflected, the monumental row with Anthea had been no bad thing. It had propelled their relationship more quickly in the direction in which it had been inevitably heading. A short-lived reprise in September, as hot and brief as today's burst of autumn sun, but then the unspoken understanding that it was definitely over. It was a shame about her lovely, lithe body – he would certainly miss that – but the whole thing had been getting a little too serious for his liking. The most attractive thing about Anthea when he'd first met her, apart from her cool catwalk beauty and independence of mind, had been her elusiveness. He'd liked never quite knowing where he stood. But time and familiarity had lowered those tantalising defences, and since the beginning of the year she'd clearly been edging Leo towards some kind of commitment, which was the last thing he wanted.

Leo regarded himself as a man of simplicity. He lived quietly (admittedly in a five-bedroom house in the most fashionable part of Chelsea, and occasionally at his weekend retreat in Oxfordshire), possessed only one car (true, the garaging fees for his top-of-the-range Aston Martin came to over three thousand a year), collected modern art on a modest scale (although the recent insurance premiums on some of his older pieces had been startling), and liked to think that for Oliver's sake he'd toned down his hedonistic lifestyle (these days he made a point of never having more than one lover on the go at once, of either sex, because at his age it was too exhausting). As one of London's top commercial silks he earned enough to enjoy these straightforward pleasures, and to afford handmade suits, bespoke shoes and a passable wine cellar – but the freedom to do as one pleased was something no amount of money could buy. Leading a simple life meant steering clear of the complexities which long-term relationships inevitably involved. He had loved Anthea in his fashion, but was, on balance, glad to be footloose again.

The note of finality in Mr Justice Cable's voice as he moved to his conclusion brought Leo back to the present.

'—and so, in my judgment on the evidence before me, the balance of convenience comes down firmly on the side of Kirkbride. Provided that Mr Davies is able to confirm the plaintiffs' cross-undertaking in damages, I therefore continue the injunction against the defendants until trial.' He glanced at Leo. 'I will hear counsel as to the form of the order and any other directions that may be required as to costs.'

Leo rose to his feet. 'I believe my learned friend Miss Lightfoot has in fact prepared a draft.'

'If you are content with the form of injunction, Mr Davies, is there anything else apart from costs?'

'We would respectfully ask for the plaintiffs' costs in cause, My Lord.'

The judge glanced enquiringly at Miss Lightfoot, then nodded. 'Very well. I so order.'

There was a rustling of papers and gowns, and everyone filed from the courtroom with a Friday-afternoon sense of relief. Leo paused in the corridor to exchange a few words with Alison Lightfoot, who had caught his attention at the outset of the hearing by the gentle, grave voice in which she'd made her submissions – a pleasant change from the strident delivery of most barristers – and by her dark, understated good looks and cool competence. He was just debating whether or not to ask her out for a drink, when a voice hailed him. 'Leo, you old bastard!'

The man striding across the corridor towards them was well over six feet tall, with a broad, smiling face, and the gone-to-seed physique of an ex-public school prop forward. The greying fair hair curling from beneath his well-worn wig looked as though it could do with a good trim, his frayed robe had slipped from his shoulders and was riding somewhere around his middle, and he clutched a haphazard bundle of papers in ham-like hands. Jamie Urquhart, despite his shambolic appearance, possessed one of the shrewdest minds at the London criminal Bar. His formidable forensic skills, coupled with a courtroom manner famous for its charm and incisiveness, had won him considerable success over the years, and he was much sought after, particularly by well-heeled clients caught on the wrong side of the law. He and Leo had met as students at Bar School, and their friendship stretched back almost thirty years. They tried to make a point of meeting regularly, but the summer break and a string of cases meant that they hadn't seen one another since before Easter.

Leo greeted Jamie warmly, and introduced Alison, hoping she would hang on a little while longer, but she took Jamie's arrival as a cue to leave, murmuring something about getting back to chambers. Leo watched her go with faint regret.

'Haven't seen you in months,' said Jamie. 'How are things?'

'Not bad. Somewhat overwhelmed with work, in fact. How about you?'

'Can't complain on the work front,' said Jamie, in the darkly confident voice which had been used to such persuasive effect on countless juries. He nodded towards the small knot of people conferring outside the courtroom opposite. 'Just finished a three-month fraud trial, and my client loves me. Which he should do, considering I've got him off money-laundering charges which could have seen him doing a fifteen-year stretch in Belmarsh.' Jamie lowered his voice to a murmur. 'He's actually an extremely dodgy Cypriot, but I have to go and schmooze him right now. How about a drink in an hour or so? Balls Brothers, six o'clock?'

'See you there,' said Leo.

In the robing room Leo took off his wig, bands and gown, and crammed them into his red silk bag. When he had changed, he made his way down the echoing marble corridors and stairs, exchanging greetings with passing lawyers of his acquaintance, nodded goodnight to the doorman, and stepped out into the late afternoon air. He saw Alison a few steps ahead of him at the pedestrian crossing, and caught up with her.

'Sorry we were interrupted back there,' he said, slinging his bag over one shoulder as they crossed the Strand together. Alison said nothing, merely gave him a smiling glance. Amazingly pretty eyes, thought Leo. 'I had intended to ask if you were free later this evening. For dinner, perhaps?' The drink with Jamie wouldn't last more than an hour, assuming he was hurrying home to his family.

They reached the other side of the road, and paused at the gate to Middle Temple Lane.

'No thanks. I'm afraid I'm busy.'

'Perhaps next week?'

'I have a big case starting on Monday. I'm sorry – I don't think it's going to leave me much free time.'

Leo knew when to beat a graceful retreat. 'OK, then,' he smiled. 'Have a good weekend.' And he headed through the gate.

Leo strode down Middle Temple Lane in the gathering dusk, mildly dashed by the rebuff. Perhaps he'd misinterpreted those occasional lingering glances she'd been giving him all afternoon. Or could it be that his vanity was getting the better of him, and the signals were no longer quite what he thought they were? With fifty looming, the age gap between himself and desirable young things was growing ever wider, uncomfortably so. He tried to estimate how old Alison Lightfoot might be. Late twenties? Early thirties at most. Christ, she was probably wondering what a man almost old enough to be her father was doing asking her out on a date.

Smarting with self-doubt and wounded vanity, Leo passed along Crown Office Row and through the archway into Caper Court. With a conscious and somewhat ridiculous sense of athleticism, he sprang up the short flight of steps into Number 5, and went into the clerks' room. Henry, the head clerk, was on the phone, and Felicity, his junior, was going through files, checking figures against her computer screen.

Felicity smiled when she saw Leo. 'Afternoon, Mr D!' she

called out brightly. She was an attractive twenty-four-year-old, with brown, curly hair and a buxom figure normally attired, to the distraction of the male members of chambers, in short, tight skirts and clinging tops. Today she was wearing a suit, possibly as a concession to the prevailing sombre mood in the City, yet still managing to display a tantalising flash of cleavage and thigh. She was a cheerful, capable girl, but had few natural organisational or administrative talents, and since her job as clerk required her to manage the cases, arrange the conferences and negotiate the fees of twenty-eight barristers in one of the City's leading sets of commercial chambers, she was normally either a whirlwind of fiercely concentrated activity, or in a fluster of scatterbrained panic. She was fond of a laugh, was Felicity, and she had a perky, easy-going rapport with the members of chambers which Henry, the head clerk, found occasionally exasperating. Henry, who was only in his thirties but old beyond his years, was a clerk of the old school, a man who did his job with a mixture of pride and the mildly facetious deference of a good gentleman's gentleman, and he often wished Felicity would conduct herself with more decorum and less familiarity. That said, he had long nurtured a wistful, unarticulated passion for Felicity, and the confusion of his feelings probably contributed to his generally careworn demeanour.

While Henry was busy with his phone call, Leo decided to take the opportunity to consult Felicity.

'Felicity . . .' began Leo.

'Yes, Mr D?' Felicity had finished on the computer and was sorting through late-afternoon mail.

'Felicity, do I strike you – I mean, someone of your age, as . . .' Leo paused, searching for a better word, but finding none. 'Old?' He and Felicity had always had a close understanding, and she was one of the few people with whom he felt he could be so blunt.

'Old?' Felicity wrinkled her brow. 'Well, you're getting on a bit, Mr Davies, no use pretending you're not. But I wouldn't say *old*. I mean, for your age you're holding up really well, aren't you? A bit like Terence Stamp, or Anthony Hopkins—'

Leo held up a hand. 'OK. That's fine. Stop there.'

Felicity, happy to think she'd said the right thing, leant forward and said in a cheekily conspiratorial whisper, 'I think you're lovely. Whatever.' Then she handed him some papers. 'These came in for you from Bentleys.' Leo took the papers without comment and left the clerks' room.

Felicity watched him go. What had that been about? Perhaps Mr D was having some kind of midlife crisis. He didn't seem a likely candidate. Those looks, and him so good at his job. He could charm the knickers off anyone, light up a room just by coming into it. She'd seen people smile just hearing his voice the other side of a door. It was something beyond charm, beyond sex appeal. The secret Leo ingredient. He needn't worry about getting old, with all that going for him.

These were hardly Leo's thoughts as he trudged upstairs. He went into his room, chucked his robing bag in a corner and dropped the papers on his desk. Unlike the rooms of most barristers, his was a haven of sharply defined order, no piles of books and papers littering the desk and floor, or stacks of briefs lining the window sill. Leo believed that focused thought and proper concentration required an uncluttered environment, and his polished desktop was bare except for his laptop, a PC, and a counsel's notebook and some pencils and pens. The only concessions to homely distraction were two framed photos of Oliver on a bookshelf of All England law reports, and three austere and extremely expensive Anselm Kiefer prints on the wall opposite.

Leo sank into his chair and sat inertly for some moments, staring at the walls. God, he was tired. Tired of enormous cases, increasingly resentful of the time they consumed, the amount of paperwork and preparation involved. He had another big one coming up next month, and the mere thought of it made his heart sink. It could even stretch into the early part of next year. His practice was flourishing as never before, he was earning fantastic sums of money, but at what cost? His mind drifted back to Alison Lightfoot. That particular brush-off was another wake-up call. On every front, he needed to face up to the fact that he was no longer young. He pondered it gloomily. Fifty would take him beyond middle age and inexorably towards sixty. Sixty! He didn't want to think about that. He sighed and glanced at his watch, and saw he still had an hour in hand before he met Jamie. There was plenty of work to be getting on with, including reading the papers which Felicity had given him, but that Friday feeling was upon him. He needed to be convivial, to relax and shake off his gloom.

He left his room and went upstairs to Anthony's room. Anthony Cross, one of his closest colleagues, would surely be up for a chat and some chambers gossip. Unless, of course, he was heading off to meet one of his innumerable young women. Doubtless Alison wouldn't have said no to Anthony – but then, Anthony was only twenty-eight.

When he rapped on Anthony's door, there was no answer. Leo was about to head downstairs again, when he heard voices and laughter coming from Marcus's room at the end of the corridor – a few of the junior barristers winding down at the end of a busy week, maybe about to go out and hit the pub or the wine bar. He hesitated, wondering if he should go in for a chat, then thought better of it. They could do without him.

He headed back to his room, switched on his desk lamp, and began to work.

When he arrived at Balls Brothers, the wine bar was heaving with young City types in high Friday-night spirits. Leo shouldered his way through the crowd, and found Jamie ensconced at a corner table with a bottle of Château Belgrave and a copy of the *Evening Standard*.

Jamie waved Leo over and folded up his paper. 'Come and have a glass of this very passable Pomerol.' He poured Leo a glass and refilled his own.

'You did well to bag a table,' said Leo, glancing around. 'So much for the credit crunch.'

'I got in here half an hour ago. My slippery Cypriot had to catch an early flight. I fancy he didn't want to hang round in the UK and risk getting his collar felt for various other financial transgressions. Cheers.'

'Cheers.' Leo continued to eye the other drinkers. 'Is it my imagination, or are people in the City getting younger by the day?'

'Like politicians and policemen, you mean? No, I reckon it's just that most people our age are scurrying home to Surbiton or Woking to worry about their mortgages and pensions, and whether or not they can afford the school fees.' He waved a hand. 'This lot – look at them. All under thirty, no responsibilities. What's a bonus here or there?'

'Bonuses are one thing, but jobs are another.' Leo tapped

the front page of Jamie's evening paper. 'Look at all the poor sods at Lehmans, wandering around with their cardboard boxes and black bin liners, not knowing what's hit them.'

'True. The world of investment banking is not a happy one right now. Friend of mine at HBOS is sweating every night, not knowing whether his job's going to be there in the morning.'

'Good news for lawyers, though. Nothing like a financial downturn to get clients litigating, chasing every penny, fighting every claim. I've never been busier.'

'Well, hurrah for the commercial Bar.' Jamie refilled both their glasses. 'What about us sorry criminal hacks? I could do with a few more big earners, like that case today. By the time Margo's finished with me, I'm going to need every penny.'

'What do you mean?'

'Margo and I are splitting up.' He uttered the words abruptly.

Leo set down his glass, truly startled by the news. 'My God, Jamie – I had no idea. When did this happen?' Leo had known Margo for twenty years, and had spent many weekends with her and Jamie and their two children at their house in Henley. The news was a shock.

'A couple of months ago. I assumed the Temple's rumour mill would have been grinding away,' said Jamie. 'Sorry to spring it on you.'

'What happened? I thought you two were pretty solid.'

'So did I.' Jamie let out a deep groan, his big frame hunched over his glass. 'She says she's just got tired of the whole thing, doesn't love me any more, is stifled by the idea of us staying together now the kids are grown up, wants to make a new life. Brutal stuff, Leo baby. Brutal stuff.

Maybe it's the modern woman's version of the empty-nest syndrome – my job here is done, the old bloke is boring, sex is boring, let's see what else is out there. They say fifty is the new forty. Margo seems to believe it.' Jamie drained his third glass. 'So she'll walk off with half the proceeds. Not the best time to be carving everything up, but needs must. I'm selling the house, the yacht – I'm going to keep the cottage in Scotland, though. The worst of it is' – Jamie looked grim – 'she has the idea that because Alice and Nick are over twenty-one that our splitting up won't bother them. I think she's so wrong.'

Leo studied his friend, noticing for the first time the grey pouches beneath his eyes, and the lines etched on his heavy face. Jamie and Margo divorcing. It seemed hard to believe.

'Are you still living together?'

Jamie shook his head. 'She moved out three weeks ago. She's staying with a friend till we sell the house. Another divorcee. One of the things she told me was that she gets more emotional support from her friends than she does from me.' He turned his puzzled eyes to Leo. 'What does she mean by that?'

'Couldn't tell you,' replied Leo sadly.

'I hate going back there in the evenings. Place is so bloody empty.'

'Come on, drink up. Let's go and find something to eat, and drown your sorrows properly.'

They strolled to a little Italian restaurant in Bloomsbury, where they had dinner and a long discussion ranging from Jamie's marriage to the economic crisis, then back again.

'I've taken a big hit on my investments,' Jamie told Leo over another bottle of wine. 'The slump in shares has wiped out a hefty sum, besides screwing the old pension – whatever's left of it after Margo has her cut. I don't especially care about selling the house, but I'm sad about the yacht. Had some bloody good times on the old *Mareva*.'

'Do you have to sell her?' asked Leo.

'I don't *have* to. Things aren't that bad. I could keep her if I wanted to – but the fact is, Leo, I'd rather be rid of her. Too many associations. The boat was a present to ourselves, after the kids were off our hands. Margo and I used to love going off at weekends, just the two of us, catching a flight to Nice, grabbing the hire car, picking up some food and driving down to the marina. I'd sort things out on board, make my special cocktail, and Margo would stretch out in the sun like a happy cat. Weather's always fantastic down there. Then if the wind was right, we'd take her out round the islands, drop anchor and have lunch, mess about – it felt like being young again.'

Leo signalled to the waiter and ordered two brandies, prepared to let Jamie talk on for as long as he wanted. 'Sounds idyllic.'

'It was.' The brandies came. Jamie swirled his in silence, took a sip, and said, 'I'm flying down there early tomorrow morning to lay the boat up for the winter. Then I'll put her up for sale, take out an ad in *Yachting Monthly* or whatever, and wait for a buyer.' He sipped his Courvoisier and mused, 'First time I've been down there on my own since I bought her.' There was silence for a moment. Jamie glanced at Leo. 'You busy this weekend?'

'Not particularly,' replied Leo.

'Fancy coming down with me? You'll have no problem getting a seat on the plane. The easyJet flights are never full at this time of year.'

Leo pondered this, mildly surprised. It wasn't his weekend to have Oliver, and the party he was due to go to tomorrow night – the prospect of which bored him already – could easily be ducked. A trip with Jamie could be amusing. On the other hand, it could be mildly depressing, given all Jamie had just told him.

'Come on,' coaxed Jamie. 'What d'you say? We'll have a laugh. God knows I could do with one. Show you the rocking sights and sounds of Antibes. Ever been there?'

'Only fleetingly,' replied Leo. He remembered flying down there a few years ago in the private jet of a Greek shipping heiress with whom he'd been sleeping at the time. They'd spent the weekend on her 150-foot yacht, with its crew of twelve, in the most extraordinary luxury he'd ever encountered off dry land. Dear Adriana, a great collector of things. Houses, yachts, paintings, money, men. She'd wanted to collect Leo, too, on a permanent basis. How come he'd passed on that one? He smiled at the recollection.

'What's so funny?' asked Jamie, swallowing his brandy in two gulps.

'Just remembering my last trip down there. I didn't see much of Antibes.'

'Time you did. It's a fantastic place. Come on – we'll go back to mine, get on the Internet and bag you a seat, have a nightcap, up first thing and head to Gatwick. What d'you say?'

Leo realised he hadn't done anything spur of the moment for a long time. 'Will it make you happy?'

'Are you joking? A boy's weekend away will do me the power of good.'

'OK,' said Leo, and raised his glass. 'Anything to oblige a friend. Cheers.'

CHAPTER TWO

At midday on Monday Sarah Colman came out of the Lloyd's Building, and shivered in the sharp wind that gusted along St Mary Axe. She wished she hadn't left her coat in the office. Yesterday had been gloriously mild, but today had brought a change. As she hurried down the steps she saw a tall, dark-haired young man emerging from the Willis Building opposite. Well, well – Anthony Cross. It had to be all of three years since she'd last seen him. Surprising that they hadn't run into one another before now. Sarah studied him as he paused to chat to a colleague. Less of a boy and more of a man now – those gentle good looks had hardened, and made him more attractive than ever. She watched as Anthony parted from his friend and headed towards Leadenhall Market, then strolled across the road to intercept him.

Anthony, still preoccupied with details of the oil pollution conference he had just left, didn't notice Sarah until she was almost upon him. He stopped in surprise. 'Sarah – hi. How are you?' Sarah's previously long blonde hair was shorter now, but there was no forgetting that pert, pretty face, and the full mouth with that charming, lopsided curve which always seemed to suggest some secret source of amusement. She was wearing a neatly tailored suit and high heels, and hugging a leather broker's wallet.

'Fine. And you?'

'Good, thanks.'

'Been a while, hasn't it?'

'It has.' He had mixed feelings about this chance encounter. A few years ago, when Sarah was a pupil at 5 Caper Court, the two of them had had a brief but ill-advised relationship, the fallout from which had been disastrous. It was quite something, seeing her again in the flesh. 'So – what are you up to these days?'

'Working as a broker for Portman's.'

'Right. Employing those formidable negotiating skills of yours.'

'Kind of you to say so. At least, I assume you're being kind.' She glanced at her watch. 'Look at that. Nearly time for lunch. What say we go and have a glass of wine and catch up on old times?'

Anthony hesitated. Sarah had a deserved reputation as a manipulative, scheming troublemaker. But she was also disturbingly sexy and provocative, qualities too easily forgotten until one was up close to her. The scent of the perfume she always wore hit him like a memory.

'OK, why not?' He had no reason to hurry back to chambers.

'Let's see if we can grab a table at the Market wine bar.'

They were ahead of the rush and found a secluded corner table. Sarah picked up a discarded copy of *The Times*, while Anthony went to the bar to order glasses of wine and a plate of sandwiches. 'Things must be getting bad when the big three banks go cap in hand to the government to bail them out,' she remarked to Anthony, when he came back.

Anthony glanced at the headlines and nodded. 'Gordon Brown may get what the hard Left have always wanted – the nationalisation of the banks. I can't believe it's happened so fast.'

'It's going to be hellish on the City job front soon – just like the nineties.' Sarah helped herself to a sandwich. 'Not that either of us remembers that. Anyway, let's not talk economic doom and gloom – there's far too much of that these days. Tell me what's going on at Caper Court. God, it seems like a lifetime since I was a pupil there. Everyone still as dull and worthy as ever?'

Anthony smiled wryly. 'I imagine by your standards we're tedious in the extreme.'

'Mmm. Life as a barrister would never have suited me. Far too much like hard work. Come on, give me the low-down on everyone. Is Henry still dying of unrequited love for Felicity?'

'Actually, there's a rumour – unsubstantiated beyond a sighting of Henry in a pub with some lady – that his heart belongs elsewhere.'

'I don't believe it. It was an open secret that he adored Felicity.'

'Henry probably realised it was one-way traffic. He's not getting any younger. Probably wants to settle down. Anyway, the great love of Felicity's life, Vince, is coming out of prison soon.'

'I'd forgotten him – didn't he get done for manslaughter, or something?'

Anthony nodded, helping himself to another sandwich. 'Hit some chap in an argument, and he fell over and cracked his head and died. Vince has done half of his sentence, so government policy means he'll be out before the end of the year.'

'Right.' There was a pause, then Sarah asked casually, 'And what about Leo? How's he?'

The question surprised Anthony. As he recalled, Sarah's friendship with Leo had been the reason why she'd come to Caper Court in the first place. 'You don't see him?'

'Why should I?'

'Oh, I don't know. I just assumed you were still in touch.' Anthony paused, then said, 'Leo is as well as ever. Doing all the usual Leo things.'

Sarah thought she detected a certain edge to Anthony's voice. She knew enough about the relationship he had with Leo, about the odd kind of love which existed between them. Something Leo could handle, but not Anthony.

'He should be careful,' she said. 'He'll break someone's heart one of these days.'

'I should think that happens with alarming regularity. The only person in the world he really cares about is Oliver.'

Sarah nodded. 'His Achilles heel.'

'An odd way of putting it.'

'You think? I find people's weak spots, their vulnerabilities, are always the most interesting things about them. And the most useful.' As Sarah stretched to pick up a sandwich, her jacket fell away a little to reveal a glimpse of soft, curving breast, and Anthony felt a little jolt of lust at the recollection of times spent in bed with her.

She looked and caught his swift, straying glance. 'What are you thinking about?' she asked, knowing perfectly well.

'Old times,' said Anthony.

Sarah eyed him speculatively. Anthony had always been famously and rather sweetly vulnerable where the opposite sex was concerned. It was Sarah's guess that he now considered himself a seasoned man of the world. Perhaps he even thought of himself as being in the same league as Leo, whom he so admired, capable of picking up and dropping lovers without a second thought. Very few belonged to that special breed of people. She and Leo did. Anthony never would.

'Old times as in – us?'

Sarah's assessment of Anthony was more or less accurate. He had been disappointed and hurt by love too often, and now maintained a kind of emotional veneer, a pretence at invulnerability. Deep down, he was as susceptible as ever, longing for love, for some special person, though he would have denied this even to himself.

'I wouldn't say there was ever an "us",' replied Anthony. He leant closer to her, enjoying her subtle perfume. 'We were both only ever after the same thing.'

'Love?' She spoke the word lightly, her eyes fixed on his face. She did enjoy this kind of game. Poor old Anthony, he really thought he knew where it was going, too.

'Was that ever particularly important to you? No, I think you know exactly what I'm talking about.'

'Mmm, indeed. You sound like you're still interested.'

Anthony felt strangely and pleasantly light-headed. Half an hour ago he'd been discussing the finer points of jurisdiction, and now – this. It brought home to him that his life right now was lacking in excitement and spontaneity. He had a sudden memory of sitting in some bar with Sarah years ago, when he'd first known her, and kissing her without warning. He wanted to do that now. She'd always had such a lethal effect on him. Even though he hadn't been in love with her, or romantically involved in any sense, she'd been able to manipulate him through sheer sexuality. This time, things were different. If anything was going to happen – and she clearly wanted it to – he would be the one in control. He'd show her this was a game he could play just as well.

'I could be.'

'Nice to see you taking the initiative for a change. If that's what you're doing.'

'So – what are we talking about here?' He glanced around. They were pretty much out of sight of the rest of the wine bar.

'You tell me.' She leant in closer. 'You're the one making the running.'

His glance rested on her slightly parted lips. Unable to resist, he put his fingers lightly beneath her chin, and leant to kiss her. But Sarah drew back, pushing his hand gently away and smiling.

'I think you've failed to notice something.' She held up her left hand, and Anthony saw the flash of a diamond.

He managed to laugh. 'Congratulations. Nicely concealed.'

'It was there all the time, only your attention happened to be elsewhere.'

'Who's the lucky – or possibly unlucky – guy?'

Sarah twisted the ring on her finger, letting it catch the

light. 'How ungallant of you. His name's Toby Kittering, and he's an investment banker.'

'Right.'

Sarah sighed. 'Oh, Anthony. You haven't changed. You're still so – what's the word? So tractable. Here – have the last sandwich.' She pushed the plate towards him. 'I have to go.' She stood up, picking up her folder. 'It was fun catching up. Give my love to everyone at Caper Court. Especially Leo. Bye.'

Anthony sat for a few minutes after Sarah had gone, feeling rather stupid. He was annoyed with himself for letting that happen. Presumably she had been trying to prove that he was easy, that he was predictable. It wasn't the way he liked to think of himself. But there was a basis of truth in it. He sat there, his mind wandering from the particularity of Sarah's put-down to the generalities of his life. Everything about it was predictable. What did it consist of, except for getting up, going to work, seeing the same faces every day? Even his social life was centred upon a largely unvarying, safe group of friends. The last couple of girlfriends he'd had seemed to have been cut from the same template – half-hearted career girls from nice, middle-class backgrounds waiting for the right man to come along so that they could get married and have babies. They had made him feel like a fraud, a lot of the time. His own dysfunctional upbringing, with its chronic lack of money, hadn't equipped him to deal with their expectations. He lived and worked in a world where most people seemed to have been to public school and Oxbridge, and had spent eight years working to fit in. Most of the time he succeeded, but there were also times when he wondered what he was doing there.

Anthony picked up his glass and drained its contents, his thoughts straying, as they so often did at such times of insecurity, to Leo. Like himself, Leo was an outsider from humble beginnings, an interloper in this elite world. And Leo dealt with the situation by operating on Jekyll and Hyde principles – keeping ahead of the game by being a brilliant lawyer, one of the best in his field, making as much money as he could, and using it to indulge himself in a hedonistic private lifestyle far removed from the dull, respectable conventions by which most barristers lived. Perhaps that was the answer. Instead of looking for love, hoping to find the right person to make sense of everything, he should take a leaf out of Leo's book. Live dangerously. Become less easy, less safe. Someone whom the likes of Sarah wouldn't find so – what was the word she'd used? So tractable.

He ate the last sandwich, paid the bill and decided to try and excise thoughts of Sarah by walking all the way back to chambers.

Anthony picked up his mail from the clerks' room and was talking football with Henry when Leo arrived, looking somewhat haggard.

Leo shrugged off his overcoat, flung it over a chair, and fished a batch of letters from his pigeonhole. 'Thanks for rearranging this morning's con with Beddoes,' he said to Henry. 'My flight into Gatwick last night was delayed, and I really didn't feel up to it.'

'Not a problem. He's coming in later today – four o'clock.'

'Heavy weekend?' Anthony asked Leo.

'You could say that. I spent the weekend in the South

of France with Jamie Urquhart. Did you know he's getting divorced?'

'No! Wow. That's a surprise.'

'Liam . . .' Henry addressed a thin, fresh-faced boy of eighteen or so, seated at a desk opposite Felicity, wearing a conspicuously new suit and an alert expression. 'Coffee time, if you would be so kind.'

The boy got up. 'Right. Yes. I'm on it. What would everyone—?'

'Black, one sugar,' said Felicity, without looking up from her computer screen.

Robert swivelled round in his chair. 'White, two sugars.'

'White, no sugar,' called out Carla, the office manager, from her desk at the other side of the room.

Liam began ticking them off on his fingers, looking anxious. 'OK, two white, one no sugar, one with one sugar—'

'Two,' said Robert.

'Yeah, right – white, two sugars. Black, one sugar – no, wait . . .'

'I'd write it down if I were you, lad,' said Henry, handing him a pen and a piece of paper. 'I'm a tea, no sugar.' Liam began to make his list. He glanced uncertainly at Leo.

'Would you like a coffee, Mr . . . ?'

'Davies,' said Leo. 'Yes, Liam, I would most certainly like a coffee. Make it black, strong, and no sugar, please.'

'Mr Cross?'

'Nothing for me, thanks.'

Liam left the room, frowning at his list.

'That, I take it, is our new fledgling clerk?' said Leo.

'Liam Sturgis. Very bright lad. Keen to do well. I hope to

have him in shape by the time Robert leaves us in March.'

'Let's hope he lasts longer than – what was her name, the previous one? Seemed like she was hardly here for more than a few days.'

'Julie.' Henry shook his head. 'She wasn't really cut out for it. Not everyone is. The girls seem to have higher expectations than the boys – don't like fetching and carrying. I have hopes for Liam. He's my brother-in-law's sister's son, if you follow. His father's one of the clerks at twenty Essex Street.'

'Ah, so it's in the blood,' smiled Leo.

'So to speak, sir. So to speak.' Henry reached out to pick up the phone which had just begun to ring.

Leo resumed his conversation with Anthony. 'Yes, so – as I was saying, Jamie's getting divorced, and over a very boozy dinner on Friday night he persuaded me to accompany him to Antibes, to say farewell to his beloved yacht and help him drown his sorrows. The result was . . .' Leo winced.

'What?'

'That I drank far too much pastis, and finished up becoming the owner of a thirty-six-foot yacht.'

'You bought it?' laughed Anthony. 'Do you know anything about sailing?'

'It's not that kind of yacht, thank God. It's a motor yacht.'

'I imagine there's still a lot to learn. Engine maintenance, handling, that kind of thing.'

'I know, I know.' Leo rubbed his face. 'Jamie says I'll have to go on some kind of course. But not yet. My new toy will be sitting in its berth for the next few months, with some chap called Philippe keeping an eye on it, till I feel like taking an interest.' He glanced at Anthony. 'I know what you're thinking. More money than sense.'

'I wasn't thinking that at all. A boat sounds like fun.'

'Depends how much time I manage to spend down there. But I have plans in that direction. Ah, coffee!'

Liam had returned with a large tray and several mugs. He set it down, checked his list, and began to hand them round.

'Thank you, Liam,' said Felicity. She opened a paper bag which had been sitting on her desk, and took out a large muffin, intercepting Anthony's glance as she did so.

'Get your eyes off my muffin, Mr Cross. You're not having any.'

'I was just wondering how you eat stuff like that and still keep your gorgeous figure.'

'I believe that remark may constitute sexual harassment,' observed Leo. 'I'll be happy to represent you, Felicity, if you decide to sue.'

Robert guffawed as he stirred his coffee with a pencil.

'It's blueberry,' said Felicity through a mouthful of muffin, 'so it counts as part of my five-a-day.'

Leo picked up his coffee, saying to Anthony, 'I've got a copy of the judgment in that inducement of breach of contract case, if you care to have a look at it.'

They left the clerks' room and went upstairs.

'Guess who I met today,' said Anthony.

'Someone amusing, I hope,' said Leo. He unlocked his door and they went in.

'That depends on your point of view. Sarah Colman.'

'Well, well. There's a name I haven't heard for a long time.' Leo set down his coffee and letters on the desk and hung up his coat. 'What's she up to these days?'

‘She’s working as a broker for Portman’s, and – get this – she’s engaged. To an investment banker. Toby something. Didn’t recognise the name. She seemed pretty pleased with herself generally.’

‘Dear Sarah.’ Leo sat down at his desk. ‘God, she was trouble.’

‘I pity the poor bloke she’s going to marry.’

‘I rather envy him.’

‘You can’t possibly mean that.’

‘Possibly not the marrying part. But she’s a most . . .’ Leo searched for the word. ‘A most stimulating girl. Extraordinarily sexy. And very inventive.’

‘You seem to be forgetting she’s also a prize bitch.’

‘So many of the most interesting women are, Anthony.’ He gave the younger man a searching glance. ‘I take it from the look on your face that she managed to ruffle your feathers in some way. You and she had a bit of a thing once, didn’t you?’

‘I’d rather forget about that.’

‘She’s not that easy to forget. Mind you, I haven’t seen her in – what? Four years.’ Leo sighed, then opened a desk drawer and began to thumb through some documents. He produced a slim bundle and handed it to Anthony. ‘See what you make of that. Mr Justice Dawson’s idea of tortious inducement of a breach of contract doesn’t exactly accord with mine. I seriously question the intelligence of some of the judges in the commercial division. One can only hope it’ll be overturned on appeal.’

‘I’ll have a read of it. Thanks.’

As Anthony reached the door, Leo asked, ‘Did Sarah say when she’s getting married?’

'No. Why?'

'No reason. I was just curious. See you.'

When Anthony had gone, Leo leant back in his chair, swung his feet onto the desk, and thought back to the summer when Sarah had first come into his life, a delectable twenty-year-old with a precocious sexual appetite and a penchant for risk-taking. He'd employed her in his country house near Oxford, together with some attractive young man whose name Leo could no longer remember, to cook, look after the house, and generally service his domestic and sexual requirements. Quite a summer. It all seemed long ago and far away now. Sarah had been fun, the kind of girl whose very smile encouraged complete dereliction of all responsibility, but the attributes which had made her such a perfect playmate had in the long run turned into liabilities. Her predilection for mischief-making, combined with a tendency to serve strictly her own interests, had put him in more than a few tricky spots. Still, nice to hear she was still around. She had been one of the few people to get under his skin, to get close to understanding him. Perhaps they were two of a kind – not an especially flattering thought. Dear, devious Sarah. Perhaps love and marriage would wreak some kind of miraculous change in her. Somehow he doubted it.

CHAPTER THREE

The following Sunday Sarah was sitting in the drawing room in Toby's parents' house in Surrey after a late lunch, listening to her prospective mother-in-law's interminable chatter, and wondering if the dreary day would ever end.

'The trouble with a July wedding, or August come to that, is that so many people go away on holiday, don't they? It seems everyone tends to book well ahead these days.' Caroline Kittering poured coffee from the cafetière into tiny bone china coffee cups. 'Toby, be a dear and pass that to Sarah.' She looked enquiringly at her husband. 'Jon-Jon?' Dr Kittering roused himself from his reverie and took his coffee, and Caroline went on, 'A summer wedding is by far the nicest, I always think, because there's less chance of the weather letting one down. Though nothing's guaranteed, is it? You remember your cousin Camilla's wedding last June, don't you, Toby? The weather was perfect all week, then on the day it absolutely bucketed down, and everyone had to huddle in the marquee instead of having drinks on the lawn as planned, and all the guests who had parked in the paddock were stuck in the mud, and Mervyn had to get duckboards, or whatever they call them, to get people out. They even had to use the local farmer's tractor . . .'

Sarah wound a strand of blonde hair round one finger, indulging in a fantasy which involved kicking Caroline's chair over and stuffing a napkin into her busy mouth as she lay flapping on the Axminster. Dear God, would the woman never shut up? Letting Toby's parents get involved in the wedding plans had been a huge mistake, but there was no going back now. Jonathan Kittering was her father's oldest friend, and the Kitterings had been over the moon when she and Toby had announced their engagement. It had been Caroline Kittering's idea to help with the wedding arrangements, since Sarah's mother was dead, and Sarah's father had agreed to it before Sarah could say anything. So here they were, spending the weekend at the Kittering's house near Egham, and talking about absolutely nothing but the bloody wedding.

She glanced sideways at Toby, and he slipped her a wink. She felt a small surge of affection, but it ebbed quickly away. Looking ahead to her married life, she saw a pageant of ritual visits stretching ahead. Sunday lunches. Christmases, dreary hours spent listening to Caroline Kittering – Wittering, more like – trying to animate her existence with endless talk about people and events, while Toby's father, the retired paediatric consultant, sat in a postprandial glaze of boredom and inertia, and the late afternoon light faded over the Surrey countryside, and the years passed by. She felt overwhelmed by a sense of claustrophobia. She couldn't wait to be out of here and heading up the M25 in Toby's Porsche towards London and real life.

'So perhaps June is the best month. Or maybe even May? What do you two think?'

Sarah realised that Caroline was asking her a direct question, and roused herself. 'Well, Toby and I haven't really discussed it yet.' She turned to look at Toby.

'No,' agreed Toby. 'We'll have to give it some thought. Though those are probably the best months.'

Caroline sipped her coffee. She was a small woman, with a very downy face, bright, questing eyes, and a dumpy, pear-shaped figure. Sarah, who found it hard to believe that such a short woman could have such an enormous arse, couldn't help worrying about the genes. What if she had a child with a backside that big? A tiny baby with an outsize bottom, straining its nappy the way Caroline Kittering's buttocks strained the fabric of her Country Casuals skirt. She'd just have to hope that any children they had took after Toby and his father, who were both tall and more or less conventionally shaped.

'Well, you'll have to get your skates on,' said Caroline. 'Not long till November, and next year will be on us before we know it. Lots to do! If we're going to have the wedding here we'll have to start thinking about a marquee, and booking the church.' She turned to Toby's father. 'Jon-Jon, it might be an idea if you had a word with the vicar. St Luke's gets very booked up.'

Christ, thought Sarah, a six-month run-up, and it could only get worse as the detail kicked in. To say nothing of post-wedding fallout. Camcorder footage, photo albums, fond reminiscence. She hadn't realised how oppressive being drawn into the bosom of Toby's loving family would be. Her own experience of family life, as an only child, had been quite different, everyone casually and fleetingly affectionate, but operating largely in their own separate spheres. Even before her mother had died when Sarah was fifteen, family intimacy had never been on this intense, need-to-know-and-interfere basis. How did Toby stand it? Perhaps with two sisters and a brother the effect was diluted.

Then again, maybe there were worse things than marrying into a boring family. The in-laws of a recently married friend of Sarah's had turned out to be as mad as a box of frogs. The wedding had been hilariously awful, with family rows and drunken, spiteful speeches. At least Caroline and Jon-Jon were safe and reliable. Perhaps she would come to find something reassuring in their dreary conventionality, their nice house, their nice neighbours, and their fearful self-satisfaction. The countrified middle classes hanging on by their fingertips to a disappearing way of life in the face of collapsing banks, terrorist threats, the disappearance of rural post offices, socially engineered universities, imploding property prices and The Third Runway.

Toby glanced at his watch, and Sarah's heart rose. 'I think,' said Toby, setting down his coffee cup, 'that we'd better be making a move. I need to get back to town before five.'

'Don't you want to stay and watch the rugby?' asked his father. 'Wales versus France.'

'Not this time, Dad. Sorry.'

Not this time, thought Sarah. That implied another time. Another time when Toby and his father would settle down in front of the HD telly for an afternoon of sport, while she helped Caroline with the pots and pans, listening to Caroline talk, and watching Caroline's monumental bum rolling around the kitchen. Maybe she should develop a fierce devotion to rugby. It couldn't be hard. Look at the people who played and watched it. Certainly no worse than cricket. Then she could book her place on the sofa with the boys. Somehow she couldn't see Caroline letting that happen. Traditional gender roles seemed pretty clearly defined and respected in the Kittering household.

Toby got up and stretched, fishing for his car keys. He was tall, broad-shouldered, with light-brown hair, and a face that was handsome without being remarkable, the product of solid middle-class nurturing and a public school education, with his upper 2:1 in economics from Warwick, and his job in the City. His intelligence, shaped and sustained by the narrow values of his family and social class, was of the unquestioning variety. He was able to believe in the value of the work he did each day at Graffman Spiers Investment Bank because of the calibre of the people he worked with and for. They were chaps like him, and he trusted them. He trusted everyone up the ladder. He believed in the world of finance and its value to humanity. He found the present banking crisis unnerving but exciting, regarded the dire events unfolding daily around him as a test of everyone's mettle, and not evidence of their ineptitude, and had unshakeable belief in the ability of the banks and the markets to triumph ultimately, and to restore order. Although at dinner parties and among work colleagues Toby mouthed orthodox criticisms of the government of the day, and articulate mild contempt for certain figures in the Treasury, like so many of his kind he possessed a deep-rooted, almost childlike faith in the infallibility of the British establishment. He had grown up in a Britain where certain aspects of life seemed reassuringly enduring – the chime of Big Ben on the six o'clock news, *The Archers* Sunday omnibus, the Boat Race, the Post Office, the Queen's smile, the apparent indestructibility of The Rolling Stones, hold-ups on the M25 – and knew that although that world might be buffeted and rocked by squalls, by political upheavals and economic crises, these adversities were themselves part of the stoutly woven tapestry of British life, just like the Blitz, or the Chartist riots; there to be overcome. This lack of doubt gave Toby a cheerful solidity which was reassuring to others. Just looking at him made Sarah feel warm and safe. She glanced at Dr Kittering as he rose stiffly from the sofa, no longer young, energetic and broad-shouldered, but containing the ghost of the young man he had once been, and could imagine Toby morphing into his father as the years rolled by.

'Can we help to clear up?' asked Sarah, hoping Caroline would take this offer in the perfunctory spirit in which it was intended.

'No, no. You two get back to London before it gets dark,' said Caroline, extricating herself from her armchair. 'It was lovely to see you both.'

As they emerged into the hall, Scooby, the Kittering's West Highland terrier, came tearing from his bed in the kitchen and sprang around excitedly. Hoping the Kitterings wouldn't notice, Sarah gave Scooby a furtive kick. She hated dogs bouncing around and snuffling at her crotch. Then she smiled and kissed her in-laws goodbye, stooping to peck the air next to Caroline's furry cheeks, and enduring wet, leathery lip contact from Jon-Jon. Either he hadn't learnt the art of air-kissing or he was being a bit of a lech. The latter, she suspected.

'Tell your father I look forward to seeing him at the Beefsteak next Friday,' Dr Kittering reminded Sarah.

'I will. Thank you for lunch. It was such fun.' She and Toby crunched across the gravel driveway to the car, and Sarah held her smile in place as she waved goodbye, only letting it fade when they reached the main road.

Caroline and Jonathan waved the Porsche out of sight, then went back inside.

'Lovely girl,' said Jonathan. 'Heard a lot about her down the years from Vivian, but never knew her. Astonishing, the two of them getting together like that. The world is smaller than we think.'

'Did you see the way she kicked Scooby?' said Caroline.

'I'm sure you must have imagined it. I didn't see it.' Jonathan closed the front door. 'Maybe she isn't fond of dogs,' he added, and disappeared into the living room to watch the rugby.

Caroline went to the kitchen and began clearing up. Not being fond of dogs told you a lot about a person. She wanted to like Sarah, for Toby's sake, but she certainly wasn't the kind of girl she had envisaged Toby marrying, and didn't look like shaping up to become the affectionate, respectful daughter-in-law she had hoped for.

Sarah slumped thankfully in her car seat and switched on the CD player.

Toby smiled ruefully. 'Sorry to drag you away. I could tell you and Mum were just getting settled in for a good old chat about the wedding.' Sarah glanced at Toby. He was a sweet man, but his social radar wasn't terribly acute. 'The thing is, I need to go into the office.'

'On a Sunday night? Why?'

Toby's good-humoured face tensed slightly. He maintained his smile, but the dark V of a frown appeared between his eyes. 'In case you hadn't noticed, we're in the middle of the biggest financial shit-storm for some decades.'

Sarah felt a tingle of alarm. 'But Graffman's is OK, surely?' Toby had worked for Graffman Spiers for seven years, and the job had given him his Docklands penthouse flat, his Porsche, his six-figure yearly bonus and, if Sarah was being perfectly honest, much of his appeal.

'There's some serious firefighting to be done. I got a text from my boss just before lunch, but I didn't want to mention it in case the old dear got in a panic.'

'Your job's safe, isn't it?'

Toby shrugged. His face gave nothing away. 'Safe isn't one of those words you hear a lot around the CDS department.'

'CDS?'

'Credit derivative swaps. They're trading instruments.' He glanced at her and squeezed her hand. 'Don't look so worried. It isn't global meltdown. Anyway, we've got each other, and that's what counts.'

Toby dropped Sarah at her Kensington flat, and sped off to Canary Wharf. Sarah wandered into the living room, sat down on the sofa and kicked off her shoes, welcoming the solitude. She'd decided to live alone after three years of sharing with her friend Louise – a lovely girl, but definitely a touch OCD on the tidying and cleaning front – and had fallen in love with this place from the beginning. It wasn't large, just a one-bedroomed garden flat off Onslow Square, but Sarah adored it, even if the rent was on the high side. It had beautiful hardwood floors and an odd vaulted glass roof over the passageway to the kitchen, which itself was a small, tasteful miracle of well-used space.

It was growing dark, but she could still make out the 'For Rent' sign outside, which the estate agent had put up the week before. It made sense, she knew, for her to move into Toby's Westminster riverside apartment. They would be married in a few months, after which they would carry on living there until they found a house. On Toby's income they would be able to afford somewhere in a decent area, and Sarah had already spent hours online, taking virtual tours of houses in Notting Hill and Islington, hitting the Heal's furnishing website and refining her search to the upper price range, and leafing through interior-decorating porn in WHSmith's. But no matter how many desirable residences she saw, in however many leafy avenues or charming squares, she knew nothing would ever give her the cosy, private pleasure of her little Kensington flat. She didn't like the idea of anyone else living here.

She got up and closed the blinds so that she didn't have to see the sign, and padded through to the kitchen. She made herself a mug of tea and brought it back to the living room, put on some music, and stretched out on the sofa, feeling vaguely depressed and unsettled. Ever since childhood she had hated the fag end of Sunday, the weekend gone, Monday looming. Added to which, today's visit to Colebrook House hadn't exactly been a bundle of laughs. She'd felt disconnected from Toby, who, back in the familiar context of his family, had become more theirs and less hers. Caroline Kittering had been doing a bit of dividing and conquering, of course, telling Toby gossip about local people Sarah had never heard of, and making sure Sarah realised what a good cook she was, and how she knew all the little things that Toby liked. That was territorial, and only to be expected. Today was only the second time she'd met the Kitterings. The last time had been at a wedding of one of Toby's friends, and she hadn't particularly cared for them, their solidity, their smugness. She'd thought at the time that it wasn't important. Toby was one thing, and his family were another. Today had made her realise how wrong that idea was. Toby and his family were one and the same thing, and once they were married, she would become part of it.

Sarah closed her eyes. She shouldn't be feeling like this. She should be blissfully happy. She was engaged to a charming, decent, good-looking man, who was a much nicer person than she would ever be and thereby made up for all her personal deficiencies, who was in a fabulously well-paying job, and could keep her in the luxury to which she would quite happily become accustomed. And, of course, she loved him. Toby was very loveable. Was she in love with him? No – but Sarah had long ago decided that being in love was a deluded state, and not necessarily the basis for a successful relationship. Marrying Toby was a rational act. She certainly didn't want to stay single all her life, she was pretty much fed up with the exhausting pleasures of dating, and of short-term relationships, and Toby was quite a catch. She didn't believe in a soulmate, or The Perfect Man. Life was all about compromise. And while Toby might not set her world on fire, the future with him looked secure, prosperous. She had already decided to give up her job when they were married. Being a broker didn't exactly float her boat, and they wouldn't miss the money. Toby earned enough for both of them. She would spend her time decorating whatever house they bought and then in a year or two, when she got bored with that, she might have a baby. Some of her girlfriends were already mothers, and it seemed like quite an amusing club to belong to. From babies her mind drifted to sex. She had to admit that, tender and affectionate though he was, Toby was ponderously unexciting in bed. But then, weren't most British men? She sipped her tea, totting up the exceptions in her head. It was a short list. She considered Anthony Cross, whom she'd run into the other day. Would she put him on it? Probably, for enthusiasm as much as anything else. And a willingness to learn. But top of the list, head and shoulders above the rest, came Leo. With Leo, sex had been a game, a guilt-free pleasure ride of unbridled physicality and shameless gratification. She hadn't seen him in four years, but she felt her stomach go into free fall just thinking about him. Perhaps there was such a thing as the perfect man after all. Of all the men she'd ever known, Leo's outlook and personality were closest to her own. On top of which, he had money, taste, intelligence and wit. An ideal partner – only Leo wasn't the marrying kind. Theirs hadn't been a friendship exactly, more an enjoyable mutual antagonism, with recreational sex thrown in. Not the stuff of lasting relationships. So why did she always feel, with a confidence that bordered on certainty, that she would see him again, some time, some place?

She dragged her mind away reluctantly from Leo. It

wouldn't do. She was marrying Toby, whom she loved, and who would make a satisfactory husband in every possible way. She took another sip of her tea, but found it had gone cold. She had been thinking about Leo for longer than she'd realised.

That same evening, Anthony and his brother Barry were meeting their father, Chay, for Sunday supper in a gastropub in Hackney. Chay Cross was a successful postmodern artist who spent most of every year flitting between his homes in Madrid and New York, soaking up the admiration and hospitality of well-heeled investors and socialites who, with more money than sense, were prepared to cough up tens and thousands for his works. This October he was on one of his regular visits to London to see his sons and check up on the progress of his pet project, ShoMoMa, a new museum of modern art housed in a former Shoreditch brewery which, with surprising foresight, Chay had purchased a few years earlier.

Their father's artistic success remained a deep mystery to Anthony and Barry. Throughout their childhood he had been a shifting, insubstantial presence, an itinerant hippy moving from one squat to another, smoking an inordinate amount of dope, and dabbling unsuccessfully in a variety of creative mediums. He only came to visit their mother Judith when he was in need of a handout, though he had occasionally taken the boys on outings and camping weekends. His surprising rise to fame had come about when Anthony, an impecunious student barrister, had sold some of Chay's paintings to a gallery in an attempt to pay off a debt. The gallery had found buyers for the paintings, critics had paid attention, and within a few months Chay Cross was being hailed on both sides of the Atlantic as 'a wuthering expressionist of plangent, emotional rawness' (*Modern Painters*), 'an artist with a thrillingly gestative response to the world' (*Apollo Magazine*), and 'a craftsman bringing meaning, mythology and dream alive within veiled abstraction' (*Frieze*). Since which time Anthony, whenever he was forced to consider one of his father's vast monochrome daubs, had the uneasy feeling he might have been responsible for launching one of the greatest public frauds in the history of art. Still, he seemed to sit in good company alongside Tracey Emin and Damien Hirst.

When Anthony arrived at the pub, Chay was already there, sitting at one of the scrubbed wooden tables reading the *Sunday Times Review*, wearing a startling Liberty print shirt, bright-blue Mordechai Rubenstein braces, grey flannel trousers and black canvas Oxfords. The look was distinctly, expensively New York. A halo of cropped, silvery hair shone on his bean-shaped head as he rose to greet his son.

'Hi, Dad,' said Anthony, returning his hug tentatively. They sat down.

'You look well,' remarked Anthony.

Chay nodded. 'I'm good. And you?'

'Yes, good, thanks. Busy.'

'Busy.' Chay nodded again. 'You lawyers are always busy, I suppose.'

The tone was familiar. Chay had always made plain his disdain for his son's orthodox choice of career. Not that it had put him above cadging fivers and tenners from

Anthony on a regular basis back in the days when he'd been permanently skint.

'What would you like?' he asked Anthony. 'A beer?'

'Thanks. Pint of Shires, please.'

Chay rose and went to the bar. Barry came in a moment later. He was tall, like his father and brother, but more broadly built, with a cheerful, open face and dark hair cut in a shaggy crop. He was dressed in denims, trainers, a jacket and a T-shirt that read '*Born To Chill*'. He high-fived Anthony, and went over to his father at the bar.

'Wassup, Dad? Get us a lager, would you?' He went back and sat down with Anthony.

Chay returned with the drinks. Barry slurped the foam off the top of his pint and nodded at the jacket slung over the back of Chay's chair. 'Nice threads, Dad. Versace?'

Chay smiled. 'Brioni. Seven thousand dollars.'

'Give over! How can you spend that much on a suit and live with yourself?'

Chay shrugged. 'It's all relative. I earn ten times that selling one painting.'

'Yeah, and that's a bleeding mystery to all of us.'

Chay gave a thin smile. Although apparently serene in his success, it irked him when his sons chaffed him, as though afraid there might be a grain of truth in their jokes. 'So,' he asked Barry, 'what are you doing with yourself these days?'

Barry sprawled comfortably in his chair. 'Stand-up.'

'Stand-up? You mean, like a comedian?'

'He's always been one of those,' said Anthony.

'Thanks, mate. I've seen you in court and I could say the same.'

Anthony smiled and took a sip of his beer. Since dropping out of sixth-form college six years earlier, Barry had had a variety of jobs – pizza delivery man, bouncer, barman, stripogram, cycle courier – and no one was quite sure what to make of this new career departure.

Chay mused, rasping his hand across his bristly skull. 'Comedy, I always think, has great artistic integrity. Good to see another artist in the family.'

'I don't reckon integrity has much to do with it, Dad. Or art. It's telling jokes to punters.' Barry picked up the menu. 'Let's see what there is to eat. I'm famished.'

They ordered food, and talked. Chay was full of the art world, of glamorous gatherings and people. Barry had good stories from the comedy club circuit. Anthony had a few interesting tales from the law courts. The talk came round eventually to the banking crisis.

'So much for global capitalism,' said Barry. 'Immoral businesses run by greedy people. I'd like to see the entire banking system wiped out.'

'I'm not sure you would,' said Anthony.

'I bloody well object to taxpayers' money, *our* money, being used to shore up these rotten institutions.'

'Since when did you pay tax?'

'I didn't say I did. Hey – what do you call twelve investment bankers at the bottom of the ocean?'

'What?'

'A good start.' Barry grinned and polished off the remains of his lager. 'Seriously, I'd like to see them all out of a job.'

'A couple of my friends who work in banking have been made redundant.'

'My heart fairly bleeds.'

'Well, no doubt you'll get good material for your comedy routine out of it all.'

Barry turned to Chay. 'I'll bet Dad agrees with me – don't you, you old unreconstructed Marxist? You always used to bang on about the greed and corruption of the markets. I'll bet you're delighted at the nationalisation of the banks. Totalitarian government in charge of the economy, right on, eh?'

Chay put his head on one side, and gave a wise smile. 'I have to confess my views have mellowed over the past few years. I used to be rather naive about money.'

'You mean when you didn't have any?'

'Wealth brings responsibilities. Money needs to be invested, made to work.'

'That sounds suspiciously like capitalism,' murmured Anthony, remembering Chay in his idleness, wheedling loans from friends, living on handouts from long-suffering relatives, pontificating all the while about the redistribution of wealth and the iniquities of the capitalist system.

'The rich are rich for a reason. The more of them I meet, the better I understand that. I've been lucky enough to have made some very useful contacts. Last year I met someone who has helped me to make some spectacularly good investments.'

Barry looked at his father with keen interest. 'Really?'

'What would you say if I told you I've been getting steady returns between ten and eleven per cent for the past two years?'

'I'd say it sounds too good to be true,' replied Anthony.

'And I'd say, please can I have a piece of it?' exclaimed Barry.

'That's just it. Not everyone can. This financier is very selective about his client investors. I know people who've begged him to take them on, but have been refused.'

'How did you meet him?' asked Anthony.

'I was introduced to him by a mutual friend at a country club in Palm Beach.'

Anthony recalled the terrible squats his father used to live in, the candlelit rooms, bare floorboards and damp walls, lentil stews, incense sticks, sleeping bags. Now he was glad-handing top-flight investors in Palm Beach country clubs. You had to marvel at it, really. 'And he knows something that no one else does?'

'Every field has its experts, and this guy just happens to be the best. He's absolutely solid. He's a very astute businessman and philanthropist, highly regarded in New York social circles.'

'What's his name?'

Chay shook his head. 'His name wouldn't mean anything to you. But the reason I mention him is that I was thinking I could invest the capital sums I've set aside for you both with him, if you like.'

Anthony caught Barry's keen expression, and could tell he was busy calculating how much that rate of interest would net him over the next few years. Barry set a lot of store by the couple of hundred grand that Chay had, allegedly, earmarked for each of them, and which they were to receive on their thirtieth birthdays. Barry nodded. 'Yeah, do it, Dad. I mean, ten per cent – what's not to like?'

Chay turned and looked enquiringly at Anthony. Anthony reflected, twisting his beer glass on the tabletop. At last he said, 'No, it's OK, thanks. Leave mine in the bank.'

'Are you mad?' said Barry. 'You have to speculate to accumulate.'

'He has his mother's cautious streak,' said Chay. 'Not one of life's adventurers. Not a risk-taker.'

Anthony forced a smile. He was getting heartily sick of being labelled boring and cautious, but in this particular instance he didn't feel like living dangerously. It seemed odd that anyone should be getting those kinds of returns in the present economic climate. He shrugged and said, 'I'll leave it to you wild creative types to do the bold, daring stuff.' He drained his drink. 'Just remember – if it looks too good to be true, it usually is.' He glanced at his watch. 'I've got to go. I'm in court tomorrow.'

'Go on, then, you young pillar of the judicial establishment,' said his father. 'I'll probably be over again around Christmas. I'll be in touch.'

'Fine. See you. And thanks for dinner.' He nodded at his brother. 'Barry.'

'Cheers, Tony,' replied Barry. 'See you around.' Barry tapped his pint glass. 'Come on – get them in, Dad. You're the one with the money.'

CHAPTER FOUR

Monday morning was not going well for Rachel. Her meticulously planned schedule took its first knock just as she and Oliver were about to leave the house, when Oliver had announced that he needed to take six baby photos of himself to school for a class project. Why was it, Rachel wondered as she hurried to the study to rummage through boxes, that children came up with these things at the last moment? She was already running late, and was bound to miss her train at this rate.

'There you are,' she said, slipping them into an envelope and handing them to Oliver. 'Come on – where's your reading book? We're late. Hurry!'

In the car, six-year-old Oliver took the photos from their envelope and gravely examined each in turn. The last one he gazed at longest, then remarked, 'That's me and Daddy.'

Slowing at a red light, Rachel glanced down at the photo. It was a close-up of Leo kissing Oliver's soft baby cheek. It had been taken when Oliver was just eight weeks old, in the garden of the house where she and Leo had lived briefly, back in the deluded days when she'd imagined their marriage meant something. How quickly she'd learnt. No one person could ever be enough for Leo. There always had to be some third person, an illicit, faceless lover, male or female. Her glance lingered on the picture. Even now, the sight of Leo made her heart contract. She could have done without being reminded of how in love she'd once been. She was startled from her thoughts by a car horn telling her the lights had changed, and pulled away quickly.

'So, what are you going to be doing with these pictures?' she asked Oliver.

'We have to write a story about ourselves, and then we cut it out and stick it onto . . . onto . . . something, and then we stick our pictures aaaall around the story,' Oliver made a big circle with his hand, 'and Mrs Latham puts them on the wall.'

'That sounds nice. Can I come and see?'

'If you like,' replied Oliver casually. 'I'm going to put the picture of me and Daddy right at the top.'

The next setback came when Lucy, Oliver's childminder, told Rachel that although she'd agreed to keep Oliver till seven, because Rachel was speaking at a seminar, she was no longer able to. 'The hospital's brought my mother's operation forward. She's going in this afternoon and I need to visit her this evening.'

'Don't worry, I'll sort something out,' said Rachel, without the least clue what she was going to do.

Rachel kissed Oliver goodbye and drove to the station car park, deciding on the way that her only option was to call

Leo and ask if he could get away early. She sent him a quick text, hoping he didn't have a con or a hearing arranged for the afternoon, and hurried to the platform to see her train pulling out. She would have to wait twenty minutes for the next one.

Once on the train, she tried to concentrate on reading documents in a new case in which she'd been instructed, but memories revived by Oliver's baby pictures kept crowding in and distracting her. God, how she wished she could simply erase Leo from her life and mind. But nothing was that simple. She closed her laptop and stared out of the train window. A few men had come close to displacing Leo in her heart, but only ever for a short time. She wished she could have made it work with Charles – he had been the kindest, sweetest man. The trouble was, for all his infidelity and incredible selfishness, Leo was a hard act to follow. Or was it those negative qualities which made him so attractive? She'd given up trying to work it out. The fact was, she needed someone to eclipse Leo. She needed to be in love. Easier said than done. She knew she was more than averagely attractive, and still young at thirty-three – but where were all the eligible men? The City of London should be teeming with them, but all the ones she came into contact with were either middle-aged and married with families, or young, conceited and gormless, or nudging sixty and lecherous. Her work as a solicitor meant she saw the same old faces every day, and most of her non-working hours were spent with Oliver. Where were the opportunities? Something had to change. It was ridiculous still to be brooding over one's ex after five years.

It was after 9.45 when Rachel reached the offices of

Nichols & Co in Bishopsgate. Her colleague Fred Fenton accosted her as she emerged from the lift.

'Bad news, I'm afraid,' Fred told her, as he walked with Rachel to her office. 'Ann Halliday has had to pull out of the casino case. A six-week hearing she had coming up in December has been moved forward. So she's having to bow out.'

Rachel slung her coat on a hook, and sat down with a sigh. 'That's all we need. I'd better see who else is free. Oh, and Fred, can we have a word at some point today with Andrew about that Drucker arbitration?'

'Sure. Catch you later.'

It was clearly going to be one of those days, thought Rachel. Not yet ten o'clock, plenty of time for more things to go wrong. Her mobile began to buzz in her bag. She fished it out, and saw the caller was Leo.

'Hi – did you get my text?'

'Yes. Not a problem. I'll pick Oliver up.'

'Thanks. I've got this wretched seminar after work, and I probably won't get back till after seven.'

'I'll have him for the night if you like. I was going to work from home tomorrow morning, so I can take him into school.'

'Really? He'd love that. Are you sure you don't mind?'

'Of course I don't. By the way, did you see Whiteside's judgment?'

'Yes, I did. What a hash he made of it! It seemed wrong from start to finish.'

'I couldn't agree more. A complete travesty. That's what comes of letting any Tom, Dick or Harry sit in Admiralty cases. It makes one wonder about the calibre of people getting onto the High Court Bench these days.'

'That's because hardly anyone wants the job. Would you do it?'

'I doubt if Henry would let me.' Leo paused, then added, 'I suppose it has its attractions.'

Rachel laughed. 'Tell me about them when you become Mr Justice Davies. Then I'll believe it.'

'At least I wouldn't be handing down ludicrous judgments like Whiteside's and clogging up the Appeal Court lists.'

They talked about the case briefly, then Leo said, 'I'd better go. I've got a con in a couple of minutes.'

'OK. Thanks for this afternoon. I'll ring Lucy to tell her you'll be taking Oliver to school in the morning. Bye.'

Rachel wished that all conversations with Leo could be as amicable. It reminded her of the early days of their relationship. They'd always had so much to talk about – in bed and out of it. On paper, they were a perfectly suited couple. If only it could have been as easy as talking – or even making love. She brought her drifting thoughts to a halt. That was enough. She was going to have to do something about her situation.

Later that morning she rang her friend Sophie, the mother of Oliver's school chum Josh, who lived just round the corner.

'Hi, it's Rachel. I just wondered if you were free later this evening for a glass of wine. Say around nine? My love life needs sorting out.'

'Absolutely. I'll be gasping for a drink after I've got this lot to bed.' Rachel could hear the sound of small voices and clattering in the background. 'Josh! Put that down! It doesn't go in the dishwasher. Sorry, Rachel. Yes, I'll pop round and leave Richard to do the evening shift. They're all in bed by eight, so it doesn't involve more than him sitting with a beer watching the Dave channel, and keeping an ear out.'

'Great. See you later.'

That was the evening taken care of. Now to find someone to take Ann Halliday's place in the casino case. She rang the clerks' room at 5 Caper Court and spoke to Henry, who consulted the on-screen diaries of the various members of chambers. 'Let's see . . . Mr Vane's no good, he's in court that day. Mr Bishop, no . . . How about Mr Cross? He's free to do the hearing, and he hasn't got much heavy work on in the run-up.'

Rachel hesitated. She needed someone who could get their head round what was a very complex case in a short space of time, and Anthony would be ideal. The truth was, ever since their affair a couple of years ago, Rachel had avoided briefing Anthony. They'd remained good friends, but she had the feeling it might be tricky working on a case together. Still, it seemed she didn't have much choice.

'Mr Cross will be fine.' They discussed fees, and Rachel said she would send the papers round within the hour.

Shortly after one, Leo went to Anthony's room. Anthony was sitting at his desk reading, his feet propped up on a cardboard box stuffed with documents. Unlike Leo's room, Anthony's was comfortably messy, with files and books everywhere.

Leo gave the box a kick. 'Christ, man, how can you work in this squalor? Didn't I teach you, when you were a callow and giddy youth, to keep a sense of order?'

'Don't kick that! It contains highly valuable evidence.

Besides, everything is in perfect order. I can lay my hands on any given document in seconds, if required. It just looks disordered to the untrained eye,' replied Anthony.

'Oh, yes? What's this, then?' asked Leo, picking up a random piece of paper from a pile on the table.

Anthony squinted at it. 'It's a chart. Something to do with a grounding case. Put it back. You're destroying an intricate filing system.' He swung his feet off the box. 'Rachel has just instructed me in a case that's coming up for a hearing in a few weeks' time. Rather an unusual one.'

'Tell me about it over lunch. How do you fancy beer and sandwiches at The Eagle?'

They left chambers and walked to the pub in Bouverie Street.

'Just an orange juice for me,' said Anthony, when they were at the bar. 'I need to finish those documents. We have a con tomorrow afternoon.'

They took their drinks and sandwiches to a table. 'So,' said Leo, 'fill me in. What's the case about?'

'A gambling debt, basically. Some rich Saudi gambling on credit at a private casino in Mayfair, paying for his chips by cheque. One night he writes a cheque for about three million, gets into an argument with one of the croupiers, and next day he stops the cheque. We're acting for the gaming club, trying to recover the debt – some years down the line, I might add.'

'No time bar, I take it?'

Anthony shook his head, wolfing down a sandwich.

'Sounds straightforward enough.'

'You would think so, wouldn't you? The trouble is, even though he put a stop on this whacking great cheque, the gaming club – Astleigh's – let him carry on gambling there for the next couple of years, because he was a hugely important client. The croupiers used to call him the Lion King. Something to do with the look of him, his big voice, stuff like that. Anyway, the club carried on grumbling about the debt, trying to strike a deal with him to repay it out of his winnings, but of course that never happened. In the end they lost patience, and now they're suing for their three million. And here's the interesting bit. The Lion King is arguing that by allowing him to carry on gambling after his cheque was dishonoured, the club was extending him illegal credit within the meaning of the Gaming Act, so their claim against him is unenforceable. Not only that, on the same basis he's counterclaiming all the sums he lost gambling during that period.'

'Cheeky sod,' chuckled Leo. 'Who's on the other side?'

'Linklaters. They've instructed George Freeman.'

'Sounds like one of his typically ingenious lines of argument. It'll never wash.'

'I hope you're right.' Anthony took a reflective sip of his orange juice. 'I don't understand the attraction of gambling. Surely you know the minute you walk into a casino that the odds are stacked against you.'

'Of course. That's not the point. I take it you've never gambled?'

Anthony shook his head. 'Not even as a student. There were always plenty of games of three-card brag or stud poker around, but I never played. I was on such a tight budget I couldn't afford to lose a penny.' Anthony was visited by a sudden memory from his student days, of sitting in his bedroom with all the loose change he'd collected from every pocket, cranny and chair-back set out in pathetic little stacks on the table in front of him, trying to work out if it would last the week. 'The Lion King gambled over fifty million in the space of five years. Fifty million! He could lose a couple of million in a single night and think nothing of it. If you ask me, that's not just stupid, it's downright immoral.'

'You're right, of course – in theory. But people don't only gamble for money. They do it for the buzz, the tantalising possibility that just this once, they might get lucky. Of course everyone loses in the long run, but they win often enough to keep them hoping. It's like any other high. And then there's the atmosphere. There's something supercharged about a private gaming club. High stakes, serious money, beautiful people.'

'All very James Bond, no doubt. But when you come down to it, what's the difference between a game of roulette and a game of bingo?'

'A whole world, believe me.' Leo was suddenly visited by a memory of his own, one of Anthony when he'd just arrived in chambers as a raw and inexperienced pupil, resplendent in a new Marks & Spencer suit, startlingly handsome and intelligent, touchingly naive, perfect to be moulded and educated in the ways of the world. Leo had taken it upon himself to act as a mentor, introducing him to all kinds of entirely straightforward pleasures, which young Anthony had thought the height of sophistication – West End restaurants, decent wine, art galleries, plays, concerts of classical music. It had been a delight to educate him, and to observe his intense enjoyment of things which Leo had long taken for granted. Anthony had represented his own forgotten self, a lower-middle-class grammar school boy of exceptional talents, determined to achieve success and to find acceptance in a class-ridden profession through his own brilliance and professional excellence.

'Perhaps I should take you to Crockfords some time, or Aspinalls,' said Leo. 'It's an interesting social experience, if nothing else.'

'Rachel and I have to go to Astleigh's tomorrow afternoon to talk to the management. Everything that happened took place before the repeal of section sixteen of the Gaming Act, and the club was operating its own credit system, which we need to get our heads around.'

'Well, that should be instructive – though not as much fun as a night at the tables,' said Leo.

They talked about work for a while, but Leo found himself distracted by a girl at the far end of the pub who kept glancing in their direction. She was petite, attractive, with a fine-boned face, honey-blonde hair and an intense gaze, and Leo had the feeling he'd seen her somewhere. Then he remembered where. She'd been sitting in the back of the court during the Kirkbride hearing. He remembered thinking then that she looked familiar, and supposed she was a student taking notes, though he couldn't think why any student should bother with such a boring case. Students from the Council of Legal Education were always knocking around the Temple, and he tended to notice the attractive ones. He could only assume that her presence in the pub today was coincidence, and that Anthony, who was lounging elegantly in his chair, was the object of her attention.

'You seem to have an admirer,' murmured Leo. 'Girl in the corner with the dark blonde hair.'

Anthony glanced at the girl. She was undoubtedly pretty – more than pretty. But he was pretty sure it was Leo she was staring at. He was used to Leo attracting female attention, and it invariably aroused in him some resentment which he couldn't quite fathom. Jealousy of a kind, he supposed, but of what or whom he couldn't quite determine. 'You're too modest,' Anthony told Leo. 'It's you she's looking at, not me.'

But Leo wasn't listening. He glanced at his watch. 'Come on. I need to get back. I have to leave early to collect Oliver.'

The girl in the corner watched them leave, quickly finished her drink and then, keeping a careful distance, followed them all the way from the pub back to Caper Court.

That evening, at half past nine, Sophie was curled up on Rachel's sofa with a glass of wine. Rachel was sitting cross-legged on the rug by the fire, head bent over a notepad, making a list. Sophie stroked the duck-egg blue silk cushions and glanced around, savouring the tranquillity. The room was lit by large table lamps, their soft glow reflected in the dark, polished wood of the floor, casting shadows on the pale walls hung with elegantly framed pictures. Long curtains of grey velvet shut out the autumn night. She loved being here. Rachel's house was so different from the chaos of her own home. But she was able to survey it all and feel not the slightest tinge of envy. Everything – the carefully placed porcelain bowls, the parchment-coloured sofas and chairs, the perfectly arranged pink peonies and the beautiful prints and ornaments – would drive her nuts inside a week. Not that any of it would survive that long at the hands of her offspring. She articulated the thought which had been troubling her.

'How do you manage to bring up a six-year-old boy in a place like this?' she asked Rachel. 'I mean, all these beautiful things – aren't you worried Oliver might knock something over, or get chocolate on the cushions?'

Rachel looked up, her silky black hair gleaming in the firelight. 'Oliver knows not to bring food in here. And I've trained him since he was little to be careful of everything. He's a great respecter of order. Besides, he doesn't come in here much. He has his bedroom – that's untidy enough. And his playroom, of course.' She dipped her head again, and jotted something down on the notepad.

'Right,' murmured Sophie. Oliver's bedroom untidy? Knowing Rachel, it was probably spotless, books on shelves, toys tidied away, dressing-gown hung up, slippers neatly together, pyjamas folded beneath the pillow. She thought of Josh and Billy's bedroom, the chaos of Action Men and toy cars and trucks strewn across the carpet, the overstuffed plastic dustbin of soft toys, and the mess of books and clothes. She took another sip of wine.

'So, where do we start?'

'Well . . .' Rachel gazed doubtfully at the notepad on her knee. 'I thought if I made a list. You know, of necessary qualities. The kind of things I'm looking for in a man.'

Sophie nodded. 'Fire away.'

'Well, he has to be educated, obviously. And to be a professional of some kind.'

'No proles, plumbers or scaffolders.'

'I'm not being a snob, or anything. It's just—'

Sophie waved this away. 'I know you're not. Carry on.'

'He has to be intelligent, well read, interesting, fond of cinema, books, theatre, that kind of thing.'

'Looks?'

'Oh, you know . . .'

Sophie gazed at Rachel sitting there with her head on one side, fabulous cheekbones etched by the light, her dark hair framing her face, thoughtful blue eyes contemplating the mysterious charms of some unknown lover. How could any man handle such perfection? It wasn't just the way Rachel looked. It was everything about her. She was so meticulous in every aspect of her life that to Sophie it sometimes seemed scary. Her house, for instance, the immaculate way she always dressed. Sophie remembered the first time she'd met Rachel at a school play, how intimidated she'd been by her cool, crisp appearance. Yet the Rachel she had come to know wasn't cool. Not really. Her apparent reserve masked a hesitant, loving nature that longed to be impulsive, but was somehow restrained. Passion strangled at birth.

'Tall, but not too tall,' Rachel went on. 'Good-looking – whatever that is. God, that's awful, isn't it? I mean, so vague . . . But it's hard. You just know it when you see it, don't you?'

Sophie reached down and refilled her own glass and Rachel's. The trouble was, the girl was still in love with her ex-husband. She might as well be listing the qualities of the legendary Leo.

'I'm not sure this list is going to get us anywhere,' said Sophie. 'Why don't we cut to the chase?'

'What do you mean?'

'You need to find out what's out there.' Sophie got up. 'Come on, take me to where your computer lives.'

Rachel rose obediently and took Sophie to her study. They sat down at the computer. Sophie issued commands.

'OK, type in www-dot-telegraph-dot-co-dot-uk-slash-onlinedating.' Rachel hesitated. 'Go on!'

'Why *The Telegraph*?'

'Don't worry, we'll do *The Guardian* as well. And *The Times*. We just have to start somewhere. OK, now here's where you register—' She glanced at Rachel. 'What's the problem?'

Rachel made a face. 'I'm not sure if this is what I want to do. It wasn't what I had in mind.'

'So you were just going to make a list of desirable characteristics and put it under your pillow, and hope the right man would magically reveal himself in your dreams? Come on – get real.'

Rachel sighed. 'What do I do next?'

'You register. And then all you have to do is tick the boxes, say what you're looking for. Look – they even let you specify Oxbridge-educated, if you want.'

'Leo went to Bristol,' said Rachel. She looked at Sophie. 'Oh God – forget I said that.'

'Come on,' said Sophie. 'Get ticking.'

It was well after eleven by the time they finished, and they'd had great fun inspecting various men and writing Rachel's profile, in between glasses of wine.

'I'm sure this isn't the kind of thing one should do when drunk,' said Rachel.

'Best way,' said Sophie. She stood up and stretched her arms.

'Do you think the picture I posted was all right? The one on the chambers website is the only one I've got.'

'It's lovely,' yawned Sophie. 'You're very photogenic. Couldn't take a bad picture if you tried. God, look at the time. I have to be up at half six.'

Rachel saw Sophie to the door. 'You're a true friend – thanks for coming round. Though I'm still not sure online dating is quite me.'

'You don't know till you try.' Sophie kissed Rachel goodnight. 'All you have to do now is wait for the offers to come flooding in.'

Rachel closed the door and leant against it, feeling a little drunk and already regretting what she'd just done. She tried to imagine the kind of man she hoped might be out there. But she could see only one face.

CHAPTER FIVE

The following afternoon, around quarter to four, Anthony arrived at Rachel's office to go over the papers in the casino case, and from there they took a taxi to Astleigh's in Mayfair, where they had a five o'clock appointment with the manager.

'I'm not quite sure of the point of this,' said Anthony, as the cab made its slow way through the City rush hour traffic. 'I'm pretty much on top of the case, so I don't see where it gets me to visit the place where this individual happened to chuck away his small fortune.'

'I thought you might find it useful to have the club's credit system explained to you by Mr Depaul himself.'

'I do know what a scrip cheque is,' retorted Anthony. 'And I've read the relevant provisions of the Gaming Act.'

'Well, it's often helpful to see first hand how things operate. Good to get a feel for the background to a case. You know that.'

Rachel was struck by Anthony's moody, offhand manner. He'd been like it for the past hour. Maybe his love life was as problematic as her own. She sighed inwardly. If she and Anthony had been able to make their relationship work two years ago, how much simpler both their lives might be now. But the obvious person wasn't always the right person. Her mind slipped back to last night, being persuaded by Sophie to sign up to that awful online dating thing after too many glasses of wine. How unbelievably naff. As soon as she got home she would unsubscribe. Just the thought of strange men studying her photo and reading her personal details made her cringe.

'What's that face for?' asked Anthony.

'Oh, nothing. Just something I did which I now regret.'

They both lapsed into silence.

Ten minutes later they reached the casino, which was tucked away at the end of Curzon Street. Its entrance was unostentatious, a black door set between pillars, with the letter 'A' emblazoned on the canopy above. They were buzzed in, and escorted by Mr Depaul's assistant down a plushly decorated hallway. The gaming room was at the far end, behind double doors. The assistant opened the doors and ushered Anthony and Rachel in. Although the room was large, it possessed a strange, luxuriant intimacy. An expanse of burgundy-and-gold patterned carpet was dotted with mahogany-lipped gaming tables and gilt-legged chairs. Chandeliers shimmered below the hand-painted ceiling, lamps glowed in alcoves, and at the end was a raised bar. It was expensively and opulently furnished, like a huge Edwardian drawing room, fragrant with the faint scent of cigars and brandies, redolent of serious money. Anthony found it unexpectedly exciting.

Mr Depaul crossed the floor to meet them, his feet soundless on the deep-piled carpet. He was a dark-haired, dapper Frenchman, with bright eyes and an enthusiastic manner. He was one of the most popular and well-respected casino managers in London, possessing an excellent understanding of the proclivities and vagaries of his punters, particularly the high rollers, and capable of switching from playful to serious as the situation demanded. His relationship with those who visited the casino regularly was friendly and warm, but, as he explained to Anthony and Rachel, his ultimate loyalty lay with the casino.

'One could not help liking Mr Al-Sarraj,' said Mr Depaul, as he ushered Anthony and Rachel into his office. 'He was one of our best clients. He was what casinos call a whale – someone who thinks nothing of spending millions in a night. The staff loved him because he gave such enormous tips – as much as five thousand pounds if he was in the right mood. But in the end, when the chips are down,' Mr Depaul smiled at his own little joke, 'the club must get what it is owed. Please, take a seat.' Mr Depaul sat down at his desk. 'We were sorry to lose Mr Al-Sarraj as a client. He was good for business. Winning or losing, he was always the life and soul of the casino. He liked to rub shoulders with rich, influential people – Adnan Khashoggi one night, Tom Cruise the next, the Sultan of Brunei another. He liked to play big. Two million wasn't so much to the Lion King. I have seen him lose a quarter of that sum at the roulette wheel in one half-hour session. But for some reason, in this game, on that night,' Mr Depaul stabbed the desktop with his finger, 'he said the game had not been fair, and he would not honour the cheque. Now we have to claim back our money.' Mr Depaul buzzed through to his PA. 'Adam, some coffee, please.' He smiled at Rachel and Anthony. 'OK, to business.'

Mr Depaul spent some time explaining the operation of the club's credit facilities, then the three of them went through documents and discussed the details of the case. It was half past six by the time they finished. Rachel was putting the papers back in her briefcase, when Anthony suddenly remarked, 'You know, it puzzles me that the casino is pursuing this claim.'

Mr Depaul arched his brows enquiringly. 'Why? We gave Mr Al-Sarraj every opportunity to repay the money from his winnings.'

'Yes, but you already said that two million was nothing to Al-Sarraj. Surely it was nothing to the club, compared to the amount Astleigh's stood to earn from him in the future if the debt had simply been written off and he'd been allowed to continue gambling?'

Mr Depaul shook his head. 'In the months before we brought our claim against him, the scale of his betting had declined to a mere ten thousand or so a night.' Mr Depaul gave a shrug. 'Who knows? Perhaps he ran out of money. Regardless of that, the reason the house always wins, Mr Cross, is that the house always recovers its debts.'

'I think your claim should succeed. And if it's any comfort, I don't believe his counterclaim has much chance of success.'

'That's good to know.' Mr Depaul rose from his desk, glancing at his watch. 'We open in half an hour. Perhaps you would like to take a little look round the club before you leave?'

'I'd like that,' replied Anthony. He glanced at Rachel. 'Unless you're in a hurry?'

'I have to go to pick up Oliver. But you stay. I'm sure it'll be fascinating.'

Mr Depaul took Anthony to the gaming room.

'I've never been in a casino before,' remarked Anthony.

'Really?' Mr Depaul made a discreet gesture to a passing member of staff. 'Young, sophisticated people like yourself are the kind of clients we have in here every night. Come and see what you are missing.'

The gaming room had now sprung to life, with croupiers behind every table, setting up for the evening. Mr Depaul led Anthony to a blue baize table. 'This is the blackjack table. It's a simple game, which you no doubt know. You play the dealer, and the object is to draw cards with a value totalling twenty-one, or as near as possible.' A waiter arrived at that moment with a glass of champagne on a little silver tray. 'Please,' said Mr Depaul, handing it to Anthony. 'I insist. You are our guest. There are no big payouts with blackjack, but if you're adventurous and play several boxes at once, the wins can mount up.'

'And the losses, no doubt,' said Anthony, sipping his champagne.

'Our clients aren't counting their losses, Mr Cross. They only think about winning. That's the excitement, the pleasure. Now, this is the baccarat table. In some casinos it is called Punto Banco. A very simple card game, but with a lot of suspense. The players bet on a player or on the bank, or they can play for what is called an "*egalité*", or a "tie", which pays out at eight to one. There is a nice little tension which rises when the third card, the make-or-break card, is drawn.' Mr Depaul gestured around as they moved away. 'Then we have the poker tables. There are many variations of the game. Clients here generally play for very high stakes. And lastly,' Mr Depaul led him to one of the roulette tables, 'perhaps the most popular game. Roulette was the Lion King's favourite. Very simple, as you know – you bet on a number, the wheel is spun, and the number into which the ball falls pays out.' Mr Depaul nodded at the croupier, who flicked the little ball and set the wheel turning. Anthony watched. There was something mesmeric about the gleam and spin of the wheel, and the clatter of the ball. 'In the US and on the Continent, casinos have wheels with zero and double zero, which doubles the house advantage, but here in the UK we play only one zero.'

'Not especially good odds,' said Anthony.

'Ah, but don't forget that if you win, the payout is thirty-five to one, and that is a very exciting prospect. Especially if you're playing for high stakes.'

'And if you're rich enough not to mind losing more times than you win.'

Mr Depaul smiled. 'Your approach to this is too clinical. People come here to escape, to enjoy the thrill of the tables, not to make money. I doubt if we would ever make a gambler of you, Mr Cross.'

Anthony finished his champagne. 'It's been fascinating. Thanks.'

'My pleasure,' said Mr Depaul, with a little bow. 'Perhaps one evening when our case has been successfully concluded, we can look forward to your company at the casino.'

Anthony smiled. 'Perhaps.'

He left Astleigh's and headed up Curzon Street in the

gathering dusk, and had almost reached Park Lane when he heard a voice hailing him.

'Anthony! Yo!'

Anthony turned and saw a thickset young man with tousled fair hair waving from the other side of the street. It was Edward Choke, his old rival in pupillage. Edward was from a wealthy and influential family, one of those charmed beings who happily expect the good things in life to fall into their lap without much effort or endeavour on their part, but whom it was impossible to dislike. When he and Anthony had both been pupils at 5 Caper Court some years earlier, Edward, as the nephew of the then head of chambers, had expected to secure a tenancy without much difficulty. On a chambers vote, however, he had lost out to Anthony, and it was testimony both to Edward's good nature and singular lack of ambition that he hadn't for one moment begrudged Anthony the place. Edward knew Anthony was cleverer than he was, and far more deserving of the tenancy. A career at the Bar had meant everything to Anthony, and the tenancy at 5 Caper Court had been the ultimate reward for years of struggle and hard work. For Edward, it had merely been one of a number of options available to him – family connections meant that he would never be short of a job of some kind.

Anthony watched Edward cross the street, dodging taxis. They shook hands. 'Good to see you, Ed. It's been a long time.'

'Three years at least, I'd say. Where the hell have you been?'

Anthony smiled. 'Where I've always been. Caper Court. What about you?'

'Oh, here and there. Look, are you rushing off somewhere, or have you time for a quick drink?'

'I was just on my way home. Where do you suggest?'

'Let's go to the King's Arms in Shepherd Market and grab a pint.'

They made their way to the pub and settled themselves at a table with their beers.

'So, what are you up to these days?' asked Anthony. 'Still at the Ministry for Arts and Cultural Development?'

'Good God, no. Jacked that in ages ago. Terminally boring, the civil service. Almost as bad as the law.'

'Or merchant banking?'

'Fuck me, that was the worst of the lot,' observed Edward of his brief and ignominious stint at Morgan Grenfell. 'Ghastly people, bankers. Never trusted a single one of them. Rightly, as it turns out. City screen-jockeys who've made a complete balls-up of everything. Not a day goes by without another bank biting the dust, shares crashing, chaps getting fired.' He took a long pull at his pint, then added with engaging frankness, 'Actually, I came into my money three years ago, so there's not much need to work, to be honest.'

'Lucky you.'

'Well, yes and no. I mean, loafing around is all very well – nice not to have to get up and go to an office every day, but a chap needs to keep busy. I'm supposed to be doing a bit of work managing my father's estate down in Surrey, but frankly the countryside bores me to death. I spend most of my time in town. I've been helping Piers Hunt-Thompson organise a couple of balls. Charity events, debs, that kind of stuff. He's a kind of society events fixer now, runs that club Pooks in Frith Street.'

'I remember Piers.'

'Of course – you went out with Julia before she and Piers got together, didn't you? They got married a couple of years ago. I went to the wedding. Massive bash in Gloucestershire. Completely brilliant. I got utterly wasted.'

'I didn't know they were married,' said Anthony. Julia had been one of his first loves, a leggy blonde barrister whom he had met during his pupillage. He had thought she loved him as much as he loved her, but she had betrayed his affection with casual indifference. To think she'd actually married that complete wanker, Piers Hunt-Thompson.

'So anyway, apart from throwing the odd bit of dosh at Piers' various ventures, and helping the old man out, there's not much to do except go out and have a good time, I'm ashamed to say.'

Anthony could tell from Edward's grin that shame didn't come into it. He'd always envied the way Edward managed to squeeze the maximum enjoyment out of life without feeling any of the guilt which plagued Anthony, that sense that he should be achieving, working for life's rewards, whatever they might be.

'A good time being . . . ?'

'Oh, you know – parties, clubs, hitting the odd casino now and then.'

'I was just coming from Astleigh's when I met you.'

'Bit early in the day for the tables, old man.'

'Not what you think. It was in the name of work. I'm acting for them in a case, and I needed to see how they operate.'

'Everything's about work with you, isn't it? That's always been your trouble, Tony. You take life too seriously. Listen, what are you doing for the rest of the evening? I'm meeting some friends at the Ritz for cocktails. Fancy coming along?'

Anthony could think of no reason why not. He had nothing better to do, and an evening with Edward was invariably good fun. 'OK,' he said, 'I'm up for it.'

'Excellent. Look, let's have another here, then head off. What d'you say?'

'I'm in your hands, Ed.'

After cocktails at the Ritz with an assortment of Edward's friends, they headed to the Wolseley for supper. Anthony knew most of the others from parties and clubs, rich twenty-somethings from wealthy families. They weren't necessarily people he much liked, but it gave him satisfaction to know that nowadays he could keep up with them, that he no longer felt out of place in their company in the way he once would have. He could still recall the social agonies of being unable to afford taxis, having to do frantic mental calculations about whether, if he got his round in, he would be able to afford lunch the next day, of having to bow out of evenings halfway through because people had begun to order champagne and outrageously expensive bar snacks, and he simply couldn't pay his way. His early years as a barrister had been marked by many such humiliations, and it was important to him now that he had enough money in the bank to spend as freely, if not quite as carelessly, as those around him.

After supper Edward was still in a boisterous mood and wanted to go on somewhere. Someone suggested Chinawhite, someone else the Ministry of Sound.

'Not a club,' said Edward, 'I'm bored with clubs. How about a casino?'

The idea met with general approval. 'Right,' said Edward,

'let's go to Blunt's. We can walk it from here.' He turned to Anthony. 'You'll like this place. Much less stuffy than Astleigh's. The chap who runs it is the father of a chum of mine, Darius Egan. He's a top man. I'll introduce you.'

Fifteen minutes later they were at Blunt's, a private members' gaming club in Mount Street. Edward seemed to know just about everyone there. An extremely tall, thin man in an impeccably cut suit wove his way through the crowd to greet him.

'Darius – good to see you!' Edward and the thin man shook hands. 'Meet my friend Anthony Cross.'

Darius nodded at Anthony. 'Haven't seen you here before. New member?'

'I'm Edward's guest.'

'Jolly good. You don't seem to have drinks.' He snapped his fingers and a waiter shimmied across. 'What do you chaps fancy? Cristal? Pol Roger?'

'Cristal,' said Anthony. 'My treat,' he added to Edward. God alone knew how much it would cost, but he had firmly decided he didn't care. Those days were gone.

'Where's the old man?' Edward asked Darius.

'He's around somewhere. Probably in the gaming room.'

They followed Darius into the busy casino. Anthony was intrigued by the different atmosphere at each of the tables. The roulette table was buzzing with laughter and excitement, a gaggle of pretty girls shouldering near to watch the wheel spin and the ball drop. Further on at the card tables things were quieter, with only the murmur of the croupier's voice as he dealt the cards.

Darius's father, Caspar Egan, was pacing the room, his manner relaxed but watchful. Like his son he was tall, but fleshier, with cold eyes and smooth features ready for all social eventualities. Edward, who was an excellent customer, received his widest smile and most cordial greeting. Edward introduced Anthony.

'Tony's something of a casino novice.'

'Really?' Caspar turned his razor smile on Anthony, weighing him up. 'We'll have to find the right game for you. You enjoy poker?'

'I haven't played much.'

'Try our stud poker table. You'll enjoy it.'

'I don't really gamble,' said Anthony. This confession instantly left him feeling foolish. He caught the amusement in Darius's eyes.

'Well, tell you what – as you're a friend of Edward's, allow the house to make you a little present of twenty pounds' worth of chips. Just to get you started.'

'No, really—'

A waiter arrived with the champagne and glasses. 'Come on,' said Edward, 'let's splash this around, buy some chips, and get down to business.'

Anthony decided the most politic thing would be to accept the chips, but not use them. He would remain a disinterested spectator, and let Edward and his friends do the gambling. He followed Edward to the roulette table, and watched as Edward dropped the better part of five hundred pounds in twenty minutes.

'Ed,' Anthony said, knocking back his second glass of champagne, 'stop betting on the same number. Nineteen's never going to come up. This is a complete waste of money.'

Edward shrugged, grinned, and dropped another two black chips on nineteen. Anthony groaned. The chattering crowd fell quiet as the croupier spun the wheel and the ball clattered and bounced. Anthony happened to glance up, and there, standing on the other side of the table with a group of friends, was the girl who had been in the pub the other day, when he and Leo had been having lunch. She was dressed in a very short, silver-grey dress, her hair was loose about her shoulders, and her eyes were fixed on the wheel. He didn't think she had seen him. Suddenly a shout went up and Edward was punching the air and whooping.

'You jammy sod!' exclaimed Anthony. 'How much is that you've netted?'

'Seven grand!' replied Edward. 'See? Just a question of holding the old nerve. Come on, Tony, time you had a go.'

'Unlikely, I'd say,' came a drawling voice behind them. Anthony glanced over his shoulder, and saw Piers Hunt-Thompson. It was seven years since they'd last met. Piers was a big, ugly, loose-limbed man, with a prominent chin and broken nose, but with an exceptional air of swaggering self-confidence which managed to intimidate men and charm women. He smiled at Anthony with lazy insolence. 'Probably as tight-fisted as ever. Still watching the pennies, Anthony?'

'Still cheating at cricket, Piers?' replied Anthony.

A pretty blonde appeared at Piers' side, dressed in a low-cut, tight-fitting red dress. When she saw Anthony, her eyes widened and she gave a little gasp of delight.

'Anthony! How lovely!' Julia leant forward and kissed his cheek as though they were old friends, as though the last time they'd met she hadn't been shattering his heart into a million little pieces with her lies and betrayal.

'Julia,' said Anthony.

Julia caught sight of Edward. 'And Eddie, too! This is a regular reunion.' She kissed Edward.

Edward looked perplexed. 'You only saw me last Saturday.' He turned to Anthony. 'Come on, Anthony, you can't keep those chips in your pocket all night.'

Realising he had no choice, Anthony drew the two blue chips from his pocket and, after a moment's hesitation, put them both on number five. Beneath Piers' mocking gaze he felt out of his depth, regressing to the far-off student days when he'd had no money, no status, and no sense of self-worth in the company of well-heeled contemporaries. He was so busy hating himself for allowing Edward to bring him here that he didn't even watch the ball as the wheel spun.

Then Edward was clapping him on the back. 'Who's the jammy sod now?'

A pile of chips was being shoved towards him.

'Oh, well done,' said Piers. 'Now you can afford the taxi home. East Dulwich, isn't it?'

Anthony ignored him. He pushed the chips back onto the baize. 'Let it ride,' he said.

'Whoa!' said Edward. 'Don't you want to split it?'

Anthony shook his head. As he saw it, the seven hundred he'd just won wasn't his. The house could have it back. Everyone watched as the ball jumped and clattered, and just for an instant, to his own surprise, Anthony found himself wondering with a darting sense of hope whether the ball might not land on five again. Could he be that lucky? That would wipe the smirk off Hunt-Thompson's face. But the ball came to rest on fourteen, and his chips were swept away.

'I told you you should have split it,' said Edward mournfully.

‘He’d started spinning the wheel,’ said Anthony.

‘Doesn’t matter. You can bet till the croupier declares the end of betting. You can place a bet and change it while the wheel’s spinning.’

‘How can you talk about splitting bets? You bet on nineteen four times in a row!’

‘Yes, but I know what I’m doing,’ said Edward gravely.

Anthony burst out laughing. ‘OK, Ed, tell me where I went wrong.’

Edward proceeded to explain the finer points of roulette, and the different types and combinations of bets. Anthony listened and learnt, partly out of a long-formed academic habit which made it almost impossible for him not to absorb information, and partly because he didn’t want to have to talk to either Piers or Julia.

After a while, when Piers and Julia had disappeared, Edward wandered off to the poker tables. Anthony stayed at the roulette table and watched the flow of play, and began to understand, with growing interest, the good and bad betting strategies. He’d known when he did it that putting that entire seven hundred on a straight-up bet had been stupid, but he hadn’t cared at the time. Now he began to regret it. He would do it differently if he could.

Piers wandered past. ‘Run out of money? I can make you a loan, if you’re hard up.’

The remark made up Anthony’s mind. He went and bought some more chips, two hundred pounds’ worth. He wasn’t a poverty-stricken student any more. He was a successful barrister with a healthy bank balance, and he could afford a few games of roulette.

At the end of half an hour, with a judicious spread of

bets, Anthony came away four hundred pounds up. He was elated, pleased to have quit while he was ahead. Edward congratulated him, and Anthony went to the bar to order more champagne. He glanced at his watch. It was past one o'clock and he had a con at ten the next day. He should go soon.

'Past your bedtime?' murmured a voice. He looked round and saw Julia.

She set her glass down and leant on the bar. She was close enough for him to smell her perfume. 'It really is good to see you after all this time. I mean it. I've often thought about you.'

She wondered if Anthony could tell how hard her heart was beating. It had been a genuine shock to her to see him here tonight. He looked so well. The same as ever, the same boy she had loved, but more assured now, an entirely different creature.

Anthony gazed at her for a long moment. It was true, that one's early loves left the deepest and most lasting impression. Julia was strange and familiar all at once. Her blonde hair still curled into the nape of her neck in that little-boy way. Her eyes were still beguilingly blue, clear and bright, but their warmth and sparkle had faded to something less girlish.

'I've thought about you, too. How you broke my heart and hung me out to dry.'

'Sounds like a line from a song.'

He smiled. 'It was all rather corny, wasn't it?'

As he spoke, the girl in the silver-grey dress appeared at the far end of the bar. Anthony watched the way she shook back her dark blonde hair as she spoke to the barman, puzzled as to who she reminded him of. He touched Julia's arm and nodded towards the end of the bar. 'Who's that girl?'

Julia glanced along the bar. 'Gabrielle Stanley. Why?'

'Do you know anything about her?'

Julia's lip curled in a half-smile. 'Anthony—'

'What?'

She shook her head. 'Nothing. If you're so interested, go and find out yourself.' She finished the remains of her drink. 'See you around.'

She walked away. Talking to him had been a mistake. Seeing him after all this time was bad enough. What had she expected? That he was still in love with her? That they could rekindle some old flame? She saw Piers talking to Darius on the other side of the room and went over.

'Piers, I want to go.'

'Ask the doorman to call you a cab.'

'Please, Piers. I'm tired.'

'Well, I'm not. Now fuck off home, if you must.'

Julia fetched her coat and took a taxi home alone.

Anthony left the bar and went back to the gaming room. Edward was now caught up in a game of stud poker. Anthony watched for a few minutes, but his glance kept slipping to the chattering crowd at the roulette table. He'd enjoyed his half-hour there. What Leo had said was true. It wasn't so much the gambling – though winning had been pretty good, and it was nice to come away with an extra four hundred in one's pocket. It was about having fun. It was about the room, the people. Something stirred in him, something like an itch. He crossed the room, bought some more chips, and went back to the roulette table.

CHAPTER SIX

Anthony found it hard to focus during his ten o'clock meeting the next morning. Not only was he mildly hungover, he couldn't stop thinking about the five hundred pounds he'd lost on his second, disastrous outing at the roulette table last night. It wasn't as though he'd been betting stupidly, on one number. He'd planned what seemed like a good strategy, using odds and evens, split bets and corner bets. He shouldn't have lost as badly as he had. He'd been kept going by the conviction that on the next spin of the wheel his luck would recover. If Edward hadn't called it a night he'd probably have gone on to lose even more. He couldn't believe how stupid he'd been. Never again. He kept thinking about Julia, too. He could have done without meeting her again. She was someone he would never quite get over, despite all the hurt she'd caused.

He had to fight against these distractions to focus on the complexities of the case under discussion, and by the time the conference ended at twelve-fifteen, he was feeling pretty lousy. He went to the clerks' room in search of paracetamol.

'I've only got Alka Seltzer,' said Felicity, rummaging in her desk drawer.

'No, thanks,' said Anthony. 'They give me indigestion.'

'Weird. They're meant to cure that. Sure you aren't thinking of something else?'

'No, I'm not thinking of something else.'

'All right. Suit yourself.' Felicity shut the drawer.

Leo came into the clerks' room and dumped some papers on Felicity's desk. 'These need to go over to Brian Rosebery's chambers asap.'

'I'll get Liam to do it. Liam!'

Liam scuttled over. 'Twenty Essex Street,' Felicity told him. 'Step on it.'

Leo glanced at Anthony, who was staring out of the window and fiddling with the blind cord. 'You OK?'

Anthony yawned hugely and rubbed his hand over his face. 'I've been better.'

'I was hoping to have a chat later on. With you and Michael. How about a drink in Middle Temple Bar? Around six?'

Anthony nodded. 'If I'm still alive.'

Leo shrugged on his jacket. 'Right,' he told Felicity, 'I'm off to lunch.'

'Don't forget you've got a con with Murray Holden at two-thirty.'

'I won't. See you later.'

Later that afternoon, around quarter to six, Gabrielle Stanley saw Leo coming out of chambers. She had been hanging round the cloisters for the better part of an hour waiting for this moment. She watched him pause at the bottom of the steps to button up his coat. A chilly wind drove a flurry of autumn leaves across the flagstones. She stepped out from behind the pillar and was about to head across the courtyard when a tall, thin man with glasses hurried out of chambers to join Leo. She remained where she was, her heart thudding, and watched them walk through the archway to Pump Court. She tried to make sense of her confused emotions. Part of her was actually relieved that the other man had made speaking to Leo impossible. In which case, why had she been lurking here half the afternoon, freezing her ears off? She knew the answer to that. Even if she wasn't going to be brave enough to talk to him – and she had to, she really had to, otherwise this was totally pointless – she wanted simply to be able to look at him. The longer she looked, the closer she came. That was what she'd been telling herself, but in fact, unless she spoke to him, all the looking in the world wasn't going to get her anywhere. There had been that afternoon in court two weeks ago, when she'd spent two whole hours staring at him. Watching him sit, stand, speak, sigh, smile, glance at his watch, shuffle his papers, yawn, feeling herself getting closer and closer. Afterwards, as the court emptied, she'd thought she might go for it then, just walk right up to him – but she hadn't. She couldn't. He was with people. No, that wasn't true – there had been a whole three or four minutes when he'd been walking down Middle Temple Lane on his own, and she'd simply bottled it. And if she went on bottling it, this thing was always going to remain beyond her grasp.

She set off after them, maintaining a discreet distance, a

slight figure in tight jeans, knee-length boots, and a baggy suede jacket over a cowl-necked sweater, hair pulled scruffily back in a hairband. Her eyes were fastened on Leo. He and the thin man paused at the doorway to Middle Temple Bar, waiting for someone who was coming up the lane from the Embankment end. As he drew closer, Gabrielle recognised the young man who'd been with Leo in the pub, and at Blunt's last night. She'd been careful not to meet his eye across the roulette table, but she had the feeling he'd recognised her. He might say something to Leo, and that could be a problem.

The three men went inside, and Gabrielle crossed the lane to Fountain Court, where she dithered for a while, kicking shoals of dead leaves and wondering what to do. This was getting pathetic. She had to be braver. It was tonight or never. If he'd gone for a drink, which he obviously had, he surely couldn't be more than an hour at most. When he came out she would follow him to where she knew his car was parked in King's Bench Walk. Then she'd just have to go for it. She felt her stomach drop through the floor just thinking about it. Resigning herself to another wait, she walked back to the bottom of the lane and leant against the wall, eyes fixed on the doorway to the bar.

'I'll get these,' said Leo.

Anthony and Michael Gibbon settled into a couple of armchairs. The bar was almost deserted, with only two people hunched silently over a game of chess at the far end.

'Place is dead,' said Anthony. 'Where is everyone?'

'When I was a student,' said Michael, taking off his glasses and polishing them with the end of his tie, 'this place would be absolutely heaving at this time of night. Of course, back then, you could get a treble Scotch for seventy-five pence, or near enough.' Leo returned from the bar at that moment with two whiskies and a pint of beer. 'I was just remarking to Anthony – remember how in our day this place would be full to bursting every evening? Everyone came. Students, juniors, QCs, the odd High Court judge. The bar was so heavily subsidised you could get drunk on next to nothing. Great days. Of course, that kind of thing is frowned upon now.' He rubbed the bridge of his nose and replaced his glasses, and took a sip of his Scotch.

'D'you remember Jess?' said Leo. He shook his head. 'Dear God.'

Michael smiled and nodded. 'She ran the bar thirty years ago,' he told Anthony. 'Long gone. Absolute battleaxe, face that would turn milk. Everyone was terrified of her, even the most senior people. I have never known a woman carry out the business of dispensing drinks so begrudgingly, or with such apparent loathing for her customers.'

'People used to compete with each other to get her to crack a smile,' said Leo, 'or just be civil. But the more fawningly polite they were, the more they tried to butter her up, the worse she was.'

'Andrew Carrick had the trick. Jess absolutely loved him. He was this very tall, pompous QC, who used to swan in and order drinks in the most lordly way, calling Jess "my good woman", treating her like some parlourmaid. She lapped it up. It was the only time I ever saw her smile. He would lean over the bar and tell her filthy jokes, and she would cackle. The rest of the time she had a face like stone.'

Anthony smiled. He'd heard all this before.

'Of course, it's not just the bar,' said Michael. 'It's the whole place. Did you know,' he said to Leo, 'that they've closed the buttery?'

'Really? That's sad.'

'And one evening last summer,' went on Michael, 'I came in, bought a drink, was about to take it outside, when someone told me the garden was out of bounds. Can you imagine? They were catering some outside event, so members of the inn weren't even allowed into their own garden. I frankly don't know what the place is coming to.'

'I hear,' said Leo, 'that they're thinking of turning this whole building over to offices.'

Michael tut-tutted and shook his head. He and Leo sat silently sipping their drinks, deploring the way the world was going. 'So,' asked Michael after a few moments, 'what was it you wanted to talk to us about? You've been most mysterious.'

Leo set his glass down on the table. 'I'm thinking of applying to become a High Court judge.'

Anthony felt a momentary shock. He knew Leo had been sitting as a recorder here and there for the past eighteen months, which was one of the prerequisites, but he hadn't really expected this. 'I assumed you were just going through the motions,' he said. 'With the recorder thing.'

'So did I. Maybe I am. But the idea has its attractions. I wanted to talk it over with you two, find out what you think.'

'I think,' said Michael, crossing his spindly legs and frowning into his whisky, 'that you're mad. I mean, think of the drop in earnings! You're at your peak right now.'

'I know that. On the other hand, if I want to qualify for

the full pension entitlement, I need to serve twenty years on the bench. Judges retire at seventy. I'll be fifty next year. Perfect timing.'

Anthony couldn't believe Leo, of all people, was sitting here talking about pension entitlements. Leo, who lived life for the moment, who despised conventions and those who lived by the rules, whose mercurial character he had always assumed to be above such mundane considerations, was actually making purse-lipped calculations about his retirement, like some accountant from the suburbs. 'Very prudent of you,' he observed. 'You'll be buying a pipe and slippers next. And a cardigan. How about a potting shed while you're at it?'

'You may sneer,' said Leo mildly, 'but when you're my age, such things become important.'

'What – potting sheds?'

Leo smiled, saying nothing, and finished his whisky.

'I'll get another round,' said Michael, and rose to his feet. 'Anthony?'

'I'm fine for the moment, thanks.'

'You don't seem too happy about my possible career move,' said Leo to Anthony, when Michael was out of earshot.

Anthony said nothing for a moment. A vision had been building in his head of chambers without Leo, without the sound of Leo's voice, his laugh, his footstep on the stair, his knock on the door. It would be lifeless, dead. From the first day Anthony had set foot in 5 Caper Court eight years ago, Leo had been, for Anthony, the scintillating heart of the place. His remarkable intellect, his exceptional eloquence and his brilliance as a cross-examiner set him apart from all the other solid, drab, clever members of chambers, including kind, pedantic Michael. On the surface he was the perfect embodiment of a successful barrister, destined to forge a career leading from the High Court Bench to the Court of Appeal, and to the ultimate pinnacle of the Supreme Court. Anthony knew all that. But he knew too that there was another side to Leo, a darker, more dangerous side. He knew Leo as a man who, free from the trammels of his professional life, took his pleasures where he chose, men or women, who had finessed the art of seduction, of love, of life itself. He had taught Anthony many things – including things which Anthony sometimes wished he'd never learnt. He simply didn't believe that this side of Leo would be content with the humdrum life of a High Court judge.

When he spoke, all he could find to say was, 'Chambers won't be the same without you.'

'For heaven's sake, I haven't even applied yet. Even if I do, the Judicial Appointments Commission could well turn me down. It happened to Jeremy. Twice.'

'I doubt if they'd turn you down,' said Anthony. 'You're too good. And they're crying out for decent people.' Michael returned at that moment with the drinks, and Anthony added, 'Michael's right – it'll mean a massive drop in income.'

'I'm not too concerned about the money. As long as I have enough to live comfortably, and to educate Oliver. One has to keep a balance in all things. No point in earning huge fees if the work is killing you.'

'I didn't realise it was that bad,' said Michael.

'Perhaps that's overstating the case, but the fact is, I'm tired. I just seem to go from one big case to another, and the workload is beginning to get to me. In fact, I feel exhausted most of the time.' Leo picked up his fresh drink. 'Plus, I'm not getting any younger. Cheers.'

'Of course, the title's always an attraction,' mused Michael. 'I imagine more than a few chaps finish up on the bench because their wives fancy being called Lady whatever.'

'That certainly isn't high on my list of priorities.'

'They say it can be a lonely life. Did you know Hugh Laddie?' Anthony shook his head. 'Leo will remember him.'

'Patent barrister,' said Leo. 'Invented the Anton Piller order. Nicest man you could hope to meet.'

'Tremendous chap,' agreed Michael. 'The least stuffy person you can imagine. Great fun. Exceptionally clever. Became a High Court judge, but found the job so boring and lonely he packed it in. First and last judge ever to do so.'

'It's not the most convivial life, I grant you,' said Leo. 'That said, grafting away on big cases gets pretty lonely. As for boring – I've reached the point where I feel as though I'm doing the same work over and over.'

'I suppose,' said Michael, 'that at least being a judge allows you to try out new areas of law.'

'Mmm. Then again, do I want to be sitting on fraud trials? Or hearing rape cases, for that matter?' Leo swirled his Scotch in its glass. 'But it shouldn't just be about me – what I get, or don't get out of it. There is the altruistic point, the public service aspect. Becoming a judge is a way of contributing. Maybe it's time I put something back.'

'Have you discussed it with Henry?' asked Anthony.

'Not yet. I'll have a chat with him next week. I wanted to sound you two out first.'

'Did you expect us to talk you out of it?'

'No. I merely wondered if you had any arguments against that I hadn't already thought of.'

They carried on talking it through for the better part of an hour. When they left the bar, it had grown dark, and the late October air was chilly. Michael said goodnight and headed off to the tube station.

'I'll walk with you to your car,' Anthony said to Leo.

They crossed the road together. 'Did you mean that stuff about public service?' asked Anthony.

'You think I'm not sincere?'

'Of course not. I was just surprised. I mean – and don't take this the wrong way – that I don't automatically think of you as . . .' He hesitated. 'That's to say, I've always regarded you as more—' He broke off, groping for the right words.

'Selfish. Out for the main chance. Only interested in number one.'

'I didn't say that.'

'Only because you're too polite. But it's true. I'm all of those things. I know myself better than anyone. I take what I want when I want it, and am prepared to let very few things stand in the way of my enjoyment of life.' They had reached Leo's car. He turned, the street light etching the sharp planes of his face, glinting on his silver hair. His gaze sought Anthony's. 'As regards my private life – by which I suppose I mean my sex life – I have few morals and even fewer scruples. However, where my professional life is concerned, you know how I've always striven to maintain the highest standards, to work with the utmost integrity. I suppose the law is one area of my life where I actually want to be a force for good. I believe in the common law of our country, I'm proud to be one of its practitioners, so I think maybe it's time I did my bit. Not a bad aspiration. Look at Tom Bingham, and the legacy he's left. The work he did as a judge will shape the law for years to come. Not that I expect my contribution would ever amount to as much, but still.'

'Very noble.'

This remark seemed to exasperate Leo. 'It's not about nobility, Anthony. I remember the day I won my first scholarship from Middle Temple. It wasn't much, but it was enough to allow me to keep studying, to do my pupillage without starving. I knew then that despite everything, despite growing up piss-poor in a Welsh mining village and having none of the advantages of all those public school types around me, my intellect and ambition were recognised and valued. This profession would let me climb as high as I wanted, if I was prepared to work hard enough. I've never stopped striving. Maybe now it's payback time.' Anthony was aware that the lilt of Leo's Welsh accent had grown slightly stronger. 'Do you understand? Because if you don't, you should.'

'I think I understand.' There was a long silence. When Anthony spoke again, his voice was bleak, lost. 'I just don't want you to go.'

'Nothing's decided yet. I'm still thinking it through.' Leo gazed at Anthony. 'Whatever happens, I'll never go. Not in that way.'

From where she stood in the shadows, Gabrielle could hear the low murmur of their voices. She wished she could hear what they were saying. And she wished the younger one would just go, and leave the field clear. If she didn't make her move now, maybe she never would. As she watched, she suddenly saw Leo lean forward, silhouetted in the gleam of the lamplight, and kiss the younger man. Not a light kiss, but passionate and lingering. And the kiss was returned. Gabrielle stood rooted to the spot.

Leo unlocked his car, got in and turned the engine, and the moment when she could do or say anything had passed. The Aston Martin purred over the cobbles and out of the Inn.

Gabrielle walked slowly down to Embankment. This was all getting too confusing. Was Leo Davies gay? She couldn't believe it. It didn't make sense. She thought about it as she walked to the station, and came to the conclusion that it made no difference whether he was gay or not. The point was that yet again she'd blown her chance. It was the last time she could afford to let that happen.

Anthony headed aimlessly through the dark courtyards and alleys of the Temple until he reached the Strand. He stood there for a moment, pretending to himself that he had been intending all along to go home, catch up on some work and have an early night, and that he was only now changing his mind. But if he'd meant to do any of that, he would have gone to the Tube. What was the harm in going to Blunt's two nights in a row? Rigging up in his mind the little pretence that he was doing this because he might bump into Edward, he flagged down a cab.

When Rachel went upstairs to put Oliver to bed, she found him sitting on a beanbag, deeply absorbed in a Richard Scarry book which Leo had given him for his last birthday. She crept across the room, pouncing on Oliver and tickling him till he squirmed giggling off beanbag. 'Come on,' she said, picking him up together with his book, 'into bed.' She dropped him onto the bed, then lay down next to him as he scrambled under the duvet.

'Is Daddy coming to my concert on Friday?' asked Oliver, thumbing through the book for his place.

'I don't know, darling. He's got a very, very important case on at the moment, and he's working every evening.'

Oliver lay back, his eyes distant. Sometimes he looked so like Leo. She smoothed his dark, soft hair. 'I could ask him. You never know.'

His eyes brightened. 'Yeah?' Rachel nodded. As far as Oliver was concerned, it was as good as accomplished. 'Wait till he hears me play the recorder. I'm sick!'

'No, you mean you're very good. "Sick" isn't the right word.' That was one problem about having a childminder. Oliver tended to pick up some unfortunate street slang from Lucy's teenage children.

Oliver shrugged. 'Whatever.' He buried his nose in his book again. 'Can you read to me?'

'Which story would you like?'

'The one where the bears go to the hospital,' said Oliver, handing the book to Rachel and snuggling down expectantly. 'And you've got to do the doctor's funny voice, the way Daddy does.'

Rachel propped herself up on the pillow next to Oliver and found the page. 'I'll try,' she said, 'but I'm not promising anything.'

She wasn't promising anything about Leo going to the concert either, but that wasn't the way Oliver saw things.

When she'd finished the story, Rachel tucked Oliver in

and kissed him goodnight, then switched the light off and went downstairs and rang Leo's home number. He answered on the first ring.

'You're working,' said Rachel.

'Too right. The hearing's coming up soon, and I have to prepare my cross-examination.'

'Oliver asked me tonight if you would be coming to his concert on Friday.'

'I don't know. This case is killing me. I've still got—'

'You don't have to say yes,' she interrupted. 'Just maybe.'

'Maybe, then. It's not as though I don't want to. What's he doing?'

'He's in the recorder group, and he's been practising like mad. I tell you, listening to a six-year-old play Bob the Builder over and over on the treble recorder every evening for three weeks should come under Amnesty's definition of torture. Forget waterboarding.'

'I'd love to be there. I'll try.'

'I said I'd ask you, and he thinks it's a done deal.'

'The pressure is registering, trust me.'

'OK. Let me know.'

Rachel hung up, then went to her study and switched on the computer. She had already made up her mind to deregister from those online dating sites. How had she ever let herself be talked into it? At the time, with two glasses of wine inside her and Sophie at her shoulder, signing up had felt amusing and daring. Now it seemed utterly demeaning. When she went on to *The Times* site, she was surprised to find three messages in her inbox. Why should she be surprised? Just because she didn't take this seriously, didn't mean there weren't men out there who did. She hesitated, then curiosity got the better of her and she clicked them open. The first was from a man called James, a tree surgeon from Luton who listed among his hobbies paragliding and white water rafting. 'Sorry, James,' murmured Rachel, and moved on to the next. This was Andy, a banker from Barnes. His photo showed a tubby, cheerful man with a moustache, and the photo's ragged edge, not quite meeting the side of the frame, indicated that some partner had been excised from it. His letter was sweet, but Rachel didn't think she shared his interest in heavy metal music, nor did three teenage sons sound like a good thing. Why was she even reading these? She had absolutely no intention of taking this ridiculous thing any further.

At that moment the phone rang. Rachel picked it up. 'Hello?'

'Rachel, it's Sophie. How are you? I've been meaning to call and see how you got on with the online dating thing.'

'Well, strange coincidence,' said Rachel, 'I'm just looking at some replies as we speak. They're awful. Actually, I only logged on to delete my registration. I've decided this really isn't my kind of thing.'

'Don't be daft – you haven't even given it a chance. Listen, I've just put the kids to bed. I'll come over and have a look with you.'

'You don't really—' But Sophie had already hung up.

She arrived a few minutes later, and followed Rachel through to her study and sat down next to her at the computer.

'God, I see what you mean,' she said, peering at James and Andy. 'Let's see the third one.'

Rachel opened the email. '*Hi, my name is Andrew*,' read

out Sophie. '*I liked what you say about yourself, and think we have possibilities*, blah blah. Works as a commodities broker, likes films, books and art.' She put her head on one side. 'His picture's nice.'

'It doesn't matter. I told you – I'm not up for this.'

'Rachel, you know the rule. Give it a chance. Give *him* a chance. He looks OK, he ticks all the boxes – what have you got to lose by going for just one drink? He may be awful, and he may be really nice. You won't know till you try.'

Rachel sighed. 'I only logged on to delete myself.' She stared at Andrew's picture. He was fair-haired, broad-faced, smiling, quite attractive. 'I suppose it wouldn't hurt to meet him.'

'Well, let's take a look and see what replies you've got on the other—'

'No! I'll do one, and that's all. Then I'm deregistering and never doing this again.'

Sophie nodded, still gazing at the screen. 'You've got a good compatibility rating. Look.'

'All right,' sighed Rachel. 'If it'll keep you happy, I'll email him and suggest meeting for a drink. He works in the City. But that's it. After this, no more.'

'Fine. Whatever you say. Let's do it now. D'you think a glass of wine would help?'

Rachel laughed. 'There's an open half-bottle in the fridge. Get pouring.'

CHAPTER SEVEN

Thursday morning, and life in the clerks' room at 5 Caper Court was trundling along at its usual sedate pace. Robert was talking on the phone, receiver cradled between shoulder and ear, swivelling in his chair and idly stringing paper clips on a length of pink legal tape. Henry, taking a break from sorting through the morning mailbag, was sipping coffee and delivering pearls of clerkly wisdom to young Liam.

'Barristers need training, see – like puppies. When they first come into chambers, with their degrees and that, they think it's all about the law. But a successful practice is built on good PR.' Felicity burst into the room at that moment, bearing a large cardboard box and a sheaf of papers between her teeth. She dumped the box on a table and dropped the papers on top. 'It's all about the three "A"s,' continued Henry. A look of enquiry crossed Liam's thin, pimpled face.

'Availability,' Henry ticked them off on his fingers, 'Affability, and Ability. Three prerequisites of a good barrister. They have to be good at their work, but they need to present an acceptable face to the world as well, and that's where we come in. It's our job to make decent human beings out of them. No good being a brilliant lawyer if you're an arrogant sod that no one likes.'

'When you've finished your masterclass, Henry,' said Felicity, 'I'd like to borrow Liam.'

Henry waved Liam away and returned to the mailbag. Liam went over to the table, where Felicity was producing bundles of ring-bound documents, sheets of paper and a pile of laminated labels from the box. 'I need these name cards slotted into these labels,' she told Liam. 'Mr Bishop's got a seminar this afternoon, so I need them all done before lunch. OK?' Liam nodded and settled to work.

Felicity sat down at her desk. Henry glanced across at her. She was looking exceptionally pretty that day, dressed in a plum-coloured angora sweater and a tight skirt, wearing her hair in a way that he liked, caught up at one side.

'How's Felicity today?' asked Henry.

'Fine,' said Felicity. Their eyes met, and Henry could tell from her expression that something wasn't right, that she was debating whether or not to tell him. In the end she said, 'I got a call from Vince's mum.'

'Oh?'

'Yeah.' Felicity glanced at Robert, who was still chatting away on the phone. 'Listen,' Felicity went on, leaning across, 'can we have a bit of a chat at lunchtime?'

'Of course,' said Henry.

Leo put his head round the door. 'Henry, do you have a minute?'

Felicity gave Henry a smile and a wink. 'Man in demand.'

Henry followed Leo upstairs to his room. Leo sat down and put his feet on the desk. Henry closed the door and leant against the bookcase, waiting. He'd never known Mr Davies to beat about the bush.

'Henry, I'm thinking of applying to become a High Court judge.'

Henry nodded. His face was inscrutable. 'I had wondered. What with you sitting as a recorder this past year.'

There was a silence. Leo waited for Henry to say more. As the silence lengthened, Leo observed, 'You're not telling me what you think.'

'What I think?' Henry's gaze wandered round the room. He wasn't going to betray his true feelings to Leo, which were of alarm and dismay. Leo was his top earner. Not that this was entirely a mercenary issue. He had Leo's best interests to consider. 'I'll be honest with you, Mr D. I'm surprised. I mean, by the timing. You're one of the best commercial silks in the Temple. A couple more years and you'll have the world at your feet. Not being presumptuous, or anything, but are you sure you've thought this through?'

Leo sighed. 'As best as I can, given how bloody tired I am these days. To be frank, Henry, lately I feel as though I'm on a treadmill. The work doesn't stimulate me the way it used to. I'm physically and emotionally exhausted.'

Henry raised his eyebrows. 'Maybe you need to say "no" more often. Manage your clerk. Don't let him work you too hard.'

Leo smiled in return. 'True. You are a pushy bastard.' His smile faded. 'Seriously, though, it's getting hard to muster enthusiasm. With some of these recent big cases, it's like pushing a boulder uphill.'

'You have to face the facts. Solicitors aren't going to instruct you on winning cases. It's the big losers they need you to manage. They know you can take on something that looks like it's a no-hoper, and turn it around. That's why they pay the fees.'

'I know that. But it gets wearing. I'm beginning to feel I'd like an easier life.'

'Now, if you were to say to me in three or four years' time that you're thinking of going upstairs, I'd say that was the right time. But now? When you're at the top of your game?'

'From where I'm sitting, Henry, three or four years seems like a long time. My son is six. He's growing up. I don't want to miss all that. I really begrudge working long weekends on big cases. For what? Money I don't necessarily need.'

'You're a lucky man to be able to say that, Mr D, in the present climate.'

'I don't mean to sound arrogant.' Leo rose impatiently and went to the window. He stared down at the courtyard below.

Henry sighed. 'What can I say, sir? There's no denying you'd do well on the bench. A credit. But I'd be sorry to lose you. And like I say, I'm not sure it's the right time.'

Leo turned and nodded. 'I hear what you say. Thanks for listening.'

Henry left Leo's room and went downstairs, pondering the conversation. It would be a big blow if Mr Davies left 5 Caper Court, no question. In common with the other clerks in chambers, Henry depended for his living on taking a slice of the fees the barristers earned, and in that regard Leo was important, his best earner. In fact, without Leo, chambers would be seriously short of good QCs. There was Jeremy Vane, who had tried and failed twice to become a High Court judge, so he wasn't going anywhere. And Stephen Bishop. Michael, too, but Henry wouldn't be surprised if he tried for the bench in a year or two. The rest were all younger, without Leo's reputation and experience. He would be a huge loss. There was no way of telling how far Leo had made his mind up, but Henry happened to know that the Judicial Appointments Commission were looking to fill twelve posts by next October, and if Leo did decide to apply, he couldn't see them turning him down. Not if they had any sense. Mind you, from what you heard these days, sense was in short supply in the JAC. Not like the old days, when the Lord Chancellor's Office ran the show, the dependable Mr Dobie at the helm.

Henry went back to his desk and worked through the morning, and at lunchtime he and Felicity went round the corner to a sandwich bar.

They sat perched on high stools next to a counter by the wall, Felicity with a can of Fanta and a chicken salad roll, Henry with a coffee and a cream cheese and smoked salmon bagel.

'So, what did Vince's mum want?' asked Henry.

'She wants to throw a party for Vince when he gets out of prison next week. And she wants me to help organise it.'

'That's nice,' said Henry, privately thinking there was something a bit iffy about throwing a party for your son who'd just done a stretch for manslaughter, but not liking to say.

Felicity shot him a look. 'No, Henry, it's not nice.'

'No.'

'It's going to be hard enough seeing him again, without having to put up bunting and let off party poppers.' Felicity took a moody swig of Fanta.

'Maybe—' began Henry, then thought better of it.

'Maybe what?'

'Nothing.'

'Come on – out with it.'

'Maybe it would have been better if . . . well, at the beginning, when he was convicted, if you'd, you know, if you'd—'

'Dumped him?'

Henry stirred his coffee. 'Sounds hard, but yes. Maybe finishing then would have been for the best.' He waited for Felicity to bite his head off, tell him he was a heartless sod. But she didn't.

'I thought of it at the time. Let him down gently.' She swirled her can of Fanta. 'But it didn't seem fair. He was so . . . so crushed by everything. I mean, that whole thing, hitting that bloke, and him dying. It was all an accident. I couldn't just turn my back on him.'

'But you wanted to?'

Felicity was silent, remembering the way things had been between her and Vince before he'd gone to prison. He'd been out of work as usual, and she'd been carrying him, paying for everything, including his booze and dope. Admittedly he'd been trying to haul himself out of the waster culture he'd inhabited for so long, hoping to get his black cab licence somewhere down the line, but that prospect was shot now. What was he going to do when he got out of prison? On recent visits he seemed elated at the prospect of release, but the last Felicity had asked him about his plans, all he'd said was, 'My main plan is just to be with you, babes. That'll do for the moment. Then I'll see.' She remembered, too, her short-lived pregnancy, and the guilt and miserable relief she'd felt after the miscarriage. A baby would have trapped her, tied her to Vince for ever.

When she said nothing, Henry persisted. 'Is he going to be living with you?'

Felicity raised sad, brown eyes. 'It hasn't come up. But I reckon he thinks everything will go back to being the way it was.'

'Is that what you want?' Henry hated to see her so troubled. He wanted to be able to put out a hand, comfort her. In truth, he wanted to do more than that. He wanted to enfold her in his arms, kiss away her anxieties, tell her he was here now and that Vince was an irrelevance, a nowhere man. In indulging this wish, he didn't think of himself as being in any way disloyal to Cheryl. The fantasies bred by his unrequited love for Felicity had been going on for so long that they occurred in a parallel universe, a place apart from reality. He was in that place right now, wishing Vince out of her life, putting himself at its centre, in a kind of happy daydream. His adoration of Felicity was so habitual, so devoid of possibility, that it didn't even depress him any more.

Felicity shook her head. 'I dunno. It's like it's not up to me. Everyone's making assumptions. Vince, his family. They kind of include me in everything to do with Vince's future without even thinking. Like this party. And here's me, too weak to say anything different. I've put my life on hold for the past few years, because I didn't want to hurt anyone. I didn't want to make things harder for Vince than they already were. I didn't want to upset his mum, with everything she's been going through. And now I'm stuck. Am I mad, or what?'

'You're kind, is what you are. Too kind. You think too much about other people and what they might want. So you end up doing what might not be best for you. Let me ask – if Vince hadn't gone inside, do you think you and he would still be together?'

Felicity shook her head. 'I can't say. If I'd had the baby – well, I don't much want to think about that. How it would have been. The thing is, with Vince being in prison, I've put off asking myself questions about him and me, what's going to happen. Now they're staring me in the face.'

'I think the truth is, too.'

Felicity struggled against this. Henry was giving her an honest answer, yet she wasn't prepared to accept it. 'Maybe I should just wait till he gets out, see how things are then, take it from there.'

Henry nodded. *Let all that happen*, he was thinking, *and it'll be too late.*

Felicity was painfully aware of her own cowardice. To change the subject she asked, 'So, how's things with you and Cheryl. Everything OK?'

Henry nodded. 'Coasting along. You know.'

Dear Henry, thought Felicity. He always looked so morose, even when he smiled. Like a sweet spaniel. She hoped this Cheryl wasn't stringing him along. He deserved someone decent. She knew how Henry felt about her. It brought out some weird, deep-seated guilt that she couldn't return his feelings. He really was the nicest man she knew.

Suddenly, half-embarrassed, Henry added, 'We're thinking we might get married next year.'

'No!' Felicity feigned delight and surprise.

'Well . . .' Henry toyed with his teaspoon. 'We've been seeing one another for the better part of eighteen months. Seems about the right time. I'm not getting any younger.'

'Well, that's lovely. I'm glad for you both.' Felicity laid her hand over Henry's and smiled into his eyes. The uncertainty of her own feelings puzzled her. She should be pleased for him. Perhaps she felt this way because he'd found something she hadn't, and wasn't ever likely to find with Vince.

'Thanks.' Henry wasn't sure why he'd told her that about him and Cheryl. It wasn't even true. Well, not yet, though Cheryl had been hinting that way, and Henry was hard-pushed to find reasons not to. He suspected he'd said it to provoke some reaction in Felicity that he was never likely to get. And there she was, smiling away at him as if it was the best news she'd ever heard. And her hand over his in a way that meant they were really good friends. Just good friends.

Sarah took Toby's call just before lunchtime.

'What's wrong?' asked Sarah. 'You sound weird.'

'I've been canned,' said Toby. 'Sacked. We've been told to clear our desks by noon.'

'Oh God.' Sarah's stomach felt like it had hit the floor. 'Oh God, Toby, that's awful. What are you going to do?'

'What am I going to do? Well, I'm filling a black bin bag as we speak, and when I've done that, I'm heading to the pub to get off my face.' He hung up.

Sarah sought out her broker friend Miranda, an American

woman in her thirties whose husband had been sacked by his investment bank just weeks earlier.

'Another casualty,' said Miranda. 'Saul said that Graffman Spiers would probably go to the wall.' She glanced at Sarah's stricken face. 'I'm truly sorry. I know how you feel. Come on, why don't we drown our sorrows?'

They went to a wine bar in Fenchurch Street to discuss the crisis over glasses of Sauvignon Blanc.

'At least Toby told you straight away. Saul didn't let on for four whole weeks,' Miranda told Sarah.

'Four weeks? What was he doing all that time?'

'Going to the gym. Boozing with friends. Having expensive lunches. Doing the denial thing. He rinsed through his final pay check in under a month. I was mad as hell, until I realised the poor guy was actually in shock. Works eighty hours a week for fifteen years, suddenly he wakes up one morning and he doesn't know what he's for any more.'

'And now?'

Miranda shrugged. 'Now he's meant to be looking for another job, obviously, but I don't know *what* he does all day. I leave him watching TV at breakfast, and I come home eight hours later and it's like he hasn't moved. I thought of letting the nanny go, but somehow I don't see Saul turning into a house husband, picking up the kids, doing the chores. He's a banker, for Christ's sake. A master of the universe. We just have to hope this picks up, that the economy turns around and he gets another job.'

'It must be hard, with the children.'

'Sure it's hard. The house is on the market, we're living on our savings, but if he doesn't get work in the next six months, God knows what's going to happen. I'm trying to sort out a nanny-share to cut down expenses. I'm not the only Notting Hill mother in this boat. And we may have to take a long hard look at those nice private schools the girls are at. Still, at least one of us is working.'

Sarah nodded. To think just a couple of weeks ago she'd been contemplating the comfortable life she would lead once she was married, giving up work and living on Toby's earnings in a beautiful London house, with no money worries. Why had she ever imagined it was going to be that easy? Because no one had told them this crash was coming, was why. Because just twelve months ago the whole world had been on one big roll, and the good times looked like they'd never stop. Well, they'd stopped as of noon today, and she and Toby were going to have to do some serious rethinking. He had to get straight out there and into the market. No question of him sitting around watching daytime television and feeling sorry for himself. He needed to find a job just as good as the last, if not better. He had to. Otherwise the future was far from orange. The future was bleak. And marrying someone who didn't have a six-figure salary and excellent prospects simply wasn't part of Sarah's game plan.

Leo had spent the entire day working on the cross-examination in a case involving a collision between a container vessel and an LPG carrier in the Gulf of Aden. The hearing was two weeks away, and so far the main stumbling block in the case was a conflict of evidence regarding the lights on the container vessel on the night of the collision. Leo's phone rang at five o'clock. It was Robin Maudsley, the instructing solicitor.

'Bit of a turn-up for the books. You know the Portuguese officer who was on watch on the night of the collision? We've tracked him down. He's a crew member on a ship coming into Tilbury tomorrow afternoon. He says there was definitely no light on the container vessel on the night of the collision.'

'My God.' Leo jotted a hasty note. 'That drives a coach and horses through their defence. Fantastic.'

'Obviously it's going to change your entire cross-examination, so you'll want to speak to him after we've taken his statement. His ship sails the next morning, so if you get down there around six, that should be good timing.

Oliver's concert. Leo's heart sank. There was simply no way round this. This was the only opportunity he'd have to talk to the officer and go through his statement with him, and he couldn't miss it. It was a miracle they'd tracked him down. It meant the difference between winning and losing the case.

'I'll be at your office within half an hour to discuss the witness statement,' said Leo.

He rang Rachel on the way and explained the situation.

'Poor Ollie,' said Rachel. 'He's going to be gutted. He so wanted you to be there. I knew something like this would happen. I shouldn't have got his hopes up.'

'Don't. I'm feeling bad enough.'

'It isn't your fault. These things happen.'

'What time does the concert end?'

'It's only an hour long.'

Leo sighed. 'There's no way I can make it. Tell Oliver . . .' He paused. 'Tell him how sorry I am. Explain it. Tell him it's a big case, a really important one. And that I'll see him at the weekend.'

'I will.'

Leo clicked off the hands-free and sighed. This was exactly the kind of thing he'd meant when he was talking to Henry earlier. Missing bits and pieces of Oliver's life. It would go on happening over the next few years. And at the end of those years, when you put those bits and pieces together, there would be a great big gaping hole.

He made his decision as he wove through the evening traffic to Maudsley's office. Enough of this. Enough of the stress and strain. As a judge he'd be working regular hours, able to see much more of Oliver and be a proper part of his life. And at the end of twenty years, when Oliver was grown up, he'd cop a nice, fat pension and retire. No more sitting on the fence, canvassing other people's opinions. He would do it. He would download the application form first thing tomorrow.

After work Sarah went to Toby's flat and let herself in. She'd been trying his mobile since mid afternoon, but he'd evidently switched it off. She'd stopped off at Waitrose to buy groceries, intending to cook them both a meal, over which they would talk through the situation calmly and rationally. All the time a thread of panic was running through her thoughts. How much did Toby have saved? How big was the mortgage on his flat? How quickly could he get another job? Toby might not be the most electrifying person in the world, but the flip side of that was that he was stable and dependable. She reassured herself with that thought. He wouldn't let their dream future go to the wall. He'd find a way through.

But when Toby arrived home four hours later, it was all he could do to find his way through the front door.

'Have you been in the pub all this time?' asked Sarah, as Toby slumped on the sofa, his keys in one hand, his black plastic bag in the other. His tie was loose and his hair a mess. 'You look like shit.'

'Yup,' said Toby, nodding slowly and emphatically.

'It's not the answer, you know.' The panic she had been supressing all day began to rise to the surface. He didn't look safe and dependable at that moment, or like a man ready to square up to his problems and find an answer. He looked like a big, drunken schoolboy.

He raised bleary eyes to hers. 'And the answer is – what, exactly? 'Cos if you know, please tell me.'

Sarah had seen Toby drunk before, getting convivially sloshed at dinner parties along with other well-heeled, successful young brokers and bankers. But that was a bright, joyous kind of drunkenness, with the sheen of success about it. At this moment Toby looked wrecked and deflated, the prosperous glaze replaced by the dull, seedy misery of a man out of a job. She knew there was no point in reproaching him. Things were bad enough without a row.

'I bought some steaks,' she said. 'I thought we could have supper and talk about it. Why don't you shower and change while I cook?' Maybe he would sober up enough for them to discuss things. In her panicky state, Sarah was desperate to receive reassurance from Toby, as if sitting and talking together they would find a solution.

He shook his head. 'Not hungry.' He rose from the sofa, leaving car keys and black bin liner behind, and headed in the direction of the bedroom. 'Going to sleep.'

When Sarah went through, she found him already spreadeagled on his back on the bed. His eyes were closed, and he was breathing deeply. If he wasn't already asleep he soon would be. Hopeless. She pulled off his shoes, and Toby groaned and rolled on his side. Sarah looked down at him. The last thing she wanted to do was to share a bed with him in this state. She would leave him to sleep it off, and they would talk tomorrow. She switched off the lights, left the flat, and went back to Kensington.

CHAPTER EIGHT

The next morning Sarah waited until after eleven before ringing Toby, assuming he'd be sleeping it off.

'How do you feel?' she asked.

'Like crap, naturally. But I'm going to force down some breakfast, then go out for a run.'

'Good idea.'

'I'm sorry I wasn't in a fit state to talk last night. The whole thing was a bit of a nightmare. It all happened so suddenly.' He gave a miserable laugh. 'One minute you're pulling down three hundred K, the next you're on the pavement with your stapler and no identity. Going out and getting slaughtered seemed like the best option at the time.'

'I can imagine,' said Sarah, marginally reassured by his tone. At least he wasn't sitting around feeling sorry for himself. 'We do need to sit down and talk about it, though. It makes a difference to a lot of things, potentially.'

'Yes, I know. Why don't we go out for dinner tonight?

Somewhere decent. Pétrus, perhaps. I need cheering up.'

Sarah opened her mouth to say that perhaps they should go somewhere cheaper, given the circumstances, but stopped herself. It was important to keep him upbeat.

'Nice idea. You book for seven-thirty, and I'll see you there.'

Over dinner, Toby described the events of the previous day, the terse management announcement, people's shell-shocked reactions, employees clearing their desks, wandering off to pubs and wine bars, not willing to contemplate in sober detail the impact losing their jobs was going to have on their lives. Plenty of time for that in the days ahead.

'Mind you, I'm luckier than most,' said Toby. 'There are guys on my trading floor with mortgages, kids in private school. They're the ones I feel sorry for.'

Sarah nodded, absorbing Toby's words. If Toby was feeling sorry for people with mortgages, presumably the docklands flat didn't have one. That was something – even in the present market it must be worth three or four hundred grand. She thought about her friend Miranda, and realised that she and Toby were relatively fortunate. They only had themselves to worry about. 'So – when will you start looking for another job?'

'In case you hadn't noticed, there aren't any jobs out there. The world's in financial meltdown.'

'I know things are hard, but at least you're going to try, aren't you?'

'I'll do what everyone else does, and sign on with some agencies, but don't get your hopes up.'

'Well, at least you don't have a mortgage. That's one

good thing. The flat must be worth a fair bit, even in today's market.'

Toby stared at her. 'I don't own the flat. I rent it. I thought you knew that.'

Sarah was aghast. 'But you've got savings, right?'

'Not much to speak of. A few grand.'

'A few grand?' Sarah couldn't believe what she was hearing. 'But you've been earning a fortune for the past few years. Not to mention bonuses. What have you been doing with it all?'

'Spending it, having a good time. Made a few investments here and there. But they're all shot to hell. Most of my portfolio's been wiped out. I told you that a couple of weeks ago.'

'Toby! All you said was that you had some shares that went down the pan! You didn't say it was everything you owned!'

'No point in making a big fuss about it. Everyone's in the same boat.' He caught the distraught look on her face and reached out a hand to cover hers. 'Don't look like that, angel. It isn't the end of the world. You've still got a job. We can manage till I find something else. Things will turn around. It'll be fine.'

'What about the wedding?'

'The wedding? I don't see how that's affected. Dad mentioned something about footing the bill for the drink, but I always assumed your old man would be good for the rest. Isn't that what happens? Father of the bride shells out?'

'Things are done a bit differently these days, Toby, in case you hadn't noticed. People usually pay a bit towards the cost of their own weddings. Frankly, I don't know if my father can afford what we had in mind. The marquee, two hundred guests, outside catering. I thought you and I would be meeting some of the cost.'

Toby looked doubtful. 'Might have to scale back a bit, in that case. We should have a word with your father. We'll be seeing him next Friday at his champagne and hotpot party. My parents will be there, too.'

'Oh God – I'd forgotten about the party. I'm not sure I feel like going now.' When the Kitterings heard about Toby's job, the emotional fallout would be awful. 'Going to be a bit of a blow to your parents, their golden boy out of a job.'

Sarah caught the look of hurt bafflement on Toby's face. 'I'm sorry,' she said quickly. 'That wasn't nice.' She suddenly realised how conspicuously Toby's job as an investment banker had figured in his appeal, in her plans for their future together. She had never, till this moment, deconstructed him, taken him apart piece by piece to work out who and what it was she loved. Recent events had begun to do it for her. Without his status, his work, he was like a different person. The whole situation required some careful thinking. She said gently, 'I'm sure things will get better. The recession can't last for ever.'

'It's got to get worse before it gets better.' He put his hand over hers, his lost-puppy eyes searching her face. 'But at least we've got one another. You make me feel like I can handle anything. Even poverty.'

'What a sweet thing to say,' murmured Sarah, thinking that had to be the ugliest, most frightening word she'd ever heard in her life.

It was well after nine when Leo got back to Chelsea. He parked the car not far from the house, switched off the engine, and sat for a few seconds watching clouds drifting across the moon through the bare branches of the tree in the square. The day had been long, the drive to Tilbury and back exhausting. What he needed now was a stiff drink and some supper. He glanced at the windows of his house and found himself wishing that they weren't dark, the rooms empty of life, no one waiting for him. Strange. Until now he had always relished the peace of his contained world, welcomed the silence. He picked up his notes from the passenger seat. Well, at any rate, Oliver would be there tomorrow evening to liven it up with his prattle and toys. He got out and locked the car.

He was halfway across the road when a figure stepped out of the shadows and came towards him. He paused, startled. It wasn't so long ago that a particularly unpleasant Ukrainian gangster had come to visit him here, and being accosted by someone lurking around the square was unnerving. Then he saw that it was a girl. Whoever she was and whatever she wanted, he thought wearily, he could do without it.

She stepped into the light of a street lamp, and he recognised her straight away. It was the girl who'd been in court during the Texmax hearing, and in the pub when he was having lunch with Anthony. She said nothing, just stood looking at him for several long seconds, and he had time to take in her features: the small, square face with its prettily defined cheekbones, the large blue eyes and the messy mane of honey-blonde hair. She had her hands deep in her pockets, her coat collar was turned up against the cold, and the tip of her nose was pink.

'Hello,' she said, still looking at him intently.

Leo nodded warily. 'Hello.'

'You're Leo Davies.'

'I am.' He waited for a few seconds. 'And you are?'

'I'm Gabrielle,' said the girl. She took a deep breath, and when she spoke again, her breath was like smoke on the chilly night air. 'I'm your daughter.'

For a split second Leo felt the bafflement of one who has just been told something patently absurd. But the automatic processes of thirty years of legal training kicked in, and against the evidence, he found himself weighing the possibility that what she had said was true. He had no way of knowing. Behind this flurry of rational mental activity he felt deeply shocked. He groped for something to say.

She helped him out. 'Don't you believe me?' Her manner seemed composed, but her eyes, fastened on his, seemed to be brimming with some indefinable emotion – hope, perhaps even fear – that threatened to spill out and overwhelm her. A girl on the brink. Leo was used to knowing instinctively the right questions to ask, depending on the answer he sought, but in this non-courtroom situation, he wasn't even sure what answer he wanted. 'How do you know?' was all he could find to say.

'How do you think? My mother told me.'

Leo said, as gently and kindly as he could, 'That rather begs the question.'

'Look,' said Gabrielle, 'we can stand out here on this freezing pavement, or we can go into your house and talk about it.'

He nodded, gazing at her, absorbed in her features, trying to see himself there and almost, but not quite succeeding. The shock of her revelation still hadn't left him.

'Well?'

'Fine. Come in, and we'll talk.' He took his keys from his pocket and together they crossed the square.

Leo unlocked the door and switched on the lights, then went to hang up his coat and put his papers in his study, feeling dazed. Gabrielle wandered from the hallway into the living room, shrugging off her jacket. She gazed around, taking in the austere, stylish contents of the room, the pictures and sculptures, the expensive furnishings, the subtle lighting. She turned as Leo came in.

'Not keen on clutter, are you?'

'Not much. I prefer order.'

'In which case, I suppose it's rather shaken you, me turning up like this.'

She sounded so assured, so much on her mettle, that he followed her cue.

'I'm used to surprises in my line of work. Generally all they require is a bit of deft footwork.' He unstoppered the whisky decanter. 'Would you care for a drink?'

'Do you have any Coke?'

'I'll see.' He disappeared into the kitchen. When he returned, Gabrielle was sitting in one of the capacious armchairs, legs crossed. He handed her a can of Coke and a tumbler of ice. 'Sorry it's not cold. There's ice, though.' He rattled the cubes in the tumbler.

'Thanks.'

Leo poured himself a Scotch and sat down opposite. They sipped their drinks in silence, too wrapped up in the moment to notice the similarity of their attitudes and timing.

'So,' said Leo, 'we need to unravel this. Just what exactly has your mother told you?'

'That's very lawyerly of you. Are you sure you wouldn't rather refer to her as my "alleged" mother?'

'Lawyerly?' Leo smiled. 'I'm not sure I know that word.'

'You know what I mean. Approaching the subject side on. Going for the third-hand hearsay evidence, instead of asking me directly.'

Leo, despite the surreal situation, was amused. 'Strictly speaking, it's second-hand hearsay. Anyway, what do you know about hearsay evidence?'

'I've been studying it at Bar School.'

'Really?' He sipped his Scotch, interested.

Gabrielle decided to make herself more comfortable, kicking off her boots and tucking her feet beneath her. She was very pretty, Leo thought, and she had an air of challenge about her which he found quite touching.

'What made you want to become a barrister?'

'I thought I'd be good at it.' She looked down at her glass, swirling the Coke and ice. 'And maybe it had something to do with you. Finding out who you were, what you did.'

'I see. Which takes us back to the main storyline. Who your mother is, and why she thinks I'm your father.'

Gabrielle looked at him almost defiantly. 'My mother is called Jacqueline.' She pronounced it in the French way. 'When you knew her, she would have been Jacqueline Pujol.' Her eyes were on Leo's face, waiting for his reaction.

Leo racked his brain. Jacqueline? He couldn't remember anyone of that name. Hardly surprising, given the number of women he had slept with over the years. It was embarrassing, given that the apparent fruit of their union was sitting opposite him, eyes fixed expectantly on his face. What the hell had he been up to twenty-however-many years ago? Much the same as now, he supposed – working all hours, making money, and trying to have as much fun as was compatible with the standards of his profession.

'Doesn't the name mean anything to you?' She frowned as she said this, and Leo noticed that her brows were dark, thick and delicately winged, like his own mother's.

'I'm afraid you have me at a disadvantage. Twenty years is a long time ago. There were a lot of people in my life. Do you have a picture or something?'

She shot him a glance, then reached down to rummage in her bag. 'I can't believe you don't remember her.'

Although she said this, Leo realised she had come prepared for the possibility he might not remember, and wondered just how fleeting his association with this Jacqueline person had been.

She handed him a photograph, and as soon as he looked at it he was astonished by the force of the recollection it triggered. Jackie. Of course. A lovely French girl he had met at a party. Whose party? His mind stumbled back to a summer night, a flat in Notting Hill, windows wide open to the summer night. Some actor friend – Philip, Patrick some name like that. He looked up at Gabrielle, then back at the photo. It was a publicity picture such as an agent might use, from which Jackie gazed out provocatively, her tawny hair tousled. They had been lovers for just a few fleeting weeks. Then she'd disappeared. Someone said she'd gone back to France. Back then, people weren't glued together by mobile phones, emails and Facebook. You might know someone, love someone, then circumstances would change and they would leave your life for ever. As Jackie had done.

Gabrielle could read the astonishment, the recognition

in Leo's face. 'So you do accept it? That you're my father?'

'I suppose it's a possibility. Why didn't she tell me?'

'She said she didn't know until she was back in France. She said she was going to write to you, but she decided there was no point. That it would have been a mess. You and she weren't in love.'

Leo said nothing for some moments, staring at the photo, astounded by this revelation. Finally he asked, 'What happened?'

'When she found out she was pregnant, she moved back with her parents. A few years later my grandfather died, and the year after that, my grandmother. She sold their house and moved back to England. She'd always loved London. She made a living doing a little modelling work, some acting. Then she met my stepfather. I have two stepbrothers. My stepfather's pretty wealthy. I love him to bits, but I've always known he's not my real father.' She stared down at her hands, spreading them out in her lap. 'When I was a kid it never occurred to me to wonder who you were. I had a very happy life. Then about a few years ago I got curious, the way teenagers do, and started asking my mother questions. She told me what she knew, which wasn't much.' Leo looked at her quizzically, and again she shrugged. 'Your name, that you were a lawyer, or had been when she met you. That you were very good-looking, funny.' Gabrielle smiled. 'When she talked about you, I got the impression she'd liked you a lot. So I wanted to find you.'

'Why now? Why not sooner?' He gazed at her, the reality only just sinking in that this creature in the leather jacket and Ugg boots, sitting opposite him and sipping Coke, was part of him. His daughter.

'I was only seventeen, for heaven's sake. I didn't know how to do it. Anyway, I was frightened. Frightened you might not be interested. Or that I might not like you.' She threw herself back in her chair, letting out a long breath. 'You don't know what the past few weeks have been like, watching you, hanging about, trying to get up the courage to say something. But here I am.'

'Yes,' murmured Leo. 'Here you are.' He gazed at her, still trying to fathom his feelings. 'So,' he said after a moment, 'tell me about yourself. You're a barrister?'

'Not yet. I'm in pupillage, Fox Buildings.'

'Criminal law? Interesting choice.'

'I certainly didn't want to do the kind of thing you do. Commercial law is so-o-o boring!' She rolled her eyes. 'I went to see you in court a couple of weeks ago—'

'I saw you sitting at the back. I wondered who you were.'

'—and I can't tell you how dreary it was.'

'Sorry about that. Not spine-tingling drama, admittedly. But it has its moments. I'm afraid criminal law is often dirty work for poor rewards.'

'How do you know?'

'I spent five weeks sitting as a criminal judge in the Crown Court. Part of my training to become a High Court judge.'

She shrugged. 'I don't mind. It's what interests me.'

'Fair enough. I happen to find ships and other people's money rather riveting.'

Gabrielle nodded. 'You earn a fair bit, don't you? This house, and everything.'

Leo drained his whisky. 'How much do you know about me? Beyond what your mother's told you.'

'Not much. But more than you do about me.' She smiled

and drained the remnants of her Coke. It was a bewitching smile, lighting up her young face, enlivening her blue eyes. Eyes, Leo realised, which were exactly like his own. He felt his heart dip unexpectedly. 'We should get to know one another,' she added.

'I would like that. I would also like to speak to your mother at some point.'

'Why?'

'Obvious reasons. I feel I've shirked my responsibilities.'

Gabrielle narrowed her eyes, then cracked the empty Coke tin between her fingers and shook her head. 'You want to check my story. You can call her if you want.' She searched in her bag for pen and paper. 'Here's her number. I'm sure she'd like to hear from you. I'll give you my mobile number while I'm at it.' She put the piece of paper next to her crumpled Coke can. 'I feel weird, now I've actually done it. Met you, I mean. Spoken to you. It's been haunting me for months. And now it's done . . .'

'A bit of an anticlimax?'

'Just different to what I expected. I thought it would be more dramatic. Emotional.'

'Sorry.'

'No, this is nice. You're OK.'

There was a long silence. Leo found himself utterly bereft of things to say. At last he said, 'I feel I'm not rising to the occasion. Finding out about you is something of a shock. A twenty-one-year-old daughter I never knew I had.'

'I'm twenty-two. My birthday's March the seventeenth.'

'Mine's March the ninth.'

'Really?' She seemed delighted. 'That makes us both Librans.'

'If you say so. Another Coke? I need a top-up.' She shook her head. Leo crossed the room and poured himself another Scotch. 'Have you eaten?' he asked.

'Not since lunchtime.'

'Come through to the kitchen and help me make supper.'

Between them they cooked scrambled eggs and bacon and talked for over two hours. Gabrielle poured forth a torrent of information about herself, her family, her upbringing, her likes and dislikes, her dreams and ambitions. In return, Leo told her about Oliver, about his own mother and his childhood in Wales. Gabrielle was thrilled to discover she had a half-brother.

'Is Oliver like me? In looks, I mean?'

'No, he's very dark. You're more like your grandmother.'

'Can I meet her? Would she like me?'

'I don't see why not. Yes, I'm sure she'd like you.'

'Have you got any pictures of Oliver? And your mother?'

Leo duly fetched some, and Gabrielle examined them closely. 'He's really sweet. I'd like to meet him. You haven't said much about your ex-wife – what was her name again?'

'Rachel. She's a solicitor. Very . . .' Leo searched for words. 'Very cool and collected.'

'Uh-huh. Why did you get divorced?'

Leo hesitated. 'A number of reasons.' Which was true. That he had been shagging the nanny was perhaps the least of them.

Gabrielle watched his face, remembering the night not long ago, when she'd seen him and that younger man, the kiss they'd exchanged. She couldn't ask him about that. The relationship was new and fragile right now, but she couldn't imagine a time when she would dare to broach a subject like that. Not that it mattered. What mattered was that she had finally done it, found her real father – and he was OK. In fact, he was more than OK. She grinned.

'What?'

'Nothing. I'm just glad.' She glanced at her watch. 'Shit, I have to go. I've got an essay to finish.'

'Where do you live?'

'Barons Court.'

'Let me drive you.'

She was putting on her boots. Then she got up and slipped on her jacket. 'No thanks. I'm fine. Anyway, you've had two Scotches.'

At the front door, he said, 'I'll call you next week. We can have lunch in the Temple.'

She nodded. Standing there on the step, she hesitated, then quickly kissed him on one cheek.

'Thank you for coming,' he said.

He watched her cross the square and disappear into the night, then closed the door. He went back to the living room and picked up the piece of paper on which she had written her phone number. He fetched his mobile and entered it carefully, checking twice to make sure he had it right. Then he put the piece of paper in a desk drawer, and went to the kitchen to clear up, feeling strangely elated, and rather old.

CHAPTER NINE

A week later, at quarter to one on Friday, Rachel tidied her desk and headed to the Ladies. She was due to meet Andrew Garroway in a wine bar in Creechurch Lane in fifteen minutes, and she wished the whole thing was already over. She stared at her reflection, anxiously dabbing on a little more make-up, when a cubicle door opened and, to her surprise, Felicity emerged.

'Felicity! What brings you here?'

'Hiya. I'm here with Robert, having lunch with a couple of your people. Little marketing exercise, really. Nice to see you again.'

Felicity had been a secretary at Nichols & Co some years ago, and had worked briefly for Rachel – not the most illustrious episode in her career. In fact, she'd just been recalling, as she flushed the loo, that the last time she'd been in these bogs it had been to knock back a couple of amphetamines to keep her awake after a heavy night.

'How are things?' asked Rachel. 'Oh, here – you've got your skirt tucked in your knickers.'

'Thanks.' Felicity groped behind and tugged it free. 'Wouldn't have done to go off to lunch showing my arse to the world, would it? Yeah, things are OK, thanks.' And then, because it was the foremost thought in her mind these days, and because in the old days Rachel had been a haven of calm in the troubled seas of Felicity's life, she added, 'Vince is getting out of prison this afternoon. I'm taking the afternoon off to go over to his mum's to help with the party.'

'That's good.' Rachel caught sight of Felicity's troubled face in the mirror. 'Isn't it?'

Felicity began to wash her hands. 'I dunno. I'm a bit all over the place. You know, in my head. I feel like I have to be there for him, but all I wanna do is run away.'

'Why?' Rachel decided Andrew Garroway could wait for a few minutes.

'Because I reckon he thinks that everything's going to go on between us like it was before. But I'm not sure it's what I want. In fact, I pretty much know it isn't. I've really got myself together these last couple of years, and I just don't see myself going back to – well, how it used to be.'

Felicity might have been the world's most exasperating secretary, but Rachel had always been deeply fond of her, and she hated to see her looking so baffled and despondent.

'You want my advice?'

'Oh, God, yeah – anything, please.'

'Tell him what you've just told me. Make it clear to him that your relationship can't be the same as it used to be. It's your opportunity to draw a line under the past, to say, look,

I don't want that relationship any more. It's going to be like this from now on. I'll be your friend, I'll support you, but I'm not the person I was, and you have to respect that.'

Felicity listened, impressed. She nodded. 'Yeah. You're right. He's coming out, he's got to start over. He can't expect me suddenly to take on responsibility for his whole life.' She paused. 'It's just—'

'What?'

'Well, I've been visiting him while he's been inside and all, and I kind of feel like he'll think I've been leading him on and that, if I tell him it's not going to be the way he expects it to.'

Rachel took her hairbrush from her bag. 'You've been his friend. The fact that you didn't abandon him doesn't mean he can make assumptions.'

'No. No, I see that.' Felicity looked doubtful. Then her face brightened as she looked at Rachel in the mirror. 'You look nice. Off somewhere?'

'I'm meeting someone for lunch.' For a second Rachel thought of confiding in Felicity about the online dating thing, this awful meeting she'd set up, but the moment passed.

'That's good.' Felicity glanced at her watch. 'I'd best be off. See you soon.'

'Stay in touch.'

After Felicity had gone, Rachel brushed her dark, silky hair and gazed at her reflection, her mind moving from Felicity's problems back to her own, and the lunch date ahead of her. Why was she doing this? It was ridiculous to go looking for love. Things should happen spontaneously, not in this tacky, manufactured way. She sighed and closed her bag. Maybe he would be great – kind, amusing, normal, easy to like. Maybe he would be 'the one'. But she knew in her heart that she'd already met 'the one', and he was probably irreplaceable.

Simon Wren was standing at the bar with friends when the dark-haired girl came in. A gust of cold air from the opening door caused him to turn, and suddenly there was this miraculously lovely creature, just a foot away. Most City women had a tendency to exaggerated self-assurance when they entered any room, be it pub or trading floor, but this one had a look of gentle wariness. Her eyes skimmed the busy wine bar, then she began to thread her way through the crowd of lunchtime drinkers. Simon craned his neck, curious to see who she was meeting, and saw her stop at a table by a pillar, where a bulky, middle-aged man with thinning fair hair, dressed in a chalk-stripe suit, was sitting, busy on his Blackberry. He looked up and got to his feet, slipping his phone into his pocket, smiling and saying something. They shook hands. Simon could see a plate of smoked salmon sandwiches and two champagne glasses on the table, and a half-bottle of champagne in an ice bucket. A romantic rendezvous, or a business meeting of the upper-end variety? It was hard to tell. The man took the girl's coat and hung it on a nearby peg. She put a hand to her neck to lift her dark, silky hair away from her shoulders as she sat down. Simon was struck by the grace and fluidity of her movements, like those of a dancer.

'Come on, Simon – Sauvignon or Pinot Grigio?'

Jeremy was waving the wine list in front of him. 'What? Oh, just an orange juice for me, thanks. Got a meeting with clients this afternoon.'

'Bor–*ring*.' Jeremy turned back to the bar and his conversation with Clive, leaving Simon free to watch the dark-haired girl, and wonder about her.

Rachel's first thought was that Andrew Garroway was a bit older and fatter than his online photo. Her disappointment made her feel faintly ashamed.

'I ordered some sandwiches,' Andrew said. 'Crayfish and rocket. Didn't have a clue, really. Hope that's all right.'

'Fine,' smiled Rachel.

He nodded. 'Good. And I thought a little champagne might be a nice way to break the ice.' He filled their glasses and handed one to Rachel, raising his own.

'To new friendships.'

Rachel smiled and took a sip. She didn't really want to drink at lunchtime. She wasn't hungry, either, but she put a sandwich on her plate.

'So – time to get to know each other,' said Andrew. 'You're a lawyer?'

'That's right. I'm a partner in a City law firm.'

Andrew pushed out his lower lip and raised his eyebrows. 'Impressive.'

'Not really.'

'I don't know about that. Not many girls at senior level in our outfit. But then, commodities trading is something of a male preserve.' Andrew eyed her, keeping his smile in place. Stunning looking, but a bit on the chilly side. Definitely in need of defrosting.

Rachel, detecting her own lack of warmth, did her best. 'So, tell me all about commodity trading. Is it interesting?'

It wasn't, as it turned out. Rachel sat with her chin on

her hand, taking an occasional nibble at her sandwich, and said not a word for ten minutes while Andrew expounded on what he did all day, what the market was like, what his colleagues were like, the things they occasionally got up to after work, the enormous freebies they got by way of hospitality from generous clients – the tickets to Wimbledon, the private boxes at Ascot, the boozy private lunches at Twickenham before important matches. Did Rachel like rugby?

'Not really. I don't know much about it. My ex-husband was very keen. But then, he's Welsh.' Why on earth had she mentioned Leo?

Andrew lifted the bottle, about to refill her glass. Rachel covered it quickly with her hand.

'No, thanks. I have a meeting later.'

Andrew shrugged and refilled his own.

To rekindle the conversation, Rachel said, 'You have two children, don't you?'

'A boy of sixteen and a girl of fourteen. You have a young son, as I recall.'

'Yes. Oliver. He's just six.'

'Lovely age. Wait till you hit the drama of the teenage years. A nightmare, I promise.'

Andrew proceeded to tell her about his children, and then Rachel talked about Oliver for a while. From this the talk drifted to their homes, the problems of commuting, the usual talk of City people. The conversation wasn't exactly stilted, but it reminded Rachel of small talk that people made at parties. Maybe she could like Andrew, if she could get to know him. It wasn't his fault he'd been a bit boring about his job. People generally were. He had a handsome, sensual face, and an easy manner, but there was something missing in their conversation, a lack of connection, of genuine interest. He asked her questions, he listened to her answers, he smiled and nodded and laughed, but it seemed to Rachel that his mind was elsewhere.

They had spun out the sandwiches and the champagne for forty minutes. There was only a small amount left in the bottle. He offered to refill her glass.

'No, really. I'm fine, thanks. You finish it.'

'Waste not, want not,' said Andrew, tipping the remains of the bottle into his glass. 'What time's your meeting?'

'Half three. Why?'

'Should be time enough. I've booked us in at the Novotel round the corner.'

'I'm sorry?'

'Only an hour to get to know one another properly, but better than nothing.' He smiled openly at her, with just a hint of insinuation, as though what he'd said amounted to no more than a bit of casual flirting.

The implication of what he'd said sank in. Rachel stared at him. 'You think I'm going to sleep with you? Today? Having just met you?'

It was Andrew's turn to look surprised. 'Sorry – am I missing something? What on earth do you think this is all about?'

'It's – it's a date.'

'A *date*? You sound like my daughter.' He laughed, and then frowned. 'We seem to have some crossed wires here. I thought you understood.'

'I don't think I do.' She knew she sounded absurdly prim, but she couldn't help it.

'Right. Well, I apologise. I thought . . .' He sat for a long moment, rubbing his chin – in bemusement, it seemed, rather than embarrassment. 'Look, I need to go to the little boys' room. Back in a tick. Then we'll talk. Sort things out.'

She watched him head off in the direction of the gents, wondering whether she should just get up and leave. But how rude would that be? On the other hand, what he'd just said had been grossly insulting. Or had it? Maybe this was all online dating was about. Looking for sex partners. She felt foolish, naive. It was the way things were nowadays. Everybody rushed at everything. Even relationships. She should get over it. When he came back she would make it clear that what he'd said or assumed didn't matter, but that she'd prefer to take things a bit more slowly. At that moment the waiter slipped the bill onto the table.

Simon was coming out of the gents when he saw the dark-haired girl's companion leaving, slipping out the side door of the wine bar. Simon glanced across the room. She was still at the table. She seemed lost in thought, features in neutral. Simon went back to his friends, but his thoughts stayed with the girl, wondering what had happened, what had gone on between her and the man. He saw her turn and glance in the direction of the gents, and noticed the bill on the table. Then it dawned on Simon. She didn't realise he'd walked out on her. Cheap bastard, dumping her with the price of a half-bottle of champagne and a plate of sandwiches.

Simon caught the attention of the waiter behind the bar. 'The girl sitting over there by the pillar. I'd like to settle her bill.'

The waiter nodded. He rang up the tab, and Simon paid with his card. He watched as the waiter went to her table.

Rachel glanced up in surprise as the waiter picked up the bill. 'Sorry – we haven't paid yet.'

'Gentleman over there paid.' The waiter nodded in the direction of the bar. A tall, lanky man with light-brown hair, who had clearly been waiting for her to catch his eye, came over and sat down.

'Your friend left, I'm afraid, sticking you with the bill. Not very gentlemanly.'

Rachel's surprise was only momentary. Of course Andrew Garroway had left. Why wouldn't he? Clearly for him online dating was just a way of finding lonely, compliant women to sleep with. Still, she felt an icy shock of humiliation.

'I can pay my own bills, thanks.' She fished in her bag for her wallet. 'How much do I owe you?'

'Nothing. I was happy to do it. Truly. I'm glad he left. It gives me a chance to get to know you. I've been wanting to do that ever since you walked in.' Simon had astonished himself. He hadn't intended to say what had been in his mind, but looking into her perfect face, her amazing eyes, it seemed easy and obvious.

'Well, I'm afraid I don't especially want to get to know you.' Rachel put two twenties on the table, got up, slipped on her coat and left the wine bar. The chilly street air felt cleansing. She strode across Leadenhall Street in the direction of her office, her heart thudding with shame and anger. Did every man in London think she could be bought for the price of a sandwich and a glass of champagne? As soon as she got home tonight she would remove her profile from every single one of those ridiculous dating websites. She must have been mad to let Sophie talk her into it.

She reached her office building and swung open the glass door. Stepping into the vestibule, she headed for the lift and stabbed the button, exchanging a nod with the security guard on the desk.

'Hold on,' said a voice behind her. 'Won't you at least talk to me?'

She turned round. The tall young man from the wine bar was standing there, wearing a baffled, almost desperate expression.

'Look,' said Rachel, 'I've had an encounter I'd rather forget about, and now I just want to get back to work. I suppose you thought you were doing me a favour, paying the bill, but I didn't ask you to. OK?' The lift arrived and she stepped into it. Simon put out a hand to stop the doors closing.

'All I wanted to—'

The security guard came forward and interrupted him. 'Excuse me, sir. I take it you have business in the building? If so, you'll need to sign the visitors' book and get a pass.'

Simon watched as the lift doors closed on the woman of his dreams. 'No,' he said to the doorman. 'It doesn't matter.'

The lift took Rachel to the fourth floor, where she went to her office and closed the door.

An hour later, Felicity was arriving at Vince's mum's council house in Deptford. Denise lived in a shabby, pebble-dashed box opposite a villainous-looking comprehensive school surrounded by a high wire fence. Most of the small front gardens of the houses in the street were overgrown, weedy repositories for discarded household items, but Vince's mum's front garden was tidy and well tended, with a low, plastic-linked chain fence. As she stood on the doorstep, Felicity wondered how many people were likely to turn up to a welcome-home party for an ex-con on a weekday. In Vince's world, maybe more than a few.

Denise answered the doorbell dressed in a short lycra skirt, black tights, and a plum-coloured satin blouse. On her feet she wore fluffy house slippers. Her hair was dyed an extravagant orange-red, and her long, square-cut fingernails were intricately painted and studded with tiny jewels. She was still good-looking for a woman in her mid fifties, but the clothes were too young, and the make-up too much.

Denise gave a yelp of delight when she saw Felicity. 'Fliss, babes!' She hugged her and kissed her on either cheek. 'Big day's here at last! Come on through and meet the girls.'

Felicity took off her coat and followed Denise into the back room, where three women of Denise's age, all decked out like ageing barmaids, were busy arranging plates of food on a gateleg table. Denise introduced Shelley, Rhona and Barbara, and they twinkled their fingers at Felicity in welcome. When Denise told them how Felicity had been waiting faithfully for four years for Vince, they all let out little murmurs of sympathy, and Shelley gave her a hug of solidarity.

Felicity glanced around. There was a 'welcome home' banner strung over the fireplace. She glanced round, but no balloons, which was small mercy. 'Can I do something to help?'

Denise grasped Felicity's hand. 'Come and help me sort out drinks in the kitchen.'

A serious mountain of booze was crammed into the tiny kitchen. Bottles of vodka, whisky and wine covered the surface of the kitchen table, and four boxes of Stella lager were stacked behind the door.

'The offie threw in a free box of wine and beer glasses, but I'm still worried there won't be enough. We've got a ton of people coming over,' said Denise. 'Here, you get unpacking these, and I'll sort out what I've got in my cupboards. He'll be here around four.'

No need even to say his name, thought Felicity, as she began unpacking glasses from the box. How had Vince attained this heroic status? Simply by being absent, she supposed, like a Beirut hostage. Forget the real reason.

'Ossie and Quills are picking him up at three, and they're taking him for a beer first – you know, just to get him acclimatised, first day out and all that.' Denise gazed speculatively at two baking trays of sausage rolls. 'I reckon those should go in the oven at quarter to four. What d'you think?'

Felicity nodded. 'Sounds about right.'

When she'd finished with the glasses, Felicity went through to the living room, where Denise and the others sat perched on the edges of two sofas, skirts riding up their thighs, making inroads into a bottle of Chardonnay. Denise was holding forth on the iniquities of the British criminal justice system, how Vince should never have been sent down, how he'd only ever been defending himself in a fair fight.

Felicity had heard Denise spin this record countless times over the past few years, always the same old tune. Felicity had her own thoughts about it all. Sure, Vince had been unlucky. He had punched someone in a brief fight in Soho, and the man had died after hitting his head on the pavement. Vince had never meant that to happen. No question it could have turned out differently. But why, in the recounting of it, was it always Vince who was the unlucky one? How come Vince's family and friends never mentioned the even unluckier bloke, the one who'd been on the receiving end of that vicious punch? It was like that time she'd ended up at the foot of a flight of stairs, losing the baby, thanks to Vince and his drunken temper. All that agonised contrition on his part. Unlucky old Vince. She hadn't wanted that pregnancy in any event – so lucky her.

'Come on, Fliss, have a glass!' Denise wagged the bottle of Chardonnay.

'I'm all right for now, thanks. I'll have one when he gets here.'

The women nattered on. Denise opened another bottle, glasses were refilled, long-nailed fingers scrabbled in the bowls of peanuts and Bombay mix. After a while Denise glanced at her watch.

'Omigod! Look at the time.' She scuffed out of the room in her slippers, and returned moments later in shiny, plum-coloured platforms. The shoes dramatically altered her height and posture, thrusting her bust forward, balling the muscles on her spindly calves. The doorbell ding-donged and she hurried out to answer it. Seconds later came the sound of Denise's squeals of welcome mingling with the voices of the new arrivals. Two middle-aged couples entered the living room, bringing with them the cold smell of outside, and two carrier bags full of cans of lager. Felicity didn't know any of them.

Denise began introductions, but the doorbell rang again

and she went to usher in more people, this time an entire family of three generations – gran, mum and dad, and brood of noisy youngsters.

The tiny living room was suddenly filled with shrill talk and laughter. Felicity made a discreet exit to the relative peace of the kitchen, and decided to station herself there and dispense drinks. She really didn't want to mingle with these strangers.

She stayed there for the next hour as more and more people arrived, handing out cans of lager and Coke, mixing gin and tonics, cracking the caps of wine bottles and pouring drinks. Denise seemed to have forgotten about her, for which Felicity was grateful. She'd been worried Denise would drag her through to the living room to introduce her to everyone as the love of Vince's life. Barbara, mildly pissed, came through and relieved the tedium by talking to her for twenty minutes about what a darling Vince had been as a teenager when he was at school with her Ryan, before splashing some Bacardi into her glass and wandering away.

There was still no sign of Vince, Ossie and Quills.

Felicity mixed herself a vodka and Coke and gazed through the window at the little huddle of smokers hunched against the drizzle by the rotary clothes line in Denise's patch of back garden. Denise came through, her face tense and anxious.

'I dunno what's happened to them. What d'you think's happened?' She bit her lip, then picked up a half-empty vodka bottle and poured a couple of inches into her wine glass. She pulled her mobile from her skirt pocket and hit the redial button, listened, sighed, put the phone back in her pocket and swallowed the vodka in one. 'Quills has got his phone switched off. I haven't got Ossie's number.'

‘Not to worry,’ said Felicity. ‘They’ll be here soon.’

‘Yeah?’ Denise’s eyes scanned Felicity’s for reassurance, and seemed to find some. ‘Yeah. He’s a good boy. He wouldn’t let his old mum down.’ She glanced out at the smokers. ‘Sometimes wish I’d never given up. I could do with one right now.’ She touched her lower lip with a manicured finger, her hand trembling slightly, eyes distant.

The increasing sense of remoteness which had been growing in Felicity all afternoon felt suddenly complete. She was nothing to do with this. She was a bystander at this grotesque circus, not even part of the audience swigging drink and wolfing sausage rolls in the living room. She wanted to leave, to get out before Vince got here. But she could not abandon Denise. To leave now would be to confirm Denise’s worst fears – that this was pointless, that Vince didn’t care about her or the party, that his priority on his first day of freedom was to go on the lash with his mates.

Suddenly there came the frantic ding-donging of the doorbell, and drunken laughter from outside the front door. Denise gave a screech and hurried down the hall to open it. There on the doorstep was Vince, so pissed he could hardly stand up, supported by his friends. Watching from the kitchen doorway, Felicity recognised Vince’s Turkish friend, Ossie. The other, a thickset man with ginger hair, had to be Quills.

‘Chrissake, bring him in!’ Denise grabbed Vince’s arm and the four of them made their way down the hall, giggling and swearing.

Felicity shrank back from the doorway. She leant against the fridge, and heard a roar go up from the living room. Then Denise shouting, ‘Get ’im on the sofa! Move, Darren!’

Laughter, then someone shouted, 'Get that man a drink! He looks like he needs one!' More laughter.

Denise tottered into the kitchen and grabbed a can of Stella from one of the open boxes. She was laughing, her eyes pink and manic. She grabbed Felicity's elbow. 'He's here, babes! Come on!'

Felicity resisted. 'I just need to go to the loo first. Freshen up.'

Denise put one taloned finger to the side of her nose and winked. 'You go and make yourself gorgeous!' She left with the can of Stella. Wife-beater, thought Felicity. That was what Vince and his friends always used to call that particular lager. The thought had come into her head from nowhere.

She stepped quietly into the hallway, hoping no one would see her through the half-open living room door. She found her coat buried beneath others on the banister, and for a panicky moment thought she'd left her handbag in the living room. Then she saw it beside the hall table. She picked it up and opened the front door, closing it behind her as quietly as she could, even though the sounds of the homecoming celebration were too loud for anyone to hear her leave.

At half past five Rachel left her office. As the lift descended she leant back and closed her eyes briefly. What a hellish day. A wasted morning when she'd been too nervous to do any serious work, leading up to a squalid lunchtime rendezvous that had left her feeling humiliated and stupid, followed by an afternoon of self-loathing. To top it all, she'd been chased by the client on the casino case, and had had to ring Anthony up and nag him, which she didn't like doing, and which he hadn't much cared for either. The work just wasn't getting done on time. It wasn't like Anthony. He was normally so conscientious, so on top of his game. Probably distracted by some new woman, thought Rachel gloomily, as the lift doors opened.

She stepped out onto the pavement into the swirl of evening commuters and found it was raining hard. She groped hopelessly in her bag for her umbrella, before realising she must have left it at home. Great. She was going to get soaked walking to the station, on top of everything else. Suddenly someone touched her arm. When she saw it was the young man from the wine bar, she sighed in annoyance.

'Are you stalking me, or something?'

'Sort of.' He held his own umbrella over her. 'Look, don't get angry, and don't get wet. I just want to talk to you.'

She stared at him. 'Have you been waiting here all afternoon?'

'Hardly. I only work across the road.' Rachel liked the way he laughed when he said this. But she had had enough of men for one day. She turned away and started to walk in the direction of Bank station. He hurried along next to her, holding his umbrella gallantly over her head.

'Come for a drink with me? Please?' She kept walking. 'Just one?'

She glanced at him, noticing that he had deep-set grey-green eyes, and was probably older than she had first thought. Early thirties, probably, though his slightly round face made him look younger. 'You're very persistent, aren't you?' she replied.

'It's my best quality. If you won't come for a drink with me tonight, I'll just have to wait outside your office again tomorrow night.'

'Tomorrow's Saturday.'

‘That’s true. OK, Monday night.’ He bumped into a fellow pedestrian and apologised, lost Rachel in the crowd, then caught up with her again. ‘So you might as well give in now.’

They had reached the junction of Gracechurch Street and Cornhill. Rachel stopped, and he did too. They stood together beneath his umbrella, the rain teeming down, people bustling past. He gazed hopefully at her, and she found herself thinking how random this was, unplanned, out of nowhere. The way things should be. She also found herself thinking that there was nothing to hurry home for – Oliver was having a sleepover with Josh.

‘It’s Friday. Everywhere’s packed.’ She realised she’d just said yes.

He realised it, too, and smiled. ‘I booked a booth at Abacus.’

‘Wasn’t that just a bit presumptuous?’

‘Do you have to talk to me like you’re constantly telling me off? I haven’t done anything particularly wrong, you know. I just saw you and liked you, and hoped we might get to know one another. Frankly, I thought booking Abacus showed a bit of foresight.’

Rachel smiled. ‘That’s one way of putting it.’

He put out his hand. ‘Simon Wren.’

Rachel shook it. ‘Rachel Davies.’

‘Come on, then, Rachel Davies. Before the lights change.’ He took her arm just above the elbow and hurried her across the road. Rachel found she didn’t mind the proprietorial gesture at all, nor the assumption that lay behind booking the cocktail bar. It was quite nice to be taken charge of. She would just go with it, and see where the evening took her. Maybe she would even have reason to be grateful to Andrew Garroway.

CHAPTER TEN

That evening, Sir Vivian was hosting his celebrated champagne and hotpot supper party at his spacious apartment in Westminster. Sir Vivian was a person of some eminence in the legal world. He had lately been Recorder of London, was a Bencher of the Inner Temple and a Judicial Appointments Commissioner, and had interests which extended beyond the law and into the arts. Besides being an accomplished cellist and chairman of the Trustees of Glyndebourne Arts Trust, he had also written a well-received history of the Dutch Republic, and a biography of the painter Duncan Grant. Sarah was his only child, the product of a late marriage. Sarah's mother had died when Sarah was just fifteen, and he had never remarried – partly because he had loved his wife too deeply to wish to replace her, and partly because he found the rewards of middle-aged bachelorhood too varied and enjoyable to want to tie himself down again. Although now in his early seventies, he remained suavely good-looking, and was one of the most popular 'spare' single men of a certain age among London hostesses.

Tonight's party was one he held every autumn, and to which he invited prominent people from the world of the law and the arts to eat lamb hotpot and quaff champagne. (It was well known that the arriviste Jeffrey Archer had appropriated this idea, as he had so many other things, after being taken in the early seventies to one of Sir Vivian's parties by the young David Mellor, then a pupil in Sir Vivian's chambers). There was always much demand for invitations among the great and the good, and every year Jonathan Kittering and his wife Caroline, though merely a retired couple from Woking with no standing in either the world of law or the arts, were sure to receive theirs. Jonathan Kittering and Sir Vivian had been close friends for many years, ever since their schooldays, and one incident in particular had had a lasting effect upon Sir Vivian and had shaped certain of his attitudes.

In his teenage years Vivian Colman had been slender, golden-haired, and a precociously gifted cricketer, good enough to be chosen at the age of sixteen to play for the First XI against Uppingham. Daunting though it was for a year-eleven boy to be batting and bowling in the company of the gods of the upper sixth against the school's fiercest rivals, he had acquitted himself exceptionally well. On that sunny afternoon in early June 1956, he had taken four wickets and achieved his first half-century, and been named man of the match. Young Vivian's quiet pleasure in the day was, however, sadly spoilt when, later in the pavilion, after the others had gone to tea, Edwin Challoner, the captain of the First XI, tried to seduce him. Vivian was deeply upset and horrified, and it was by the merest good fortune that Jonathan Kittering had come into the pavilion at that moment and interrupted the incident. Challoner left swiftly, leaving Kittering to calm and reassure his schoolfellow.

Throughout the long years of friendship which followed, neither of them ever referred to the incident again, but its legacy to Sir Vivian was a lasting gratitude to his friend, and a profound distaste for the unnatural tendencies displayed by the captain of the First XI. He had never been able to reconcile himself to the increasing tolerance towards homosexuals, and what he regarded as their ghastly practices.

When Sarah had announced her engagement a few months ago to the son of his oldest friend, Sir Vivian had been not only delighted, but relieved. Dearly as he loved his daughter, theirs had always been a somewhat awkward relationship, particularly after the death of Sarah's mother. Without his wife to bridge the communication gap, Sir Vivian approached sole parental care of his extremely attractive and sexually precocious daughter with bafflement and anxiety, feeling the best he could do was to give her a generous allowance and hope she'd be bright enough not to make any disastrous mistakes. When Sarah left her boarding school to go to Oxford to study law, he had naturally been pleased, but wasn't convinced that she had the necessary drive and tenacity to make much of a career of it. In his view, the best any girl could do was to find some decent man with a fair amount of money, and settle down. That Sarah had chosen to do this with the son of his best friend was more than Sir Vivian could have hoped for.

On the eve of his party, fifteen minutes before the

guests were due to arrive, Sir Vivian wandered through the reception rooms, surveying the array of glasses and bottles of champagne cooling in their baths of ice. He had toyed with the idea of cancelling the party a few weeks ago, fearing that, with a recession impending, it might look overly extravagant. But he was glad that he hadn't. Besides, the simplicity of hotpot hinted at austerity. This year's gathering would be more than a mere social event – it would also be a special celebration of the fact that his only daughter was to marry the son of his oldest friend. Smiling with satisfaction, he went through to the kitchen to see how the caterers were getting along.

While her father was inspecting trays of hotpot, Sarah was still in the office, trying to catch up with the last of her work. She'd already received more than one frosty reproof from her boss, Hugo, about sloppiness and bad timekeeping. Two weeks ago she couldn't have cared less, confident that as soon as she was married she was going to dump the job. But Toby's redundancy had changed everything. Until he found something else, they badly needed Sarah's money. Only an hour ago, Hugo had dropped an urgent new matter on her desk, barking, 'I need it tied up by the end of the day, so make sure you get it done tonight.'

She was leafing through the file when her mobile buzzed. It was Toby.

'I've just had a shower, and I'll be leaving the gym in ten minutes. Do you want me to pick you up?'

'I'm still at the office. Probably going to be here for another half-hour at least. Bloody Hugo dropped something on me at the last minute. One of our major clients wants reinsurance cover for a tanker going to Yemen. You go on without me. I'll see you there.'

'OK. Don't work too hard.'

She clicked the phone off. That was a laugh. At least she had a job. All very well for people with time to spend in the gym. Why wasn't he out there trying to find something? So far as she could tell, he'd done nothing all week. She turned back to the file. She'd got cover for seventy per cent of the risk, with the last thirty per cent still to get. In theory, she could go straight to her father's bash from the office, but she really wanted to go home and have a shower and change, and not turn up in her office scruffs. So she needed to wrap this up in the next fifteen minutes, if possible. She pondered for a moment, then picked up the phone, deciding to give Gerald Last at Haddow Syndicate a shot. With any luck she'd catch him before he headed off to the wine bar for his Friday night drinking session. Gerald was a smooth operator, one of the old-school, long-lunching brigade who gave the lie to the notion that the City was no longer a sexist institution. He largely despised City women, but he liked Sarah because she was attractive, had decent legs and nice tits, and was a good sport. As a result he and Sarah had done a fair amount of business over the past year or so. Sarah, with robust cynicism, knew exactly how Gerald's mind worked and was prepared to flirt and massage his ego to get the job done.

She found Gerald still in his office and, after some preliminary banter, explained what she needed.

'Who else is on the slip?' asked Gerald.

Sarah gave him the names of the other underwriters.

'Fine,' said Gerald. 'Don't see a problem.'

‘Great. Can I bring the documents over now for you to sign?’

‘Darling, I was just on my way out. Let it wait till Monday. You can take it you’re covered.’

Sarah hesitated. Strictly speaking she should get Gerald to initial the slip, but clearly he’d rather be heading off to Corney & Barrow than waiting around at the office for her. Besides, she was in a hurry, too. ‘OK. We’ll do it first thing on Monday. Thanks for that. Maybe see you for a drink soon?’

‘Charming idea,’ said Gerald. ‘Enjoy the weekend.’

Sarah put the phone down. Job done. She logged all the information on the computer, saved it, and hurried back to the flat in Docklands to shower and change.

By the time Sarah arrived at her father’s house, the party was well underway, the rooms ringing with well-bred chatter and laughter. It had taken Sarah longer to get ready than she’d anticipated. For some reason she felt the need to dress bravely, and had opted for a stunning little black Marc Jacobs number with the sheerest black stockings, which made the most of her legs, plus a pair of new Manolos with four-inch heels. Even without the dress and the heels, she knew she was the youngest and sexiest woman there. One glance round the room told her it was the usual crowd of Daddy’s moulting old birds and buffers. She gazed round at the crowd of lawyers and artists and writers, and reckoned the average age must be sixty.

Sir Vivian greeted his daughter with a kiss, dwelling on her appearance with a mixture of pride and anxiety, and reflecting that, like her mother, she was too extravagantly pretty. He introduced her to a brace of elderly Benchers, one tall and crumpled, the other short, round and bald. They beamed with pleasure at the sight of a pretty girl and, forgetting their years and imagining themselves thirty again, they battled with one another to occupy the small talk high ground while pretending not to eye her cleavage. Sarah made a show of listening as she scanned the crowd for familiar faces. After a few minutes she saw Caroline Kittering heading straight for her, bright-eyed and clutching her champagne glass. Her face was pink, possibly from the effects of champagne, possibly because she was kitted out in full Country Casuals rig, wearing a woollen skirt, boots, and a quilted navy gilet over a cashmere jumper.

Sarah excused herself from the Benchers and greeted Caroline, stooping a little, because of the heels, to kiss the air either side of Caroline's downy cheeks.

Caroline scarcely bothered to return the kiss, but launched straight in. 'Toby told us the other night about losing his job. It's simply ghastly. You poor children. Of course, I blame this wretched government.' She glanced around. 'Where is Toby? I've been looking for him everywhere since we arrived.' She took a gulp of her champagne. 'What was he thinking of, letting a whole week go by before telling us?'

'He probably didn't want to worry you.'

'Of course, it means you'll have to put the wedding back—'

But whatever else Caroline had to say, Sarah wasn't listening. She had just caught sight of Leo on the far side of the room. He was leaning against a doorway, glass in hand, deep in conversation. The sight of him was a jolt to her senses – the handsome, well-defined features as youthful as ever, his intelligent gaze and the flash of his disarming smile as familiar to her as though she'd last seen him yesterday, rather than four years ago.

She tore her gaze away and tried to pay attention to Caroline.

'Because,' Caroline was saying earnestly, 'who knows how long this recession will last? Toby doesn't seem to realise that things have changed. He has commitments now.'

'Don't you think this is something we should talk about when Toby's around?' said Sarah. She glanced again in Leo's direction. She had to talk to him. He might leave at any minute. The two elderly Benchers were hovering hopefully a little way off. Sarah grabbed Caroline by the elbow and steered her towards them.

'Caroline, may I introduce you to Mr Justice Waddell and Mr Justice Huntsby-Stevens?'

Having parked Caroline with the Benchers, she made her way quickly through the throng of people to the doorway. But he had disappeared. People were coming and going, but there was no sign of Leo. She felt an unnerving, unexpected sense of panic. Then a voice in her ear said, 'Hello, young lady.' She turned, and there he was.

She smiled, intent on remaining cool. 'Leo. How lovely to see you.'

'And you. What a long time it's been.' He drained his glass of champagne. 'You look, if I may say so, as lovely as ever.'

'Thank you.' She was conscious that her heart was thudding.

'You do realise, I've been coming to these parties of your father's for the last three years, hoping you might show up?'

'You've had other ways of getting in touch.'

'True. But we always had a – what's the word? – a capricious friendship. I was fairly confident that our paths would cross again. I enjoyed leaving it to fate.'

'And letting fate decide whether the moment would be auspicious – or inauspicious?'

'Inauspicious, it seems. I gather I've lost you to some lucky young man.' He lifted her left hand, so that light glittered from her engagement ring.

The combination of his touch and the ridiculously affected nature of their conversation was too much. 'Leo, can we stop this bullshit? I need another glass of champagne. I feel like getting rat-arsed. God knows, I've reason enough.'

Leo caught the eye of a passing waitress, and she refilled their glasses.

'OK, bullshit over,' said Leo. 'So, tell me about your fiancé. He must be an exceptional individual to make you want to settle down. I never saw you as a one-man girl.'

'You know how it is. The mating game gets exhausting after a while.'

'Really? I recall you as having considerable stamina.' Leo's smile was just short of suggestive, but in his blue eyes she felt she could read their whole history, every sexual encounter, every bed-warmed conversation, every tetchy disagreement, every pleasurable weekend passed in the ease of one another's company. What had happened to all that? As though reading her thoughts, he added, 'I've thought about you a lot. In fact, when Anthony told me you were engaged, I felt—'

'What?'

'Something selfish. Proprietorial. Totally unjustified, of course.'

'Of course.'

'So tell me about him. Who is he, what does he do?'

'His name is Toby Kittering, and he's – that is, he *was* a merchant banker, until a week ago. He got canned.'

'That's bad luck.'

She couldn't meet Leo's eye, not wanting to find herself, and her disloyal thoughts reflected there. 'Yes, well . . . It makes things difficult.' She glanced around the room. Anywhere but his penetrating gaze.

'But not difficult enough to change your plans?'

'God, no!' She drained her glass swiftly.

'Pity. We had a good thing once. Friendship, with recreational sex thrown in. The ideal relationship.'

'Look, Leo, just because we happen to have bumped into one another doesn't mean I'm suddenly going to jump into bed with you for old times' sake.'

'That was the last thing on my mind. I was thinking more of the friendship part. We've let things slip.'

'And whose fault is that?'

'I think we both bear some of the responsibility.'

Sarah saw Toby nearby with a group of people. He smiled as she caught his eye. 'There's Toby. I'd better go – I haven't spoken to him since I got here.'

Leo followed the direction of her gaze. Toby was everything he'd expected. Tall, conventionally good-looking, safe, uninspiring, and if he was fresh out of a job, probably quite needy, too. Leo felt disappointed for Sarah. And in some strange way, responsible. 'I mean what I say,' he added, as she turned to go. 'If you want to talk – or anything else – you know where to find me.' He fished in his jacket for his Blackberry. 'In fact, why don't you give me your number?'

She hesitated. 'If you like.' She gave him the number, and he keyed it in. 'Let's stay in touch.'

He watched her go, and felt a pang of – what? Desire? She had always been desirable, and was now, being unattainable, even more so. But it was more than that. There was a certain inescapability about Sarah. And now she was marrying a man who probably wouldn't be enough for her. As she walked away, Sarah's emotions were a mixture of anger and bewilderment. She'd never known any encounter with Leo be so painfully superficial and strained. From the first day they met seven years ago at an Oxford garden party, from which they'd escaped together to the nearest pub, and then to Leo's bed, their relationship had been characterised, even in its most vitriolic moments, by a kind of callous, loving sympathy, a harmonious conflict in which they loved and detested one another. But the best they could do now, after four years, was stale banter. Yet the one thing she'd wanted to do, as soon as she'd seen him standing in the doorway, was to escape with him again. Get out of here, away from all this, and be together. But that was never going to happen now. No more escapes. She warmed her face into a smile as she approached Toby.

Toby kissed her. 'You look good,' he said. 'Who was that you were talking to?'

'Just someone from my old chambers. Oh God, here come your parents. Your mother cornered me a while ago, wanting to discuss our plight. You'd think the fucking atom bomb had dropped. Have you spoken to them yet?'

'Don't worry. I've kept a pleasant surprise up my sleeve. I wanted you all together before I told you.'

Sarah realised there was a clarity and brightness about him. He looked happy. 'Shit! You've got a job.'

'Sort of. But not quite. You'll see.'

Jonathan and Caroline arrived, and Toby kissed his mother. Sarah decided she could even forgive the way Toby called her 'Mumsy', if only he would tell them all that everything was going to be all right.

'Managed to tear your mother away from two batty old judges,' said Jonathan Kittering. 'Now, what's this summit meeting all about?'

Toby glanced from face to face, preparing his announcement. 'I wanted to let you know that I'm taking a change of direction. My life's going to be about something entirely new from now on.' No one said anything. Sarah found her eyes meeting Caroline's briefly. 'I was coming out of the gym at Canary Wharf,' went on Toby, 'when I saw this notice in the lobby of one of the buildings. I went inside, and I spoke to the guy, and – well, to cut a long story short, I went along to a recruitment meeting. Well, not exactly recruitment, it was more some kind of information forum—'

'For God's sake, Toby! Will you just *tell* us?' exclaimed Sarah.

'I'm going to be a teacher.'

There was a stunned silence.

'A *teacher*?'

Rather than let Sarah's appalled note sound for the rest of them, Caroline said, 'I think that's a wonderful idea, darling. An excellent stopgap. Better than sitting around idly, waiting for the economy to improve.'

Toby looked momentarily discomfited. 'It's not a stopgap. It's a complete career change. I'm never going back to banking. It's a soul-destroying business, and I never much liked it. Since I met Sarah . . .' Sarah felt Toby twining her fingers into his. 'I've realised there's more to life than making money. Massive bonuses, expensive stuff we don't need – it's all meaningless. I want to make a difference to people's lives. I want to wake up in the morning and feel good about myself. I want to think about what I'm going to put into the world, not what I'm going to take out of it.'

Toby's father nodded slowly. 'What kind of teaching had you in mind?'

'My degree's in economics, so that's the obvious choice. Usually you have to do a one-year postgraduate teaching qualification, but there's a chance I'll get fast-tracked.' He smiled at Sarah. 'In six months' time I could be facing my first class.' This time the smile was straight into her eyes, warm and trusting, and she had to return it. 'And with Sarah's support, I know I can do it.'

'But . . .' Sarah paused, trying to blend enthusiasm and caution in her tone. 'Darling, are you sure it's the right career change? I mean, if you were some middle-aged banker who'd been chucked on the scrap heap with no hope of ever finding another job, it would be one thing. But you're young! Surely it's just a matter of time before you get another banking job.'

'But I don't *want* another banking job.' Toby was calm and earnest. 'Getting canned by Graffman's has let me see there are other possibilities in life. Possibilities that may not involve making a shedload of money, but which I think—which I *know* will make us both much happier.'

In which life, wondered Sarah, did Toby think that not having a shedload of money would make her happy? She said nothing, scanning his face, realising this was serious. Whatever else he might be, Toby, when he made up his mind about something, could be doggedly implacable. She would have a job of work to do, talking him out of this disastrous idea, but she would do it, come what may. A teacher? She couldn't go through life married to a teacher! Still, now wasn't the time to say anything. She smiled and squeezed his hand, while Jonathan Kittering made encouraging noises and said stuff about momentous decisions, full backing of your mother and myself, crossroads in life, and so forth, and Caroline twittered anxiously about probably taking more time to think it over, one read such awful things about schools these days, and what if Toby finished up in a comprehensive on some sink estate, had he really thought it through *properly*? Sarah felt she could almost begin to like the woman.

CHAPTER ELEVEN

Sarah arrived at work just minutes before the Monday morning team meeting was due to start. Hugo emerged from his office just as Sarah reached her desk, coffee in hand. He shot her a grim look.

'Good of you to turn up at last. Bring that Lindos file into the meeting – we need to sort out the claim.' He stalked off in the direction of the meeting room.

Sarah dumped her bag on the desk. 'Claim? What claim's he talking about?' she asked Colin, who sat at the next desk.

Colin looked at her in disbelief. 'The *Lindos*? The supramax that ran aground off New Zealand over the weekend?'

Sarah's heart tightened momentarily. It was the tanker she'd been asked to get reinsurance cover for on Friday evening. Thank God it was covered, and that Gerald was good for that last thirty per cent. Still, it would have been better if she'd got it in writing. She wasn't looking forward to telling Hugo that Gerald had yet to sign the slip. She found the file and headed for the meeting.

'OK, first things first,' said Hugo, as Sarah closed the door and slid into her seat. 'The *Lindos*. As you've all no doubt heard, she seems to be a casualty. Sarah, I left the matter of the reinsurance cover with you on Friday – I assume you dealt with it?'

Sarah nodded. 'Yes. I've got it covered.' Her mouth felt dry. 'Sort of.'

Hugo's gaze was steely. 'Sort of? What the fuck are you telling me? Either it's covered or it's not.'

'It's covered. Gerald Last agreed to write the last thirty per cent. But there wasn't time to get his signature. It was Friday, it was late—'

'Jesus Christ, Sarah. Go and get it sorted. Straight away! You know we can't post this claim without his mark on the slip. We've got a vessel insured for a hundred million. We've only secured lines for seventy per cent, which leaves us a cool thirty three million to find. And if Gerald isn't going to sign, and your trust fund isn't good for it, we're in shit. So get his signature. Now!'

Sarah picked up the file and left the room, crimson-faced. Swearing beneath her breath, she stalked back to her desk and called Gerald on his mobile.

Gerald Last was driving along Chelsea Embankment when his hands-free rang. He glanced at the display, and saw Sarah's name come up. He reached out, pressed a button, and cut the call off. He'd heard about the *Lindos* over the weekend. He knew exactly why she was ringing.

* * *

Unable to reach Gerald, Sarah began to feel panicky. She tried to reassure herself that it would all be fine, that she was worrying needlessly. But things wouldn't be fine, she knew, until she got Gerald's signature. She flung on her coat and headed out of the office. At Lloyd's, the usual line was forming at the box. Sarah had a quick look round for Gerald, though she knew that as a senior underwriter, he was unlikely to be there. She went up to his office, but was told by Gerald's sour-faced PA that Gerald wasn't in yet.

'When do you expect him?'

'I couldn't say. All I know is that he's on his way. I can't tell you any more than that.' Gerald's PA wasn't a fan of Sarah's.

'Look, can you tell him to ring me when he gets in? He's got my number.'

'I may *ask* him,' replied the PA frigidly. 'I certainly won't tell him.'

'Whatever, bitch,' muttered Sarah beneath her breath as she turned to go.

She retreated to Starbucks and sat with a large latte and a copy of *The Times*, her mobile on the table next to her, ignoring a series of increasingly urgent messages from Hugo. She didn't dare go back to the office until she'd got Gerald's signature. Please, please let him ring soon. Her head had begun to ache.

Half an hour later, when no call had come, she rang Gerald's office again.

'I'm afraid Mr Last is still in his meeting,' the PA was happy to tell her.

Sarah didn't have a clue what to do next. She rang the office to check where everyone was, and got Colin.

'How's Hugo?' she asked.

'Spitting teeth and blood. He's gone off to a management meeting. The last thing he said was for you to ring him as soon as you can.' Sarah closed her eyes briefly. She could guess what the management meeting was about. Hugo was busy doing some damage limitation, waiting for her to assure him she'd got the signature on the last thirty per cent. 'Where are you, in case he asks?'

'Tell him I've gone to the market – no, wait – tell him I've fixed up a meeting with Gerald later this morning.' Maybe that would keep him off her back for an hour or so.

She drained the cold dregs of her latte, and because she could think of nothing better to do, headed off aimlessly to the shops in Liverpool Street station and hung around there for a fearful half-hour, before going back to Lloyd's, and to Gerald's office.

'I'm afraid Mr Last has gone into another meeting until twelve,' the PA told her. 'Then he's out to lunch.'

'But I really need to talk to him!'

'As do a lot of people.' She gave Sarah a meaningful look. 'He does know you're trying to reach him.'

Sarah didn't want to face the truth which she read in the PA's cold eyes – that Gerald was deliberately blocking her. She felt close to tears. How could he do this? She returned to Starbucks, and sat hunched over another coffee. When she tried to drink some, she felt sick. Several times she tried Gerald's mobile, and each time it went straight to voicemail.

At twelve-thirty she knew she had no choice but to go back to the office, and tell Hugo. Just as she was crossing Leadenhall Street, she saw Gerald on the other side, heading towards Caravaggio's. Dodging taxis and cars, she raced across the road, and accosted him just as he was about to go into the restaurant. She was dimly aware that the person he was with looked very like the Chairman of Lloyd's.

'Gerald!' she said breathlessly. 'I've been trying to get hold of you all morning. I need you to sign the slip – you know, for the thirty per cent of that *Lindos* risk you agreed to take on Friday?'

Gerald looked bemused. 'I said I'd look at it. I didn't say I'd sign it.' He opened the restaurant door for his companion. 'In future, you should get these things properly sorted out, before dashing off for the weekend.' The Chairman of Lloyd's passed through the doorway, and Gerald lingered for a second. 'I spoke to Hugo half an hour ago. We agreed that these things will happen if you employ incompetent staff. He blames himself entirely.' He gave Sarah a smile. 'Nice try, sweetie.' He disappeared into the restaurant.

Sarah stood rooted to the pavement, her heart thudding. He'd given her his word, the bastard! Did he realise what it meant if he didn't sign the slip? Of course he did. He knew only too well, and he didn't care. He was hanging her out to dry. She was momentarily tempted to follow Gerald inside and tell him exactly what she thought of him. But she didn't. Even in her present state of hopelessness, she knew it wouldn't be a wise move to make a scene in front of the Chairman of Lloyds. There was the future to think of, even if right now it didn't look as though she had one.

She went back to the office. Hugo had recently returned from the management meeting. His face looked grim, grey. His job, too, was on the line when this kind of thing happened.

‘I didn’t get his signature,’ she said simply to Hugo. ‘But then, you know that.’

‘Yes, I do,’ said Hugo. ‘Clear your desk.’

He turned without another word and went into his office, closing the door behind him.

Henry was on his way out of the clerks’ room. He paused by Felicity’s desk.

‘Just going round the corner for a sandwich. Want me to get you anything?’

Felicity shook her head. ‘No, thanks. I brought something from home.’ She nodded at her computer screen. ‘Doing a bit of online shopping. I need a new electric toothbrush and some hair straighteners.’

Henry’s eyes shifted to Felicity’s unruly dark curls. ‘Right. OK.’

When he had gone, Felicity sighed to the empty room. The hair straighteners were meant to help in achieving the new image she had dreamt up for herself the night before, as a sleek, poised career woman. Who was she kidding? The phone rang, and Felicity answered it. ‘Five Caper Court. How can I help?’

‘Fliss?’ Vince’s voice sounded rough, unused, and slightly surprised. ‘Wasn’t expecting you to answer. It’s me. Vince.’

Felicity wasn’t sure what she felt. After she’d walked out of the coming-home party, she had half-hoped he might just leave her well alone, that she could put his part in her life behind her. Like the sleek, poised career woman she was going to be from now on. But she’d always known that wasn’t going to happen. She didn’t say anything immediately.

‘Fliss?’

'Yeah. Hi.'

'I've been meaning to ring you all week. To say sorry, and that. For being like I was on Friday. Mum said how much you'd been looking forward to seeing me, waiting all afternoon.'

'Did she?'

'And I fucked it up.' A pause. 'You forgive me?'

Felicity swallowed a sigh. 'It doesn't matter. Honestly.'

Never one to take things at face value, Vince latched on to what he thought she meant. 'No, listen, it does. You mustn't let me get away with that kind of stuff. That's not gonna happen. OK?'

'Whatever.'

'I've been feeling so bad about it. I kind of hoped you'd call, though.'

'Me? Why would—?'

'Look, can I come round tonight? Maybe take you out, make it up to you? I want it all to be different. You and me. Starting again.'

'Do you?' Felicity could hear her own voice sounding weak and flat. She glanced up as Leo came into the clerks' room. Vince was still talking, making his useless noises, his promises and plans, reassuring himself. She remembered Rachel's advice: tell it to him straight, make it clear he can't just expect things to be the way they were. Well, she would. She definitely would. It had to be done. Only not here, not now on the phone, with Leo five feet away.

When Vince was eager to please, he was hard to shut up. She had to interrupt him. 'Vince – stop talking. It's all right. You can come round. But I've got to go now. I'll see you later.' As she hung up, she looked at the box Leo was holding. 'What's that?'

'I was lunching in Soho with a long-lost love, and on my way back I passed Patisserie Valerie, and I thought – when did I last see Felicity with cake? Cake and Felicity belong together. So here you are.'

She smiled at him. 'Thank you. I needed cheering up. But not fattening up.'

She opened the box. 'Wow! I can't eat all those.'

'I suspect others will help you out. See you later.'

Felicity gazed at the cakes. Gingerly she lifted one from the box, transferring it to her other hand and licking the cream from her fingers. When Leo was in a good mood, he was a darling. She wondered who his long-lost love was, whether it was a woman or some bloke. You never knew with him.

Lunching his daughter at Arbutus had been one of the most delightful things Leo had done in a long time. In a habit developed in boyhood, when memorably pleasurable experiences had been few and far between, he deliberately tucked the recollection to the back of his mind and did not take it out and examine it until the early evening, when he had finished his work. Abandoning his shipbuilding case, he leant back in his chair and spent fifteen minutes recalling everything about Gabrielle at lunchtime; her bright, wary glance, the way she had of tucking her hair behind her ears when she was feeling unsure of herself and less sophisticated than she wanted to appear, the slight lift of her shoulders when she laughed, the rough little catch in her voice when she talked about things that meant a lot to her. He recalled the glances she'd drawn from every man in the restaurant, and his own startled pleasure in realising she wasn't even aware of them, that she had eyes and ears for no one but him, her new-found father. It reminded him of the way Anthony had been in the early days – attentive, fascinated, and so heartbreakingly young. He felt his heart swerve, and he passed his hands over his face as if to obliterate some unworthy recollection. God, he must not let her down. He must not do anything to devalue this.

Disturbed by his train of thought, he switched off his laptop and tidied his papers, deciding to go in search of company, of familiar faces.

He headed to Middle Temple Bar, and found Anthony there with another member of chambers, David Liphook. David, whose wife had given birth a few days earlier, was dwelling in doting detail on the marvels of his new daughter, oblivious to Anthony's polite concealment of the fact that he wasn't much interested in babies. Leo, however, once he had settled himself a large Scotch, was in exactly the right mood to indulge in a little transference and listen to everything David had to say.

This left Anthony free to pursue his own thoughts. He had felt irritable and restless all week, and never more so than today. Just a week ago he had dropped almost three thousand pounds at the poker table at Blunt's. At the time, caught up in the mood of the table, the rising stakes drawing him in, it hadn't seemed such a big deal. But the next morning he had seen it in a different light, and had decided maybe he should give the gambling thing a rest – partly to show himself that he could take it or leave it, and partly because he was aware it was affecting his work. He hated the fact that Rachel, with all the grace and tact in the world, had had to nag him about work left undone. He had always prided himself on being thorough, meticulous and punctual. Leo had taught him the importance of those qualities, without which one could not hope to be counted among the elite. Her phone call had left him feeling humiliated and second-rate.

Tonight, however, those feelings had slipped away. The loss of that three thousand had returned to haunt him, like an unrecovered debt that he had to call in. And today Henry, bursting with cheerfulness, had given him the news that the one hundred and twenty thousand pounds he was owed by solicitors for his work on a four-week trial last November had finally been paid. One hundred and twenty K! The most he'd ever earned on a case. It gave him every reason to celebrate. He'd agreed to go to see Barry in his first gig at the Comedy Store this evening, but after that he decided he would head to Blunt's and see if he couldn't make good the losses of the week before. Where was the harm? He wouldn't go wild. Just recoup the three thousand, put himself back in the black, and never gamble such ridiculous sums again. He could almost laugh at himself now, thinking of the way he'd got roped into staking such high sums. It wouldn't happen again.

He was aware Leo was talking to him. 'Sorry – what? I was miles away.'

'Just asking if you'd like another.'

Anthony glanced at his empty glass. 'No thanks. I'm meant to be in the West End in half an hour. My brother's doing stand-up, would you believe. Have to show support.' He rose, anxious to get away from Leo's relaxed scrutiny, which always made him feel as though Leo could see into his very heart and soul.

* * *

Ten o'clock, and still no Vince. Felicity had spent the evening in a state of agitation. No point in hoping he wouldn't come – even if he didn't, he was bound to show up some other night. As the hours ticked by, she couldn't settle to anything, not even making supper. She had no appetite. At a quarter to eleven, just when she was thinking of going to bed, he rolled up. She opened the door to the sound of the buzzer, and there was Vince, slouched against the door frame, dressed in a thick combat jacket over a black T-shirt, hands in his jeans pockets. His dark hair was shaggy, and he had two-day stubble. He flashed her a darkly charming smile and leant forward to kiss her lightly on the lips. To her surprise, he didn't smell of alcohol or dope.

'I thought maybe you'd changed your mind.'

Vince put out a hand and stroked her hair. 'Would I let you down?' He strolled past her and into the flat. The suggestion that this evening was her idea, and she'd be disappointed if he didn't show up left her momentarily speechless. She closed the door.

Vince glanced around the living room, pulling off his jacket. His body had grown leaner and more muscular during his time in jail, and Felicity couldn't help thinking how good he looked, narrow-hipped and broad-shouldered. She was aware of a little surge of lust, and tried to suppress it. It wasn't something she wanted to feel right now.

Vince delved into his jacket pocket, held up a bottle of Smirnoff Blue Label, and set it down on the coffee table. Reaching into a second pocket, he produced a bag of dope and other paraphernalia.

Felicity sighed. 'Vince, no. It's not what this evening's about.'

‘Oh? What’s it about, then?’ He came towards her. She realised she was standing defensively, arms folded. Gently he pulled her arms apart and drew her against him, and kissed her. It was such a long time since she’d been kissed in that way, she just let it happen, unable to resist. After a moment he let her go. ‘Come on, then – get the glasses.’

She fetched glasses, and Vince cracked the bottle open and poured the vodka. They sat together on the sofa, and Vince gathered Felicity into the crook of his arm. She didn’t resist. He smelt good, familiar, and she wanted to be at peace for a while. He started to talk about what he’d been up to since the day of Denise’s party. Felicity was barely listening, busy trying to work out when would be the best time to set things straight, to say the things Rachel had told her to say. Now, probably, before things went any further and he began to make assumptions. But somehow she couldn’t think of the words. She took long swigs of vodka, letting the warmth of it spread through her body, hoping it would inspire her with courage, unlock her tongue. But then Vince, tired of talking, began to kiss her again, fondling her in a lazy, proprietorial way. Felicity knew this was her moment, that she should stop this right now, explain to him that he wasn’t going to come in here and take her for granted like this . . . But, oh God, it felt so good, it had been such a long time, and she had to admit she liked being taken for granted. In fact, she liked being taken, full stop. She returned his kisses with a passion she had forgotten, helping his hands explore her body, unzipping his jeans and pushing up his T-shirt to run her hands over his warm, hard body.

Twenty minutes later, she lay slack and replete, watching as Vince picked up his T-shirt from the floor and slipped it on. He poured more vodka. She drank it unthinkingly, wanting the warmth and sensual satisfaction she was feeling to go on for ever. She knew that none of this was good for her, but she didn't care. They could sort out the future later. Tonight was just a bit of abandonment. She deserved it. She hadn't let herself go in a long, long time. She watched Vince roll a spliff and light it, and when he handed it to her she took a deep drag. Not at all what she had intended this evening to be about. She began to laugh.

'What's funny?' asked Vince, smiling.

Felicity shook her head and laughed again. She reached to pick up her bra from the floor, and began to slip it on. Vince stopped her. 'You won't be needing that.' He bent his head and kissed her breast, his tongue grazing her nipple, and Felicity arched her back with pleasure.

'I feel pissed,' she said. 'I've had nothing to eat all day. Just a cream cake Leo bought us.'

'Leo, eh? How is the old shirt-lifter?'

'Stop it,' murmured Felicity. She eased herself off the sofa and stood up. 'I'm going to make something to eat.' She bent down and took the spliff from him and took another drag, slopped some more vodka into her glass and drank. 'Need something to mop up the booze.' Vince gazed with idle appreciation at the creamy curves of her body as she strolled naked to the kitchen with her glass, her dark, curling hair falling round her shoulders. He reached out and took a long swig of vodka, listening to the sound of cupboards opening and closing.

'Fajitas all right?' she called.

'Whatever. Anything'll do me.' Vince leant back and smoked contentedly. He'd been worried there might be problems tonight, that she wouldn't be prepared to let him back into her life and pick up where they'd left off. Things had been a bit rough between them before he'd got banged up. But the evening was shaping up very promisingly. If he played his cards right, he'd be moving in in a couple of weeks. Living with Fliss would definitely ease the pressure of having to find a job and sort himself out. It was the perfect set-up – a girlfriend with a nice flat, a car, money in the bank, food in the fridge and booze in the cupboard. Oh yeah, and that beautiful body. Sweet.

CHAPTER TWELVE

Leo had spent an entire afternoon filling in the online High Court judge application form, so when Henry knocked on his door and looked in, he was grateful for the diversion.

'Spare a moment, Mr D?'

'By all means, Henry. Come in. This Judicial Appointments Committee form has just about finished me off. If there's one thing I loathe, it's self-assessments, having to make up spurious guff to demonstrate one's leadership qualities and independence of mind. This bit about my intellectual capacity – I think I lost it around page three.'

'No need to worry. You're tailor-made for the job.'

'You say that, but I'm not entirely sure I tick all the JAC's politically correct boxes. Besides which, I've probably managed to offend at least one member of the committee at some stage in my professional life.' He tapped the page and scrolled down the committee list. 'Here's a shining example – Gregory Hind.'

'Senior partner at Reed Smith?'

'The very same. He instructed me when I was a junior on a ship grounding case. We had a slight falling-out over the presentation of the technical evidence. Well, more than slight. He threatened to disinstruct me. Didn't help that I was ultimately proved right. I have the feeling he's loathed me ever since.' He nodded at the screen. 'Sir Vivian Colman's on the committee, too – father of our ex-pupil, Sarah. He's one of the professional members. Anyway . . .' Leo closed his laptop. 'How can I help you, Henry?'

'It's that time of year, Mr D. We need to make a decision about the Christmas party. Where and when, who to invite, how much champagne to order. The usual.'

'I'm happy to say that you've come to the wrong person, Henry. That ball is now firmly in the court of the social committee. Headed by our young Mr Cross, if I am not mistaken. He's the man you want to see.'

'Oh. Right. Budget and everything?'

'Budget and everything. It's one responsibility I am very glad to be rid of, frankly.'

'OK. I'll go and have a word.'

'You do that. By the way,' added Leo, as Henry turned to go, 'how is our fledgling clerk coming along? He seems very keen.'

'Liam is turning out very nicely, thank you, Mr D. Shows aptitude. Very quick on the uptake. I'm hoping by the time Robert leaves I'll have him well in harness.'

'Glad to hear it.'

When Henry had left, Leo opened his laptop and pondered the members of the JAC. He knew none of the lay members, though some of the names – Baroness Paradeep, and Dudley Callow, for instance – were vaguely familiar, but all the judicial members were known to him. Gregory Hind was probably the only one he didn't get on with, and in all truth he didn't believe that Hind would let any personal animosity interfere with his judgment. He had met the Committee Chairman, Alastair Flockton, at various functions, and recalled him as a rather highly strung, irritable man. His Honour Judge Ian Cole, so far as he could recall, was an immigration lawyer. Mervyn Woodall he knew only by reputation – a Treasury counsel, Bencher of Grey's Inn, and an amiable eccentric. Julian Hooper was a fellow silk with whom he got on well, and on whom he felt he could count.

Leo moved down the list and smiled when he saw the name of the Committee's Vice-Chairman. The Right Honourable Lady Justice Daphne Hunter might look formidable enough in her photo, a slim, handsome woman in her early sixties with a piercing gaze, but having appeared before her on numerous occasions, Leo knew that she was as susceptible to his charm as the next woman. In a hearing a couple of years ago, before her elevation to the Court of Appeal, she had even gone so far as to indulge in some judicial flirtation with him during the cross-examination of an expert witness.

Sir Vivian Colman he knew very slightly on a professional level – Leo had appeared before him when Sir Vivian was Recorder of London, and was on the guest list for Sir Vivian's champagne and hotpot parties – but one would hardly call it a friendship. Probably just as well, since Leo had been sleeping with his daughter on and off for some years. Well, not lately, which was a pity, really. Why had he let things slip? Had something happened which had brought about a cooling off? He couldn't remember. The relationship had always been volatile. He thought about the last time he'd seen her at her father's party, wearing that outrageously sexy dress, and felt a little surge of lust. God, she had been something else in bed. Only now she was engaged to a characterless banker, and beyond his reach.

Leo shut his laptop. He would finish the application form later. He got up and strolled to the window, gazing down at Caper Court, thinking about Sarah and her banker boy. What was his name? Tony, Toby, something like that. Hadn't she said something about him becoming recently unemployed? The credit crunch had spat out any number of young bankers. Not much chance of him getting another job any time soon. A blow for Sarah, no doubt. Leo guessed that the six-figure salary and hefty bonuses had been a large part of Tony or Toby's attraction. In fact – and in merely thinking the thought, Leo felt an odd sense of clarity, as though he could read Sarah's mind – might she not be thinking twice about the whole marriage thing? He smiled to himself. Perhaps he was doing her a disservice, doubting her love and loyalty. Somehow he didn't think he was.

Leo returned to his desk. Even if he was right, he knew that persuading her back into his bed was going to be far from easy. Fiancé or no fiancé, she had a new air of defensiveness about her. No – that was the wrong word. Of strength. Coolness. Sarah had always known what was good for her, but had been too busy having a good time to care. Nowadays she probably cared a good deal. Her appetites had very sensibly given way to extreme self-interest. This wasn't going to be a pushover. Which, of course, made it all the more interesting. He took out his mobile phone, scrolled down to her number, and pressed 'call'.

'Grand Night? What the hell's Grand Night? Sounds a bit northern to me.' Toby was slumped on the sofa in the Docklands flat, laptop on his knees, filling in the online teaching training application form.

'It's a big swanky dinner in the Inns of Court, usually with some visiting dignitary they want to make a big deal of. Everyone has to turn up in white tie, and the crumbliest old Benchers put on their medals. There's a champagne reception, and a dinner – not that the food's any better than usual – and a thing called the "loving cup" that gets passed round for everyone to drink from, and is basically unhygienic. All extremely archaic and posh, but in reality just another opportunity for people to get hammered.' Sarah spoke in an offhand manner, but Leo's phone call had left her with a feeling of elation, and a sense of possibility which she hadn't felt in a long time.

'Sounds a bundle of laughs. This Leo that you're going with – isn't he that oldish bloke you were chatting to at your father's party? Should I be worried?'

'Hardly. He probably only invited me because I'm a member of the Inn, and outsiders aren't allowed.' She leant over Toby's shoulder. 'This teaching course you're applying for – when does it start?'

'January. And you'll have another job by then, so we'll be OK.' He turned and stretched his face up to kiss her.

Sarah returned the kiss half-heartedly. 'You're more optimistic than I am. I'm going to struggle to get a half-decent reference from Hugo, remember.' She stared over his shoulder at the screen of his laptop. 'Honest to God, Toby, I wish you would rethink this teaching thing. It's mad to throw away seven years of City experience just because of one crash. Think where the banks would be now if everyone had walked away from banking during the last crisis! You should be holding your nerve, maintaining your confidence.' She knelt down, and laid her cheek against his arm. 'You don't have to run away. You'll find another job. I believe in you.'

'I know you do. That's why I'm doing this. How many times do we have to go over this? Everything that's happened – the recession, getting sacked – has enabled me to re-evaluate what I want to do with my life. Deep down, I think I've always wanted to teach. This is my chance.' He stroked her hair. 'And it's because I have you here, believing in me, that I can do it.' He returned to his laptop.

Sarah flopped into an armchair and picked up the paper, then realised she'd read every page already. Who knew not working could be so boring? It felt claustrophobic being cooped up here in the flat with Toby day after day. She had moved in the week before Toby had lost his job, when the flat was meant to be a temporary measure before buying a house. A house. What a distant dream that had become. She felt as though the world was closing in on her. She knew even as she had uttered her words a few moments ago that they had been futile. After Hugo had fired her, she'd hoped the fact that they were both out of a job might make Toby reassess the situation. But he was sticking doggedly to his plan. Every time she so much as hinted at all the material advantages they would have to forfeit, he just smiled in that patient, killing way of his and told her he wasn't interested in materialism any more, that he'd had his fill. He was positively evangelical about it. She didn't see how the relationship was going to survive this. It wasn't about love. Marriage was a package, and love was just a part of it – other things had to be right, too. The future – the kind of future Sarah wanted – required more than love to keep it afloat. Money, comfort, security, decent clothes and holidays, being able to afford private school fees – without these things, marriage was scarcely worthwhile. But how could she explain to Toby that if marriage meant living in a suburban semi on a secondary-school teacher's pay, then the love she felt for him simply wasn't enough to sustain such an existence? It would mean telling him that *he* wasn't enough. And that was the awful truth she was having to wake up to and face every day now. Toby was kind, handsome, and a much more decent person than she could ever be, but the fact was that without a six-figure income he simply wasn't such an attractive marriage prospect any more. Other people might think her a heartless cow, but Jane Austen would have understood.

Toby's voice interrupted her thoughts. 'I'd love a coffee, if you're making one.'

'Sure.' She headed for the kitchen, glad of something to do.

As she waited for the kettle to boil, a sense of sad determination overwhelmed her, and she felt her resolve crystallise. There really was no going back now – or rather, forward. It was simply a question of how to end things. She thought of the Kitterings, and of her father, and of their collective disappointment, but she wasn't going to abandon herself to a life of penury simply to avoid upsetting them. It was Toby she was most worried about. If she simply dumped him now, when he was at his lowest ebb, it would destroy him. Well, he was going to be destroyed one way or another, so better that it should happen in such a way that he could salvage some pride. She had to put herself in the wrong. A bit of self-abasement was called for. It wouldn't be the first time. She thought of Leo's phone call half an hour ago. The fact was, he wanted her, and he needed to find a way back in. Perhaps they could do each other a favour.

It was almost midnight at Blunt's, and Julia was feeling hellish. She had taken a line of coke half an hour earlier to lift the boredom, but all it had done was to make her brain buzz within the confines of its own ennui, like a trapped and angry wasp.

'I see your boyfriend's in again,' murmured Darius Egan.

Julia followed the line of his glance and saw Anthony at one of the tables. 'I wish you'd stop calling him that. It's childish.'

'Don't get so defensive. Anyone would think he's important to you. He's certainly becoming that way to us.'

Darius took a sip of what looked to all intents like a glass of champagne, but was in fact fizzy water tinted with a drop of Angostura bitters – a tip he had picked up from his father. Seeing the casino boss with a glass of bubbly made the punters feel convivial, like guests at a party.

'What d'you mean?'

'Just that he's in every night, dropping a ton of the stuff. He used to have the odd win here and there, big enough to keep him going, but he's been losing heavily recently. I'm afraid he doesn't do himself any favours. Doesn't know when to stop.' Darius scanned the room. 'Now, where's that husband of yours? I have a little business to discuss with him.'

As Darius went off in search of Piers, Julia crossed the room to the roulette table where Anthony was playing. In three spins of the wheel she saw him lose four hundred, then another two, then claw back eighty.

'Bad luck,' she murmured.

Anthony gave her a glance and shrugged. She read indifference – both to her and to the situation.

'Darius says you're pretty much a regular here.' She watched as Anthony pushed forward two blue chips onto number five. 'Says you lose a lot.'

'And what's that to you?'

'Anthony, seriously – I don't like to see you being taken for a mug. You're a novice at all this. And I don't believe you can afford it.'

Anthony said nothing. His eyes were fixed on the spin of the wheel and the skipping clatter of the ball. The wheel slowed and the ball dropped into number five. Anthony scooped in his winning pile of chips and turned to Julia. 'I suppose when it comes to taking me for a mug you're the leading expert in the field, I'll give you that. But I'm not the person I once was, Julia. You have no idea what I can and can't afford.'

Gabrielle had been watching them from the other side of the room. She knew from gossip that Julia and Anthony had once been an item, and she could tell from Julia's subtle body language that Julia would like to rekindle that. Given the state of her marriage to Piers – which Gabrielle gave a year at best – it was hardly surprising that Julia was looking for a new flame. Or an old one. But even though she couldn't hear the words exchanged, it was obvious to Gabrielle that Anthony wasn't interested.

She was curious about Anthony, and somewhat fascinated by him – a fascination darkly connected to the kiss she had witnessed that night in Middle Temple. She had thought often about this, confused by her conflicting emotions. Far from being revolted, she had found it faintly arousing, and realised she wouldn't mind kissing Anthony herself. How weird did that make her? To desire someone her own father found attractive? She didn't care. Normal rules didn't apply to Leo, so maybe they didn't apply to her. There was only one way to find out. She crossed the room to where Anthony was standing looking indecisive, touched his arm lightly, and said, 'Hello. I don't think we've met.'

Anthony glanced round in surprise. He had been contemplating what to do with his winnings. Common sense dictated he should cash in his chips, have one last drink, and go home. But the relief at having at last covered his mounting losses and put himself back in the black had been swiftly followed by the now-familiar adrenalin rush, the sense that he could ride his big win like a surfer, go back to the tables and win even more. Even though he knew the pattern which was developing was not a good one, coming to the casino three nights in one week, making heavy losses which simply drove him to bet more, he couldn't resist the urge to have one more spin of the wheel. And here was this beautiful girl looking into his eyes.

'My name's Gabrielle.'

‘I know.’ He smiled. ‘I asked someone. I’m Anthony Cross.’

‘I know.’ She smiled. ‘I asked someone.’

Anthony knew she was waiting for him to offer to buy her a drink. Much as he wanted to spend the next couple of hours sitting over drinks getting to know this delicious girl, he was itching to get to the poker tables and carry on gambling, though he knew he would probably end up losing it all, and leaving with less than he had come in with.

She seemed to read his thoughts.

‘Come on,’ said Gabrielle. ‘Quit while you’re ahead. Cash in your chips and buy me a drink. Something non-alcoholic. I’ve got lectures in the morning.’

‘Orange juice all round, in that case. I have to be in court at ten.’

‘So you’re a lawyer?’ she said, even though she knew. She was interested in hearing Anthony’s own version of himself.

‘A barrister.’ Anthony bought drinks, and they carried them to a corner table and sat down. ‘So,’ asked Anthony, ‘what are you studying?’

‘Law.’

‘Well, well.’ He raised his glass. ‘Cheers. Here’s to the law. I thought I’d seen you around. It was in a pub near the Temple.’

‘I’m flattered you remember.’

‘You have a kind of unforgettable look.’

She smiled. ‘Tell me about your case tomorrow.’

‘It’s only a case management conference. The case is to do with a casino, actually.’ He told Gabrielle about Astleigh’s and the Lion King and the bounced cheque, but she only half-listened, too busy concentrating on his face, his eyes, the way he occasionally frowned or smiled as he talked. The attraction was immensely powerful, and every time he met her gaze she could tell he felt it too. Yet at the same time she couldn't get rid of the image of her father and Anthony together. Whatever was going on was wildly strange. She was curious to know about her father's relationship with Anthony, but she realised she had to approach the subject obliquely. She certainly wasn't about to tell him that Leo was her father.

'I've got a pupillage in criminal chambers starting next July,' said Gabrielle. 'If I pass my Bar finals, that is.' She hesitated. 'It must be quite an intimate set-up. Working with the same people all your life in such an enclosed environment.'

'No different from most workplaces, I imagine. And it's not always for life. People come and go. Admittedly not that much.'

'But you must make really close friendships.'

'Of course. Some people make the mistake of letting their social lives become too bound up with other people in chambers. Same old dinner parties, holidays together, that kind of thing. There's only one person in chambers I regard as a really close friend.'

'Who's that?'

'My head of chambers, Leo Davies. He was sort of my mentor when I first came to chambers. Taught me a good deal about many things. Anyway . . .' Anthony finished his drink and glanced at his watch. 'I should really be heading.'

'Me too. Where do you go to?' As they left the table Gabrielle was aware of Julia watching them.

'South Ken. What about you?'

'Holland Park. The slummy end.'

'We can share a cab.'

They left the casino, and a few minutes later were heading together in a taxi towards Kensington. They said very little to one another on the way, but just before they reached Gabrielle's flat, Anthony pulled out his mobile phone.

'Let me have your number, and I'll give you a call. Maybe we can have lunch. Or you could come along to the casino hearing once it starts. You might find it interesting.' Her expression was unreadable in the shadowy interior of the cab. 'Or not, depending.'

'I'd like that.' She gave him her number, and Anthony tapped it in. She leant towards the driver. 'Number seven, please, on the right.' She turned to Anthony. 'See you soon, then.' The curiosity which had been burning in her for the last hour or two suddenly took hold. She wanted to know what it was like to kiss the mouth which her own father had kissed and enjoyed. She leant forward impulsively, and in the dimness of the cab her mouth found his.

Anthony returned the kiss, which lasted only a few seconds, then she was out of the cab and heading towards the steps of the house. 'Night,' she called, without turning round. He watched her disappear inside. Then he said to the driver, 'I'll get out here, too, thanks.'

He paid the fare and walked back through the quiet, chilly streets to his flat, reflecting on the remarkably pleasurable kiss, and wondering where it might lead.

CHAPTER THIRTEEN

It was Friday morning, and Toby was getting ready for a trip north with old university friends.

'Don't forget this,' said Sarah, picking up his washbag from the bed.

'Thanks.' He dropped it into his overnight bag. 'Right, I think that's everything. Let's see – ticket, ID, wallet, keys . . .' He shrugged on his jacket, adding to Sarah, 'You know, I honestly don't see why going out with your girlfriends on Saturday means you can't make it down to Mum and Dad's for Sunday lunch. You've got this Grand whatever-it-is thing tonight. I'd have thought that would be enough excitement for one weekend. If you stayed in tomorrow night you'd be OK to make it to the parents for Sunday lunch. I'm heading straight there from Gatwick.'

'I'd hardly call Grand Night exciting. You're going off to Scotland for the rugby for two whole days with your friends, so I'm entitled to a girls' night out, OK? Following which I intend to have a long lie-in, then spend the rest of the day in my dressing gown with the Sunday papers, recovering. I don't want to have to drag myself all the way down just to eat roast lamb in Surrey.'

He sighed. 'OK. I'll see you on Sunday evening.'

She kissed his cheek lightly. 'Have a lovely time. I hope England win.'

The door of the flat closed. Sarah glanced at her watch. Nearly half three. Only four more hours, and she would be with Leo.

That evening Leo waited inside the arched vestibule of Middle Temple Hall, as the great and good of the Inn thronged past in their evening finery. Cut-glass accents and gentle, confident laughter filled the air. He nodded and spoke in greeting to friends as they passed, but he didn't allow anyone to catch his attention for long. He was on the lookout for Sarah, combing the faces, aware of an unfamiliar teenage edginess. He could only assume that this was because he knew only too well how fabulously unreliable she could be – and tonight really would not be a good night for her to be late. These formal evenings were always engineered with stopwatch precision, and with the clock ticking towards the kick-off time of half seven, the ushers were already hovering as the last guests trickled in. Where the hell was she?

A taxi coming up Middle Temple Lane swung round, its lights brushing the cobbles. Leo glimpsed blonde hair in the interior. It had to be her.

'Hold on a moment,' he said to one of the ushers who stood ready to close the huge wooden doors. He headed towards the taxi. Sarah stepped calmly out, wearing a strapless dress of pale cream silk, and a cloudy-pink cashmere wrap against the cold air.

'About time,' said Leo, chucking a twenty at the driver.

He hurried her up the stone steps and across the vestibule, and the ushers closed the wooden doors behind them, the sound causing the guests, milling around with drinks, to turn to look in their direction.

'I could almost believe you planned this late entrance,' murmured Leo, picking up two glasses of champagne from a tray and handing one to Sarah, 'just to grab everyone's attention. But I think you have it, anyway. You look delectable.'

'Thank you,' smiled Sarah. 'You look pretty tasty yourself.'

They mingled for a short while until the signal came for the guests to be seated, with the minor European royal who was the guest of honour taking pride of place at the centre of the high table. Since Leo was a Bencher, he and Sarah were seated at the high table, too.

'I hadn't realised that you'd become an official member of the old farts' brigade,' observed Sarah, as they took their places.

'Pipe down,' said Leo. But the elderly Bencher on Sarah's right had either failed to pick up her remark on his state-of-the-art hearing aid, or was too happy to be in the proximity of such warm, enticing flesh to care. He nodded and beamed at Sarah, then delivered some innocuous remark regarding the grace of the occasion. Sarah murmured in agreement, and gave Leo a smiling glance.

After some gavel-banging and the intoning of grace, the meal began.

'Is the food still as bad here as it used to be?' asked Sarah, watching the waiters bring in the first course.

'Actually, it's improved,' said Leo. 'A bit.'

Sarah gazed around at the sombre panelled walls and the stained-glass windows. 'I haven't been here in years, literally. Not since I had to eat all those horrible dinners before call. Give or take the odd Christmas champagne party. It's as dismal as ever.'

'How can you say that?' asked Leo. 'This place is astonishing. It never fails to move me every time I come here, and I've been doing that most weeks for the better part of thirty years.'

'Yes, but that's because you're an impressionable grammar school boy from the valleys. It represents everything you ever aspired to, it reeks of intellectual and social elitism. One of the most exclusive clubs in the world, and they let you in. No wonder you love it.'

'An interesting analysis, but quite some way off the mark. It's not what the place represents that I love, but what it is. It's alive with history. Do you realise that this table we're sitting at is almost five hundred years old, a present from Queen Elizabeth to Middle Temple? Cut from a single oak and floated up the Thames from Windsor Park. And Sir Walter Raleigh came to this very hall, this same hall, and took a standing ovation after tanking the Spaniards at – somewhere or other. I forget. How can you fail to be impressed by that?'

'Probably because I'm a dreadfully shallow creature,' murmured Sarah. 'Is there any more wine?'

Sir Vivian, seated at the other end of the high table, was surprised to see his daughter. He hadn't known her to attend any of the Inn's functions in years, and he wondered at whose invitation she was here this evening. Old Hugo Leveson, seated on her right, was hardly a likely candidate. He could see Hugo leering goatishly at Sarah's cleavage, and shot him a glare, but Hugo appeared not to notice. Sir Vivian doubted if he could see that far. He peered past the arm of the waiter setting down the soup plates to get a glimpse of the person on Sarah's left. He recognised his face and distinctive silver hair. Leo Davies, wasn't it? He'd been at the party a couple of weeks ago. Suddenly the Bencher opposite, Colin Fryer, remarked to his female companion, 'I see Leo Davies has turned up with some stunning girl, as usual.'

'Quite a striking couple,' observed the woman, glancing down the table. Then she added, 'He's tremendously attractive. What did you say his name was?'

'Leo Davies. One of our top commercial silks.' Fryer dropped his voice, but Sir Vivian caught the words, 'The stunning girl could as easily have been some stunning young man, from all I've heard. There are more than a few rumours flying around concerning Leo Davies' private life. Boyfriends, and so on.'

Sir Vivian was agog. He tried to fasten on the rest of what Fryer was saying, but a rather deaf retired Law Lord, the Right Honourable Lord Dutton of Chelmsley, chose that moment to enquire loudly what soup they were eating. 'Is it some kind of vegetable? I can't make it out.'

Sir Vivian seethed with irritation. He thought Fryer had just uttered the words 'male lover', but he couldn't be sure.

'I believe it's broccoli and stilton,' replied Lord Dutton's neighbour.

Lord Dutton nodded. 'That accounts for the colour.' Sir Vivian was still trying to home in on the conversation opposite, and could just pick up '—in a sense one would prefer it if he were one thing or the other, rather than bisexual.'

'I thought at first it was courgette,' observed Lord Dutton. 'I think I prefer courgette to broccoli. In soup, that is.'

'My wife makes courgette soup with mint. Very pleasant in summer.'

'Does she grow her own?'

'Oh yes. Courgettes, broad beans, tomatoes, lettuces. She has a veritable *potager*. Quite the good life. We're a regular Tom and Barbara.'

As the polite chuckles died away, Fryer was saying, 'I mean, what woman would care for the idea that her lover's previous fling was with some man? A bit iffy.' Sir Vivian saw Colin Fryer's guest glance at Leo with a faint smile, and she said, 'That depends, I suppose.'

Sir Vivian was appalled and dismayed. He was aware that certain Members of the Bar were homosexual – how he detested the misappropriation of the word 'gay' – and he always tried to avoid their company, without letting it be apparent. Somehow the notion of bisexuality seemed even more disgusting. He leant forward to try to get a better look at the man Davies. He now recalled Leo appearing before him a couple of times when he was Recorder of London. A clever advocate, no doubt, but he could wish that Sarah had not chosen such a person to escort her this evening. No doubt she knew as much as Colin Fryer did, but the young seemed not to let such matters influence their judgment. In that they were misguided. Old-fashioned notions of morality were too readily discarded. He could only be thankful that she was marrying someone as decent and upstanding as young Toby. Sighing at the sorry state of the world, Sir Vivian returned to his soup.

When dinner was over, speeches were made – interminable speeches, it seemed to Sarah – and port was passed.

Sarah sniffed at the contents of her glass. 'This stuff is like the blood of dead relatives. Do we have to stay much longer?'

'Probably not.'

For the past twenty minutes Leo had been preoccupied with the question of whether or not he would be able to persuade Sarah into his bed this evening. Once upon a time, in a situation such as this, he would have been pretty confident of success. He and Sarah had always had a relaxed, straightforward approach to sleeping with one another whenever both of them felt like it. But Sarah was engaged now, and while his instincts might tell him she could well be having second thoughts about marrying Toby, the fact was that she had a pretty substantial diamond glittering on her left hand. Nothing – if anything – could be taken for granted. This would require delicate handling. But the sooner they got away from here, the sooner he would find out.

He turned to her. 'Do you remember the first time we met?'

Sarah sipped her port. 'Vaguely.' This was far from true. She would carry with her for ever the memory of that afternoon, of seeing Leo for the first time across the lawn at a Pembroke College garden party. The chemistry, the attraction, had been instant. She had been twenty, and Leo had seemed to her excitingly sophisticated and – it had to be admitted – pretty old at forty-one. Mutual desire had kindled after just twenty minutes of conversation, and after that each simply wanted to get the other into bed as fast as possible. They had left the garden party, escaped in Leo's car to his house, and had finished up having sex in the garage, too overcome by lust to get as far as the house, let alone Leo's bed. The hours that had followed, once they reached his bed, were a long tangle of mutual pleasure, the details admittedly indistinct. But for some reason the events later in the evening were imprinted on her mind: stepping barefoot into the darkness of the garden, trailing a rug across the cool grass, sitting cross-legged, waiting for Leo to bring out wine and the only food he could find – cold cocktail sausages and a punnet of strawberries. It was the summer solstice, the day had been long and full of heat, and the glimmer of morning lay just behind the darkly fragrant night as they lay there, eating, drinking, talking, kissing, making love. It sounded romantic, but in fact it hadn't been. Exciting, erotic, intensely pleasurable, but both of them had been too self-aware and self-absorbed to give anything of themselves. She had stayed the next day, and the day after that, and eventually for the entire summer, a mutually satisfactory arrangement for both of them. It enabled Sarah to escape London and the limitations of living with her father, and enjoy the pleasures of a life in Leo's enchanting country house, which he had only recently bought, while Leo had someone to look after the place while he was in London, and oversee the builders during the renovations, and to cook when he came down at the weekends. Sex was a fringe benefit for both of them, long, intensely pleasurable hours of it. The idyll had only come to an end when Leo introduced into the household a young man he had picked up in the village pub, James. The threesome lasted a couple of weeks, and then it had all gone disastrously wrong. Still, it had been a glorious summer while it lasted.

'Maybe we could repeat our great escape,' said Leo.

'What? Get in your car and drive all the way to Oxfordshire?'

'Not that part. Just slipping away on our own. You could come back to my place for a drink. Unless there's somewhere else you have to be.'

'No, nowhere I need to be. Toby's away. In fact, he's away for the entire weekend.' She paused. 'I'm good to go, if you are. But I'd better say hello to my father first.'

'Right. I'll join you outside shortly.'

Leo watched her as she made her way down the table towards her father. He felt fixated by his need for her, tantalised and tormented by the idea that now, after all their casual sexual encounters down the years, he might not be able to have her. He relished the uncertainty. How much sweeter, how much more exciting success would be, if he achieved it.

Sir Vivian rose to greet his daughter, excusing himself from his fellows.

'Why didn't you tell me you wanted to come tonight? I would have been happy to bring you,' he reproached her, accepting her gentle kiss on his cheek. 'I thought you didn't care for formal occasions at the Inn.'

'I don't usually. But I could hardly turn down an invitation from Leo Davies. He's a silk in the chambers where I did my pupillage.'

'I know very well who he is, and frankly I could wish you weren't with him.'

Sarah laughed. 'What on earth are you on about?'

'He doesn't have the most salubrious of reputations.'

'Really, Daddy, you shouldn't listen to gossip. He's clever and he's fun, and he's been a good friend to me, one way and another. Besides, you see fit to invite him to your annual bash.'

'Hmph. I can't imagine Toby would be best pleased if he knew you were out with some other man.'

'Oh, for heaven's sake, give us both a little credit. He does know. Anyway, he's in Scotland for the weekend. Now, lovely to see you, aged parent, but I have to be off.' She gave him another light kiss.

Twenty minutes later Leo's Aston Martin pulled into Carlyle Square.

'When did you move out of Belgravia?' asked Sarah, as they crossed the street to his house.

'About four years ago. I wanted somewhere with a garden for Oliver.' Leo unlocked the door and put on the lights. Sarah followed him into the living room. 'Make yourself comfortable. I'll fix us both a drink. What would you like?'

'Whatever you're having,' said Sarah. She wandered round the room, checking out the pictures and pieces of sculpture, some of them familiar, others not. Then she slipped off her heels, picked up a cushion, and sat on the floor with her back against the sofa, tucking the cushion behind her.

Leo returned with their drinks. He handed her a tumbler of Scotch, thinking that she looked no older than she had when he first met her, sitting on the carpet with her arms round her knees, blonde hair glinting in the glow of the single lamp. He sat down in an armchair opposite, setting the decanter on the floor next to the chair. He stretched out his legs, unfastening his bow tie and the top button of his dress shirt.

Sarah took a sip of her drink. 'Nice malt,' she said. 'Why do you spoil it by putting ice in it?'

'Sorry. Didn't realise you were such a purist.'

'You knew. You've just forgotten.' She swirled the contents of her glass. 'So – what's going on in the wonderful world of 5 Caper Court?'

'Not a great deal. Things roll on much as they ever did. I'm thinking of making some personal changes, though. I may be applying to become a High Court judge.'

'That'll be the day. You'd be bored stiff. I know Daddy found it pretty tedious.'

'Actually, I don't know why I say "may be applying". The fact is, I am.'

She stared at him over the rim of her glass. 'Seriously? You'd be prepared to go from earning what you do as a silk, to a pitiful hundred thousand grand a year? I find that hard to believe.'

'Life's not all about money.'

'Really? Since when?'

'I've gained a great deal from being in the legal profession. It's shaped my entire life. Now I feel it's time to give something back. One can't just go on taking for ever. And the financial sacrifice is hardly as great as you make it sound. I earn far more than I need. Life can be lived quite comfortably on a judge's salary, you know. If one is doing something one loves and believes in, it's not hard to make adjustments, to relinquish a standard of living which most people would find ridiculously extravagant anyway, for a single man.'

'Leo, I don't think I've ever heard you sound so horribly pious.' Sarah took a swig of whisky. But his words had touched her on the raw. It was exactly what she wasn't prepared to do where Toby was concerned – to lower her expectations and accept, for love of him, a life less easy and affluent than she had hoped for. She struggled to rationalise it. Whatever sacrifices or changes Leo had to make, at least they were for his own ideals. She was being asked to sacrifice herself for the sake of someone else's.

Leo saw the clouded look on her face, and asked, 'What's eating you? Not something I said?'

'Sort of. You seem to be turning into an altogether good person. Not something I'm ever likely to become.'

'Goodness hardly comes into it. I should have thought that you, of all people, would realise that I'm doing this for purely selfish reasons. I want less pressure, and to be able to see more of Oliver. I'm not as young as I was. I need a bit of balance in my life.' He paused. 'What makes you think you're a bad person?'

Sarah set down her glass and ran a tired hand through her hair. 'Oh, Leo – of all the people in the world, I should be able to tell you . . . but I daren't. I'm too ashamed.'

'Try me.'

She rested her chin on her arms, staring at nothing. After a long silence, she said, 'It's to do with Toby. We're meant to be getting married next year. Everyone's thrilled – my father and his father are old friends, it seems to them like the perfect set-up, everyone's all geared up for a big summer wedding. The thing is – I'm not sure I can go through with it.' She flexed the fingers of her left hand, staring at the diamond.

Leo took the stopper from the decanter. 'Another?' She shook her head. He poured himself another finger of Scotch. 'Well, you won't be the first woman in the world to call off her wedding. It's over six months away – hardly a last-minute change of mind. Why so ashamed?'

Sarah shook her head. 'You don't understand. It's my reason for not wanting to go through with it. You see, as long as Toby was a banker, I was quite happy to be marrying him. I mean, someone sane, sweet and decent, so easy to love, earning a six-figure salary, with a whopping great annual bonus on top. What more could a woman ask? I thought our future was secure, perfect – well, as secure and perfect as one can hope for. But then Graffman Spiers went to the wall . . .' She drew in a deep breath and reached for her glass. 'And now he's decided to turn his back on the banking world and become a teacher.'

'A teacher?' Leo couldn't help feeling amused. Poor Sarah.

She swallowed a mouthful of whisky and shook her head. 'And that's why I don't think I can do it. I can't face that life, Leo. I can't live in a terraced house in . . . in wherever, and work nine to five, struggling to pay school fees, worried about money all the time. I can't become that kind of person. It's all down to money. So what kind of a wretched individual am I?'

'You simply don't love him enough. If you did, you

wouldn't care how much he earned, or what he did for a living. At least you've found out before it's too late.'

'You still don't get it,' said Sarah impatiently. 'I know exactly what I feel about him. I don't think I know how to love that way. Unconditionally, passionately, regardless of everything. I'm not made that way. But what I feel for Toby would have been enough. I would still have married him, been prepared to spend my life with him, if—'

'—if he'd been able to keep you in the style to which you've become accustomed?'

'God, you make it sound so trite.'

'Life often is trite. It's a matter-of-fact business. I think you should congratulate yourself on your pragmatism.'

'Leo, don't laugh at me! I can't stand it! I'm trying to tell you something—'

'I'm not laughing at you.' He set his glass down on the carpet and crossed the room to where she sat hunched against the sofa. 'You think you know yourself so well, but I know you better. Stand up.'

'You're saying you already knew what a selfish cow I am?' She set her glass down and stood up.

'Oh, yes.' He drew her towards him, holding her close.

'But Toby doesn't know.'

'Then he's going to have to find out. You can't pretend to be a better person than you are. Or to love him in the way he expects you to.'

'I know he deserves better. But I don't think I can bear the moment when he finds out. He's going to hate me. Despise me.'

'That's the price you have to pay.' His lips brushed her neck, and he felt her shiver.

She drew away. 'I should go home.'

'That's hardly going to make things any better in the long run.' He drew her close again, and kissed her for a long, intense moment. 'Please stay. I want you. I don't think I've ever wanted you more.' His fingers slipped the thin satin straps from her shoulders and gently tugged down the bodice of her dress. Leo kissed and caressed each of her breasts in turn. Sarah shivered as his hand strayed from her breasts down across her stomach. He slipped his hand between her legs and she gave a little whimper, her mouth seeking his.

'I suppose,' she murmured after a moment, 'that I might as well start as I mean to go on.'

'That's my girl,' said Leo softly. 'That's my lovely Sarah.' He kissed her again, easing her dress down to her hips, till it slipped with a rustle to the floor.

CHAPTER FOURTEEN

The next morning Leo woke to find Sarah's side of the bed empty. He sat up, wondering if perhaps she had slipped out of the house early and taken a taxi home, filled with guilt. Unlikely. Then he heard sounds coming from the kitchen. He lay back on the pillow, surprised by his own sense of relief.

Moments later he got up, put on a dressing gown, and went downstairs, picking up the morning paper from the doormat. Sarah was in the kitchen making breakfast, barefoot and wearing Leo's dress shirt from the night before. Coffee was brewing, and on the table stood a pitcher of freshly squeezed orange juice, a basket of warm rolls, and dishes of butter and cherry jam. The radio was tuned to some music station.

'Morning,' said Leo, dropping the copy of *The Times* on the table. He picked up one of the rolls. 'Where did these come from?'

'Found them in your freezer and warmed them up in the oven. You haven't got any oranges left, I'm afraid. I juiced them all.'

'Good of you to bother.' He poured out two glasses of juice.

She came to the table and set down plates and knives. 'Napkins?'

'Over there. Third drawer down.'

She returned to the table with the napkins and the coffee pot.

'Which bit of the paper do you want?' asked Leo.

'Magazine, please.'

They breakfasted in companionable silence, the radio murmuring in the background. Sarah, though she appeared to be immersed in *The Times* supplement, was still busy with the thoughts which had occupied her as she prepared breakfast. She didn't feel remotely guilty about the night before. It had been bound to happen – though not, she liked to think, if Toby hadn't lost his job and made his disastrous career-change decision. Marrying him, however, was now out of the question. She had known that for a while. But she also knew that extricating herself from the relationship was going to be tricky. Apart from Toby's feelings, there would be the reaction of her father and the Kitterings to contend with. Damage limitation was going to be of the essence. She couldn't emerge from this without reproach – that was impossible. But she might be able to shift a little of the blame.

She lowered the magazine. 'Leo?'

'Mmhm?'

'I need to ask you something.'

Leo lifted his head from the sports section and gazed at her enquiringly.

'Well, just before Toby lost his job, I gave up the lease on my flat and moved into his place in Docklands. The idea was that we would live there till we found a house. The thing is . . .' She paused, and poured more coffee. 'Once I've told him that the wedding's off, obviously I can't go on living in his flat.'

'Obviously.'

'And I'll have nowhere to go.'

Leo sipped his coffee. 'Can't you rent somewhere else?'

'That's just it. I can't. Not for a while, at any rate. You see, I lost my job, too.'

Leo was surprised. 'How did you manage that?'

'Credit crunch. It's been bad for everyone. So . . .' she added quickly, before he could say anything, 'I was wondering if I could stay here for a while. It wouldn't be for long. I should find another job pretty soon.' She crossed her fingers under the table and gazed at him, waiting.

Leo was silent as he considered this. He could see advantages. Since the demise of his relationship with Anthea, the house could sometimes seem lonely in the evenings, even when he had work to do. The company of someone as intelligent, amusing and sexually stimulating as Sarah was quite an appealing prospect. He liked the idea – but it would have to be strictly on a short-term basis. However sweetly she might smile at him over the freshly squeezed orange juice, however delightful sharing a bed with her might be, she was bound to bring trouble in the long run. She always did. Plus, there was a risk he would get bored. He didn't want to find Sarah boring, ever.

As if reading his thoughts, she added, 'It could be like that first summer. A few weeks of mutual enjoyment, I perform a spot of cooking and housekeeping while I look for another job, then we both go our own sweet ways.'

Leo folded the paper. 'On that basis – and it would have to be on that basis, mind – I'll say yes. Though you'll have to make yourself scarce on the weekends Oliver comes to stay. He gets my undivided attention. And you know what Rachel is like.'

'Not a problem. Thanks, Leo.' She stretched her arms languidly above her head, then picked up her magazine, sipped her coffee, and resumed reading.

Leo marvelled at her cat-like serenity, and the apparent ease with which she was discarding what should have been the most important relationship of her life. However well he might know her, he would never properly understand her. He was suddenly conscious that the music from the radio was some unpleasantly insistent rap.

'What station is that?' he asked.

Sarah looked up. 'XFM.'

'Right. Well, that has to go for a start.'

'OK, boss.' Sarah got up and padded over to the radio, and switched it to Radio 3, smiling to herself.

The following morning in Brixton, the breakfast scene was less appetising. Felicity woke in a mucky tangle of sheets with a splitting headache and a mouth that felt like the bottom of a birdcage. She pulled herself to the edge of the bed, grasped the tumbler of water from the bedside table with a shaky hand, and drained it. She lay for a few moments with her forehead pressed to the pillow. Why had she gone with Vince to that club? Why had she let him persuade her to drop those pills, and then smoke dope on top of it all? Then there had been the vodka when they got home . . . She hauled herself slowly out of bed, and found her robe under a pile of other clothes at the foot of the bed. She hadn't done any washing in a week. She uncrumpled it and put it on, then wandered through to the kitchen, where she could hear the radio blasting, feeling shivery and sick.

Vince was sitting at the table in his boxers, eating leftover pizza from a cardboard box and drinking a can of lager.

'Jesus, Vince – how can you?' Felicity went to the sink to fill the kettle.

'Hair of the dog, sweetheart.' He turned and glanced at her as she stood hunched over the sink. 'Feeling a bit rough?'

'Rough's not the word.'

She stood blankly by the sink, staring out at the white December sky, filled with familiar feelings of self-reproach, but too hungover to care. She was aware of Vince dropping the empty pizza box down beside the overflowing swing-top bin. He stood behind her, running his hands around her body, nuzzling her shoulder. She wasn't so hungover that she couldn't feel instantly randy when he put his hands on her.

'Come on back to bed,' he murmured, fondling her through her robe.

She turned and kissed him. His mouth tasted of lager, but she didn't care. She probably tasted worse, and he didn't seem to mind. Her mind and body took comfort in the feel and touch of him. Sex, the great healer. They would go back to bed for an hour or so, keep the reality of Sunday at bay for a little while longer. But then, Felicity decided, they would make something civilised of the day.

'I'll come back to bed,' she said, 'if you promise to take me for a nice lunch later. Somewhere we can sit and read the Sunday papers. Down by the river, maybe. A gastropub.'

Vince groaned. 'I hate those poncey places. Posh waitresses, sawdust and no spit, and the beer's usually rubbish. Can't we just go down the Kempton Arms? Ossie'll be there. They do burgers and stuff, if you want lunch. And they've got Sky. Arsenal are playing Juventus.'

'No, Vince. I want to have a nice day. A civilised day.'

'All right. But you'll be the one paying. I'm skint.'

'I don't mind.' She would pay a fortune not to have to sit in the Kempton Arms with Ossie and his weird girlfriend, watching football all afternoon while Vince got slowly pissed.

He kissed her again. 'It's a deal, then. Come back to bed.'

'OK. Let me just make my tea first, and bring it with me.'

Choosing The Heron in Chiswick for Sunday lunch had been Rachel's decision. She was nervous about Oliver and Simon meeting for the first time. Her relationship with Simon had been chaste so far, consisting of that first evening at Abacus, a lunchtime drink, and supper and a play at the Menier, after which she had gone back to Simon's flat in Bermondsey for coffee. Rachel knew that her wary approach to sex, based on bad experiences from long ago, had a tendency to confuse and deter men, and she had been apprehensive about being alone with Simon. But he seemed remarkably sensitive to her mood and her feelings, and an hour after their first kiss and all that followed, she had found herself desperately wishing she didn't have to go home. But there was Oliver to think of, the babysitter to pay, work and school the next morning. Rachel knew that the only way forward was for Simon to stay at her place some night, and that would have to be very delicately played where Oliver was concerned. So she had suggested that Simon and Oliver should get to know one another, that the three of them should spend a Sunday together. She liked Simon very much, more than any man she had met in a long time. He was easy, funny, and uncomplicated. And, rather gratifyingly, he seemed pretty smitten with her.

So on a bright, chilly December Sunday, Rachel and Oliver met Simon in Kew at noon, and the three of them took a long ramble along the river, aiming to get to The Heron between half one and two. Initially Oliver, who was quite jealous of his mother's company, treated Simon with marked indifference. Simon took this in his stride, and didn't try too hard to engage him in talk. Twenty minutes into the walk, in the course of a conversation prompted by the sight of rowing eights practising on the river, Simon revealed that he had been a rowing blue at Oxford. Once the term was explained to Oliver, he seemed grudgingly impressed. He was even more impressed when he discovered, in the course of a lengthy discourse about X-Men, that Simon had decided views on whether Cyclops's ability to shoot red beams of force from his eyes was superior to Sabretooth's accelerated healing powers and resistance to disease. By the time they reached the pub, Oliver had accepted Simon as a worthy friend, and was busy filling him in with information about the ancient Egyptians, whom he was studying at school.

The Heron was big and busy, but the early lunchtime rush had subsided, and they found a table at the far end by the window and ordered lunch. There was a deck outside, fenced around, and Rachel and Oliver went outside to feed the ducks on the river with some stale bread Rachel had brought. Simon stayed inside, leafing through the Sunday papers. After ten minutes Rachel came in.

'Too cold for me.' She pulled off her gloves and sat down. 'Oliver's determined to stay out there till the bread's all finished. What's in the papers?'

'Oh, mainly the Bernie Madoff story. You do wonder why people weren't more suspicious. Didn't they ask themselves how he was managing to get people twelve per cent returns on their money in such an appalling economic climate?'

'People are greedy, I suppose. And they like to have faith. Obviously Madoff inspired that.'

'Some of the victims I feel sorry for – not all of them are rich. Some of them are charities.' Simon sighed and folded up the paper. He glanced out at Oliver, who was still crouched down on the deck outside, his woollen hat down over his ears, patiently waiting for ducks to paddle past so that he could throw them pellets of bread.

'He's a very good little boy,' observed Simon. 'I'd have been roaring round the place at his age.'

'He can be a terror when he wants to, but he's very focused when he wants to be. Just like his father.'

'I take it you and his dad still get on?'

'Better than we used to.'

'How long ago did you split up?'

'A year after Oliver was born.'

'Can I ask what happened? I mean, you don't have to talk about it if you don't want—'

'No, it's fine.' Rachel paused, glancing out to check on Oliver, who had finished the bread and was leaning against the palings, watching the river. 'Leo just wasn't – isn't – very good at commitment. Which is a nice way of saying that he was having affairs with other . . . people. Some I knew about, some I didn't. I wasn't prepared to put up with it.' She sipped her wine. 'What about you? No one reaches thirty-six without some kind of back story.'

'Oh, fairly typical stuff.' Simon sipped his beer. 'The usual girlfriends before, during and after uni, nothing serious. Then a long-term girlfriend that I lived with for about six years. We broke up just after my thirty-first birthday. Messy, splitting up with someone after that long. Carving things up. Possessions, the flat.'

'At least your relationship lasted longer than my marriage. Why did it end?'

Simon shrugged. 'She wanted to get married. I didn't.'

'Another man afraid of commitment. The world seems to be full of them.'

'Not entirely fair. I ended it because I thought, well, if I didn't love her enough to marry her – what was the point? I was wasting time. Hers and mine. I do want to get married some day, have children, the whole family thing. Most men do, I reckon. But it has to be the right person.'

At that moment Oliver barged back in from the deck area, bringing a gust of chilly air. 'Mummy, when's lunch?' he demanded. 'I am so unbelievably hungry.'

Simon spotted their waitress heading towards them with a laden tray. 'I think your roast beef is on its way right now.'

He grinned and ruffled Oliver's hair. Rachel winced – it was something Oliver generally hated. But Oliver let his hair be ruffled and grinned right back, then wriggled onto his chair and watched appreciatively as his food was set in front of him.

Twenty minutes later, on her way to the Ladies at the very back of the pub, Rachel saw Felicity. She was sitting at a table with a dark, broad-shouldered man dressed in jeans and a combat jacket. He had two-day-old stubble, and seemed mildly, cheerfully drunk. He was sitting with his legs propped on a chair, paying no attention to Felicity, conversing with two couples at a neighbouring table. Felicity's attitude was one of defeat and boredom, verging on apprehension. Although the two men at the next table were responding to whatever Felicity's friend was saying with wary tolerance – it seemed to be something to do with football – it was clear that their girlfriends were fed up with the intrusion. Rachel took this all in at a glance. She stopped by the table and said hello.

Felicity looked up, startled. 'Rachel, hi!' Rachel could sense her embarrassment. Felicity glanced across at Vince, who had been sufficiently distracted by Rachel's arrival to stop chatting to the two men. 'Rachel,' said Felicity, 'this is Vince. Vince – this is Rachel Davies. She was my boss, once upon a time.'

Vince smiled at Rachel woozily, giving her an appreciative once-over. 'Was she now?' He lifted his feet from the chair and stood up. Rachel, not quite sure what was coming, put out her hand. Vince shook it, then leant in to kiss her cheek. He reeked of both beer and whisky. 'Rachel, you are most welcome. Like to sit down? Get you a drink?'

'No thanks. I'm just on my way to the Ladies.' Rachel

turned to Felicity. 'I'm here with Oliver and a friend. We took a long walk along the river before lunch. Isn't it a glorious day?'

'Glorious!' exclaimed Vince loudly, imitating Rachel's proper vowels. 'I say, isn't it absolutely glorious?' He laughed and turned to the two men at the next table for confirmation and approval, then sat down clumsily. One of them grinned sheepishly and looked away. The other muttered something into his drink, not smiling. Vince gave him a bleary, searching glance, then decided to let it go. He looked back at Rachel. 'Glorious. *You're* fucking glorious, you know that?'

Felicity put her hand on Vince's knee. 'Vince! Stop it!' she urged. People at nearby tables were glancing round.

Rachel pretended it was all fine. 'Listen, good to see you, Fliss. Give me a call some time.' She turned and headed to the Ladies.

When she came out a few moments later, something had clearly kicked off between Vince and the men at the next table. He was shouting incoherent abuse, and one of the men stood up and fetched Vince a punch that knocked him off his chair. The girls began to scream, and then the table went over, sending drinks crashing and spilling across the floor. Bar staff raced across. Felicity crouched down to try and help Vince up, but he pushed her away so forcefully that she went sprawling backwards.

Rachel stood on the edge of the commotion, uncertain what to do. Felicity was getting unsteadily to her feet. Rachel went over to her. 'Come on,' she murmured, 'you don't have to stay here if you don't want to. Let him look after himself.'

Felicity gave her a stunned, frantic look. 'I can't just leave him! Look at the state of him!'

At that moment three bar staff waded in, grabbing hold of Vince and his assailant, and hustling them both towards the back entrance. Felicity went after them. Rachel watched her go.

Sarah sat by the window in the half-darkness, staring across the river at the glimmering lights of Canary Wharf, waiting for Toby. One small lamp cast a muted pool of light in a far corner of the room. Her heart felt numb. She was about to inflict a terrible injury on someone to whom she had once – almost – been prepared to give her whole life. She couldn't feel sorry for him. He was lucky to be making his escape. She had pretended not only to him, but to herself, that she loved him enough to marry him, simply because it meant a life of relative ease and prosperity, and freedom from certain kinds of menial cares. But take away those pleasing prospects, and the affection she felt simply wasn't enough. She had been put to the test, and found utterly wanting. She had never felt less capable of love in her life.

She picked up her gin and tonic from the black lacquer coffee table and took a sip, thinking that a bit more self-reproach and spiritual abasement might be in order. But she'd done enough of that. She needed to move on, calculate the likely fallout with Toby's family, and with her father.

Then the sound she had been dreading all day interrupted her thoughts. She heard Toby's key in the door, the sound of it opening and closing, the thump of his overnight bag on the hall floor. His tall figure appeared in the doorway, silhouetted against the glow of light from the hall. He stood there a few seconds, accustoming his eyes to the gloom.

'There you are.' He crossed the room. 'What are you doing sitting in the dark?' She said nothing. He gazed at her for a moment, then sat down on the sofa, but not next to her. Something in her silence, perhaps in her tense posture, put him on his guard.

Sarah swallowed the remains of her gin and tonic, and set the glass down. 'How was your weekend?' she asked.

'Excellent. Always gratifying to beat the Scots. Paul's wife and Alan's girlfriend came along. They went shopping on Princes Street. You should come next time.'

'Be a WAG, you mean.'

Toby laughed uncertainly. 'Well, it's a weekend away. I just thought, if other people take their wives . . .' He decided to leave the subject, and leant over to pick up her empty glass. 'Another?'

'Thanks.'

'Think I'll join you.' He stood up and went to the drinks cupboard. Sarah wondered if he was as aware as she was of the level of tension in the air. She had no way of behaving normally. It was merely a question now of getting from A, this instant moment, to B, the point at which she would put on her coat, pick up the bag that was already packed and sitting in the bedroom, and leave.

Toby uncapped the gin bottle and poured drinks. 'Annabel was down for the weekend,' he remarked. Annabel was Toby's younger sister, already earmarked as a bridesmaid. 'Mummy was trying to persuade her to suggest some colour or other for the bridesmaids' dresses. Annabel said she should leave it up to you and stop interfering.'

Sarah could think of nothing to say. Toby brought the drinks over and sat down, still keeping a distance between them, but stretching out an arm along the back of the sofa. He stroked her hair, and asked, 'You OK?'

Sarah took a swallow of her drink. 'No. Not really.' She waited for him to ask what was wrong, but he didn't. When he lifted his glass, it was almost like a defensive movement. Sarah wondered for a fleeting instant if he suspected, or guessed what was coming. If he did, he wasn't going to help her out. She had to continue. 'I'm afraid something happened this weekend.'

He turned to look at her. 'What do you mean?'

She looked down at her glass, which she was clutching between both hands in her lap. 'Saying it like that makes it sound as though it was out of my control. But it wasn't. It didn't just happen. It was something I did.'

Toby set his drink down sharply on the table. 'For God's sake—'

She carried on quickly, not letting him speak, just wanting it to be told, out of the way, the hellish moment over. 'I slept with Leo Davies. On Friday. After Grand Night. I wasn't drunk. I wasn't anything. I did it because I wanted to.' She had wondered earlier if she would have to try to manufacture tears, but they came naturally. Saying it out loud charged her with genuine, ice-cold guilt, and she began to cry. 'I did it, and it changes everything.'

She wept, pausing once to sniff and take a long pull at her gin and tonic, thinking what nice, strong ones Toby made, while Toby sat with his head in his hands.

After a while he lifted his head, staring straight ahead at the lights of Canary Wharf. She was appalled to see that he had been crying, too, and her first impulse was to take him in her arms and comfort him. But she resisted it, and when she heard his next words, was glad she had. He turned to look at her. 'It doesn't have to change everything. I don't want it to. People do these things. I'm not . . . it's not like, well . . . that is, it's not like I haven't had a bit of a moment myself.'

'Sorry?'

'I mean, it didn't go anywhere – it was when we went on that cricket tour last summer. It honestly didn't matter, it meant completely nothing, and that's why – that's why I don't want this to make any difference. To us.'

Sarah allowed herself a moment to digest this unexpected revelation. 'Toby, it's more than just a casual fling. I'm moving in with Leo.'

'What? You slept with him once and you're moving in? What are you talking about? This is mad!'

'It's complicated. It's also much more than you think. Leo and I go back a long way. It's made me realise' – she spread her hands – 'that there's no way I can marry you. I don't want to. I don't love you. It's simply no good.'

Sarah knew that a point had been reached where this either escalated into a full-scale row with attendant histrionics, more tears, and abuse hurled – which would be a waste of time since there couldn't be any of the customary reconciliation – or she cut to the chase and left. So she stood up. Toby stood up too, and grabbed her by the wrists.

'Sarah, please. This is ridiculous. You don't mean any of this. You can't just walk away. Please, baby.'

'Toby, let go. I'm sorry. I never wanted this. But it's over, completely over. Let me go.'

'Do you love him?' he demanded.

'Let me go.'

'Come on – I want to know!'

Sarah wanted to say no, but to her surprise she found that she couldn't disown Leo. It was one lie she would not tell. 'That's not the point. The point is, I don't love you, Toby. That's all that matters.' Perhaps the gentle finality with which she said this made him realise there was no further point. He let go of her.

'I've packed some of my things. It's best if I just go now. I can get the rest another time.'

He said nothing. She went to the bedroom. Her case lay on the bed, her handbag next to it. She took out her mobile and rang for a cab, then sat down on the bed and waited. After five minutes or so, Toby appeared in the doorway.

'Look, do what you want now. Go where you want. I can't stop you. We'll talk later. No matter what you say, it can't be over. Not just like that.'

Sarah knew it was best to say nothing. At that moment an alert buzzed on her phone. The cab was downstairs. She put on her coat, picked up her belongings, left the flat, and went down in the lift.

When the cab reached Chelsea, the driver missed the house, and Sarah got out a few doors down. She was just paying the fare, and as she glanced towards Leo's house she saw the door open, and Leo emerge with a girl. The cab purred away up the street, and Sarah quickly picked up her case and retreated to the edge of the central garden and the shadow of the trees. At this short distance Sarah could see the girl was young and extremely pretty. Leo and the girl spoke briefly, then she kissed him and went down the steps and unchained a bicycle from the railings. She waved once at Leo, and cycled away. Leo went inside, closing the front door.

Sarah waited for the clenched, painful feeling in her gut to subside. She shouldn't be surprised. Just because they'd slept together on Grand Night didn't mean he wasn't seeing someone else. She of all people should know that. How ridiculous to hope that because he was letting her live in his house for a few weeks, he was interested in rekindling a relationship. After all, what kind of a relationship had they ever really had? Mutual use and abuse, no more. Well, at least now she knew the terms on which she would be living with him.

She picked up her bag and walked towards the house, fixing what she hoped was just the right smile on her face.

CHAPTER FIFTEEN

Leo realised that he could no longer put off the business of getting in touch with Gabrielle's mother. Every time he spoke to her Gabrielle asked if he had done so, and his stock excuse – that he would do so when he felt the time was right – seemed to be wearing thin.

They were lunching together in Chancery Lane, Leo snatching time between court hearings, Gabrielle between lectures and tutorials, when she brought it up again.

'I don't understand what difference it makes if I get in touch with her or not,' said Leo. 'I would have thought my relationship with you is all that matters. How do you know she even wants to speak to me? It could be difficult for her. Embarrassing. Have you asked her if she wants me to get in touch?'

'No,' admitted Gabrielle. 'I suppose it's up to you.'

'Exactly.'

'I just think you should. I don't know how you can't

want to. It's like – it's like the whole thing is one big jigsaw, and this is the last piece that needs putting in place.'

'Well, maybe you'll get married some day, and she and I can meet again at your wedding. A fittingly romantic conclusion?'

'It's not about anything being romantic.' Gabrielle frowned, and Leo could tell his remark had hit home.

'Really? I think some little-girl part of you wants the long-lost lovers reconciled.'

She shrugged. 'Yeah, OK. I suppose I want you two to . . .' She cast around for words. 'To, well – *acknowledge* one another. Otherwise it's like there's something you're both ignoring, pretending doesn't exist.'

'By which you mean – you?'

'Maybe. Anyway, I'll keep on nagging you. And by the way, I am *not* romantic. I hate that word. I hate everything it stands for.'

'I see. So you're a material girl who doesn't believe in love.'

'No. I just don't like sentimentality. I believe in love. I'm seeing someone now, as a matter of fact. Someone pretty special.' She thought of Anthony, of how they had seen one another almost every night for the past week. What would Leo say if he knew?

'That's nice. A he or a she?'

Gabrielle sat back in her chair. 'What a random thing to say! A man, of course.'

'Why of course? One should never presume, these days.'

'Either you're trying too hard to be right-on, or—' She broke off. Something slipped into place.

'Or what?'

'Nothing.'

Leo signalled for the bill, not really wanting to take the conversation any further. For all the ease and intimacy they had created over the past month and a half, occasionally they would hit these jarring pockets of incomprehension, which made them realise they didn't really know one another.

'I'd better get going,' said Gabrielle. 'I have a tutorial in ten minutes.'

'And I have to get back to court,' said Leo, fishing out his wallet.

'I might come along and watch you after my tutorial. Nothing else to do.'

'You're very welcome. Although you might find my discourse on what constitutes an unsafe port somewhat tedious.'

She smiled. 'I'll be the judge of that. I like watching you in court. You're pretty cool, you know.'

'I wish some of my younger colleagues in chambers thought that.'

'Maybe they do.' She bent and gave him a light kiss on one cheek. 'Catch you later.'

When he got back to chambers at five, Leo decided to grasp the nettle. He sat down at his desk, found the piece of paper Gabrielle had given him with Jackie's number, and rang it. The photograph of Jackie had acted on his memory like an evocative trace of scent, or a snatch of music, but no matter how hard he tried to recall the places and events of that summer, he couldn't bring them to life. One of so many affairs. Even the fact that she was French didn't help – yet how many French women had he slept with? He was in the middle of counting when a woman's voice, light, smoky, answered.

'Hello?'

'Jackie?'

There was a pause. He could hear traffic sounds at her end, then she said, 'Yes. Who is this?'

'Leo. Leo Davies. Gabrielle gave me your number.'

'Oh.' She let out a breath, as if giving in to something. Leo realised she must have been preparing for this for some time.

'I meant to call before now.'

'No – it's I who should have called you,' she replied hurriedly. 'A long time ago.' The emotion in her voice made him realise that the subject of Gabrielle was not one to be dealt with in the blundering clumsiness of an out-of-the-blue phone call.

'I thought . . . I thought perhaps it would be a good idea to meet and have a talk.'

'Yes. Yes, of course. Hold on a moment – I'm sorry. I'm just paying a taxi.' A moment later she came back on the line. 'I'm in the West End right now. I could come over to the City and meet you somewhere in, say, half an hour?'

Leo hadn't envisaged anything so sudden. He felt unprepared. But he could think of no good reason for putting it off.

'Yes, if you like. There's a wine bar in Chancery Lane – Hunter's. It's usually fairly quiet early in the evening.'

'Fine. I'll see you there.'

Leo clicked off his phone and sat musing. The casual, almost perfunctory nature of the exchange seemed at odds with the significance of the fact that he had just spoken, after a silence of twenty-two years, to the mother of his child, a child whose existence he had been unaware of until very recently. Apart from her initial surprise, Jackie had sounded composed, unflustered by the idea of meeting up with him. But then, people of her age – his age – generally knew how to maintain a facade of imperturbability whatever their emotions. He guessed, however, that her feelings must be as turbulent as his.

Even at half five the basement wine bar was busy. There was a rowdy group of office workers crowded round the bar, the fag end of a Christmas lunch party. Not that he could have found anywhere quieter. Every bar and pub in the City was permanently busy in the run-up to Christmas. Leo glanced round, but could see no solitary females. He seated himself at a table as far away from the raucous office crowd as possible, and ordered a bottle of Rully Blanc and two glasses. He felt nervous, glad he had brought papers with him to read while he waited.

Jacqueline didn't arrive till six. Leo had glanced up every time someone came into the bar, but when an expensively dressed middle-aged woman, unmistakeably not a City type, appeared in the doorway clutching a number of designer carrier bags, he knew it had to be her. She glanced around, then began to forge a path through the knots of drinkers. The closer she got, the more distinct her features became, and suddenly, extraordinarily, Leo recognised not just the girl in the photo, but the girl from that summer so long ago. She was older, her once dark hair streaked with blonde highlights to hide the grey, but her face was the same – not a girl's face, but that of a beautiful, poised woman. The physical sight of her seemed to open a door in his mind, and a thousand memories came cascading in. How could he have forgotten? The rush of recollection – of Jackie leaning over a window sill to call to him in the street, of Jackie sitting on a riverbank with her feet in the water, of Jackie tapping out a Gitanes and asking him to teach her to blow smoke rings – was so overwhelming that when he stood up and she recognised him, he was momentarily lost for words.

'Leo,' she said. 'I'm sorry – it took me longer to get here than I thought.' He stood up and shook the hand she held out. She set down her bags and took off her coat, and he hung it up for her. They both sat down. She clasped her hands together on the table, and smiled at him. 'What a very long time.'

'A very long time,' he replied. He picked up the bottle. 'I bought some wine. I can't remember if you . . . ?'

She nodded. 'Please. Just a small glass.'

He poured the wine. She took a sip, then set the glass down. She met his gaze and let out an awkward laugh. 'My God, this is so strange.'

Leo smiled. 'Isn't it?' He was fascinated by how much she was still the girl he had once known, and yet not. Their initial exchanges were slow, each hesitating before they spoke.

'So – I think I must apologise.'

'For what?'

'For the shock all this must have been to you. For not telling you at the time. I should have realised Gabrielle would want to find you some day.'

'As shocks go, it's been a very pleasant one. Truly.'

'Maybe. But I should have told you a long time ago.'

'It doesn't matter now. Things are as they are.'

Nothing was said for several seconds. They were two strangers, locked in silence, struggling to deal with the intimacy which connected them. When Jackie spoke again, her tone was polite and friendly, like a woman making small talk at a drinks party.

'Gabrielle tells me you've met – what, several times now?'

'That's right. We meet just about every week. It helps that she's a lawyer. I mean, that we're working in the same area.'

'She's doing that because of you. Studying law, I mean.'

'I doubt that's entirely down to me.'

'You're her father. She sets great store by who you are, what you have achieved.'

'I'm only her father in one sense. You and your husband have brought her up, you are her true parents.'

There was another long pause, then Jackie said, 'I'm relieved to hear you say that. Daniel, my husband, has been—' She broke off, trying to find words. 'Anxious about all this. There was a time when you seemed to have become a fixation with Gabrielle. She knew about you, she made it her job to learn a lot about you, but she was so nervous about actually going to find you. It took her a long time. We didn't encourage or discourage. It had to be something she did as and when she wanted to. We were worried she was building you up into something – Daniel thought you might . . .' She shrugged. 'I don't know . . . eclipse him in some way. That he would lose something. Not her, but – well, something. The fact of Gabrielle being his daughter.' She spoke hurriedly, as though glad to be releasing her fears. She looked up at him, her eyes bright with unshed tears. Leo remembered what a very emotional girl she had been. So much was coming back to him.

'Gabrielle is more his daughter than mine,' he replied. 'She knows that. We've talked about a lot of things. Whatever balance there is to find in situations like these, I believe she's found it. I don't think she expects anything from me.'

Jackie shook her head. 'You don't know her very well. Not yet. Gabrielle is – she is, well, not a demanding girl, exactly. But she is passionate, very wilful. We've had some very tempestuous, difficult times with her. It's better now she's older. She seems to have found some stability. I'm glad she's doing what she's doing. And I really believe the fact that she has persevered with her law studies, that she has made it this far, is to do with you. To make you proud.' Jackie laughed uncertainly. 'Or the person she has made you up to be. This ideal she's had.'

'I'm far from ideal. As I'm sure she realises, now that she's getting to know me better.'

Jackie put her head on one side and gave Leo an appraising look. 'Self-deprecating. That's not the way I remember you.'

Leo realised that over the years Jackie must have thought about him often, in a way he had never thought about her. Finding out she was pregnant a few weeks after they stopped seeing one another must have acted like a catalyst, crystallising the recollection of the relationship, and of him, for ever.

'I can't remember the person I was then.'

She drew a deep breath. 'It's probably not the right moment to start going back over old times. I don't even think I want to. Do you?' The look she gave him was searching, almost challenging. Leo didn't know how to respond. By saying nothing, he felt he was failing her. She went on, 'Gabrielle, the here and now – that is what counts. I want you to understand, Leo – Daniel and I want you to understand – that you will have a lot of influence over Gabrielle, now that you are in her life. As I say, she has been something of a wild child. Perhaps we indulged her too much. A lot of her friends are rich, spoilt kids, maybe not the best people for her to hang out with. It will be good if you can help to keep her steady.'

Leo poured a little more wine, giving himself time to think how to respond.

'I'm not sure if I'll be much use in that department. I don't know anything about the rest of her life. But I'll do what I can – if she needs my help, that is. She doesn't seem to.'

'Don't worry – I don't mean to burden you with responsibility for her, not after all these years. It's just that if things go wrong, or she has problems, you might have some influence with her, in ways we don't. You know what young people are like.'

'I think I understand what you're saying. I'll keep an eye on her. She seems fine, though.'

'Yes, I hope so.'

There was another silence. It felt as though the subject of Gabrielle had been disposed of for the moment. 'So,' said Leo, 'Gabrielle tells me that you and your husband live in Richmond? And you have two sons?'

The next twenty minutes were filled with a courteous exchange of information. By the end of it, Leo felt more remote from Jackie than he had at the beginning of their meeting. It was as though they were retreating from intimacy, rather than making headway.

She broke the tension by glancing at her watch. 'I'm afraid I have to go.'

She slipped on her coat. Leo helped her pick up her raft of carrier bags. 'So much Christmas shopping,' she said. 'I seem to finish up buying presents on behalf of everyone else in the family.' She lifted her hair free of her coat collar. 'I envy you, having a little boy to buy presents for. I always think Christmas is for children, really. Grown-ups just go through the motions. It's when you're a child that it's magical.'

'Oliver's very excited, certainly,' replied Leo. She put out her hand, and he touched it, then they both laughed awkwardly, and Jackie leant over and kissed him on either cheek. 'Goodbye, Leo,' she said.

Her fragrance was one he knew, but couldn't name. He wasn't sure where he had last encountered it. Surely not twenty years ago? He smiled. 'Goodbye.'

He watched her leave, then sat down. He poured what was left of the wine into his glass, marvelling at what could both connect and disconnect people over time. Then he took out his reading glasses and tried to read the papers he had brought. But the encounter with Jackie, with his own past, had left him disturbed. Jackie was on her way home now, happily laden with Christmas presents, to prepare supper, to be with her family, to become immersed in a life entirely unconnected to his own existence. Confused, bleak thoughts beset him. Of Rachel. Of Oliver. Of how different his life might have been if he had known twenty-two years ago that Jackie was pregnant.

Pointless thoughts, he told himself. His life had been good. *Was* good. Some mistakes, certainly. But things were as they were. Gabrielle was still a secret he had told no one about. Now he badly needed someone to share it with. He had thought that he might tell Sarah – there was little she didn't know about his life already – but since moving in she had been somewhat remote. The easy, relaxed sensuality with which she usually behaved when they were together had disappeared. Tactfully he let her alone, assuming she was still raw from the break-up with Toby, that it had been harder for her than she had expected. Maybe she'd even had regrets about it, and about the events after Grand Night which had led to it all. He told himself he had nothing to feel guilty about; there had been no need for her to tell Toby that she had slept with him. The truth was that she had probably let it happen simply to give her an excuse to break off the engagement. With that achieved, presumably she'd had no further desire – except for somewhere to stay. The idea that something had been lost between himself and Sarah made him feel even more isolated and depressed. He glanced at his watch. Almost seven. He drained his glass, gathered up his papers and made his way back to chambers, hoping Anthony would still be there.

Anthony was sitting at his desk, going through his online bank statement in a mild state of shock. The only light in the room was that from his desk lamp, its glow etching gaunt shadows on his face. He couldn't believe the figures. That he had gone through so much money in one month was unbelievable. The debits to Blunt's cascaded down the page, night after night, thousand upon thousand. He felt his stomach tighten with fear. Why was he afraid? Because he knew only too well that he couldn't just shrug these losses off, quit gambling and wait for his finances to recover. He didn't have the strength of will. A part of him knew – was convincing itself even now – that inevitably he had to go back to the tables to try to make good what he had lost. The disastrous scenario lay all too vividly before him, and he could think of no escape.

There was a light rap at his door, and he glanced up and saw Leo.

'Your light was on, so I thought I'd say hello.' Leo stepped into the room and closed the door. 'Working?'

Anthony logged off the page and leant back in his chair. 'Just casino stuff.'

'Ah. Your Lion King case. Rachel's told me about it. The hearing's in a couple of months, isn't it?'

Anthony could feel the knot of fear still twisting his insides. He badly wanted to unburden himself to Leo, find a way to loosen the dread. 'I didn't mean that. I meant my ridiculous gambling losses.' He added, with an effort at lightness, 'I blame Edward, leading me into bad habits, luring me to poker games when I should have been in bed.' He began to feel his anxiety relaxing. He would confess to Leo, and Leo would absolve him, help him.

But Anthony's words and manner irritated Leo. Gambling amused him only vaguely, and the idea that anyone should allow themselves to rack up losses struck him as incredibly weak.

'Spending your evenings gambling? I imagine that's why you were so badly prepared for that interlocutory disclosure hearing the other day.'

Anthony gave him a sharp glance, all thoughts of

confession and absolution dismissed. 'What do you mean? Who told you that?'

'George Webb from Holmans mentioned it to Henry. Henry mentioned it to me. Doesn't do to let down instructing solicitors, you know. Especially someone like Webb. He's the kind of person you should be looking to for reliable future income. But if you spend your nights in casinos and turn up ill-prepared—'

'Oh, for God's sake, the hearing has nothing to do with anything. Felicity messed the days up. I didn't have time to get my head round the case.'

Leo said nothing for a moment. 'If you say so.' There was an uncomfortable silence. 'So, how much are you talking about?'

'How much what?'

'Your losses.'

But Anthony knew the moment had passed. 'Forget it. It's not that bad. I don't know why I mentioned it. Anyway,' said Anthony, seeking now to deflect the conversation from himself, 'why are you in chambers at this hour?'

'I was meeting an old friend for a drink. I needed to come back to chambers to drop some papers off.' He knew he could say nothing now about Gabrielle and Jackie. The mood was wrong. Anthony was angry, troubled, and he himself felt tired and confused. The faint trace of Jackie's perfume clung to his face from where she had kissed him, and was a source of irritation rather than pleasure.

Anthony nodded. They gazed at one another, aware of a loss of connection.

Leo rose. 'I should go. I'll see you tomorrow.' He paused. 'Can I give you a lift home?'

'No thanks. I have some things to do. Papers to look at.'

As he listened to Leo's footsteps fading on the stairs, Anthony wished he had accepted the lift. He wasn't seeing Gabrielle till eight. It would have been a chance to rewind the clock, confide in Leo and find some wise counsel. For an instant he almost got up and went after him. But the seconds ticked by, and silence reclaimed the empty chambers. Anthony locked up, and made his way home, glad of the thought of having Gabrielle to take his mind off his problems, even if she couldn't solve them.

It was ten o'clock when Gabrielle reached across to the bedside table to check the time on her phone. She rolled back to face Anthony. He was lying on the pillow with his hands clasped behind his head, staring at the ceiling.

'What are you thinking about?' She traced a line with her finger down his chest, and kissed his shoulder.

He didn't answer for several seconds, then suddenly turned to her. 'Sorry – what?'

'Don't worry. You were miles away.' She sat on the edge of the bed, fishing on the floor for her underwear. 'I have to go. I've got an essay to finish.'

'Will I see you tomorrow?'

'My parents have some family friends coming for dinner. They asked me to be there. Sorry.'

Anthony got out of bed and pulled on his boxer shorts. He padded to the kitchen to fetch a glass of water. When he came back, Gabrielle was dressed. He took her in his arms, stroking her face. 'It's weird. I've only been seeing you for a couple of weeks, and yet it feels like I've known you much longer.'

She gave a crooked little smile. 'Maybe we met in another life.' She pulled a brush from her bag and dragged it through her hair. 'So, what do you plan to do tomorrow night, now that I'm blowing you out? It's Saturday, after all.'

'Not sure. Maybe I'll pop along to Blunt's. Edward might be there.'

'As will the lovely Julia, no doubt. She and her husband practically seem to live there.' Gabrielle turned to a mirror and checked her reflection.

'I'm not remotely interested in her,' replied Anthony. 'As well you know.'

'But she's interested in you. Watch yourself.' She picked up her coat. 'And don't gamble too much. You always seem to lose shedloads. I can't believe you can afford to chuck so much money away.'

When she had gone, Anthony put on some music and tried to clear his mind. With Gabrielle he had been able to forget his anxieties, but now they returned. He thought of the calculations he had done earlier, reckoning up his mortgage, outgoings, chambers' rent, the cost of the new car he'd recently bought, against his monthly losses. Maybe the answer was just to stop. Just stop, cold. But how would that help? It was a panicky reaction, and the wrong one. Looked at rationally, the losses were only the cumulation of a losing streak. Nothing lasted for ever. What he really needed to do was to stop panicking and be patient. Quitting now would mean losing entirely the possibility of a big win. And really, that was all he needed – just one big, solid win to rebalance everything. Just fifty or seventy-five grand to set him back on an even keel. It was possible. It had happened to him before. And what about that guy who had won a hundred and eighty grand the other night? It would be mad just to stop. The truth was, he didn't like the idea of giving up his nights at the casino. He enjoyed spending time there, seeing Edward and the new friends he had made lately. The answer was to cut down. Instead of lashing down a few hundred on every bet or poker game, he could bring it down to sensible levels. That was the solution. Thirty or forty pounds could just as easily net him a big win at higher stakes. He liked to think that he was cultivating a better idea of judicious betting. He even had a bit of a system going. It was just a question of hanging in there till his luck turned.

His deliberations had made him feel better about everything. He glanced at his watch. Only half ten. He might as well start his new regime now. He felt happier, could sense luck waiting round the corner for him.

He dressed, left the flat, grabbed a cab, and fifteen minutes late he was in the plush, warm, well-lit womb of the casino.

CHAPTER SIXTEEN

Toby stood at the kitchen window in his parents' house, a mug of coffee in his hand. His mother's car drew up, and he watched as she got out and crossed the yard to the house, Scooby bounding at her heels. She came into the kitchen, pulling off her coat, and saw Toby.

'Toby, what a nice surprise! When did you get here?'

Toby crossed the kitchen to give his mother a kiss. 'About half an hour ago.'

'You should have told me you were coming. I wouldn't have spent so long in town.'

'Just thought I'd pop down and see how you old folks are getting on. I have a lot of spare time these days.'

'Well, I have just come back from Waitrose with the most enormous shopping, so you and your father can bring it in from the car. Where on earth is he?' She went to the door leading to the hallway and called into the house. 'Jon-Jon, I'm back!'

Toby went out to the car, happy to postpone, if only by ten minutes or so, the business of telling her about the break-up with Sarah. He had been calling and texting her several times every day since the night she'd left. Yesterday she had eventually answered one of his calls, and by the end of their conversation he finally accepted that it was over, and that she was never coming back to him.

He opened the boot and started to take out bags of shopping. His father emerged from the house to join him.

'Have you said anything to Mum?' asked Toby.

Jonathan Kittering shook his head. 'I'm leaving that to you.'

They carried the bags into the kitchen, and Caroline began to bustle about, putting groceries away.

'Mum,' began Toby, 'the reason I came down today—'

'In a minute, darling. Let me sort all this out, and then we can have a chat. Make yourself useful and put on the kettle. I'm dying for a cup of tea. Shopping always wears me out.'

While Toby made tea, Caroline unpacked bag after bag, talking nineteen to the dozen about her trip into town.

'I met Denise Hannon at the delicatessen counter and I hardly recognised her. You wouldn't believe the amount of weight she's put on since summer. Here,' she handed a bag of frozen food to Jonathan, 'all this can go in the freezer.'

'Here's your tea,' said Toby.

'Thank you, dear. Just pop it on the table. Nearly finished.' She started to empty the last bag of groceries. 'Actually, I'm glad you popped down, because we need to discuss arrangements for Christmas. It's only a week away, you know. The way it creeps up! Annabel gets back from Florence on the nineteenth, though she doesn't know yet if

Marcus will be here or not. Daniel and Ffion can't get here till the afternoon on Christmas Day, because they're driving down from Wales, so I thought I would do the meal in the early evening, if people don't mind. I was also thinking it might be a good idea if you and Sarah were to come down the day before, so that Sarah can give me a hand with preparations. I know she's not all that keen on domestic chores, but if she's going to be one of the family, she'll have to learn to muck in—'

'Sarah won't be coming for Christmas,' said Toby abruptly. 'We've split up.'

Caroline stopped, open-mouthed, a packet of milk chocolate digestives in one hand. 'Split up?'

'She ended it. Said she didn't want to marry me after all.'

Caroline put the biscuits on the kitchen table and sat down. 'Good heavens. Oh, Toby – how awful for you. How truly awful.' She turned to her husband. 'Did you know?'

Jonathan Kittering nodded. 'Toby told me as soon as he got here.'

Caroline looked piteously at her son. 'Darling, I am so sorry.'

'Don't be. I'm glad I found out now the kind of person she is.'

'What do you mean?'

'When I was away in Scotland – you know, at the rugby – she slept with someone else. She told me when I got back. She's moved in with him. For all I know, she could have been seeing him for months.'

'What? How absolutely dreadful! Who is he?'

'No one you know. A barrister called Leo Davies. Someone she used to work with. So you see, I'm probably well out of it.'

'Yes. Oh, what a shock. I can't believe it. You poor, poor boy.' Caroline got up and went to hug him, standing on tiptoe to get her arms around him.

'Mum, honestly . . .' Toby tolerated her embrace for a few seconds. 'I'll get over it.'

Caroline stroked his arms, then returned to the table and sat down, picking up her tea, her gaze growing distant. 'I shall have to make some phone calls. What a good thing we decided on a marquee for the reception and didn't book Calcott House. I imagine the deposit—' She broke off, glancing at Toby. 'Oh, I'm sorry, darling. I shouldn't be thinking of such mundane things at a time like this. Too practical for my own good. How awful for Vivian. He was so thrilled when you and Sarah got engaged. His best friend's daughter. So perfect. And now . . .' She raised her eyebrows eloquently. 'Though I have to say, sad as it is that you and she have split up, that Sarah was really never quite my idea of—'

'Not now, Mummy,' said Toby brusquely. 'I think I'll take Scoobs for a walk.'

Jonathan sat down at the kitchen table. 'I have to talk to Vivian, obviously.'

'And say what, exactly? That Sarah has behaved appallingly? I should think he must be heartily ashamed of her.' Caroline sipped her tea, and added, 'That's assuming he knows.'

'Sarah must have told him, surely?'

Caroline shrugged. 'Who knows? I should wait until he rings you. In the circumstances, it's really up to him.'

'I suppose. I'll give it till Wednesday. But if he hasn't been in touch by then, I shall have to call him.'

* * *

That Wednesday, Sir Vivian spent the hours between ten and two at the London Library, engaged in research for his new book, a history of the Cambridge Apostles. When he got back to his Westminster flat he felt he had pretty much earned an afternoon in front of the telly. He put on his slippers, toasted and buttered some crumpets, poured himself a glass of beer, and settled down on the sofa to watch the racing from Uttoxeter, the phone by his side so that he could ring his bookmaker if the urge overtook him. He had just taken one bite of crumpet and a sip of beer, when the phone rang.

'Buggeration,' he muttered. He hesitated, wondering whether to bother, then pressed the 'mute' button on the remote and picked up the phone.

He recognised Jonathan's voice at once. 'Jonathan, my dear fellow. You've just caught me putting my feet up, watching the racing. How can I help?'

'Vivian, I'm sorry to disturb your afternoon, but I had to call you. Toby came to see us a couple of days ago.' A brief silence elapsed. 'He and Sarah have broken off their engagement.'

'What?'

'I'm sorry to be the bearer of bad news. I would have thought Sarah might have told you. It happened over a week ago.'

'She hasn't said a thing.' Sir Vivian tried to quell his alarm with words of reassurance. 'Probably because it isn't as serious as you think. You know what young people are like. It's probably just a trivial tiff.'

'I really think it's more than that.' Jonathan spoke his next words with evident difficulty. 'Apparently Sarah has gone to live with another man.'

'What?'

'His name is Leo Davies. Toby thinks it's possible she's been seeing him for a while.'

The spark of instinctive concern Sir Vivian had felt for his daughter on the news of the break-up was immediately extinguished. Shame and anger washed over him. He recalled Grand Night, the conversation he had overheard. Sarah had been with him that very evening. How could she do this to Toby – to everyone? 'Jonathan, the girl has taken leave of her senses. She adores Toby. I'm sure there must be some explanation, some way of sorting this out.'

'From the way Toby was speaking, I don't think there's any way back. We may just have to accept it.'

There was a long pause before Sir Vivian spoke. 'I cannot find words at the moment, Jon. You must let me speak to Sarah.'

'As you wish, Vivian. As you wish. We are so sorry – about all of it.'

When the conversation had ended, Sir Vivian was in no mood for beer or crumpets. He rang Sarah's mobile, but it went straight to voicemail. He left a message asking her to ring him as a matter of urgency.

Sarah didn't pick up her father's message until the following morning, as she was leaving the offices of an insurance company in Lombard Street where she'd been for a job interview. A few days earlier she had made a tentative approach to her ex-boss, Hugo, and found his wrath had cooled to the point where he was prepared to write her a reference – albeit a fairly equivocal one. As he himself had said, if every person in the City who'd ever screwed up was never able to work again, most major financial institutions would be in a state of collapse. The interview had gone well; Sarah was one on a shortlist of three, and instinct told her she had it in the bag. With any luck, by New Year she would be back in work.

When she switched on her phone and heard the message from her father, she guessed that he had heard at last about her split with Toby. It had been a calculated decision not to tell him, to let him hear the news from the Kitterings. Since the tone of his message had been irate rather than sorrowful, she assumed he also knew that she was living with Leo. She stopped outside the entrance to Cannon Street station, about to call him back, when she thought better of it. She would go and see him instead.

Fifteen minutes later she emerged from Westminster tube station and made her way to her father's house near Smith Square. When he opened the door, Sir Vivian's expression was one of surprise, and then gloom.

'Come in,' he said, and she closed the door and followed him into the living room. He permitted a stiff exchange of kisses. 'What's this about you and Toby? And why was I the last to know?'

Sarah composed her features into an expression somewhere between sadness and anxiety. 'I'm sorry, Dad. I think it was because I knew how upset you'd be that I couldn't face telling you.'

'Upset about what? You breaking off with Toby, or the fact you've taken up with some other man? I simply do not understand you, Sarah. God knows, you were trouble enough when you were a teenager, but behaving like this at your age! You and Toby had everything ahead of you, and now you're throwing it all away. For what? Explain it to me, because I simply do not understand.' He sat down in an armchair, crossing his legs and staring at her with angry expectancy.

Sarah leant against the fireplace. 'I'm not sure what you want me to tell you. It sounds as though you know everything already. I was stupid. I did something idiotic. Toby found out. He's right not to forgive me.' Sarah allowed her eyes to brighten with incipient tears, then she looked away.

Sir Vivian looked uncomfortable, and his manner softened. 'I'm not sure that it's my place to say anything about your behaviour. You're a grown woman. I don't pretend to understand the morals of today's world.' He sighed. 'But if, as you say, it was simply a mistake, and no more, why on earth can't you and Toby patch things up?'

'It's not as simple as that. Things have gone too far.'

'So it's true about this man Davies – that you've been living with him for the past however many weeks?'

'Yes.'

'My God. Poor Toby.'

'Look, I don't know how to explain it. When Toby came back from his weekend away – the weekend it happened – I felt I had to tell him. He was so devastated, I couldn't stay in the flat. I had nowhere else to go, so . . . well, I was at a low ebb, and when Leo offered—'

'So it was his idea? Pah! He is clearly a disgusting creature. Another man's fiancé – unspeakably low behaviour.' Sir Vivian frowned in disgust. Sarah had undeniably behaved badly, but he couldn't help feeling that the real culprit in all this was the odious Davies.

'The blame lies with me,' said Sarah meekly, and in a manner intended subtly to suggest to her father the exact opposite, that she had in fact been the victim of a callous seduction.

'Hm. Yes and no,' replied Sir Vivian. Then he added, 'You have been foolish beyond belief. Moving into that man's house has merely compounded the problem. But I don't see that the damage is irreparable. You and Toby could still—'

'It's completely finished, Dad,' said Sarah quickly. 'There is absolutely no way we'll ever put it right. I won't be marrying Toby.'

There was a long silence. Sir Vivian sighed and said, 'Sarah, I can't hide from you the fact that all this makes me profoundly unhappy. Naturally I cherished the prospect of my daughter marrying the son of my oldest and dearest friend. I remember when you and Toby got engaged, thinking that it seemed to be too good to be true.' He rose from his armchair. 'I suppose there really is nothing left to say. Obviously it is impossible for you to speak to the Kitterings. I shall have to make what reparations I can.'

Sarah was inclined to observe that it was nothing to do with the bloody Kitterings, that it was between herself and Toby, but she restrained herself. She crossed the room and gave her father a gentle kiss. 'I'm sorry you're so disappointed, Dad.' He made a movement of impatience, refusing to look at her, and she added quietly, 'I'm pretty miserable myself, in case you hadn't realised.'

He nodded glumly. Sarah picked up her handbag and let herself out.

Sir Vivian sat back down in his armchair to mull over the whole wretched business. It seemed such a waste, all so unnecessary. Sarah and Toby had been admirably suited. Obviously Sarah must take her share of the blame, but clearly the influence of this odious man Davies lay at the heart of it. He was, if Colin Fryer and others were to be believed, a man of foul perversions. Bisexual, indeed. The world might nowadays smile on such people, but Sir Vivian believed such distorted lusts had to be evidence of deeper corruption. To think he had seen the man's name in the applications list for the High Court Bench, too. Well, even if he couldn't salvage the mess of Sarah and Toby's relationship, there were certainly other things he could attend to. He would make investigations.

Mission accomplished, thought Sarah, as she headed back to the station. Her father was angry and sorrowful, as expected, but at least she'd managed to deflect his wrath towards Leo, and that would burn itself out harmlessly over time. As for how things worked out between her father and the Kitterings – well, she really wasn't bothered. At least she'd escaped from the prospect of having Caroline Kittering for a mother-in-law. And an economics teacher for a husband.

She decided to put the conversation with her father to the back of her mind and concentrate on the rest of the day. The job interview had left her feeling pretty upbeat and in the mood for some retail therapy. It was almost eleven, so maybe she should get in a couple of hours of shopping, maybe rustle up a friend for lunch. Then in the afternoon she would buy some delicious food, and later on cook dinner for herself and Leo. She felt bad about the way things had been between them lately. Sarah had been convinced that Leo was having an affair with the girl she had seen leaving his house, and that he hadn't told her because he was hoping to have the best of both worlds. So, not prepared to let herself be played like that, she had kept a cool distance, and stayed out of his bed. Whatever he thought, Leo had said and done nothing to alter the situation. But the girl, whoever she was, seemed to have faded from the scene. Leo was home most evenings, working, reading, with no sign of any woman in his life. So perhaps she had been wrong. In which case she should start making up for lost time. They could spend the evening together and see where things went from there.

On the way to the station she rang and arranged a late lunch with a friend who worked in a firm of solicitors in Chancery Lane, then she took the tube one stop to Embankment and walked up to browse the shops around Covent Garden.

Leo and Gabrielle were snatching a hasty lunch at a restaurant in Holborn, just round the corner from the arbitration rooms where Leo was involved in a two-week hearing.

'I only ever see you for an hour here and there,' complained Gabrielle. 'It's hardly quality father-and-daughter time. In fact, that evening when I first came to your house is probably the longest we've ever spent together.'

'OK. So, what are you up to this weekend?'

Gabrielle thought of Anthony, and wondered if she should tell Leo she was seeing him. No, not till she got to the bottom of whatever strange relationship the two of them had. And it wasn't something she could see herself exploring right at this moment. 'Nothing in particular. Why?'

'Feel like spending it in Antibes with me?' He signalled for the bill.

She smiled. It sounded like an idea. 'What's in Antibes?'

'I'm in the process of buying a small property down there. A friend of mine had a yacht down there that he wanted to sell, and in a somewhat rash and inebriated moment, I bought it. I think I had the vague idea I could live on it, but it's not really practicable. Not at my age. So I decided I needed somewhere to stay as well. What started out as a minor indulgence seems to have snowballed into a major extravagance. I'm going down there first thing on Saturday to look at a couple of places I've earmarked. I think I know the apartment I want. It's in a building tucked away in a cobbled courtyard behind the main market street.' Gabrielle was delighted with the notion of helping Leo buy a house. 'Yeah, OK – I'm up for it.'

'Excellent.' He paid the bill and got up. 'In which case you're going to have to let me dash back to my laptop and try and book flights. Come on.'

It was half one when Sarah emerged from Nicole Farhi with the last of her purchases, a very sexily cut pair of blue trousers and a wrap-over dress. She'd spent far more than she'd intended, but was feeling very happy about it. She was strolling up Long Acre with bags on either arm, heading towards the wine bar in Holborn where she had arranged to meet her friend, when suddenly she saw Leo coming out of a restaurant not ten yards away. Sarah stepped into a shop doorway. He was with a girl – the same girl Sarah had seen coming out of his house on the night she had moved in. She watched as they stood talking on the pavement for a moment. Leo said something to the girl which made her laugh, then he lifted a strand of hair from her face and kissed her lightly on either cheek, and they parted, Leo turning and heading towards Kingsway.

The girl walked past Sarah, oblivious. Sarah had time to look at her properly, see how young and lovely she was. So there it was. She'd been right from the outset. He was obviously in a relationship with her, this girl who looked barely more than a teenager. No wonder he had left her alone, made no moves towards her. Well, at least she knew where she stood now. He was only letting her stay in his house out of kindness – making love to her the night that Toby was away had been a piece of opportunism. Naturally he had behaved as though there was no one in his life, because that was what he wanted her to think. The plans for a cosy dinner and a pleasant evening of sex suddenly looked like a dismal joke. It was as well there was a job on the horizon. The sooner she got away the better, to rid herself of the delusion that there could be anything lasting between herself and Leo.

On Saturday morning Leo and Gabrielle arrived in Nice a little before noon, and drove in a rented car to a hotel in Juan-Les-Pins, where Leo had booked rooms. Then they drove round Cap d'Antibes to the town and had a late lunch at a bistro before heading to the estate agent's office.

'I looked at a few places online,' Leo told Gabrielle, as they waited for the agent to fetch the keys, 'but this was the one that really caught my eye. I hope it's as good as its pictures.'

Gabrielle was flicking through one of the brochures. 'The

way you described it makes it sound a bit poky. Why don't you go for one of these apartments with a pool? Something a bit more modern and luxurious?'

'Because I like the old town. I want to feel a part of it when I come here, be able to step out and buy croissants first thing, watch the market come alive at weekends. Anyway, who needs a pool when you have a beautiful beach a couple of minutes away? Not a huge fan of chlorine, personally.'

The estate agent, a slim, self-important young man, appeared with the keys and escorted them on the short walk to the apartment, which was on the third floor of an old building overlooking the Cours Massena. The ground floor of the building was a café-patisserie, and the apartment entrance was at the back, in a narrow cobbled street, through high wooden gates leading into a charming courtyard dotted with pots and shrubs. A gnarled bougainvillea creeper, wintry and naked, shrouded the doorway to the building.

The agent led the way upstairs to the apartment, and showed them around with great aplomb. 'Vair light and airy. Vair unusual for the Old Town,' he told them, leading them through the empty rooms. 'Bedrooms are at the back, so all is quiet, *oui*? But the big living area through here has a balcony, quite *charmant*.' He unfastened and flung back the wooden shutters, then opened the long windows to a balcony, with a high, wrought-iron surround.

They stepped outside, and the estate agent gestured towards the castle, whose medieval ramparts were visible. 'That is where the Picasso Museum now is. Vair important tourist destination.'

Gabrielle leant on the iron railing and gazed down at the

busy street which sloped away to the harbour. She smiled and turned to Leo.

'It's absolutely amazing. I take it all back. Imagine sitting out here in summer, sipping pastis, watching the world go by.'

They went back into the living room, and at that moment clouds parted in the winter sky outside, and the parchment-coloured walls and scrubbed floorboards were suddenly washed with sunshine. Gabrielle gazed around.

'It's beautiful. Makes me want to go out and start buying things to furnish it.'

'I hoped that particular task might appeal to you.'

She laughed. 'Is that why you brought me down here? To do the place up?'

'Only partly. You also speak French very much better than I do. I thought we might get through the formalities faster if you were here. Seriously, I wanted to see what you thought of the place.'

'Well, I love it, and I don't mind helping out with red tape.'

They went back to the agent's office and completed a volume of paperwork. The agent seemed mildly discomfited to discover that Gabrielle spoke perfect French. It was half past three by the time the lease was signed, and the keys handed over. Leo and Gabrielle took a leisurely drive back along the coast, had cocktails in Juan, then ate dinner at Tetou. The next day they spent browsing furniture and antique shops, ordering beds, tables, chairs and sofas, and buying kitchen and bathroom equipment. At the end of the day they had dinner at the hotel and talked over the day's purchases.

'That was such fun,' said Gabrielle. 'Like furnishing a doll's house. And so lovely to be spending someone else's money.'

'I'll have to take a few days off in the New Year to come down and take delivery of the furniture. Which reminds me,' Leo fished in his pocket and pulled out a set of keys and handed them to Gabrielle, 'these are for you. I had them cut before we went out yesterday evening.'

'Keys to the apartment?'

Leo nodded. 'I can't see anyone else using it. I like to think I have a project to share with my daughter. Come down whenever you like, bring a girlfriend, enjoy Antibes and Juan in season. Sometimes I'll be here, sometimes I won't.'

She leant across and kissed his cheek. 'That is so amazing. Thank you.'

'I say girlfriend, but you're welcome to bring your boyfriend down, too, if you like.' Leo paused. 'You still haven't told me anything about him.'

Gabrielle knew that to hesitate or equivocate would be fatal. She said calmly, 'Actually, he's someone you know. I only found out recently.' She glanced down, stirring her coffee. 'He's in your chambers. Anthony Cross.'

As soon as she spoke his name, she could feel the tension crystallise. When she looked up, Leo's face was giving nothing away, though a muscle had tightened in one cheek. 'Really? You should have said something before.' His expression might be unreadable, but Gabrielle could detect an edge to his voice.

'I told you – I didn't know. We haven't being seeing one another very long.'

Leo nodded. He picked up his coffee and took a sip. 'Does he know about me?'

'What? That you're my father? Of course not.'

'I'd have thought it would be a point of interest.'

'To be honest, I haven't told anyone. No one knows, except my family. Not even my best friends.'

Leo nodded, saying nothing.

'What's wrong?' asked Gabrielle. She asked the question in apparent innocence, knowing full well what was wrong. Far from being appalled or disgusted at the knowledge, confirmed now by Leo's behaviour, that there was something going on between him and Anthony, she felt excited and curious. The knowledge gave her a strange sense of power over both of them. She tried to imagine, thinking of her own affair with Anthony and the hours spent in his bed, Leo enjoying the same pleasure.

'Nothing's wrong.' Leo gave a smile, but it didn't reach his eyes. 'When were you thinking of mentioning it to people? About my being your father?'

'I don't know. I probably won't, unless it comes up. I mean, it's hardly the kind of thing you go around telling people randomly, is it?'

Leo didn't know how to respond. He was stunned by the misfortune that, of all the people in the world, she should be seeing Anthony. Sleeping with him, too, no doubt – possibly even in love with him. Why was it his immediate instinct that the relationship should be destroyed? Was he jealous? Afraid? The lightning thoughts and impulses prompted by her revelation began to settle and rationalise. She was right to say that the information that Leo was her biological father was not something she was going to broadcast. She would only tell people who mattered to her. Thus, she was only likely to tell Anthony if the relationship developed into something serious. God alone knew what would happen then. It would be beyond anyone's control. If Anthony found out now – and it wouldn't be from Gabrielle, it seemed – his reaction would probably be to end the relationship. That would probably be for the best. She herself had said she hadn't been seeing him for very long.

He tried to relax his manner. 'Well, life is full of coincidences, I suppose. He's a lovely chap. Very bright.'

'He speaks very highly of you.'

Leo studied Gabrielle, wondering if there was something which he wasn't quite grasping. She was his daughter, after all, and devious behaviour was very probably in the genes. But he could read nothing in her expression, which was as sweet and open as ever. Best to let it go, while he worked out how to deal with the situation. He glanced at his watch.

'Probably a good idea to turn in. We've got an early flight tomorrow.'

They went to their separate rooms. Gabrielle lay in bed, thinking, wondering how and when she would ever be able to tell Anthony that Leo was her father. She wasn't sure, after this evening, that it was necessarily a good idea. But how, in all conscience, could she not?

CHAPTER SEVENTEEN

Every year, when Christmas came to 5 Caper Court, Felicity cast herself as the unofficial Mistress of Revels, and would go around chambers decked out in her flashing Santa Claus earrings, humming cheesy Christmas pop songs, and draping pieces of tinsel over everyone's PC. Her special pleasures were decorating the Christmas tree in reception, and arranging the food and drink for the chambers Christmas party, at which she would later get happily hammered.

But this year she didn't seem to have the heart for it. She couldn't even be bothered getting out the box of tinsel from the coat cupboard. The Christmas tree stood in reception as usual, tastefully decorated by a couple of the secretaries, but the clerks' room was sombre and bare. Everyone noticed, and everyone was privately dismayed – even the senior members of chambers, who every year pretended to shudder at Felicity's enthusiasm for sparkle and for singing 'I Wish it Could be Christmas Every Day' while doing the post.

'Not very festive round here,' remarked Jeremy Vane to Leo, as he fished his mail from his pigeonhole. 'Not even a Christmas card in sight.'

'Everyone sends electronic ones now.'

'I know. Ghastly.' He glanced at Leo. 'How was your weekend?'

'I spent it in the South of France.'

'Oh? Whereabouts?'

'Antibes, the old quarter. I bought a boat from Jamie Urquhart in the autumn, and realised I need a place to stay if I was going to be serious about sailing her, so I've rented an apartment down there.'

'Antibes – bit of a glitzy place, isn't it?'

'It can be. But I don't think I quite make the glitzy category. The apartment's tiny, and my yacht looks laughable compared to the enormous things on the international quay—' Leo broke off at the sound of raised voices on the other side of the room, and he and Jeremy turned to see Felicity shouting angrily at young Liam, who was looking aggrieved and upset, while Henry seemed to be doing his best to calm things down. Suddenly Felicity burst into tears and fled from the room.

Jeremy stared in astonishment. 'What on earth—?'

Leo crossed the room to find out what was going on.

'Angela Butler and Chris Tebbins from Hill Dickinson have turned up for a ten o'clock conference with Michael,' explained Henry. 'They're waiting in reception. But someone mistakenly put in Michael's diary that he was meant to be going to their offices. So they're here, and he's there.'

'And Felicity's saying it's my fault, when it's not,' put in Liam.

'Fuss about nothing,' muttered Jeremy, and departed with his mail.

Leo sighed. 'Well, it's hardly the biggest deal in the world. Liam, call Michael on his mobile and turn him around. Then get reception to apologise to the solicitors, tell them that Michael will be with them in ten minutes, and give them coffee.'

When Liam had gone, Leo turned to Henry. 'Is there more going on here that I should know about? Even if Felicity is responsible for the diary cock-up, it's hardly important enough to make her storm off in tears.'

'I don't know what's up with her lately, Mr D. Liam absolutely wasn't to blame, and she knows it. Last week she forgot to tell Roger Fry that a hearing date had been brought forward, and we had the solicitor ringing up from court in a state demanding to know why Roger wasn't there. Felicity tried to make out that was Liam's fault, too. We all make mistakes, but her putting the blame on young Liam – well, it isn't on. He feels like she's got it in for him, and it's shaking his confidence. He's shaping up very nicely, and I don't want to lose him.' Henry shook his head. 'But I'm worried for Felicity, too. She's not been herself lately. Not since that bloke of hers came out of prison. When I try to talk to her about it, she just clams up.'

Leo nodded. 'I think I'd better have a talk with her.'

Felicity had taken herself off to a sandwich bar in Fleet Street, and was sitting miserably in a corner with a cup of tea, hating herself. She knew that the cock-up with the solicitors from Hill Dicks was down to her. She shouldn't have blamed Liam. The fact was, she couldn't get her head straight these days. She'd let Vince walk in and take over her life. Every day was the same. Waking up hungover and depressed, despite the good resolutions of the day before. Feeling better by lunchtime, telling herself for the hundredth time that things were going to change. Making a series of resolutions – one, Vince would have to start taking responsibility for keeping the flat clean; two, Vince would have to make a bigger effort to find a job; three, Vince would do more shopping and cooking. Then getting home in the evening and being defeated by either the pigsty state of the place, or Vince's already half-sozzled cheerfulness, or by her own weariness, and forming resolution four – tell Vince to get out. Then postponing that difficult moment by knocking back a large vodka and tonic.

After which the evening would just slide away. Supper would be whatever was in the fridge, or a takeaway from Pizza Hut or McDonalds, with another stiff drink to take the edge off the fact that she was failing herself yet again, and then another, maybe a bit of whatever Vince had scored down the pub. Then bed, and sex she couldn't even remember in the morning.

Too much dope, too much booze, too little self-control and rapidly dwindling self-respect.

Felicity glanced up and saw Leo at the counter, buying a coffee. He came across and slid into the chair opposite her.

'I thought I might find you here.'

Felicity said nothing.

Leo sipped his coffee. 'Want to tell me what's up?'

She turned her gaze to the window, and the street beyond. Leo let a silence elapse, then he went on, 'Come on, we're old friends. Think of all the times I've told you things I wouldn't tell anyone else in chambers. Don't shut me out.'

Felicity's eyes grew suddenly bright with tears. 'Oh, Christ, don't be nice to me.'

'Is it to do with Vince? Henry mentioned something about him coming out of prison.'

She let her gaze meet Leo's, and nodded. 'He came out last month. I was never going to get back with him. Somehow it just happened. He's there in my flat. He's there right now. My little flat that used to be so nice, and he's turned it into a tip.' Felicity told Leo the whole story, how manipulated she felt, and how she couldn't seem to find the strength to alter the situation. 'He keeps saying he'll get a job, but he doesn't. If I have a go, he just laughs. It doesn't matter how angry I get, he thinks I don't mean it. It's like – like punching wet lettuce. Or like one of those dreams where you're trying to get somewhere, and it doesn't matter how hard you try, you're running on the spot, getting nowhere. I feel completely helpless, and it's all my fault, because I still fancy the hell out of him, and he knows it. Like he's got some sort of hold over me. I hate myself for being so weak.' She shook her head. 'You probably don't understand.'

'I understand all too well. I know what it's like when someone has that effect on you. Your life isn't your own. The only time you can think clearly is when you're away from them. Then you make all kinds of decisions, promises to yourself about how things are going to change. But as soon as you're with them again, your plans vanish into nothing. You might as well have never made them. And the knowledge that you keep failing yourself just compounds it, takes you lower and lower.'

Felicity nodded, her eyes fastened on Leo's face. 'That's

exactly how it is. And you know what? I never even wanted him back in the first place. Rachel was right. She told me to lay it on the line to him from the start, tell him he couldn't go making assumptions that things were just going to automatically go back to the way they were. But what did I do? I let him waltz right back in and plonk himself down. I must be the weakest person I know.'

'Do you love him?'

'No. That is, I do and I don't. I mean, I know he's no good for me, that in the long run he's just going to fuck up my life as well as his.' She glanced at Leo. 'It's got a name, that – hasn't it?'

'Codependancy, I think. Something like that.'

'Yeah? Well, he knows just how to play me, the buttons to press, my weak spots.'

'We've all got weak spots. But you really need to find some strength. You know this relationship is disastrous, and you need to sort it out. You have to ask yourself – how is this going to be in six months' time? Am I going to let this guy run my life, jeopardise my career . . .' Leo paused, catching the look on Felicity's face. 'You know it could happen. It's obvious your work is suffering because of your personal life. Nothing major, so far, but with the kind of work we do, mistakes can have huge repercussions.'

Felicity buried her face in her hands. 'I know.' After a moment she looked up. 'I feel like I'm in some kind of self-destructive nightmare. Like you said, I can decide here and now that he's got to go, but when I get home, it makes no difference. The same old shit, over and over.'

Leo drained his coffee cup. 'Then you need to take drastic action. Change the locks. Wait till he goes out, collect all his belongings and put them outside, and never let him back in.'

Felicity contemplated this unhappily. 'How would I work it? Even if I could get him out of the place long enough to change the locks, he'd come back and talk me round.'

'Only if you let him. That's where strength of will comes in, and I can't help you there.' Leo contemplated her despondent face. 'But as both a friend and an employer, I have to say – you can't go on like this. One, you're making yourself wretched, and two, you're in danger of doing yourself out of a job.' Leo knew this was a hard thing to say, but he also knew instinctively that Felicity needed something to stiffen her spine. Maybe fear would give her the gumption she needed to get rid of this waste of space of a boyfriend. He hoped so.

She gazed at Leo, stricken. 'You're telling me I need to sort myself out, or else.'

'I am.'

'OK.' She nodded. 'OK.'

Leo touched her hand gently. 'Good. See you back in chambers.'

Felicity worked throughout the afternoon in tight-lipped silence. Everyone tiptoed round her, sensing her mood. Henry shot her surreptitious glances now and again, wishing he knew what was going on in her head. At six o'clock, as he was about to leave, she was still tapping away at her keyboard. He went over.

'Fancy a quick one? I'm not meeting Cheryl till half seven.'

Felicity shook her head. 'Thanks, but I've got a lot to catch up on.' Then she stopped tapping and looked up. 'Going anywhere special?'

'Just a movie, then maybe a pizza.'

'That's nice.'

In the silence that followed, Felicity found herself wishing that she was going out for the evening with a normal bloke who had a job and who wasn't a loafer and a sponger, and Henry found himself guiltily wishing that he was going out with Felicity instead of Cheryl.

'OK,' said Henry abruptly, hating himself for his disloyalty, 'I'll see you in the morning. Don't work too hard.'

Felicity worked for another hour, then went home. She sat on the bus, staring out of the window. Perhaps she should try and make Vince hate and despise her, so he would want to leave. But she didn't know how to make him hate her. She would have to hate him first, and she didn't. She didn't hate anyone except herself. Leo was right. She couldn't let this crap set-up lurch on any more. Tonight she would spell it out to Vince. Then she remembered the other times she'd spelt it out, and how nothing had changed, and felt her resolve waver.

When she got in, Vince was sitting with his feet up, drink in hand, watching television.

'You're late,' he remarked.

'Some of us have to work,' replied Felicity. She hung up her coat, and sniffed. 'What's that smell?'

'Supper,' replied Vince. 'Thai green curry. I picked up some chicken breast and a jar of stuff from the supermarket. Found some boil-in-the-bag rice in the cupboard.' He swung his feet off the table, stood up and went to the kitchen, returning with an overfull glass of wine. 'Here. Sit down and put your feet up.'

Felicity's heart sank. This happened every so often. Vince

would realise he'd been pushing his luck, trespassing too far on her goodwill, and so he would go through a pretence of making amends, of cooking supper and giving assurances of looking for work. Meaningless gestures which, she now knew, went nowhere. She stared into her wine, took a large swallow. 'Vince?'

'Uh-huh?'

'I know why you're doing this.'

He dropped a kiss on her head and sat down next to her. 'Because I love you, babes.'

'Because you know how fed up I am of all this, and you're trying to butter me up.'

'Hey—'

'No "hey" about it. You think you can play me like a piano, don't you? Here's me working my arse off every day to pay the bills, while you spend your jobseeker's allowance down the pub like it's pocket money. And every time you see me getting fed up with the whole malarkey, you think all you have to do is tidy up a bit, buy a bottle of wine, open a jar of cook-in sauce, promise to look for a job, and it'll all be fine. 'Cause you've got everything you want, haven't you? A roof over your head, a bed, telly, food in the fridge – naturally you want to make sure you don't lose it.'

He seemed genuinely wounded. 'Fuck me. Is that what you think?'

Felicity drained her glass of wine. 'Roughly, yeah.' She stood up and stalked to the kitchen to pour herself another. She had never been so forthright before. This could be his cue to go off on one, to start throwing things around and shouting. On one level she hoped he would. An out-and-out stormer of a row might provide a good excuse to chuck him out. She took another swig of her fresh glass of wine to set her up, and returned to the living room. What she saw was not what she had expected. Vince was sitting on the edge of the sofa, hands clasped over his bent head, crying softly. Immediately she sat down next to him, stroking his shoulder, filled with anxious remorse for what she'd just said, forgetting the entire truth of it. Felicity couldn't bear to see anyone cry, especially a big, strong bloke.

His voice sounded broken. 'You don't know what it's like, Fliss. Prison wrecks you. It shatters your confidence.' He wiped his tears away with the back of his hand. 'I know it looks to you like I'm just some kind of sponger, and it kills me that you think that. I'm doing my level best to get work, straight up. Thing is, it's going to take time to get my self-esteem back to where it needs to be.' He turned to look at her. 'How bad do you think I feel about not bringing anything in? Tonight was just my way of trying to do something right. You're the only thing holding me together. If it wasn't for you, I wouldn't even care what happens to me . . .'

It was when he turned to look at her that she realised how fake it was. She could see it in his eyes. She let his plausible words, all the bogus self-justification and whining protestations wash over her. She felt unutterably weary. *Enough*, she told herself. *Enough*.

She let him finish talking, then stroked his arm. 'Forget what I said. Let's eat supper. I'm hungry.' She got up and went to the kitchen. She picked up her glass of wine and emptied it into the sink, got the rice out of the cupboard and put plates to warm in the oven. Behind her she could hear Vince, cheerful now that he was off the hook, rabbiting on about things Ossie and Quills had done and said, examining the navel fluff of his empty, useless day.

He came through and picked up the bottle of wine to refill Felicity's glass.

'It's OK,' said Felicity. 'I don't fancy any more to drink tonight.'

'That's not like you. Hey, you're not . . . ?' Vince grinned, raised his eyebrows.

'No,' said Felicity. 'I'm not.' She stared at him for a moment. That he could even think that would be a good thing, a reason to smile – it put the lid on everything, finally, once and for all.

As they ate Vince's Thai green curry, Felicity asked casually, 'You done any Christmas shopping?'

'What kind of a question's that? You know I'm skint.'

'Just you need to get your mum something nice. She'll be expecting it.'

Vince nodded. 'She's asked us round there Christmas Day.'

'Lovely.' If there was one place Felicity did not intend to be on Christmas Day, it was Denise's house. She added, 'Tell you what, I get paid Friday. Why don't I give you a bit of a loan and you can go and do some shopping up Westfield? Get your mum a handbag or something.'

Vince mused. 'Yeah, all right.' He finished his curry, then added, 'I'll pay you back. When I get fixed up, I mean. I reckon I'll find a job in the New Year.'

'Yeah.'

He leant across and kissed her, then sat back replete and comfortable. 'I did the cooking, your turn to clear up.'

Felicity's face was inscrutable as she cleared the plates

away. When she came back, Vince was skinning up a large spliff. She watched for a few seconds, thinking about the amount of money he must spend every week on dope.

He lit up, took a long drag, then handed it to Felicity. She shook her head. She badly wanted to feel the curling warmth of the skunk slowing her mind, letting her cares leach away, till nothing mattered. But she knew if she was going to see this through, she had to detach herself, stay hard-hearted and clear-headed.

They lounged on the sofa together, watching television. Vince smoked the spliff down to the end, then got up and poured himself a large vodka. 'Sure you don't want one?' he asked. She shook her head, eyes fastened on the TV. Normally by this time they would have smoked a joint together, and would be starting to neck more booze, and she would be curled up lazily, hazily in his arms. A little bit of her ached for that. She got up and went to wash the dishes. Then she sorted out a neglected basket of clean washing, and did some ironing in the bedroom, listening to Capital FM.

She went to bed early and read for a while. It was a long time since she'd done any reading. Before Vince had moved in she'd been getting through a book a week. She became so engrossed that she was still reading when Vince came through, pulling off his T-shirt, scratching his chest and yawning. 'Thought I'd join you for an early night.' He sat down on the edge of the bed and plucked the book from her hands, then leant in to kiss her, his hands sliding beneath her pyjama top to caress her breasts.

Felicity pulled away. 'Not tonight. I'm not in the mood.'

'Not tonight, Josephine,' murmured Vince, and wandered

to the bathroom. Felicity picked up her book and carried on reading, her nipples tingling from his touch.

Once in bed, he tried again, but Felicity elbowed him away gently, and carried on reading. Vince lay back, blinked, yawned, tried to talk a bit, but the dope and the booze got the better of him and he fell asleep in minutes.

When she heard the regularity of his breathing, Felicity switched the light off and lay in the darkness, thinking ahead. She had no idea how the next week was going to play out, but she was determined that by the end of it, Vince was going to be out of her life and her bed for good. Her stomach lurched with fear. What if she couldn't do this? Then she thought of what Leo had said. He was one of the few people in the world whose opinion she really cared for. She wasn't going to let him down, or herself.

Felicity had booked the locksmith for eleven, but the way things were going, she was beginning to wonder if she wouldn't have to call him off. She hadn't even given any thought to what would happen if Vince didn't go out. How could she have the locks changed right in front of him? Picture the scene. It simply wasn't going to happen.

Vince was wandering round the flat, hungover from the night before. Felicity made him coffee and a bacon sandwich.

'Nice day for Christmas shopping,' she said brightly, glancing at the clear sky.

Vince lolled back on the sofa, feet on the coffee table. 'Not sure I fancy it.' He took a bite of his bacon sandwich, then made a face. 'I've told you I don't like it when you don't cut the fat off. My mum always cuts it off. I don't like bits of stringy fat.' He pulled a piece from his mouth and set it on the side of the plate, then wiped his fingers on the side of his boxers and took a swig of coffee.

'Up to you,' said Felicity casually. 'But it's your last chance. You know what your mum'll be like if you don't get her something, specially if we have to be round hers Christmas Day.' The little piling up of deceits was not pleasant, but she had to get him out of the house. She thought about everything Leo said. She had to do this to save her own life. 'Go on – get it out of the way, then you can meet up with Ossie and Quills and watch the football round The Kempton. I'll pop down later.'

'Yeah, maybe. I'll see.'

Felicity was worried that she'd said too much, been too pushy. Vince didn't react well to pushy. She picked up his empty plate. 'Anyway, there's fifty on the side in the kitchen. You can pay me back later.' Leaving the money out for him, avoiding the business of directly handing it over, was part of the game. She glanced at her watch. Ten past ten.

Vince drained his mug of coffee, got up, stretched, and scratched himself under his T-shirt. 'I'm off for a shower.'

She listened to the water splashing in the bathroom, counting the minutes.

Vince emerged, showered and dressed, at twenty to eleven. Felicity was sitting making up a to-do list. She glanced up. 'You off?'

'I don't fancy shopping on my own. You come too. You know the kind of thing Denise'll like.'

'Vince, I've got a million things I need to do. Working all week, the chores really pile up.'

He gazed moodily around, then dropped onto the sofa

and picked up yesterday's *Standard*. He flipped through it for a few minutes, while Felicity pretended to concentrate on her list. Then he got up and sauntered into the kitchen. She knew he was pocketing the fifty. How much of that would go on a present for Denise, and how much of it down the boozer?

'Right, I'm off,' said Vince. 'I'll see you later down the pub?'

'Yeah, most likely,' said Felicity. She looked up and smiled. 'Bye, Vince.'

An hour later, the locksmith had been and gone, and Felicity had two bright new sets of keys.

She found some black bin liners in the kitchen cupboard and went round the house, stuffing in Vince's possessions. They were pitifully few. She paused in the act of folding up one of his shirts. He was thirty-three, with almost nothing to show for his life. If she discarded him, he would probably go from bad to worse. When Vince said she was all he had, it was just about true. She stared at the shirt for a few seconds, then thrust it into the bag, followed by his electric razor and toiletries.

When she had finished, she rang her friend Maureen.

'Mo? It's me. I need a favour. I need to come and stay with you tonight, if that's OK. Just this one night.' She explained about Vince, about changing the locks, about not wanting to be here when he came back and found out she'd kicked him out.

'About time, girl,' said Maureen. 'Well done. I never liked to say it, but he is such a loser.'

'You don't have to tell me. I've known a long time. Too long.'

Twenty minutes later Felicity's car pulled up outside Denise's semi. She walked up the path and rang the bell.

It took Denise so long to come to the door that Felicity began to think perhaps she was out. Maybe she could leave Vince's belongings up the side path near the bins, and pop a note through the letter box, scuttle away without confrontation. But eventually she heard the rattle of the chain being taken off. The door cracked open a few inches and Denise peered out. She had obviously just woken up. With her frowsed dark-orange hair and smudged eyeliner she looked strangely like Vivienne Westwood.

'Hello, Fliss, darlin'!' The enthusiasm was forced, but she opened the door wide to let Felicity in, clutching closed the front of her peach sateen kimono. Felicity stepped inside, bringing the bin bag with her.

'What's that?' asked Denise.

'Some stuff of Vince's.'

Denise nodded, not comprehending. 'I'll put the kettle on.' She headed for the kitchen, and Felicity followed.

'You caught me on the hop,' said Denise, filling the kettle, then reaching for cigarettes and a lighter lying on the worktop. She gave a throaty laugh. 'Or rather, off it. I was out on the piss with Shelley and Rhona last night.' She pulled out a fag, snapped the lighter, and took a deep drag. 'Getting too old for this caper. But we had a laugh.' Her gaze wandered for a few seconds, then returned to Felicity. 'So – what brings you round here on a Saturday?'

'Like I said, I've brought Vince's things.' She set the bag against the leg of the kitchen table. 'I can't have him living with me any more.'

Denise's eyes widened. 'What you on about?'

'I've told him a million times – things aren't working out between us. We're bad for one another. I need him to leave. But he won't listen. So I had the locks changed this morning, while he's out. I didn't know what else to do. And I've brought you his things.'

Denise set her cigarette carefully to one side, its tip clear of the work surface. Then she grasped Felicity's forearms gently and looked intently into her face. 'Fliss, don't do this. You're the best thing that ever happened to him. He needs you.'

'Well, I don't need him,' replied Felicity stonily. 'And he's about the worst thing that ever happened to me. Not that he's a bad person. But I can't carry him. He's lazy, he's a sponger, and I don't want him any more.' Denise let go of Felicity. Her expression was stunned, pained. 'I don't mean to hurt you, Denise. But this is . . . this is non-negotiable.'

Denise raked a hand through her hair. 'What makes you think I want him here?'

'I don't, necessarily. But I couldn't think of anywhere else to bring his stuff.' She sighed. 'No point in tea. I'd best be off.' She turned and went down the hall. Denise padded behind her.

'He's not going to let it end here, you know,' said Denise, when they reached the front door.

'It's not up to him. Vince has got to sort his life out without me.' She leant forward and gave Denise a peck on the cheek. 'Good luck.'

'Thanks,' replied Denise. She sounded weary. Felicity left and drove home, astonished at how accepting Denise had been. But then, she was Vince's mother. She knew better than anyone what Felicity had been putting up with.

* * *

Vince went to the local market and did some desultory shopping with Felicity's money, dropped in at the bookies, and then went to the pub, where he spent the afternoon watching the football and drinking with his mates. It wasn't until seven o'clock that he began to wonder where Felicity was. He rang her mobile a few times, but got no answer. He and his friends decided to move from the Kempton Arms to another pub for more drinks, and from there to a club in Brixton, and although Vince tried ringing Felicity a couple of times throughout the evening, he wasn't especially bothered when she didn't answer. He tried his luck in the club with a redhead called Candice but, being pretty drunk by this stage, didn't get far. He left the club with Ossie and Quills, and they went to buy kebabs. Vince suggested going back to Felicity's place for a few more drinks and some dope. Felicity, he assured them, would be cool about it.

Fifteen minutes later, Vince was battling boozily with the lock. Eventually he gave up and started banging on the door. When that produced no result, he tried the keys again. After more struggling and swearing, Ossie took over.

'They don't work, mate,' he concluded. 'They don't fit. You sure they're the right keys?'

'Course they're the right keys. They're the only ones I've got.'

'This the right door?' ventured Quills.

'Course it's the right fucking door!' Vince began to beat on it again.

'I reckon she changed the locks, mate,' said Quills.

'Happens,' agreed Ossie.

Vince stared at them for a moment, then started banging on the door again, shouting Felicity's name.

A man in a vest and boxers emerged from a flat down the corridor.

'You lot gonna stop that effing noise? I've got a baby in here.'

'Fuck off!' Vince began kicking the door.

Felicity's neighbour stormed down the corridor. He was enormous and beefy, and sufficiently enraged not to feel intimidated by three drunks. 'Right,' he said.

The next few minutes were mayhem. Two other male neighbours woken by the row came down from the floor above. Vince and his friends were too drunk to put up a proper fight, and after much barging, tussling and a few erratically thrown punches, they were forcefully ejected from the building.

Out on the pavement they swayed and swore for a while, then eventually wandered off into the night.

On the landing by Felicity's front door lay a carrier bag containing the Christmas presents Vince had bought in the market, and the remains of a half-eaten kebab.

CHAPTER EIGHTEEN

On Christmas Day, Sarah came downstairs at eleven o'clock to find Leo wrapping Oliver's Christmas present on the kitchen table.

'Merry Christmas,' said Leo. 'Coffee's on.'

'Thanks. Merry Christmas to you, too.' She poured herself some coffee. 'You want a cup?'

Leo shook his head. 'I'm meant to be at Rachel's in half an hour. Oliver's putting off opening his presents till I get there.'

'What have you got for him?'

'A Playmobil fire station. Rachel's got him the fire engine. The trouble is, the box is so big that it's not easy to wrap,' said Leo, wrestling with the roll of paper.

'Cut another piece. Here . . .' Sarah took the scissors and deftly cut another piece from the roll and wrapped it round the end of the box. 'Pass me the Sellotape. There. And the other end. See?'

'I'm not much of a hand at wrapping things. Lack of practice.'

'That's the first time I've ever heard you admit that there's something you're not good at.'

'How are you spending the day?' asked Leo, suddenly wondering if she was going to be there all on her own.

'I intend to do nothing for the next few hours, beyond soaking in a long, hot bath and contemplating my future. I had rather a heavy night . . .'

'So I gather, given that it was well past three when I heard you come in.'

'Sweet. You sound like my father,' smiled Sarah. 'With whom I happen to be spending the rest of the day. I'm helping him cook Christmas dinner for some of his friends. Just hope they're not all fossils. Are you going to be at Rachel's all day?'

'Till six or so. Some people in Kensington have invited me for drinks, but it's only a loose arrangement.' Gabrielle had been insistent that he should meet the rest of her family, but he was still in two minds about going. 'If I do go, I won't hang about for long.'

Sarah poured herself a cup of coffee. 'Right. Well, have a lovely day. I'm off for a bath. Oh, something I've been meaning to tell you, but I haven't seen you since Thursday – I've got a new job.'

'Really? Where?'

'London and International Insurance Brokers Association. On the legal side.'

Leo paused in the doorway. 'Well done.' He wondered if this was the moment to say something about the way things had been over the past few weeks, to explain that he understood, and that he was there if she wanted him – in whatever way. It seemed sad that their relationship had reached this odd stalemate. 'So . . .'

'So I'll be out of your hair in a couple of weeks.'

'Right.' He paused. 'Well, congratulations.' Then he added, 'By the way, there's something for you under the Christmas tree.'

Sarah raised an eyebrow, trying not to look pleased. 'So Santa's been?' She smiled. 'I left your present there, too.'

'So I saw. I intend to open it later.'

'OK – see you whenever.'

When Leo had gone, Sarah wandered into the living room. She crouched down under the tree – a tree which had been bought largely for the satisfaction of Oliver, for whom Christmas, and everything pertaining to it, was sacred. Her present to Leo and his to her were the only ones there. Sarah knelt there for a moment, staring at the two gifts, thinking how empty their lives were in some ways, hers and Leo's. Neither of them had ever known anything else, she supposed. No siblings, few relatives, or not enough that cared, friends whose loyalties did not extend to the intimacies of gifts. It would have been different with Toby. She pictured how it would be at the Kitterings house in Surrey, and closed her eyes. No doubt they were all happy together, relieved at Toby's lucky escape, reassured in the knowledge that she really hadn't been good enough for their precious, golden boy. She wondered if she'd ever be good enough for anyone. She opened her eyes, and picked up the present from Leo and unwrapped it. Inside was a Tiffany box. She untied the white ribbon. Inside the box was a little blue suede pouch. She untied the pouch and drew out a delicate chain necklace studded with three tiny diamonds. She held it up to the light, letting it slide through her fingers. Enough to make a girl think she was good enough for someone, after all. But the fact was that Leo was seeing someone else, and he wasn't even brave enough – or kind enough – to tell her. Even the nicest present couldn't change that.

The toy fire station and fire engine went down well with Oliver. Apart from his stocking presents, Christmas sweets, and some books, the only other presents he received were a remote control car from Leo's mother in Wales, and a Harry Potter Lego Knightbus from his godparents. Leo and Rachel had always agreed not to spoil him by buying him too many toys and games.

'You wouldn't believe what some of his school friends are getting for Christmas,' said Rachel, as they watched Oliver carefully steering the fire engine into the fire station and reversing it out again. 'I've talked to other mothers. Playstations, laptops – Gabriel Sutton's parents have bought him a quad bike.'

'Too much stuff is not what they need. Not at his age, not at any age. When I think back to Christmases in Wales back in the sixties . . .'

'Yes, we all know,' murmured Rachel, smiling. 'You were lucky if you got an orange and a pack of coloured pencils. Amazing you weren't sent down the mines as well.'

Leo raised an eyebrow. 'That was touch and go too, in the long run. Thank God for Llanryn Grammar. If there's one thing I don't mind spending money on, it's Oliver's education.' Leo reached into the inside pocket of his jacket hanging on the back of the chair and took out a small, pale-blue box tied with white ribbon. He handed it to Rachel. 'I almost forgot. Merry Christmas.'

Rachel took the gift doubtfully. 'We haven't exchanged presents since . . .' She unwrapped it and stopped, gazing at the box. 'I wish you'd said. I haven't got you anything.'

Leo shrugged. 'So? Open it.'

Rachel unfastened the white ribbon, and from the little suede bag that nestled inside she drew a chain necklace, studded with three tiny diamonds. She held it up, smiling. 'It's beautiful, Leo. Far too extravagant. In fact, I'm not sure it's—'

'For God's sake don't use that ghastly word, "appropriate". I can buy the mother of my son whatever I like for Christmas.'

Rachel slipped the thin chain round her neck and fastened the clasp.

'Thank you.' She gave him a swift kiss on one cheek. 'It's beautiful.'

Leo shrugged and smiled. 'Nothing special.'

Anthony spent Christmas Day at his mother's house. In the years since his commercial success, Chay Cross had tried to be generous to his ex-wife, but Judith had never wanted or accepted from him any more than she felt was just repayment for the handouts and support she had provided throughout Chay's impoverished hippy years. She still worked as a primary school teacher, and still lived in the same terraced house in East Dulwich in which, as a struggling single mother, she had brought up their two sons. Today she had cooked Christmas lunch for Anthony, Barry, her cousin Cora, Cora's ninety-two-year-old father Sidney, and Yvonne, a fellow teacher.

Anthony had found the day tedious, and the atmosphere round the table in the cramped dining room claustrophobic. Cora managed to suppress everyone's appetite by dominating the early part of the lunchtime conversation with a detailed account of her father's bowel problems and his countless hospital visits. Then when the conversation shifted to more general topics, an initially mild disagreement between Yvonne and Cora on the subject of state versus independent education threatened to escalate, as a result of too much wine, into an unpleasantly acerbic row. But Judith managed to divert talk to the recession, and to the recent shock closure of Woolworths just three weeks earlier, so that the prickly mood was dispelled and everyone was unified by a general agreement that the country was in a shocking state and that it was hard to see where it would all end. Barry's contribution throughout all this consisted of cynical remarks and off-colour jokes which everyone tried to ignore, but which Anthony found extremely tiresome. By the time six o'clock came Anthony was very glad of an excuse to leave.

'I thought you'd be staying for a game of Pictionary and some turkey sandwiches,' said Judith sadly, as they stood together in the kitchen, putting away the last of the glasses. 'It's one of the few times in the year I get to see anything of you.'

'Sorry, Mum,' said Anthony. 'I promised my girlfriend I'd see her this evening.' He felt entirely guilt-free, having cleared away the dishes with Barry, loaded the dishwasher, and washed every pan in sight.

Barry sauntered in. 'You doing a runner? Think I might join you.'

Judith looked even more pained. 'Why can't you stay a little longer? Catch up with great-uncle Sidney – he loves a chat.'

'Mum, I can't safely get within two feet of great-uncle Sidney. If farting was an Olympic event, he'd be bagging gold for Britain.'

'Well, he's had his problems. Cora told you at lunch.'

'Yeah, how delightful was that?' Barry opened the fridge. 'You won't be wanting these lagers, will you? Mind if I take them?'

'Go ahead,' sighed Judith. 'Are you two seeing anything of your dad over the holidays?'

'I haven't heard from him,' said Barry.

'He said he was coming over, that he'd be in touch. Must have changed his mind.'

'Oh, well . . .' Judith folded a tea towel. 'Thanks for coming – and for the lovely presents.'

'No problem, Mum. Lunch was great.' Barry gave his mother a kiss.

'Yes, thanks, Mum. Sorry I have to go so early. It's just I told Gabrielle—'

'Don't worry. You get off. Don't forget to say bye-bye to Cora and Sidney.'

Out in the cold of the quiet street, Barry asked Anthony, 'What did you get Mum?'

'A voucher for a day at some spa in the West End. It's the kind of thing she'd never buy for herself. What about you?'

'Egg timer. She said she needed a new one.' He caught Anthony's look. 'What? I just don't happen to be loaded like you.'

The remark gave Anthony a momentary pang. He'd recently been shocked to discover how little was left in his current account, the day after he'd spent eight hundred pounds on a bracelet for Gabrielle. That was the trouble with splashing out hundreds – even the odd thousand – at casinos. You got used to dealing in big figures, even when it came to things like Christmas presents for your girlfriend. Still, there were quite a few outstanding fees that he would get Henry to chase up in the New Year, and a couple of decent wins at the tables could easily set things to rights, if his luck would just turn. Which it had to. No need to worry.

'Need a lift?' asked Anthony.

'Depends where you're going.'

'South Ken.'

Barry shook his head. 'It's OK. I'm heading to Deptford to see some mates. I'll catch a bus.' They paused on the street corner. 'By the way, I'm compering a gig at a club in Greenwich at New Year, if you fancy coming along. Bring your girlfriend.'

'Yeah, could be fun. Email me.'

Anthony left Barry to wait for his bus and headed to where his car was parked. It was a BMW Z4, and he had bought it just three weeks ago, when he was still flush with the giddy sensation of having banked a hundred and ten thousand pounds from one single case. Its purchase had given him immense pleasure at the time. Now, as he pressed the remote through his coat pocket and heard the expensive slitch of the central system unlocking, he felt a faint sickness at the thought of having spent so much on a car. *It's not like you're Leo*, he told himself. But Leo was who he so badly wanted to be. Successful, in demand, work flooding in, plenty of spare cash to spend on the good things in life. He wanted to feel that everything was fine, that he was entitled to be behaving as he was.

He stopped by the car and drew in a long, deep breath of frosty air, wishing that he could just drive to Oxfordshire, to Leo's house, and find him there with a welcoming glass of whisky, ready to listen to it all and understand and help him. But in the place he was, he felt he couldn't reach out to anyone. He opened the car, its interior fragrant with the faintly sickly smell of new leather, and drove through the quiet streets to meet Gabrielle's parents.

It was almost half five. Leo and Oliver had spent the last half-hour on the rug in front of the fire building a football stadium out of Lego. Rachel came into the living room carrying a tray with mugs of coffee for herself and Leo, and a glass of juice for Oliver.

Leo got up, and Oliver rolled over onto his back. 'Mummy, can I eat my Smarties and watch my *Wall-E* DVD now?'

'OK. You know where it is?'

Oliver nodded, fetched his DVD and put it on, then sat down cross-legged on the rug with a giant tube of Smarties from his Christmas stocking. Rachel curled up in a corner of the sofa and Leo sat down next to her. 'What's Wally?'

'*Wall-E*,' corrected Rachel. 'It's a film about a robot. It's really pretty good. You should watch it.' She sipped her coffee and added, 'You don't have to go, you know. You could always stay and meet Simon.'

Oliver had started to talk about Simon over lunch. Later, during a walk in the park, while Oliver was busy cracking ice at the pond's edge, Rachel had filled in the details.

Leo grimaced. 'I'm not sure that's a good idea.'

'Why not? You have to meet him sometime.'

'Do I? Is it that serious?'

Rachel hesitated. 'Possibly. I don't know.'

She had coloured faintly, not meeting his eye, and Leo could tell all he needed to know simply from her manner. He wasn't sure quite how he felt. He only knew that he didn't want to be reminded twice in one evening of his status as the outsider. He would be meeting Gabrielle's parents later, and having it brought home to him how much he had missed – lost – in the twenty-two years of not knowing about her was going to be bad enough. Making small talk with Rachel's new boyfriend, of whom Oliver appeared to think so highly, was not something he felt up to.

'Anyway, I have to be somewhere.'

'So you said. Who are you meeting?'

Leo knew she assumed he was seeing some lover – man or woman. He glanced at Oliver, making sure he was absorbed in his film. He needed to tell someone about Gabrielle. Rachel seemed like the ideal person.

'It's someone I met three months ago.'

Rachel gave a wry smile, twisting her coffee mug in her hands.

'It's not what you think. I need you to listen. Please. This is something I haven't told anyone else. Three months ago this girl, she walked out of nowhere one night as I was getting out of my car, and told me she was my daughter.'

'What?' Rachel stared at him.

'I have a daughter. From an affair I had with a French girl twenty-two years ago. It was just a brief thing. When we split up I had no idea she was pregnant. I don't think she did either. Anyway, her name's Gabrielle – my daughter, that is. So Oliver has a half-sister.'

'Are you convinced it's true? That she is who she says she is?'

'Oh yes. We've talked. I met Jacqueline – her mother – just a week ago.' For the next twenty minutes Leo told Rachel the whole story, describing Gabrielle, trying to explain his feelings, the extraordinary, momentous effect of the arrival of this unknown child in his life. Rachel listened, asking occasional questions.

When he'd finished, Rachel shook her head. 'How extraordinary.'

'I want you and Oliver to meet her. You'd like her.'

'So that's where you're going now?'

Leo drained his coffee mug. 'Gabrielle says she wants me to get to know her father and her brothers. I'm not sure.'

'About what?'

'About being the spectator, looking in on other people's happy lives. Realising what I could have had, if I wasn't so . . .' He rubbed his chin. 'So selfish. Self-absorbed. I suspect it's rather the reason I don't want to meet Simon.'

Rachel looked down at her half-drunk coffee. 'You needn't feel that way. About Simon, I mean.' There was a long silence. Leo waited, half-expecting what she would say. 'If being part of our lives, Oliver's and mine, is really what you want, that can still happen. Properly. The way it was.'

Her eyes met his. 'The way it was?' He reached out a hand and lifted the diamond studded chain that hung at her neck, lightly touching with his thumb the pulse that beat in her slender throat. The sound of Oliver's cartoon rose in the room and filled the silence between them. 'I am part of your lives. Anything more than this wouldn't work. We've been there once before. And I'd only disappoint you again. I know it. You know it.'

She let her gaze drop, and Leo took his hand away. Suddenly the doorbell rang.

'That's Simon,' said Rachel.

As she got up to answer the door, Leo joined Oliver on the rug and paused the DVD. 'Daddy has to go, I'm afraid.' Oliver wormed his way onto Leo's knee and put his arms round his father's neck, still clutching his tube of Smarties. He had chocolate around his mouth.

'Have you had a nice Christmas?' asked Leo.

Oliver nodded. 'Would you like one of my Smarties?'

'Thanks. Can I have an orange one?'

Oliver inserted a finger into the tube and prised out an orange Smartie. He watched Leo put it in his mouth. 'Have you had a nice Christmas too, Daddy?'

'Yes, I have. Very.'

'Did you like the calendar I made you?'

'It's my favourite present. I'm going to put it on my desk at work.'

Oliver nodded, gratified. 'My fire station is brilliant.'

'Good. I'm glad you like it. You know you're coming to spend a whole week with me next weekend?'

'Yeah, I know.' His soft smile filled his face, made his eyes glow, and touched Leo to the core of his being. Oliver glanced round as Rachel came into the room with a young man.

'Simon!' Oliver scrambled to his feet and went to hug Simon.

'Hi, mate. Merry Christmas.' He hugged Oliver and handed him a present. 'For you.'

Oliver tore the paper open. 'Geomag! Wow! That's genius!'

'Say thank you,' said Rachel.

'Thank you.'

Simon laughed. 'Glad you like it.'

While this had been going on, Leo had quietly fetched

his coat, and was fishing for his car keys. He and Simon glanced at one another.

'Leo, this is Simon – Simon, Leo.'

They shook hands awkwardly. 'I was just leaving,' said Leo.

'Simon,' said Rachel, 'why don't you help yourself to a drink? There's some wine in the fridge.'

Simon dutifully headed to the kitchen, leaving Leo to say goodbye to Rachel and Oliver.

'Seems a nice enough young man,' said Leo.

'Not so very young. He's thirty-six.'

'I guess it all depends on your vantage point.' Leo smiled, and bent to scoop up Oliver and kiss him. 'Be good for Mummy. I'll pick you up next Friday evening. And I'll be speaking to you on the phone before then.'

'OK, Daddy.' Leo set him down, and he headed back to his DVD and his Smarties.

Leo turned to Rachel. 'Thanks for today.'

'It was fun. Oliver likes us all being together.' She smiled. 'So do I.'

Leo kissed her face lightly, and opened the door to step out into the chilly evening air. He turned. 'Speak to you in the week. Merry Christmas.'

'Merry Christmas.'

If only she would let go, thought Leo, as he opened the car door. Then someone like Simon might stand more of a chance. He got in and turned the key in the ignition, letting the engine run for a moment, wishing he didn't have to go to South Kensington. He really wasn't in the mood for meeting Jacqueline's family, for coping with a situation where small talk and the usual rules of social engagement were bound not to suffice, given the weirdness of the situation, making things even more awkward. Gabrielle was enough for him. He had no need of the rest. But Gabrielle and Jacqueline seemed to want to knit him into the family fabric.

He sighed and leant back against the headrest. His phone buzzed and he pulled it from his pocket. Jamie's name appeared on the screen, and he answered.

'Jamie?'

'I'm sorry, Leo, I shouldn't be calling you on Christmas Day.'

'That's OK. I've just left Rachel's. What's up?'

Jamie made a sound halfway between a groan and a sob. 'I don't know. Christ, I just needed to talk to someone.'

'Hey, it's fine,' said Leo gently, alarmed by the distress in his big friend's voice. 'Talk to me.'

'I've been with Margo and the boys today. And a couple of other family members. Her family.' Leo heard him draw a deep, shaky breath. 'Fucking misery from start to finish. She and I – we've been having some disagreements recently about property and money. That is, her lawyers have persuaded her she deserves more. Christ knows I've been generous – what option do I have? Anyway, we'd agreed that whatever is happening in the divorce, we'd try to keep things pleasant today. You know, because it's been hard on Alice and Nick, and we promised them at the time that whatever happened, their mother and I would stay friends. But today at lunch she started on about the money. Why? Today of all days? With the kids there? They were great, tried to stop her, talk her down, but she – well, Margo had had a bit to drink, and she started on them, and the whole thing got out of hand.'

'God, I'm sorry.'

'Nick took it pretty badly. He's having a tough time in his final year at uni. The last thing he needed was that kind of crap on Christmas Day. Alice took him off for a walk. I tried to calm things down, but I was left with Margo and her family, so you can imagine . . . I don't know how we came to this, Leo. What the hell happened? It wasn't like I did something, like I had an affair or anything. One day I think I'm happily married, and the next – this.'

'Where are you now?'

'A service station on the M25.' Jamie managed a sad laugh, which was a good sign.

'Right. Well, why don't you head to my place in Chelsea? I'll be home in ten minutes. We can spend the evening there. One of my clients gave me a very fine twenty-year-old Macallan, and I need some help drinking it.'

'Are you sure? God, Leo, that would be a lifesaver. I just don't want to be on my own.'

'To be honest, I'm feeling somewhat vulnerable myself. I could do with the company.'

'OK. I'll be there in about twenty minutes. There's bugger all traffic about.'

'Good. I may even warm up some mince pies.'

Leo ended the call. He stared at his mobile for a few seconds, then keyed in Gabrielle's number to tell her he wouldn't be there that evening after all.

The drawing room in which Anthony sat, nursing a glass of champagne and waiting for Gabrielle to return, was vast and expensively furnished. Gideon Hatch rugs lay scattered on the silk-pale polished wooden floor, and on the smoke-coloured walls were hung contemporary prints and photographs. The curtains remained undrawn on the windows which overlooked Ennismore Gardens, and the black night threw back reflections of the Adam fireplace, the long, black leather sofas and low glass tables, and the eighteen or so guests gathered in the room, talking and laughing with their hosts.

Anthony wondered if they'd left the curtains undrawn deliberately, to offer passers-by a tantalising glimpse into their privileged world, rich people enjoying themselves, cocooned in their warm, brightly lit rooms. He remembered when he was younger, walking past windows such as these, wondering about the inhabitants, what it must be like to live in such style. Now he sat on the other side of the window, a glass of champagne in his hand, feeling slightly bored. He had had a cursory conversation with Daniel Stanley, Gabrielle's father, whose swiftly appraising gaze and faintly impatient manner left him feeling oddly unworthy, and a longer one with Gabrielle's mother, who was sweet, but overly fascinated by anything he had to say, as though she needed to obscure her own personality by finding her guests transfixing. Gabrielle's brothers were decent enough, but they had invited their own group of friends, and were busily engaged in gossip and plans of their own at the other end of the sofa.

Gabrielle came back into the room, her mobile phone in one hand, and a dark look in her eyes. She wasn't smiling. Anthony sighed inwardly. Gabrielle in a bad mood was no fun. He got up and met her halfway.

'What's up?'

'Nothing. It doesn't matter. Someone I invited tonight can't make it, that's all.'

'Who? Obviously someone important.'

She said nothing. She had been pretending to herself that bringing Leo here tonight would be a painless way to present Anthony with the fact that Leo was her father. But she now saw that it had been a very bad idea. Whatever the truth of Anthony's relationship with Leo, a surprise of this kind would have gone down very badly. Leo probably wouldn't have been particularly pleased, either. She was confronted with the fact that she must have some ulterior motive which she herself didn't understand. She only knew that as her feelings for Anthony grew, so did her need to uncover the relationship between him and Leo, to lay it bare. Was she jealous? She must be. But of what? She had no idea. That was what burnt her, consumed her. Whatever she had hoped to achieve this evening, she would not have discovered what there was between her father and her lover. Perhaps it was all much more straightforward than she had thought. Perhaps it was simply a question of asking. But which one to ask?

She forced a smile. 'Just someone I wanted you to meet. But it's not important.' She put an arm round his neck and kissed him. 'Not as important as you. Let's give this another half-hour and go back to yours. Or did you have other plans?'

Anthony looked into her blue eyes. 'Absolutely not. I can't think of a nicer way to end the day.'

Sarah got back to Chelsea late in the evening. The day had been better than she'd anticipated, with her cousins Alice and Hugo turning up unexpectedly with their mother, Sir Vivian's half-sister. Her father also seemed to have forgiven her for Toby, which was a relief.

Seeing light from the living room, she looked in. Leo was stretched out on a sofa, reading.

'Glad to see you like your present,' said Sarah.

Leo looked up and smiled. '*The Lost Railways of North Wales*. Inspirational. Not even my mother could have come up with this.'

'Why are you whispering?'

Leo put a finger to his lips and pointed. On a sofa on the other side of the room lay Jamie, head propped on a cushion, deeply asleep.

'Who's that?' whispered Sarah.

'Just a minute.' He left the room and came back with a duvet, which he draped over Jamie.

'He's an old friend who's going through a bad divorce. He had a not very happy Christmas Day, so I've been helping him drown his sorrows.' He motioned to the door, and they went out, closing it behind them.

'You don't look or sound like you've been drinking a lot.'

'I haven't – Jamie has. I've had just one small Scotch in the past three hours. I was waiting for you.' He put his arms around Sarah. He looked into her eyes for a second, then kissed her. 'Thank you for the book.'

'Thank you for the necklace. You have very good taste.'

There wasn't much he could say to this, since he had in fact asked Felicity to go to Tiffany's online, choose something in the £800 to £1,000 price range that she liked, and buy two on his credit card.

'There's a bottle of champagne in the fridge. Why don't we open it, and take it up to bed? Unless you're too tired, of course.'

Sarah wanted to ask him why he was doing this. Did he really think he could just take and leave her as he pleased? No doubt his girlfriend was busy elsewhere, and Sarah herself was here and, as he no doubt presumed, available.

Leo gazed into her eyes, trying to read her thoughts. She was always marvellously inscrutable, but in this moment she possessed an air of remoteness which he had never detected before. It made her even more desirable than usual.

They looked into one another's eyes, neither of them able to say what they felt, because neither properly understood what it was.

He tried to lift the mood, prompting her. 'This is where I say, "I'll get the champagne", and you say, "I'll see you upstairs".'

She smiled sadly. 'I don't think so, Leo.' She drew away from him. 'It's simply not that easy.'

'Why not?'

'I'm not . . . I'm not actually the person you want me to be any more.' She crossed the hall. At the foot of the stairs she turned to him. 'I think it's best if I leave tomorrow. I'll stay with my father until I move into my new flat.'

She disappeared upstairs. Leo was left wondering how this had happened, what had extinguished the spark between them. After Jamie had fallen asleep he had spent a long time thinking about her, about what she meant to him. Tonight he had been going to suggest that she shouldn't leave, that she should stay until she got over Toby, and that they should see what they could find together. But that, it seemed, was never what she had wanted.

CHAPTER NINETEEN

The new year crept in, and London came sluggishly to life after the long break. Commuters from the suburbs filled the trains once more, spilling out of the stations and into their offices, offering each other listless new year greetings. The wheels of commerce gradually picked up their pace, and the City hummed once more.

Felicity, to her amazement, had heard nothing from Vince. Optimism gave her confidence, and a few days into the new year she was confiding the whole saga to Carla, the office manager, over early morning coffee in the clerks' room. Turning Vince into an anecdote was a way of consigning him safely to the past.

'And the neighbours said he and his mates turned up that night absolutely hammered, and started trying to break the door down.'

'No!'

'I know. Just as well I'd gone to stay with my friend Maureen. She put me up for a couple of nights.'

'I don't blame you. Sounds a nasty piece of work.'

Felicity dunked a Hobnob. 'Not nasty as such. Just a bit aggressive when he's had a few. A big, silly useless waste of space the rest of the time.'

'I know a lot of men like that.'

'Men like what?' asked Henry, who had just come in, his first day back after a two-week Christmas break in Tenerife with Cheryl and her family.

'Like Vince. Good-for-nothing layabouts. I was just telling Carla, I finally kicked him out. Changed the locks.' Felicity dusted her hands together. 'Boom. Gone. Never to be seen or heard of again.'

'Congratulations,' said Henry.

'Now you're footloose and fancy-free,' said Carla, 'we should arrange a girls' night out. Maybe next—' Her phone began to ring.

Felicity turned to Henry. 'So, how was your holiday? Feeling all loved up? You've got a bit of a tan.'

'Bit of red, more like.' He skipped her question. It had been a revealing experience, being on holiday with Cheryl, her parents, and her sister. Cheryl, he had realised, was very like her mother. It wasn't hard to imagine Cheryl, much as he loved her, or thought he did, as she would be at fifty-seven. 'What about you? How was your Christmas? Apart from Vince, I mean.'

'Yeah, not bad. I went to my cousin Trish's for Christmas Day. She and her husband Ian have got four-year-old twins. My aunt and uncle were there, too. We had a lovely time. And I went out a bit, couple of parties, few pubs and that. Trouble was, everywhere I went I was looking over my shoulder in case Vince was there. But I think he's got the message.'

'I'm glad. Really I am.'

She gave Henry a warm smile. 'I know you are.' At that moment Leo came into the clerks' room, and she added, 'Here's the man I should really thank.'

'For what?' asked Leo.

'For getting rid of Vince. For telling me to change the locks and bin his gear.'

'Ah. So the deed has been done? Good girl.'

Henry sat down and switched on his screen. He glanced at Felicity as she bubbled forth to Leo the story of Vince's departure. She seemed a bit overexcited. Probably just the relief of getting shot of him. Funny, though, Vince disappearing without so much as a murmur.

Leo and Henry began to go through Leo's diary for the week.

'We'll need to change the meeting with Sullivan next Tuesday. I've got an interlocutory hearing on that redelivery dispute.'

'I'll move a couple of things around.'

'And we need to arrange a courier to pick up a load of box files from Mays Brown on that grounding case. I'd like them before lunchtime, if possible, so I can start going through them this afternoon.'

'I'll get Liam on it straight away.' Henry tapped at his screen and added, 'I'm told the Judicial Appointments Commission is meeting next week. Going through the applications.'

'I hope you'll keep your fingers crossed for me.'

Henry smiled, staring at his screen. 'You don't need my luck, sir. I reckon it's in the bag.'

'Take nothing for granted, Henry,' said Leo, before heading off to his room.

* * *

Simon was spending the evening at Rachel's. He spent most evenings there now. The routine was easy, pleasant. Simon would come over around half six, usually straight from work, play with Oliver or help him with his homework, then begin to prepare supper while Rachel put Oliver to bed. When Rachel came down she would take over in the kitchen, then they would sit down to eat together and talk about the day. Sometimes Simon stayed over, and sometimes he went home. It was Rachel who had suggested that he leave a couple of shirts in her wardrobe. Shortly after that, he bought a second electric toothbrush and left it in Rachel's bathroom.

Oliver and Simon had spent fifteen minutes working on a map of Oliver's route to school for geography.

'Right,' said Simon, 'you can colour it in. I'm going to see what needs doing for supper.' He got up and went through to the kitchen, where Rachel was slicing vegetables.

'How's he getting on?' asked Rachel.

'Fine. Go and see. I'll finish this.'

Rachel went through to the living room. 'That's very good,' she said, looking over Oliver's shoulder. 'I like the compass in the corner.'

'That was Simon's idea.' Oliver busily swapped a red crayon for a blue one. 'Is Simon staying the night?'

'He might.' Rachel felt a little guilty. Maybe Simon shouldn't be staying. There were probably a few of the mothers at Oliver's school who would disapprove. She remembered the fuss she herself had made when she found that some girlfriend of Leo's – or was it a boyfriend? – had been staying overnight on weekends when Oliver was there. And he'd been barely two, not even old enough to pay attention. Now Oliver was six, so she could well be accused of having double standards.

'Why?' she asked.

'Nothing.' Oliver carried on crayoning, then added, 'I like it when he's here in the morning. Instead of just you and me. It makes the day better.'

Later, when Oliver was fast asleep, and when supper was over, Rachel and Simon nestled together on the sofa.

'Oliver said he likes it when you're there in the mornings. He said it makes his day better.'

Simon laughed. 'That's sweet.'

'Makes my day better, too.'

Simon kissed her. 'That's good to know.' There was silence for a moment, then he added, 'I thought it might be an idea if the three of us took a holiday together. In the February half-term.'

She looked at him. 'Are you sure?'

'Well, the first idea I had was that you and I should go away somewhere together at the end of the month, and that Oliver could stay with Leo. Then I thought, much as I love being with you – much as I love you – it seemed sad, Oliver not coming along.'

Rachel traced a line with her finger from his brow to his chin. 'You just said you love me.'

'Of course I love you. Don't look so surprised.'

'You've never said it before.'

'I've been in love with you since the day you walked into that wine bar in Creechurch Lane—'

'Oh God, don't remind me.'

'Hey, that was one of the best days of my life. Meeting you.'

'I didn't mean that. I meant that man. The blind date.'

'He was all part of the plan. Without him, I would never have met you. Though getting to know you took some effort.'

'You were persistent, I'll give you that.'

'And aren't you glad I was?'

Rachel smiled. 'Very.' It was true. It frightened her a little to think how differently things could have turned out if Simon hadn't been so tenacious.

'So,' he added gently, 'the question is – do you love me, too?'

She looked into his eyes. Just a few months ago it had seemed she would never find anyone to take the place of Leo. She knew that she never would, but she realised now that it was still possible to fall in love with someone new. 'I must do. I haven't been as happy as this in a long time. Yes, I do love you.' They kissed, then she added, 'I think Oliver does, too.'

'So the half-term holiday sounds like a plan?'

'It does. Oliver will be thrilled. And I think you'd better stay tonight.'

Simon kissed her for a long time. 'I think so, too. Make everyone's day.'

Julia and Piers were having a late dinner at Le Caprice with Darius Egan and his Russian girlfriend. Piers was talking about new clients, two Saudi brothers and their cousin, who were looking for property in London.

'These guys have serious truckloads of money,' said Piers. 'One of them drives a Pagani Zonda. His brother has a Bugatti Veyron. Not to mention a fucking stable full of Ferraris and Lamborghinis.'

‘I’d sooner have a Hennessey Venom,’ observed Darius.

‘Bugatti’s faster.’

‘Who would want to drive a fast car in London?’ asked Julia. ‘The traffic doesn’t go above fifteen miles an hour.’

Piers and Darius ignored her and carried on talking. Julia realised that she had been relegated to the status of second-class citizen, just like Darius’s girlfriend. The Russian girl, whose name Julia couldn’t remember, was sitting toying with her cocktail as though nothing was expected of her. And in truth, as far as conversation went, nothing was. Julia thought for a moment of trying to talk to her, but the effort seemed too much. Besides, she didn’t think there was anything about the girl she cared to know. She tried to tune back into her husband’s conversation with Darius.

‘What I really want is to get some investment from them,’ Piers was saying. ‘A serious injection of that kind of money would mean a chain of clubs. I think it’s there, but I need to keep them royally entertained while they’re here.’

‘If it’s women you’re talking about, that’s no problem. And if they’re into gambling, why don’t you bring them to Blunt’s? I don’t just mean the tables. I could set up a big game in one of the private rooms. High stakes, high rollers. Give them a real taste of excitement. The towel-heads love that kind of thing.’

Piers pondered this. ‘That’s not a bad idea. Of course, there are fringe benefits for you, too.’

‘Of course,’ grinned Darius. ‘That’s why I suggested it. If you think they’d be interested, I’ll see if I can come up with a few names.’

On the way home in the taxi, Piers appeared to be asleep. Julia stared out at the dark streets, thinking nothing.

Suddenly Piers opened his eyes, laid his hand on Julia's, and said in his drawling voice, 'If Darius sets this game up, it might be amusing to rope Anthony Cross into it. He seems to get a kick out of losing money.'

'Come off it. He's a novice. Darius is talking about serious players.'

'You're rather missing the point. I don't want my boys to come out of this on the debit side. That's not going to be much of a fun night out for them. OK, we need some decent players to make it exciting, but a few gullible losers around the place wouldn't come amiss.'

Julia said nothing for a few moments. A small, vindictive part of her wouldn't mind seeing Anthony getting into something he couldn't handle. She felt he'd behaved extremely badly towards her since they'd renewed their acquaintance last autumn. OK, maybe she had let him down cruelly in the past, but good manners dictated that he should grow up and get over it. As for his relationship with Gabrielle – it seemed to her that sometimes he flaunted it just to annoy her. But deep down, and mixed up with all this, was the knowledge that in Anthony she had lost something precious. He really had loved her once. Only in the last year or so of her marriage to Piers had she come to realise what a rare and valuable thing that was. A part of her wanted it back, but she knew it was impossible. Anthony hated her. For that he deserved to be punished.

'Why mention it to me? You don't usually involve me in any of your schemes, business or otherwise.'

'Don't whine, Julia. I mention it to you because you still have a little thing for Anthony – don't pretend you don't. And he probably does for you. You were the love of his life, after all. Or so he said, in his somewhat callow way. I'm sure you can persuade him that gambling with the big boys is right up his street.'

'I'll think about it.'

'Please do.' Piers took his hand away and closed his eyes again, and the taxi purred on its way to Holland Park.

When the Judicial Appointments Commission convened the following week to review the various applications to the High Court Bench, its chairman, Sir Alastair Flockton, was not in the best of humours. His irritable bowel syndrome, to which he was a martyr, was manifesting itself in bursts of flatulence which he was trying with great difficulty to contain. The medication which he had taken didn't always work, and holding in wind made his insides roil and bubble in a most unpleasant way. Concentration was not easy.

'So now we come to . . .' He glanced down the list. 'Ah yes, Leo Davies.'

'An excellent candidate, in my view,' observed Ian Cole, himself a High Court judge.

Lady Justice Daphne Hunter nodded. 'I know the candidate. I believe he is of absolutely the right calibre. And he performed exceptionally well in the structured discussion stage of the assessment process.'

'He certainly has all the right credentials,' agreed Baroness Paradeep. 'And I think his background helps, too – state school, and so on. The judiciary needs to demonstrate that people from disadvantaged backgrounds can rise in the profession.'

Dudley Callow OBE, a former commander of the Royal Anglian Regiment and one of the lay members, gave her a sharp look. 'Disadvantaged? He's fifty. He went to a grammar school. He's not exactly a product of New Labour educational policies.'

Mervyn Woodall thought he could see where Baroness Paradeep was tending, and assumed some politically correct qualities were being sought. 'He's Welsh. Doesn't that help?'

'In what way?' enquired Sir Alastair, shifting a little in his chair. His stomach growled audibly.

Mervyn blinked. 'Aren't they classed as a minority? I mean, isn't being Welsh some form of . . .' He gestured vaguely.

'It's not classed as a disability. Not yet,' murmured Gregory Hind.

'To come back to the point,' said Lady Daphne firmly, 'I think Mr Davies' experience and professional qualities speak for themselves. I really don't see how his application can be faulted.'

There were general murmurings of agreement, and Sir Vivian sensed his moment had come. He leant forward. 'Am I not right in thinking that the issue of good character is one which is just as important as professional attributes?' There was a silence. 'In fact,' went on Sir Vivian, 'if I may quote from guidance specifically offered to candidates on the JAC website, "public confidence will only be maintained if judicial office holders and those who aspire to such office maintain the highest standards of behaviour in their professional, public and private lives".' He laid careful emphasis on the penultimate word.

Magdala Keel, a lay member, and co-founder of an activation forum for gender equality, spoke for them all. 'I'm not quite sure what you're saying.'

Sir Alastair, his IBS momentarily forgotten, added, 'If

there are matters which you feel prejudice his application or disqualify him in some way, they really should be made known to the committee.'

Julian Hooper, a bookish, well-meaning QC who both liked and admired Leo, came to what he thought was Leo's aid. 'Look, if you're talking about rumours about Davies' private life, I frankly don't think they're relevant.' All eyes swivelled to Julian. 'I say rumours, but actually certain facts have been pretty well known to most people for some time.' Julian became aware that he might not be helping, but floundered on. 'I mean, surely what someone gets up to in their personal life is neither here nor there.' He glanced around the faces. 'Is it?'

'Personal?' Baroness Paradeep asked Julian. 'By that, you mean . . . ?'

Julian realised he had started something, and it had to be finished. 'The fact is, he's been married and has a child, but the word is that he . . .' Julian wasn't quite sure how to put it delicately. 'That he also associates with young men.'

'You mean he's gay?' said Mervyn brightly.

'Well, not gay exactly. Not in the accepted sense of the word—'

'That's a pity,' said Mervyn. 'We don't have enough gay judges.'

'Or lesbian judges,' pointed out Magdala.

'Indeed. Gay or lesbian. Gay *and* lesbian.'

'Have we *any*?' asked Ian Cole.

'Any what?' asked Sir Alastair.

'Gay judges.' Mervyn caught Magdala's eye. 'Or lesbian.'

'I have not the faintest idea,' sighed Sir Alastair. 'Julian, you were saying?'

'Well, as I understand it, he has been known to have . . . ah . . . relations with both men and women, but I really don't see how—'

Magdala interrupted. 'You mean he's bi.' She glanced round the group and met a few perplexed expressions. 'Bisexual.' Faces cleared.

'Yes, I believe that's the term,' murmured Julian.

'Well, that's wonderful!' exclaimed Mervyn. 'To have a bisexual on the bench – it makes us look very liberal and open-minded. I don't suppose there's any chance that he's TG?' Faces looked perplexed once more. 'Transgender. I went to a diversity workshop about all this. Or undergoing GR? Undergoing gender reassignment? It's when they perform surgery to remove—'

'TMI,' said Dudley abruptly. More perplexed faces.

'Too much information,' said Magdala impatiently. 'Can we—?'

'Because,' went on Mervyn, 'that really would be a feather in our cap.'

'The government is very keen on that kind of thing,' agreed Ian Cole. 'Wasn't Gordon Brown going on recently about celebrating BLTs, or something?'

'No, no.' Baroness Paradeep shook her head. 'A BLT is a kind of sandwich. It was something else. LGTG? Yes, that's it, I think – lesbian, gay, transgender, maybe.'

'It's lesbian, gay, bisexual and transgender,' sighed Magdala. 'LGBT.'

'Gordon Brown wouldn't know anything about that. He just parrots these things out.'

'I think we're straying from the point,' interjected Lady Daphne. 'A candidate's sexual life is neither here nor there.

And I think it's rather patronising to seek to elevate people because of their sexual orientation.' Mervyn folded his arms. 'The fact is, Leo Davies is an outstanding candidate. He certainly appears to fulfil all the intellectual and professional criteria and I, for one, am not prepared to look beyond that.' She glanced at Sir Vivian. 'Does that answer your concerns?'

Sir Vivian inclined his head gravely. 'I merely feel I have a duty to ensure that this committee is fully informed of matters which may affect a candidate's acceptability. I fully accept that a person's sexuality should be neither here nor there, but when in their private life an individual has strayed more than once into areas of potential – or actual – scandal, one has to ask if there is not a danger that at some point in the future that person's behaviour might affect their ability to discharge what is, after all, a vitally important public office, and one which calls for the very highest standards of personal integrity and responsibility.'

These portentous words had the desired effect on the rest of the committee.

Sir Alastair looked solemn. 'You say scandal. I was not aware—'

'Wasn't there something a few years back,' mused Gregory Hind, 'about some woman attempting to commit suicide, and he was involved in some way? I forget the details.'

'You are correct. It was a matter involving a female journalist who, I believe, had incriminating information concerning Mr Davies which he was anxious should not get into the public realm,' supplied Sir Vivian. This was more than a slight distortion of the truth, but he knew that no one's memory would be long enough to recall the real events. The incident in question had involved an obsessed and somewhat batty tabloid journalist who had stalked Leo for months, and who had ultimately made a botched suicide attempt to gain the attention not only of Leo, but of the rest of the world. The story had made it to the front page of *The Sun*. 'She tried to kill herself,' went on Sir Vivian, 'but failed, and thereafter the matter was hushed up.'

The faces of the committee registered concern, not to say interest. Sir Vivian continued, 'A year earlier Mr Davies' name was also linked to the death in suspicious – indeed, somewhat unnatural – circumstances of a civil servant, whom I shall not name, though he was in fact the principal private secretary to a prominent member of the cabinet of the day. That individual was known to frequent male brothels – a subsequent police raid on one of these places revealed the involvement of underage youths who were supposed to be in the care of the local authority. And after his death it was also revealed that the individual had been involved in blackmailing men in public office who were in fact gay, but who did not wish it to become publically known. He and Mr Davies were close friends, and their social paths often crossed, so how narrowly Mr Davies avoided being caught up in these scandalous events is not for me to say—'

Gregory Hind cut in. 'No, quite. And I think we have to be very careful not to make potentially libellous allegations in this committee room.'

Again Sir Vivian inclined his head. 'I have no intention of overstepping the mark. There are certain other matters relating to this candidate within my personal knowledge, but it is the very fact that I cannot speak openly about them which has persuaded me to refer to events which are already within the public domain, albeit from a few years ago, which themselves raise questions about this candidate's suitability. I shall say no more.'

The beautiful fluency of Sir Vivian's utterances had had a somewhat numbing effect on the minds of the committee members, but had at the same time awoken in them concerns which, had they been better defined, might have troubled them less. As it was, they were left with the distinct – or indistinct – impression that Leo Davies was, or could become, a liability.

'Well,' said Sir Alastair, 'I am not entirely convinced that these matters affect—'

He stopped. 'Then again, the issue of good character is very important, if not crucial . . .' He paused once more, frowning. He was conscious of the accumulation of a considerable amount of painfully bloating wind, and felt he could not safely remain in his seat without imminent risk of embarrassment. He badly needed to escape to a lavatory, or to some other private place. 'I think in the circumstances we shall have to defer this candidate's application and possibly – I say possibly – return to it another time. Does anyone have anything to add?'

Lady Justice Hunter seemed to be about to say something, but didn't. Gregory Hind frowned, evidently not entirely happy, and shook his head. The others said nothing.

'Then perhaps we can end this session here.'

There was a murmuring and a shuffling of papers, and the committee members rose and filed from the room. Sir Vivian, the last to leave, was well satisfied. He doubted very much if Leo Davies would be on the High Court Bench this time next year. Or any year.

CHAPTER TWENTY

Jacqueline and Gabrielle were having coffee on the fifth floor of Harvey Nichols after spending Saturday afternoon trawling the fag end of the sales. The acquisitive companionability of clothes shopping had given way to a mother-daughter lull, and Jacqueline was looking for topics to brighten the conversation.

'So,' she asked, 'are you still seeing that very good-looking man who came to us on Christmas? I've forgotten his name.'

'Anthony? Yes. We're having dinner at some new restaurant in Mayfair tonight.'

'How lovely to have a boyfriend who can take you to expensive places.'

Gabrielle shrugged, glancing around the restaurant. Then she asked, 'What kind of thing did you and Leo do when you were going out together?'

'Well . . .' Jacqueline thought for a moment, trying to extract something suitable from her recollections, which consisted largely of long hours in bed, making love. 'I suppose the usual things that young people do. We both worked in the day, so it was just evenings and weekends. Nights. Summer nights. There was a pub on the river we used to go to. We just . . .' She shrugged. 'Spent time together. It was only six weeks. Not long. There were a lot of parties. We met at a party.' She stopped. 'You know, now that he is in your life, I find it odd to talk to you about those times.'

Gabrielle was silent for a moment. 'I suppose it must be weird.' Then she added, 'You must have been amazingly careless to get pregnant.'

'I suppose I was. I was on the Pill, but these things can happen. Sometimes it's a subconscious desire. Maybe that sounds silly?'

'No.'

Jacqueline gave her a glance. 'Don't you be careless.'

Gabrielle smiled. 'What? Are you saying you wish you'd been more careful, that I had never happened?'

Jacqueline smiled in return. 'You know I don't wish that. I could never wish my beautiful, clever daughter away. But it wasn't ideal. It was very hard for a long time.'

'You should have told him.'

'I almost did. But I knew that Leo wasn't a man who would ever be tied down. There seemed no point. It would just have been messy and unhappy. Anyway, as I say, I don't want to revisit all that.'

'OK.' Gabrielle drank the remains of her coffee. 'You want to know a funny thing?'

'Go on.'

'Leo and Anthony work in the same chambers. They're old friends.'

'No! What a coincidence.' Jacqueline pondered this. 'Maybe I should invite them both to one of my dinner parties. Would that be fun?'

'Possibly.' The waitress brought the bill. Then Gabrielle said, 'Can I ask you something?'

'Of course.'

'Now, don't go taking this the wrong way, or anything – I know you're very broad-minded, but . . . well, anyway. Do you think Leo, when you knew him, was ever interested in boys? I mean, that he might be bisexual?'

Jacqueline laughed in astonishment. 'No, I never thought that! Not for a moment! What an extraordinary thing!' She handed a twenty to the waitress. 'Why do you ask?'

'Oh, nothing. Well, something I heard. A rumour.'

'It's a long time since I knew him. Who knows the kind of man he is nowadays? Maybe . . . well, let's not speculate. Nowadays such things don't matter. People are what they are.'

'Very "*Cage Aux Folles*", Mummy. Very liberal.'

'But it's true! Don't laugh at me. I really don't care.' Jacqueline took her change. 'Do you?'

'Do I? Of course not. I'm just intrigued.'

'Well, Leo is an intriguing man. Let's leave it at that.' She put her purse into her handbag. 'Shall we go?'

It was over three weeks since Sarah had moved out. Leo was surprised how much he missed her. Even if living with her had lacked the erotic angle he'd anticipated, her presence in the house had given it energy and cheerfulness, evoking memories of the Oxford summer. The physical distance which she maintained had been puzzling and frustrating, after the passionate interlude of Grand Night, but he had put it down to the break-up with Toby. It had clearly affected her more than she had expected. Understandable, he supposed. Sex was always something that could be put on hold.

Now that she was gone, Leo found himself mulling over the situation, wondering if he hadn't misread it. She'd said she had changed her mind about marrying Toby – hadn't she? On the strength of which he'd set about seducing her, thinking she wanted it as much as he did, that she didn't care about the risk to her relationship with Toby. But what if his assumption had been wrong? What if, without his interference, she and Toby might still be together? If that was the case, she probably blamed him as much as herself. No wonder she'd wanted, in the end, to get away.

Leo had never much cared where his desires led him, or what chaos they wrought in other people's lives, but the idea that he might have been responsible in some measure for destroying Sarah's happiness – even if he had thought Toby not good enough for her – troubled him. She was someone he truly valued. It was as though she was a part of him. Even in the last few years, when they had seen nothing of one another, she had always been there, in some corner of his mind. And now he might have estranged her for good.

Sarah had just come back from the supermarket when her mobile buzzed. She set down the shopping, kicked the front door shut, and pulled her phone from her pocket. When she saw Leo's name on the screen, her heart dipped, and as she took the call, her fingers shook a little.

'Hi.'

'Hi. I just called to see how you are.'

'I'm fine, thanks.'

'How's the new job going?'

'It's great. I'm working hard, making sure I keep my nose clean. My boss Geraldine is vaguely insane, but really nice.'

'That's good. And the new flat?'

'Yeah, it's fine. I'm still getting used to it. I only got the rest of my stuff out of storage last weekend, so the place isn't quite straight. But I like the area. Actually, I realise I prefer Fulham to Kensington. Less up itself. More of a buzz.'

'Not much buzz around here. Without you, I mean.'

'I should think you prefer the peace and quiet. And having less mess. I wasn't a very tidy house guest.'

'I miss all that. I miss you.' There was silence for a moment, then Leo said, 'Look, I called to see how you were, but also because I felt I had to say something about – about what was going on while you were here.'

'Please, let's forget it.'

'I know why you left, and I don't blame you. I should have said something at the time.'

She saw he was intent on being serious. Her heart sank a little. Why tell her now about his lover? She didn't want to know. 'It doesn't matter. Just took me a while to realise.'

So she did have regrets about Toby. The least he could do was apologise for the part he'd played. 'I'm sorry. My expectations were crass. I probably took it too much for granted, that you and I understood one another.'

'We do. Maybe that's why neither of us is very good at bringing things out into the open.'

'Maybe. I just hate to think that our relationship has been damaged.'

'Honestly, that's not something you should be worrying about.'

'Well, it is. I don't want to lose you.'

She gave a wry smile. Typical. Always wanting to have his cake and eat it. 'Leo, there is nothing to lose. That's the way it's always been between us. We just have to get on with our lives.'

'That has a ring of finality about it. I'd like to think we could see one another occasionally.'

'Why?'

'Because I don't think that things can ever really be over between us.'

She closed her eyes. The last thing she needed, at this point in her life, was to get drawn back into Leo's amoral, cruel world. These were games she was no longer able to play. But she couldn't bear the thought of never seeing him. 'Maybe we can have lunch sometime.' It was the best she could do.

'That's not—'

'Look, I have to go. Maybe I'll be in touch. Thanks for ringing.' She ended the call.

Leo stood in the silence of his kitchen, phone in hand. He wandered out into the garden, bracing himself against the cold, and paced around the lawn. He wondered if she would get back with Toby. No, he couldn't see Sarah as a teacher's wife. She had been honest about that part. But perhaps not about losing Toby's love. That had obviously been hard. Sarah, for all her callous ways, needed someone to love her. If she had stayed, who knew how things might have developed? As it was, they would never know.

* * *

That evening, Anthony and Gabrielle dined at Corrigan's in Mayfair.

'That,' said Gabrielle, as the waiter took away the dessert plates, 'was fantastic. But you don't have to keep taking me to expensive restaurants. I'd be just as happy with Pizza Express.'

'You couldn't get wine like this at Pizza Express,' replied Anthony, pouring the remains of the bottle into their glasses. 'Would you like coffee?'

She shook her head. 'I'm fine, thanks.'

Anthony signalled for the bill, and Gabrielle studied the label on the empty wine bottle. 'Vitovska, 2002,' she read. 'What's so wonderful about it?'

'What's wonderful is that it's not something you'll drink every day. It's made from a grape that grows only in the limestone region around Trieste.' He took a sip. 'That slight astringency comes from the skins. I think it's an amazing wine. Can't you taste the wild herbs?'

Gabrielle took a sip and smiled. 'Yes, now you mention it. I wish you'd told me I was drinking something special. I might have treated it with a little more respect, instead of just glugging it back.' The waiter had brought the bill; Gabrielle squinted, reading it upside down. 'My God! I can't believe you're paying that for a bottle of wine! Seriously, this is wasted on me.'

Anthony leant across and kissed her. 'You're worth every penny.' He gazed into her blue-grey eyes. 'Do you know how amazing you are?'

She smiled. 'You're pretty special yourself. But seriously, I would be just as happy with a Four Seasons and a Peroni.'

'I'll remember that next time.'

'So, where did you learn about wine? All that stuff about limestone.'

'Leo Davies, the friend I told you about. I was a very raw and callow young thing when I joined chambers, and he decided to educate me in the ways of the world. I knew nothing about anything. He used to take me to expensive restaurants, order the best wines, and teach me about the various regions, the different grapes, what to look for. It's not difficult to learn.'

Gabrielle wished Leo's name hadn't come up. She knew very well that she should have told Anthony about Leo before. To say something now seemed ludicrously difficult. But it had to be done. She opened her mouth to speak, then hesitated. She had no idea how Anthony would react. Leo was clearly someone hugely special to him. What if the discovery changed things between them? She didn't think she could bear that. She was more than a little in love with Anthony, and the idea of estranging him in some way frightened her.

'What? You were about to say something.'

She shook her head. 'It was nothing.' She would find another moment. She leant forward, stroking his hand with her fingers. 'So, what do you want to do now? It's only ten.'

'Why don't we go to Blunt's for an hour or two? It's a while since we've been.' This was true, but only in the sense that he and Gabrielle hadn't been there together since before Christmas. Anthony himself had visited Blunt's twice in the past week, but his conscience was eased by the fact that he'd come away a winner both times. His policy of lowering his stakes meant he hadn't netted as much as he would have liked, but it was good to know he was finding his form. He'd always known it was simply a matter of time.

Gabrielle shrugged. 'OK.' She liked the atmosphere of casinos, and watching people gamble, even though she didn't do much of it herself. She went mainly to socialise; a number of her friends, and those of her brothers, were regulars at Blunt's.

It was a five-minute walk to Mount Street. The casino was busy, and Julia and Piers were there, hanging out with Darius and their usual crowd. Anthony left Gabrielle chatting to friends and went to buy drinks. While he was at the bar, someone gave him a friendly slap on the shoulder. He turned and saw Piers.

'Anthony, how are you?'

'Fine, thanks,' replied Anthony, mildly surprised.

'Excellent, excellent. Good to see you.' Piers gave him another pat on the arm, and wandered away.

Five minutes later, as he was paying for the drinks, Julia came to the bar and ordered a cocktail. She and Anthony greeted one another warily.

'Your husband is being strangely pleasant to me this evening,' remarked Anthony.

'Probably because he thinks he can sucker you into a private poker game he's organising. Some Saudi clients are in town, and he's trying to set up a game for them.'

'Sounds interesting.'

'I'm afraid you'd be rather out of your depth. They're enormously wealthy. Not quite your league.'

'That doesn't make them expert poker players.'

The bartender handed Julia her cocktail. 'Oh, I quite agree. I imagine they're more likely to lose than win. But then, so are you. And the thing is, they can afford it. If I were you, I'd steer well clear of it. Remember, I know your limitations. And so should you.' She raised her glass and smiled. 'Cheers.' Then she slipped away.

Piers caught up with her on the other side of the room.

'Give it an hour or so,' said Julia.

Piers nodded. 'Jolly good. I'd better keep an eye on how he does at the tables. No point trying to enlist him when he's on a losing streak.'

But Anthony was on a winning streak. He started out with a modest fifty pounds worth of chips, and by midnight he was several hundred up. Poker wasn't a game he often played, but his success began to convince him that perhaps he was one of those rare people who were naturally good at it. Gabrielle came and went, sometimes watching with interest, sometimes talking with friends. Anthony knew that a couple of hours of the casino were usually enough for her, and that soon she would want to go. He felt an itch of frustration at the thought of having to leave. He felt he could go on winning all night.

Sure enough, at the end of the next game, she came over and kissed his ear, murmuring, 'Quit while you're ahead. Let's go back to yours and play games of our own.'

Anthony swallowed a sigh. 'OK. Let me cash these in and I'll be with you in a few minutes.'

As he was pocketing his winnings, Anthony once again found Piers' hand on his shoulder.

'Anthony, old man – do you have a minute?' Piers drew Anthony aside and they were joined by Darius.

Darius and Anthony shook hands. 'I'll tell you what it is,' said Darius in a confidential manner. 'My father and I are trying to organise a private poker game here at the casino, something to keep some Saudi friends of Piers amused.

We need around eight players, but of course we can't have just anyone. You seem to be a pretty handy player, and we wondered if you'd be interested in joining in?'

'I might,' replied Anthony. He had been stung by Julia's remarks earlier, by the implication that he had neither the skill nor the money to participate in anything high-level.

Piers chuckled. 'I have to tell you, Tony, these boys are absolutely fucking loaded. They throw money around like confetti. And they're not exactly card sharps. Anybody who's any good stands to do pretty well out of the evening. I'm certainly going to be playing.'

'The stakes are pretty high,' said Darius. 'Lowest opening bet in any game is two hundred.'

Anthony smiled. 'I think I can manage that.'

'No, of course. I wouldn't have asked you if I didn't think you were good for it. Just letting you know.'

Anthony considered for a moment. There were risks – he knew to his cost how losses could mount up in one evening – but it was a one-off game, and if tonight was anything to go by, he might come out of it pretty well. He could even make a killing. He nodded. 'OK, count me in. When is it?'

'We were thinking next Saturday. Probably kick off around ten, make it an all-nighter.'

'Bring Gabrielle, if she wants to come,' added Piers. 'Julia will be there, and some of the other girls. Galina, probably Connie and Abigail. Gabrielle knows them all. Hate to sound sexist, but it'll be an all-male game. You know what the Saudis are like. But it should be quite a party. Plenty of food and champagne on the go. Fun for all.'

'Fine. I'll see if she's interested.'

* * *

Anthony mentioned the game to Gabrielle later, when they were in bed. 'I said I'd play. Do you fancy coming along?'

'I don't mind, if Connie's going. I'm not a huge fan of Galina – Darius's girlfriends are always weird. Like they're just for decoration. Julia's all right, in her way.' She propped her head on one hand. 'How long do you give that marriage?'

'Piers and Julia? I think in many ways they're perfectly suited.'

'Really? That's not the way it comes across to me. He can be really foul to her, you know. And it's perfectly obvious she has an eye for other men. You included.'

'Julia and I were over a very long time ago.' Anthony reached up and drew her mouth towards his. 'I love no one but you.'

Gabrielle wondered if now was the moment to tell him about Leo. No – the timing wasn't quite right. She would wait for another opportunity.

Leo found himself in a hideously restless mood that evening, and he knew exactly where it was leading. The club he ended up in at two in the morning was one he hadn't visited for over a year. Some of the faces were familiar, but there was no one there he would have called a friend. It wasn't that kind of place. He bought himself a drink and stood at the bar, watching the men cruising, eyeing one another. Even those who were obvious couples threw out stray glances. The place was loud with music and conversation, the thump from the dance floor at the far end relentless.

A part of Leo wondered what he was doing there, but another part of him knew exactly. Idly he eyed a knot of attractive young men drinking at a nearby table. He recognised one of them as Joshua, and his gaze froze. Forgotten feelings of fear, love and desperation suddenly flooded him, confusing him. It took him a moment to understand that what he was experiencing was nothing more than a conditioned emotional response, the merest remnant of love.

Leo waited for his feelings to subside, studying Joshua with the fascinated detachment of one long since cured of his passion. His features were slightly pouchy now, not as delicate as five years ago; his red-gold hair still curled at his collar, his eyes still held their implacable beauty, their Garbo-like expression. He was talking to a dark-haired young man, glancing around occasionally. And of course, after a few seconds he saw Leo.

Joshua smiled, but without surprise – Leo guessed that Joshua had perhaps seen him come in, and had waited to choose his own moment of connection and acknowledgement. Leo could not bring himself to smile, but he knew that his own expression must be one of vulnerability. How could it be otherwise?

Joshua rose and came over. He leant on the bar and surveyed Leo with a smile. 'Hello, Leo. How are you? You look as good as ever.'

'Thanks. I'm well.' Leo was interested to note that five years had given Joshua composure and maturity, but also an aura of self-awareness bordering on affectation. He still seemed, as he had at nineteen, ready for anything, but in quite a different way. 'You look well, too,' he added. 'How's life treating you?'

'Pretty well, actually. I like to think I've moved on and up in the world since I knew you.'

‘No longer a struggling artist?’

‘I’m working as a set designer.’ He nodded to the table. ‘I’m with some friends from the theatre. Why don’t you come and join us for a drink?’

Leo sat down at the table and Joshua introduced him as an old friend. Leo imagined the others knew very well what that meant. They were polite, guarded, sizing him up. The dark-haired man to whom Joshua had been talking extended a hand and Leo shook it, noting its slender strength. His entire body was lean and toned, with remarkable poise. This, thought Leo, was exactly the kind of distraction he had come looking for tonight.

‘This is Sergei,’ said Joshua. ‘He’s a dancer with the Barinov Ballet Company. They’re in residence at the theatre where I work.’

‘You like ballet?’ asked Sergei. He had a Slavic face, with sharp cheekbones and a full mouth, and large, liquid eyes. Leo thought he looked like trouble, and felt stirrings of interest and desire.

‘I do. Not that I go very often. I prefer modern ballet to traditional. That said, I rather like Matthew Bourne’s take on the classics.’

Sergei smiled, pleased. He asked Leo what he did, and Leo told him. They chatted for a while about London, which Sergei was visiting for the first time, and Leo could sense a chemistry. Joshua was talking to the others, his attention elsewhere, possibly deliberately. Leo felt he had Sergei all to himself.

‘It’s interesting that you work in the law,’ said Sergei. ‘It is one of the institutions I admire most in your country.’

‘You should visit the law courts some time,’ said Leo.

'I would like that,' said Sergei. 'Maybe you could show me around?'

'Maybe I could,' said Leo. 'Shall I give you my number?'

'Please.'

They exchanged phone numbers. Leo was just wondering how to detach Sergei from his friends and invite him back to Chelsea, when Sergei suddenly said, 'I have to go. I have rehearsals in the morning.' He rose with exquisite grace, gathering up his jacket and kissing a hand to his friends. '*Spokoynoy nochi, malyshi.*' He turned to Leo. 'And goodnight to you, Leo. I hope we meet again.' The promise in those large, lovely eyes was unmistakeable.

'I hope so, too,' replied Leo. He watched him go, wondering if it would look too crass to follow him; wondering, too, if that was what Sergei intended. As he drained the remnants of his drink, trying to make up his mind, Joshua seemed to read his thoughts.

'No point in going after him,' he murmured. 'He really means it about the rehearsals. I'm surprised he stayed up as late as he did. A dedicated professional.'

'It was the last thing on my mind.'

'Really? Remember, you're talking to someone who knows you very well.' Joshua surveyed Leo, thinking how little he had changed in five years. The features were still sharply handsome, the gaze of his blue eyes still intense, and even the silver hair wasn't ageing – quite the opposite.

'You think so?'

'Of course I do. And no one changes. Not really.'

'You have.' Leo lifted his glass, then realised it was empty.

'Have I?' Joshua seemed happy at the prospect of talking about himself. 'Have another drink. I'll buy.'

'Thanks. I'll have a Scotch.'

Joshua went to the bar. While he was waiting to be served he considered the situation, remembering the hold he had once had over Leo. It had been fun for a while, wielding so much emotional power, with such easy material gains. Leo had everything – wealth, status, possessions – yet it had been Joshua, with nothing to his name but some scrappy artistic talent and superb good looks, who had been in total command of the relationship. But the affair had eventually taught Joshua a strange truth – that freedom, even when it meant hardship and uncertainty, was better than the ease and comfort of belonging to someone you didn't love. Not that he hadn't been fond of Leo. Looking back, he wished he'd been more appreciative of the efforts Leo had made. Or at any rate, kinder to him. With several relationships with older men behind him – and the tender, fretful concern of a certain middle-aged choreographer hovering somewhere even now – he had a better understanding of what impelled their generosity.

He took the drinks back to the table and sat down.

'So, tell me how I've changed.'

'You've grown up. That is to say, you've lost the charmingly ingenuous air you once had.'

'You mean I'm not naive any more.' Joshua meant to be lightly sardonic, but Leo took the remark at face value.

'Evidently not.'

Joshua was conscious of being looked at critically by Leo – it was a new experience. Only in that moment did it occur to him that Leo was no longer in love with him. Why would he be? It was just that his youthful vanity had expected it.

‘Don’t you think you played a part in my loss of innocence?’

The ghost of a smile crossed Leo’s face. ‘That was lost well before you knew me. Why do you think you ever said hello to me in the first place? I wasn’t talking about your heart and soul. I was merely talking about your expression, your features.’

At these words, Joshua’s hand strayed unconsciously to his face. He stroked his chin, gazing reflectively at Leo, working on what he had said.

‘I’m not so very different.’ The flicker of anxiety made him look vulnerable, younger.

Leo was suddenly struck by a vivid memory – Joshua in his leather jacket, holding the rucksack hastily crammed with his belongings, turning round in the doorway to look at Leo before shrugging off his hand and leaving, walking out of Leo’s life for good.

Leo swallowed his whisky quickly. He had no wish to revisit that pain. ‘Not so very. I think I am, though. Not so good at these late nights. I have to go.’ He stood up. Joshua looked at him for a hesitant few seconds, and Leo could tell from his face that he was rapidly debating whether there was anything to be gained here. ‘There’s one thing about you that hasn’t changed, Joshua. You still have a beautiful transparency.’

He left the club, hailed a cab and headed home, cold in his heart.

CHAPTER TWENTY-ONE

Caspar and Darius Egan had gone to considerable trouble for Piers' Saudi friends, setting aside a lavishly furnished suite of rooms on the first floor of Blunt's for the occasion. In one room a blue-baize-covered poker table had been set up for the game, and in an adjoining room champagne was cooling in silver buckets, alongside a selection of spirits, beer, and an array of glasses. Platters of cold food had been laid out – crayfish in aspic, blinis, smoked salmon, caviar in bowls of ice – with warming stands ready for hot food to be served later. Next door was a large sitting room, whose windows overlooked rain-soaked Mount Street, lit by discreetly placed lamps, and furnished with deep leather sofas and low tables, with a large plasma television screen on one wall. Off this room was a bedroom with an en suite bathroom in between.

When Anthony and Gabrielle arrived, Darius, Piers and Julia were already there in the sitting room with the three guests of honour. Darius's Russian girlfriend, Galina, had brought along a trio of other Russian girls – Valeriya, Dina and Katia. All were dressed in tight-fitting short dresses and eight-inch hooker heels, and all wore expressions of ineffable boredom.

Everything about the young Saudis suggested wealth, but of a crude, unsubtle kind. They wore bespoke suits that were a little too sharp, silk shirts, and handmade Italian shoes, and sported Rolex Oyster watches and a profuse amount of gold jewellery. The air was heavy with the smell of Clive Christian No. 1 cologne. Darius introduced them. Farid Al-Rahman was a tall, well-built man in his mid twenties, with a patchy beard on a strong jaw, and a smile made disarming by the smoked glasses he wore, which hid the expression of his eyes. His younger brother, Hakim Al-Rahman, was a corpulent youth who looked barely out of his teens. He didn't get up to shake hands, but stayed lounging on the white leather sofa, grunting a greeting and extending a flabby hand studded with heavy gold and diamond rings. The third, Gabir Al-Wadhi, was a wiry man with a heavy short beard and bright eyes that glittered under heavy brows. He seemed the senior of the trio, and introduced himself as the cousin of the other two. He excused Hakim by saying, 'He has taken a holiday from his manners as well as his morals.' He threw the boy a chiding glance. 'Hey, Hakim?'

Hakim ginned and shrugged, and took another swig of his drink.

Darius turned to Gabrielle. 'Glass of champagne?'

'Lovely,' murmured Gabrielle, and sat down on a sofa opposite the Russian girls.

Darius, Piers and Anthony wandered into the adjoining room.

'What would you like?' Piers asked Anthony.

'Just a beer, thanks.' Piers uncapped a Becks and handed it to him. 'What was all that about taking a holiday from his morals?'

'Normal rules don't apply, is what he means. Back home, these boys can't drink or gamble, and they don't get much of a chance to sow their wild oats. Whereas over here – well, let's just say they like to take advantage of our ludicrously low moral standards.'

At that moment Anthony heard a familiar voice behind him, and turned to see Ed piling into the suite with a number of assorted male and female friends. He was as ebullient as ever, pulling off his scarf and unbuttoning his overcoat, and exclaiming about the filthy weather outside.

'Anthony! I heard they'd roped you into this evening's shenanigans. You must be bloody mad. Brought a few friends along to witness the carnage. Now, lead me to the champagne!'

Anthony felt reassured by Edward's presence; somehow it lessened the tension. He wanted to have a good feeling about this game, but it was difficult. He didn't care for the Saudis, and deep down, he didn't care for the Egans. Still, he was committed now.

Gradually the other players trickled in, with girlfriends in tow. Two of them Anthony already knew as regular frequenters of the casino – Tom Finnegan, a wealthy young Irishman and crony of Piers, and a German by the name of Klaus Bauer. The other two players were Piers, and a middle-aged Cypriot by the name of Markou, who was a business acquaintance of Caspar Egan's.

After drinks and some friendly chit-chat, they got down to the serious business of the evening.

'Right, gentlemen,' said Caspar, 'the buy-in is twenty thousand, as agreed. Total pot of eighty thousand. If everyone would like to take their seats?'

Anthony drew Darius aside. 'You said the buy-in was five thousand.'

'Did I? Well, we've had to up the stakes a bit. Five thousand is small change to our Saudi friends. Even twenty isn't particularly interesting, but I promised them there would be some pretty girls coming along to liven things up if the poker got dull. Which is where Galina's friends come in.' He gave Anthony a dry look. 'If you want out, just say so.'

Anthony hesitated. Twenty thousand was a ludicrously large amount to gamble, far more than he'd intended, but on the other hand, the higher the stakes, the higher the potential winnings. Apart from which, there was no way he was going to sidle out of this game because of lack of funds, with Piers and Julia looking on.

'No, I'm in. But I'm only good for five thou in cash right now.'

'Not to worry. The house will stake you the other fifteen. We know you're good for it.'

Anthony considered briefly. If he came out even or on top, which he fully expected to, the Egans would have their money straight back. He nodded. 'OK. Thanks.'

The game started, and the play for the first hour was uneventful. Anthony played cautiously at first, then as he loosened up and grew more confident, his betting did too. The Saudis were unexceptional players. Hakim played irrationally and sloppily, not much caring whether he won or lost, and kept calling for more drinks. Gabir's play was temperamental, and he was prone to wild betting, but somehow his luck held. Farid was both a lazy and an unlucky player, and by half eleven he had dropped out of the game, having lost his entire stake. By this time, Anthony had amassed a comfortable pile of chips and was feeling buoyant. Those not involved in the game seemed content enough with the little party they had created for themselves in the sitting room; the players could hear muffled music and laughter, but it seemed to disturb no one's concentration. Occasionally people wandering from the sitting room to get food and more drinks would drop in to watch the game for a short while, then drift away again.

After steady, successful play during the first hour, Anthony experienced a couple of disastrous hands. He bet too much on what he thought was a promising hand, only to have his two pairs beaten by Klaus's three of a kind. In the next hand he rashly hoped his five of hearts, six of diamonds and seven of spades might turn into a straight, and again he overextended his bet. When the flop went down, the resulting Jack of diamonds, nine and ten of hearts gave Piers two pairs. As he watched Piers gather in the chips, Anthony suddenly began to feel panicky. His pile was dwindling rapidly. If he didn't start winning, he would finish up like Farid, bowing out of the game with his entire twenty thousand stake gone, and owing the Egans fifteen thousand. He tried to calm his mind, and focus.

It seemed to work. He won three out of the following seven hands, but the betting was modest, and didn't recoup him a great deal. Still, the tension began to ease. He told himself it was just a question of climbing back up again, and not betting over-optimistically on hands which could easily go wrong.

A quarter after midnight, Hakim had drunk himself out of the game, and went to the buffet to console himself with a large plate of asparagus and truffle risotto, and a few more glasses of champagne. He wandered into the sitting room and flopped down on one of the leather sofas next to Valeriya and Dina, slopping champagne over Dina's skirt. He laughed and wiped his fat hand across her thigh, and she exclaimed, '*Dura!*' and shoved his hand angrily away. Hakim stroked her thigh again, trying to push his hand between her legs, and she shouted at him again and got up and stalked away.

'Only a pig does that kind of thing,' snapped Valeriya.

'Shut up, bitch,' replied Hakim indifferently. His drunken attention shifted across the room, to a glass-topped table where Julia was cutting some lines of coke. His eyes lit up, and he got up and went over and sat down heavily on the sofa next to her, watching and waiting eagerly. Gabrielle, curled up in the corner of the sofa, watched the proceedings dispassionately, inching her feet away from Hakim's fat thigh. She didn't touch drugs, though she didn't care if other people did.

There were now six players left in the poker game – Anthony, Markou, Gabir, Piers, Klaus and Finnegan. All eyes watched as the dealer flicked the cards across the baize. Anthony picked his up. The ace and two of spades. Promising, but everything depended on the flop, the three cards to be dealt next. More spades would be excellent for him, but just as good for any of the other players holding spades. Maybe the betting would throw up some clues. He watched the other players study their cards impassively. The betting opened. Anthony, Gabir and Piers made modest bids. Klaus gave a shrug and folded his hand. A couple of seconds later, Tom Finnegan and Markou did the same, leaving just three players in the game.

The dealer dealt the flop, and as the six of spades, the ten of diamonds, and the three of spades went down, Anthony's pulse quickened. The ace, two and three of spades, and the six – a flush draw with the potential for a straight draw, if the next two cards were the four and five of spades. The rational part of his brain knew the unlikelihood of that, but the part that had driven him over the past few months to return, night after night, to the poker and roulette tables, had taken over. In his mind he could see the dealer turning those cards over, false certainty driving illusory hope.

The betting resumed. Piers raised the stakes – but only modestly. Gabir seemed unusually reflective, stroking one thick, black eyebrow. Anthony tried to read his face, wondering if he was merely bored, or had something in his hand that merited concentration. As he studied the faces of his fellow players, he was vaguely aware of an increase in the noise and laughter from the food and drink room. Presumably staff from the casino kitchen had brought up the hot supper. He realised, with surprise, that he was hungry.

People began to drift in from the next room, curious to see how the game was going, as though the slightly heightened tension of the game was infectious. Klaus and Tom Finnegan were exchanging discreet banter, but Anthony scarcely noticed. The game was like some kind of cocoon, his own concentration soundproofing him against external realities.

After a moment or two's thought, Gabir raised Piers. Anthony, with a growing conviction that luck was with him on this hand, matched him briskly. Possibly too briskly, he realised, after he had pushed the pile of chips forward. He waited anxiously for the dealer to turn the fourth card. As the ten of spades went down he felt an almost dizzying sense of astonishment and relief. His instincts had been proved right. Now he had an ace-high flush, on the cards already down – only two pairs of ten could beat him.

Piers' own feelings on seeing the ten of spades were akin to Anthony's. He already held the ten of hearts and nine of clubs, and the cards which had just been dealt gave him three tens. What were the odds of anyone else having a better hand? Outside, surely. Then again, if either of the others held spades, they had a good chance of having a flush, which would beat his hand. Maybe some confident, tactical betting would give him a better idea of who had what. He stacked up a hefty pile of chips and pushed them forward.

Gabir pursed his lips, his dark eyes shifting back and forth from the cards in his hand to those on the table. He counted out four careful stacks of chips and eased them across the baize, doubling Piers' bet. Piers knew at that moment that his speculation had been right. Gabir must be holding spades, and he must have a flush. He glanced across at Anthony, whose expression was unreadable, his gaze focused.

Anthony felt his nerve give a little as he tried to rationalise Gabir's bet. The guy had more money than sense, so the amount he gambled didn't necessarily reflect the realities of his hand. Also, he had occasionally made wild bets throughout the evening merely to amuse himself, so far as Anthony could tell. Either he was bluffing, or he just didn't care. Or maybe he held a flush himself. Even if he did, Anthony reckoned it couldn't beat his own.

Gabir stifled a yawn, then shook himself, frowning at the cards as though trying to concentrate. The gesture made up Anthony's mind. He couldn't sit with the best poker hand he'd ever held in his life, and not go with it. The Saudi simply couldn't hold better cards. With a deliberate gesture, he drew all his chips together and pushed them into the middle of the table, going all in.

Piers was momentarily taken aback. Either Anthony's move was naive recklessness, of the kind that had made Anthony such a useful customer of Blunt's, or it was a clear signal that he held an exceptionally strong hand. Either Anthony or Gabir could be bluffing, but from the cards on the table, and from the way the betting had gone, one of them held a flush. His own chances of coming out on top depended entirely on the next card being the ten of clubs – insanely remote odds. He glanced up, and saw Julia on the other side of the table. She was watching Anthony, her gaze intense. Piers saw and read the expression in her eyes. That she should still feel anything for that lower-middle-class waste of space filled him with contempt and anger. He looked back at the cards. He knew the sensible thing to do would be to fold. But suddenly Piers wasn't feeling sensible.

'I'll call you,' he said to Anthony. Then he pushed all his own chips into the centre of the table.

Suddenly everyone became aware of the sound of shouting, and some kind of commotion in the next room. People began to look round and murmur. Anthony sighed inwardly; the chances were that Edward had started some drunken piece of nonsense, as he was prone to do. Klaus and Tom Finnegan got up and left the table to go and see what was going on. Anthony's attention returned to the game, where the dealer was about to turn the final card.

The nine of spades went down, and Anthony's heart jumped. Only in that moment did it dawn on Anthony that Gabir might have spades. He looked up. For the first time in the game Gabir was looking directly at him. Then, as each turned their cards over, Gabir smiled. Anthony's stomach seemed to hit the floor. The cards Gabir had laid down were the seven and eight of spades. The six, nine and ten lying on the table completed a straight flush, beating Anthony's. He couldn't believe it. Just as Piers was laying down his own cards in disgust, Tom Finnegan stormed back into the room and shouted at Gabir in fury, 'Come and sort out your fucking animal of a cousin!'

Gabir stood up abruptly and left the table, his face dark, and everyone followed, the game forgotten. The commotion was coming from the sitting room. Among the shrill exclamations of female outrage Anthony could hear Tom shouting, 'You unbelievable Arab bastard!'

Gabrielle met him in the doorway, white-faced. 'It's one of the Russian girls. He raped her. Or tried to.'

'Who did?'

'The fat one. The boy.'

Anthony went into the sitting room, where shouting and swearing was going on in various languages. Klaus and Edward were trying to pin Hakim to the sofa, but he was violently drunk, and they were having trouble holding him. Hakim's trousers were undone, roughly hoisted to his waist, his silk shirt loose. Gabir was standing over him, shouting furiously at him in Arabic. Katia was screeching and spitting abuse at him in Russian. Farid Al-Rahman stalked out to the hallway, pushing roughly past Anthony, barking orders into the mobile clamped to his ear. Agitated voices were coming from the room beyond, and Anthony went through the bathroom and into the bedroom. The Russian girl, Dina, was lying on the bed, being tended to by Valeriya and Galina. She was crying and talking woozily, as though she had only recently regained consciousness. Her nose was bloody. Caspar Egan stood at the edge of the room, talking on the house phone.

'How is she?' Anthony asked Valeriya, who was crying as she dabbed at the blood on Dina's face with a tissue. Every woman in the room seemed to be crying.

'That fat Arab pig raped her! He hit her and he raped her!'

Anthony fetched a glass of water from the bathroom and gave it to Valeriya, then went back to find Gabrielle. There was no sign of her in the sitting room, where Hakim was slumped on the sofa, sweating, sullen and drunk, his struggle abandoned, Klaus and Edward holding his arms firmly on either side. Caspar Egan stalked in.

'Right. I shall be calling the police in a moment, so I want all this' – he gestured to the cocaine paraphernalia – 'cleared up. I don't want there to be a single trace of any illegal substance when they get here. Not one.'

At the word 'police', Farid began shouting at Caspar in Arabic. Gabir spoke to him sharply, calmed him, then indicated to Caspar that he wanted to speak to him away from everyone else. They left the room together.

'Have you seen Gabrielle?' Anthony asked Edward.

'She was here a moment ago.'

Anthony went to the empty room and the abandoned poker game. His unlucky cards still lay on the table, and it hit him forcefully that he had lost everything, and that he was now in hock to the Egans for twenty thousand. Twenty thousand he could ill afford. He stared at Gabir's cards and remembered his own conviction that he had a hand that couldn't be beaten. There on the table lay stark proof of the folly of the past few months. It was madness, the idea that if he just hung in there, things would get better. He suddenly recognised the futility that lay ahead if he went on, the endless games of poker, evenings at the roulette wheel, making wins, trying to make bigger wins, then failing, and trying to recoup his losses. A never-ending cycle of stupidity and loss. He'd come this far and had done nothing but lose tens of thousands. There was, he realised, no such thing as winning. He felt sickened.

He felt a hand on his arm, and turned, expecting to see Gabrielle. But it was Julia.

'You really don't want to carry on like this,' she said gently. He could tell she was trying to be kind.

He closed his eyes momentarily, and sighed. 'You're right. I don't.'

Piers sauntered in. He glanced at the table, then said to Anthony, 'Shame for you that the little fracas next door didn't kick off five minutes earlier. Things turned out rather badly, didn't they?'

Julia suddenly reached across the table and gathered the cards up. She squared them, shuffled them neatly and set the deck on the baize. 'I'm not sure things turned out any particular way. Not that anyone can prove.'

'Try telling that to Mr Al-Wadhi. Or the Egans.'

'I think they're too preoccupied right now to care much,' said Julia. 'The thing is, I don't particularly want to see twenty thousand of our money go into the pockets of some rich Arab to whom it's merely so much loose change.'

'Oh, please – we all know who your noble little gesture was intended for. Reminds me of the way things were years ago, Julia coming to the rescue of poor old Anthony. Still . . .' He smiled and shrugged. 'This way no one goes home a loser. Thank you, darling.' He kissed Julia lightly. 'Enough excitement for one evening. Shall we call a taxi?'

'I thought the police were coming? In which case, we'll all have to stay.'

'Something tells me not. I think that was just Caspar putting the wind up our Saudi friends. I suspect a deal is presently being brokered, whereby the fat, would-be rapist gets flown home pronto to the House of Saud by his minders, and Caspar is the recipient of a healthy amount of hush money, as is young Svetlana, or whatever her name is.'

'She's been attacked and raped, for God's sake!' said Julia angrily.

'Oh, indeed. She may well want to press charges. Then again, once the bruising has died down, by which time Mr Al-Rahman will probably be well out of the jurisdiction and beyond extradition, she may decide that a few hundred thousand is a price she's prepared to pay for her – let's face it – dubious virtue.' He turned to Julia. 'Come on – no point in hanging round here.'

After they had gone, Anthony trawled the rooms of the suite – Hakim remained pinned down in the living room, where tidying up operations were in progress, the bedroom was still a scene of weeping and agitation – but Gabrielle was nowhere to be seen. Anthony assumed she must have left, but he couldn't understand why she had left without telling him.

'Have the police been called?' he asked Edward.

'No idea. Only a matter of time, I imagine. Hey, is there anything left in that bottle of champagne over there? Pass it over, there's a good chap.'

Anthony retrieved his overcoat and slipped out of the building, keying in Gabrielle's number. If the police were eventually called and decided they needed to talk to everyone, they could always get hold of him. But there was no reply from her phone. It was half one, but he managed to find a cab without difficulty, and headed to Holland Park.

When he reached her flat, he could see no light on. He left the cab waiting at the kerb, and buzzed the bell. But there was no reply. He stepped back out onto the rainy pavement and looked up again at the dark windows. Then he took his mobile from his pocket and keyed in her number again. Still nothing but voicemail. Whatever had happened at the poker game had left her in a state, he now realised, and he probably should have stayed with her. He guessed she had probably gone to her parents, as she occasionally did, and it wouldn't do to call there at this hour. He would speak to her in the morning.

CHAPTER TWENTY-TWO

Anthony tried Gabrielle's mobile several times the next morning, but each time it went straight to voicemail. He assumed she must be at her parents' house – she'd certainly seemed badly upset by the events of last night, for reasons that weren't wholly clear – and that she would answer his calls when she felt like it. He had learnt to deal with her occasional bouts of moodiness, and periods of radio silence.

Around half eleven Edward dropped by the flat, a bundle of Sunday newspapers under his arm.

'God, what a night! I've only had four hours' sleep. Thought you might fancy a spot of brunch to discuss it all. There's a good place I know in Chelsea. Come on, grab your coat!'

They drove to Chelsea in Edward's Alpha Romeo convertible. It was a chilly ride, because the soft top was jammed in the down position. Edward explained he kept meaning to get it fixed, but just hadn't got round to it.

'So, were the police called?' asked Anthony, keen to

know how matters had developed after he'd left. Above all, he wanted to know if he could expect any fallout from the final, disastrous round of poker.

Edward shook his head. 'So far as I know, the Saudis are buying their way out of it. Some Arab chaps came and picked up the fat, drunk one, and Caspar brokered a deal between the Saudis and the Russian girls. That may not be the end of it, of course. Turns out he didn't actually rape her – not that that's the point, trying to is just as bad – but he did assault her. Keeping it all quiet is going to cost them quite a packet. Is that a parking place up the end there?'

They continued the discussion over bacon, eggs, grilled tomatoes and hash browns, plus champagne cocktails which Edward insisted were necessary to bring about his full recovery. He drank one off straight away, and handed the empty glass to the waitress. 'Two more of those please, and a jug of freshly squeezed orange juice. So – shame about your poker game. Piers said it was just getting interesting when everything kicked off.'

'You could say that. I think it was probably just as well for both of us that it ended the way it did.'

'Rubbish hand?'

'Actually,' said Anthony, 'I was on my way to an ace-high flush. But you know how it is – it's always possible someone's holding a better hand. I think last night made me realise I'm not a very good gambler. I reckon I'll give it a rest. It's put quite a dent in my finances.'

'I suppose it's all about knowing your limitations. Caspar said he's redistributing last night's pot, so everyone gets their stake back. Tom's pretty chuffed, since he was about sixteen thousand down.'

'Well, it was twenty thousand I couldn't exactly afford to lose either.'

'So – no winners, no losers.' The waitress arrived with food, orange juice, and two fresh champagne cocktails. 'Excellent,' said Edward. 'All we need now is a round of toast, and some brown sauce.'

When they left the restaurant a couple of hours later, after sifting and yawning their way through the Sunday papers, Anthony got Edward to drop him off at Gabrielle's flat. He stood on the corner and watched Edward roaring off, bellowing farewells, the chilly air tousling his hair. Anthony went into the building and rang the bell, but still there was no answer. He contemplated making the twenty-minute walk to her parents' house in Ennismore Gardens, but decided against it. If she couldn't be bothered to take his calls, why should he go chasing after her? He walked home, stopping at Waitrose on the way to pick up groceries, and spent the rest of the day catching up on chores and preparing for an interlocutory hearing the following day.

It was late on Monday afternoon when Jackie rang Leo in chambers.

'You'll think me very stupid, calling you like this. I was actually trying to reach Gabrielle's boyfriend, Anthony. But they say he's in court.'

It was a forcible reminder to Leo of a situation which he had so far failed to address, either emotionally or practically.

'Very likely,' said Leo. 'How can I help?'

'Gabrielle hasn't been answering her phone for two days. I spoke to some of her friends, and they haven't seen her or spoken to her either, even though she's meant to be at lectures today. I know she was going to some party with Anthony on Saturday. I thought he might be able to help because, frankly, I'm worried.'

'I'm sure she's fine. Probably just lost her phone.'

'Maybe. But I have to know she's all right. Could you have a word with Anthony? Just ask him to tell her to get in touch?'

Leo hesitated. 'Gabrielle hasn't told Anthony I'm her father, you know. He's going to wonder what she has to do with me.'

'Oh, Leo – I don't really care! Why is this some big secret? Daniel has no problem with people knowing, so why should you? Tell him you're an old friend of the family, if you like – whatever. I just have to find out that Gabrielle is all right.'

He could hardly refuse. Anyway, the situation was bound to turn into some kind of ridiculous charade, if someone didn't say something soon. Anthony might as well find out now. In a way, he was glad that matters were coming to a head.

'I'll speak to him when he comes back from court. He shouldn't be more than fifteen minutes or so.'

'Thank you.'

Leo put the phone down. He was possibly about to jeopardise the happiness of two of the people he cared most for in the world. But he had no choice. How Anthony would react, what he would say or do, was anyone's guess. Leo got up and strolled to the window. Halfway through January, and the days were beginning to lengthen slightly, dusk falling a little later each day. As he gazed down, he saw Anthony come from the cloisters and across Caper Court, still in his bands, his red robing bag slung over one shoulder.

Leo sighed. Time to grasp the nettle. He went downstairs to the clerks' room to intercept Anthony.

He found him going through the post from his pigeonhole, while Henry bent his ear regarding the fees on a new case.

'I'll have no problem justifying the fees, Mr C, but whether I'll get them or not is another matter. Still, I always work on the principle that if you don't ask, you don't get.'

'Well, do your best, Henry. I've had to do a bit of financial belt-tightening recently.'

'Anthony, have you got a minute?' said Leo. 'There's something I need to talk to you about.'

'Sure. I just need to put this stuff away.'

'That's OK. We can go to your room.' On the way upstairs Leo asked, 'What was all that about belt-tightening? Don't tell me you're still losing a fortune gambling.'

'No,' replied Anthony. His manner was curt, but as they reached his room, it relented. 'If you want to know, I've given all that up. Or at least, I've decided to. I'm not sure how easy it's going to be. To be honest I got myself into a hell of a mess. Mentally, I mean. It was getting obsessive.' He slung his robing bag in a corner of the room. 'I really wanted to talk to you about it – you know, that evening when you found me here going through my bank statements.'

'I know you did. Neither of us was in the right place. If you've made up your mind to stop, I reckon you'll do it without my help. But it's there if you need it. Remember that.' Leo moved some papers from a chair and sat down. 'There was something I wanted to tell you, too, that evening. I didn't, and I wish now I had, because events have rather overtaken me, and I find I must.'

Anthony loosened his collar stud and took off his bands.

He unbuttoned the neck of his collarless shirt and sat down at his desk, waiting. He could tell from Leo's face that it was something important.

'You're going to the High Court Bench?'

Leo shook his head impatiently. 'No word about that yet. No, this is more personal. It's about someone we both know. Gabrielle.'

Anthony stared. 'You know her?'

'Yes. Quite well, as it happens.'

'You're not—?'

Leo could see that if he didn't say something quickly, Anthony would start to jump to all kinds of ridiculous conclusions.

'For God's sake, I'm her father.' There was a silence. 'There. That's it. I had an affair with Gabrielle's mother twenty-odd years ago. She went back to France without telling me she was pregnant. I only discovered a few months ago that Gabrielle is my daughter. And Gabrielle only told me recently that she was seeing you.'

Anthony let this revelation sink in. It was a while before he could speak. 'This is unbelievable. You. Of all people—'

'I know. Not a great situation, is it?'

'Why didn't she tell me about this? Why didn't you?'

'She didn't tell you because she hasn't told a lot of people. She knows we work in the same chambers, but—'

'For God's sake, I've *talked* about you! She listened to me talking about you and she said nothing! Why?'

'That's something you'll have to ask her. I didn't tell you because . . . well, when I discovered Gabrielle was seeing you, I hoped your relationship might turn out to be a short-lived thing. I gather now, from what she tells me, that's not the case.'

'I don't know what she feels. I don't know what she thinks. I realise I don't know – anything.' Anthony put his head in his hands, trying to make sense of it. Certain things fell into place, the familiarity of things about her, mannerisms. All the time she had reminded him of Leo. Was that the reason he had fallen in love with her?

Leo was silent for a moment. He knew it would take Anthony some time to come to terms with it all – if he ever did. But there was also the matter of Jacqueline's phone call.

'The reason I'm telling you this now is because Gabrielle's mother rang me this afternoon, while you were in court. She's worried about Gabrielle. She can't get hold of her, hasn't heard from her in two days. She said she knew you and Gabrielle were going to a party on Saturday, and she hoped you might know where she is or why she hasn't been in touch.'

Anthony lifted his head from his hands. 'I haven't been able to get hold of her myself. The last time I saw her was at . . .' He hesitated. 'At that place on Saturday.'

'What place?' Leo began to feel alarmed. He'd been hoping Anthony would have an easy explanation for the lack of contact. 'Tell me exactly where you were and who you were with.'

'We were at Blunt's. It's a members-only casino in Mayfair. The owners were hosting a private poker game for some Saudi playboys. The game was going on in one room, and there was some kind of party going on in another. I was playing poker.'

'And?'

'Something kicked off next door. I think one of the Saudis got drunk and tried it on with one of the girls – away from the party, I mean, in a bedroom. The word was he tried to rape her, and that he knocked her about, assaulted her. I don't really know. Like I say, I was in the poker game.'

'And Gabrielle?'

'When I left the game with everyone else to find out what was going on, she was . . .' He frowned, recalling. 'She was standing in the doorway, and Edward and some other guy were holding the man. The one who'd tried to rape the girl. She was shocked. Well, all the girls were, I suppose, but Gab seemed really shaken. White-faced. I went into the bedroom to see what was going on, and when I went back to find her, she'd gone.'

'She'd left?'

'She must have. No one saw her go. I kept ringing her mobile, and I went round to her flat, but she wasn't there. I assumed she'd gone to her parents' place. I kept ringing the next morning, and went round to her flat again. Then I gave up, decided to wait till she got in touch with me. She does this sometimes. Goes out of radio contact for a few days, for whatever reason.' He stared at Leo, as if seeing Gabrielle through him, still trying to fathom the fatefulness of it all, that Leo should be Gabrielle's father.

'She didn't show up at college today, no one's seen or heard from her,' said Leo. 'I need to know more about Saturday night. After the incident, I take it the police were called?'

'No. That is, Caspar Egan, the chap who runs Blunt's, was all set to call them, but when I spoke to Edward the next day he said the Saudis persuaded him not to, paid everyone off to try and hush it up. I don't know how it was done. I'd left before it happened.'

'So Gabrielle thought the police were going to be called?'

'I suppose so,' said Anthony slowly. 'I don't know. You think that's why she left? But where could she possibly have gone if she didn't go home, or to her parents?'

'I think I have an idea. At any rate, don't worry. No need to post her as a missing person just yet. I'll call her mother.' Leo rose and went to the door. He paused and turned. 'Look, I realise what I've told you has come as a shock. It's going to be hard for you to get your head around, but it will sort itself out in time. It's just a question of recognising priorities, making things work.'

Anthony sat back in his chair and gazed at Leo, then nodded, his face expressionless.

Leo went back to his room and called Jacqueline.

'I've spoken to Anthony. He hasn't heard from Gabrielle either. Apparently there was some trouble at whatever party they were at, and there was an idea the police were going to be called. They weren't, as it happens, but I think for some reason the possibility scared her, and she took off.' Leo was on his laptop, tapping at the keys as he talked.

'But why would she do that? And where would she go? If she was frightened for whatever reason, surely she would come to us. Why would she be scared of the police? What kind of trouble was there at the party?'

'Some man attacked a girl. I really don't know the full story, and I don't know why Gabrielle should be scared, but if she was, I have an idea where she might have gone. I bought a place in Antibes recently, and I took her down there to look at it and help me furnish it. If for whatever reason she's taken fright, she may well have gone there.'

'Leo, I want to call the police. Daniel doesn't know about

any of this – that no one's seen or heard from her in two days – and I have to tell him.'

'Will you give me a few hours, Jackie? Because if there was a reason why she was afraid of the police, it might not be a good idea to call them just yet.'

'But what if you go to France and she isn't there? Then we've wasted time!'

Leo tapped again at the keyboard. 'I've been looking up flights to Nice, and there's one in three hours. If I catch that, I'll be down there by eleven, with the time difference. It's only a fifteen-minute drive to Antibes. I'll ring you as soon as I get to the apartment. If she isn't there, then you can call the police. OK?'

There was a brief silence. 'All right. If you really think that's where she's gone—'

'I do. I could be wrong, but if I am, we'll know in a matter of hours. OK?'

He had been making the booking as he spoke, and when she rang off he completed it, checked in, and printed off the boarding card. He glanced at his watch. It was half five now, and his car was parked at the end of King's Bench Walk. Driving to Gatwick should take no more than an hour and a half, rush hour traffic permitting, which would be about right. He closed his laptop, tidied away his papers, put on his jacket and overcoat, and hurried down to the clerks' room.

'Felicity, I need you to cancel tomorrow morning's ten o'clock con with Peter Jago and rearrange it for later this week. Apologise to him, tell him I'll buy him a drink. Then – and I need you to listen carefully – I want you to go onto a car rental website and book a hire car that I can pick up at

Nice airport at eleven o'clock tonight. Any car, don't worry about the cost, just get me one. Then find me a room in a hotel in Antibes, and text me the name and location. In return, I shall take you out to lunch. I may not be back in the office till Wednesday morning.'

Hurrying out, Leo almost collided with Henry in the doorway, and flung him a hasty apology.

'What's his hurry?' asked Henry.

'Don't ask me,' replied Felicity. 'All I know is he's catching a flight to Nice in a couple of hours, and I've got to book him a hire car and a hotel room for the night.'

'Man of mystery.' Henry shook his head. He glanced at an oblong cardboard box lying on Felicity's desk. 'Looks exciting.'

'Not that thrilling. It's my new set-top box. Only trouble is, I'm worried I won't be able to set it up. The bloke said it was dead simple, but I've read through the instructions, and I can't work it out. Not very good with gadgets.'

Henry examined the box. 'I can sort it out for you, if you like.'

'Oh, would you, Henry? That would be brilliant.'

'Can do it this evening, if you're not busy. I've just got to pop round to Cheryl's first.' He tried to look matter-of-fact as he said this, but in reality the brief visit to Cheryl's would be momentous, involving as it did the return of the power drill her father had lent him, and the acknowledgement that the relationship between them had come to an end. It had begun to founder during the holiday with Cheryl and her family. He should have realised at the time that it was a mistake, but at least he had realised before it was too late that Cheryl was one thing, but Cheryl together with her family – well, that was quite another. And since Cheryl was looking for a husband, what was the point of wasting her time, or his? The pang he felt was more for the failure of romance, rather than the loss of Cheryl herself.

'This evening's fine. I can cook us something, if you like.'

'That's all right – I don't want to put you out. The set-top box shouldn't take more than a few minutes.'

'No, really.' She smiled at Henry. 'I'd like to.'

'OK. Lovely. I'll be round about eight.'

The grind through the rush hour traffic took a frustrating hour, but when Leo finally got onto the M23 after Croydon, things began to speed up. Then after fifteen minutes he saw red tail lights building up ahead, and the traffic slowed to a crawl. Listening to useless local traffic information about an accident at Junction 14, he cursed himself for not taking the train. He would have been at the airport by now. Not for the first time, he reflected on how limiting a car could be in London, even a top of the top-of-the-range Aston Martin. In fact, having a fast car made the whole thing even sadder. If he didn't make this flight, he would have to call Jacqueline, and let her take matters into her own hands.

But gradually the traffic began to ease, and he reached the airport just after half seven. Once he had parked and walked to the terminal, the flight was already boarding, and he had to run to the gate. He boarded the plane with the tail-end stragglers, and took a seat at the back, a little out of breath, relieved to have made it.

Without the distraction of a book or a newspaper, he was left entirely to his own thoughts on the flight. He found his concern was centred not on Gabrielle, but on Anthony.

Gabrielle – unless for some reason Anthony decided to tell her – need never know about his own relationship with Anthony. But Anthony was well aware of how grotesque it all was. His lover was the daughter of a man with whom he'd slept – only once, admittedly, but degrees of normality did not apply to this situation. There was no knowing the extent to which it might alter, or even destroy, Anthony's relationship with Gabrielle. Anthony knew that Leo had never stopped loving and wanting him. And it was he who had always put those possibilities out of bounds, admitting only the elements of profound friendship and unspoken emotional attachment. The incestuous nature of this entanglement would be too much for him. He would retreat, of that Leo was pretty sure. How would that affect Gabrielle? Leo had no idea. She was young. Leo wasn't even sure how deeply she felt about Anthony. By the end of the year, it probably wouldn't matter. As for himself, his part in all this was debatable. He had no reason to feel guilty – the coincidence of the circumstances would be risible if not so wretched – but for some reason he did. He decided not to explore this, but closed his eyes, trying to empty his mind of all concerns except finding Gabrielle safe and sound in Antibes.

CHAPTER TWENTY-THREE

Henry left Cheryl's with a heavy heart. A naturally kind person, he didn't like hurting anyone, and Cheryl had cried a lot. But there was simply no point in going on with a relationship with someone you didn't really love. It wasn't fair. He wondered, as he caught the train to Brixton, whether he would ever find anyone to love and settle down with. Maybe there was no such thing as the perfect person. Maybe everything in life was a compromise. He was glad he had promised to sort out Felicity's set-top box; it was something to take his mind off the business with Cheryl.

When he arrived at the flat, Felicity had laid the table for supper.

'I'm just doing us steaks and baked potatoes,' she said. 'And a bit of salad. Nothing fancy.'

'Sounds ideal. Here, I picked up a bottle of wine at the off-licence on the corner.'

'Lovely! I'll go and open it.'

Henry took off his jacket and unpacked the set-top box, while Felicity took the wine through to the kitchen.

A few moments later, as Henry was examining scart leads, Felicity returned with two glasses. 'I'll just leave yours here,' she said, setting down Henry's wine on the coffee table.

'Thanks. This shouldn't take long.'

She sipped her wine, watching Henry on his hands and knees, trying to sort out the various connections. It was nice to have a man around, helping out. Vince had rarely done a hand's turn, and even when he did it had usually ended in failure, making more work than there had been to start with. Henry wasn't like that. He was competent, industrious, and he did things conscientiously and well. She knew that from years of working with him.

'How do you like your steak?' she asked.

'Medium rare, thanks.'

'Right – same as me. They'll only take a few minutes.' It was a little thing, but it pleased Felicity. Vince had always insisted on having his steak well done, and she'd hated cooking perfectly good bits of meat to a frazzle, only to have him complain that she never got it right, not like his mum. As she watched Henry work, she wondered vaguely how Denise was coping.

'OK. All done.' Henry emerged from behind the television. 'Pass us your remote.'

Felicity left Henry to set up the channels and went back to the kitchen to cook the steaks. When she came back through, she found Henry sipping his wine and watching a shopping channel. 'There you go. All your extra channels. You'd still be better off getting a dish, though, or cable.'

'This will do to be going on with. It's brilliant. Thanks. Now switch it off and come and get some food.'

Over supper they chatted about the goings-on in chambers. It was gossipy, relaxing, and pleasantly intimate. Afterwards, they cleared up and tidied the kitchen together.

'Still a couple of glasses left,' remarked Felicity, holding up the bottle Henry had brought. 'Shame not to finish it.'

They settled themselves on Felicity's sofa and Henry picked up the remote. 'Want to watch one of your new channels?'

'Sounds daft after you've gone to all that trouble, but I think I'd rather just talk.'

'Fine by me.'

'So, how's everything with you and Cheryl? Still all loved-up?'

Henry twisted the stem of his glass. 'Not really. You know I said I was going round to see her tonight? Well, it was to tell her I was ending it.' He took a swig of his wine. 'And to give her back her dad's power drill.'

'Oh, Henry – why?'

'Because I'd finished the shelves – oh, I see. Sorry. Because . . . well, because she wants something long-term, and I don't love her enough for that. And it seems unfair to let her think it's going to turn into something it's not.'

'That's such a shame.'

'Yeah. But it would have been an even bigger shame if we'd got married and it hadn't worked out.'

'I suppose.' Felicity glanced up at the sudden sound of someone knocking on the front door. 'God, that gave me a fright. Who is it at this time?'

She went down the hallway and opened the front door. There stood Vince.

'Hello, Fliss. How you doing?' He smiled, and Felicity could tell immediately that he'd been drinking.

'Vince, I don't want you round here. You and me are over. So piss off.' She tried to close the door, but Vince held it open.

'You don't mean that. You were upset a few weeks back, but now you've had time to get over it, and you and me just need to have a little chat and sort things out. Isn't that right?'

'No, it's not right – get out!' She tried shoving the door shut again, but Vince leant against it, and a second later he was inside the flat.

'We've got a bit of unfinished business, Fliss. I mean, why did you have to do stuff like change the locks? Couldn't you just say to my face you wanted me gone?' His tone of wheedling aggression and the stink of stale beer set off a sudden explosion of anger in Felicity. Why couldn't he just get out of her life and stay out?

'Because it wouldn't have made any difference!' she shouted. 'Because if I hadn't done what I did, you'd still have been here, still a big, useless waste of space. So get out – now!'

Henry came into the hallway. 'What's going on, Fliss? You all right?'

'Oh, hello – it's what's-his-name.' Vince grinned. 'Henry, isn't it? What a surprise, you being here, all cosied up with my girlfriend.'

'I think you'll find she's not your girlfriend any more.'

'*I think you'll find*? What kind of bollocks talk is that?' Vince advanced up the hallway towards Henry. 'I think you'll find my fist in your gob, mate, if you don't shut it.'

Henry, who was stocky and by no means unathletic, squared his shoulders as Vince approached. But Vince was a good few inches taller than Henry, and unlike Henry was no stranger to casual brawling, so the contest, if it came to it, was bound to go only one way. Felicity could see this, and quickly stepped between them. She tried to speak calmly and reasonably.

'Stop it, Vince. You're wasting your time coming here. You know that. Just leave. Please.'

Vince gave a contemptuous snigger. 'You're not seriously telling me you're picking him over me, are you? This half-baked tosser?'

'Henry's my friend. That's all. And even if he was more than that, what would it be to you? Nothing in my life has anything to do with you any more, Vince. You're irrelevant to me. And you know what's sad about that? What's sad is that it didn't have to be that way. If you'd tried a bit harder, if you'd taken a bit more pride, cared more about me – we might have been all right.' Felicity's eyes brightened with tears as the truth came out. Vince's smile faded, and his gaze faltered from Henry's face to hers. Something in him seemed to slacken as he listened. 'I really loved you once, Vince. I could have gone on loving you if only you'd tried to make it worth my while. But you never did. You just took and took and took, and gave nothing. There are two types of people in this life, Vince – givers and takers, and you're a taker. You moved in here, you sponged off me, you never tried to find work or make something better of your life. You took all my love and affection and gave nothing back.' The tears spilt over and down her cheeks. 'If you'd really loved me, if you'd wanted any kind of future for us, you'd have done more to sort your life out. Maybe if you hadn't had it so easy here, you'd have tried harder – who knows? But you didn't. And I lost all respect for you. And I stopped loving you. So you coming round here after you've had a few beers and shouting the odds is going to get you precisely nowhere.' She sniffed, and wiped her nose with the back of her hand. 'Do you see that?'

Vince stared at her, baffled. She could see in his eyes that if Henry hadn't been there he would have tried to wheedle and plead, and ask for another chance. But the remnants of his pride couldn't let him do that in front of Henry. He shook his head. 'That's wrong,' he muttered. 'All of it.' He turned his angry gaze to Henry, and for a second Felicity thought he was going to go for him. But something in Vince had been defeated by her words. He simply turned and left, slamming the door behind him.

Felicity felt shaky, and oddly worn out, and began to cry in earnest. Henry came and put his arms round her. They stood there for a long moment, until her tears subsided.

'Well done. Saying what you said – that was brave.'

'Not really. I was just being honest.' She wiped her eyes. 'I feel sorry for him, more than anything else.'

'You're too nice. I've always said it.' He kissed her forehead lightly, happy just to be holding her.

'No, I'm not. You're the nice one.'

'Then we're a nice pair.' He smiled at her, hesitated, then kissed her mouth. He waited for her to resist, to push him away. But she didn't. She let him kiss her. Something sad in Henry's heart told him she was just being kind, or kissing him for the comfort of it, but he gave himself up to the pleasure of it, enjoying it while he could.

‘I’m not sure about this,’ said Felicity, when the kiss had ended.

‘No, well.’ Henry stroked a stray curl of hair from her forehead. ‘It doesn’t matter.’ He moved away from her, turning to go into the living room. ‘I should be heading home.’

She grabbed his arm. ‘Henry, it does matter. This evening was lovely. Being with you just feels so – so normal. That’s what I’m not sure about. If it’s the right thing to feel. Or whether I just feel that because I’m used to being with you. And you’re the last person in the world I would ever want to hurt.’

He smiled. ‘That’s a good start.’

She put her arms around him. ‘It is, isn’t it? A start, I mean.’ She kissed him lightly. Dear Henry. It had never occurred to her, till now, how safe and secure she felt with him. Suddenly she wanted very much to kiss him again. But instinct told her that this had to be taken slowly and gently. ‘Why don’t we do this again? I mean, you could come round another time and—’

‘Stop being such a giver. My place next time. I’ll do the cooking. OK?’

She smiled. ‘OK.’

When Leo arrived in Nice a hire car was waiting for him, and Felicity had texted the name of the hotel he was booked into. He took the motorway route, and twenty minutes later he was turning into the car park of the hotel on the harbour front. He parked the car and walked to the Cours Massena. The town had a dead feeling, only a handful of bars and restaurants open, the rest closed for the winter. As the apartment building came into view, he gazed up anxiously at the windows of the third floor, but could see no lights on. He felt a little sick inside. Perhaps his hunch had been wrong. He should have let Jacqueline call the police when she wanted to. Perhaps he had wasted valuable hours.

He let himself in and hurried upstairs and unlocked the door. The apartment was empty, but to his unspeakable relief, a canvas overnight bag sat on the floor, next to a sleeping bag. He went through to the kitchen and found an opened bag of pasta, a jar of pesto, and unwashed dishes and a pan in the sink. Leo took his mobile from his pocket and rang Jacqueline.

'She's here.'

'Oh, thank God! Can I speak to her?'

'I mean, her things are here. She's not. She must have gone out somewhere. But the good thing is, you can stop worrying.'

'I'm so relieved! But I still need to know what's going on, why she left!'

'I know, I know. So do I. I'll talk to her, and tomorrow I'll get her to call you. OK?'

'OK.' There was a pause. 'And thank you, Leo.'

'It's what any father would do.'

When he had hung up, Leo paced around the apartment. She could be in any one of the bars and clubs he had passed. The sensible thing would be to wait till she got back. But the place was still unfurnished, with not even a chair to sit in. Besides, his instincts told him that if she was troubled – and he believed she was – she wasn't looking for the company of other young people. He asked himself what he would do in her shoes, alone, here, trying to make sense of some problem. He left the apartment, walked up the quiet midnight streets to the castle, and along the deserted sweep of the ramparts that looked out over the port.

After he had gone a little way, he saw a solitary figure sitting on the ramparts wall. It had to be her. As he came closer, she turned at the sound of his feet on the cobbles.

'Hello,' he said. 'I thought I might find you here.'

'Leo!'

'You've got everyone very worried back home.' He swung himself onto the wall and sat next to her, digging his hands deep in his overcoat pockets. She was wearing a thick jacket, but she looked cold. He put an arm around her, and she leant into his shoulder and began to cry.

'I'm sorry,' she said through her tears. 'I didn't mean to worry anyone. I've just been so frightened and miserable, I didn't know what to do.'

'Hey, hey. No need to be frightened. Is this to do with what happened on Saturday?'

She took her head from his shoulder and stared at him, sniffing. 'How do you know about that?'

'I spoke to Anthony. And just so you know – the police weren't called.'

'Really?' She looked visibly relieved.

'I gather some money changed hands, and the whole thing is being hushed up.'

She buried her face in her hands. 'Oh, God. I don't know whether that's good or bad. Good for me, I suppose.'

'Look,' said Leo, 'what do you say we go somewhere and talk about this?' She nodded, wiping her eyes. 'I'm booked into a hotel down on the harbour. You might as well stay there tonight, too. That sleeping bag at the flat doesn't exactly look comfy. Come on.'

They walked down the deserted street to the harbour, and along the quay to the hotel.

'How did you know I was here?' asked Gabrielle.

'Just a hunch. I asked myself where I would go, what I would do, if I was afraid and wanted to hide somewhere.'

They checked into the hotel, and went through to the bar, which was deserted, but still open. 'Sit down, and I'll get us both a drink, and see if we can rustle up some food. I haven't eaten all day. Have you got any cash?'

Twenty-five euros persuaded the bar manager to produce from the kitchen some bread and fruit, and a hunk of brie, and they sat in the silence of the bar with a glass of wine each, and ate a late supper.

'So, what made you run all the way down here?' said Leo. 'Why were you so terrified of the police being called?'

Gabrielle had taken off her coat, and in her sweatshirt, jeans and trainers, with her hair tied back, she looked very young and vulnerable. 'OK, I'll tell you the whole thing. I should probably have told Anthony, but I was too – well, I was a bit high.'

'What do you mean?'

'I'd taken some coke.' She glanced at Leo's face. 'I know. Don't look like that. It was just there.'

'Well, for an aspiring barrister, it was a remarkably dumb thing to do. Potentially career-ending. That can't be the reason why you hopped on a flight to France, though.'

'No. But when you wrap it up with everything else that happened . . .' She sighed and pushed her plate away. 'You see, one of the Russian girls, Dina, had gone into the bedroom because she was a bit drunk and wanted to lie down. Well, I only know that now. I wasn't aware then.

And one of the Saudi guys went in after her. I wasn't aware of that, either. The first time I realised there was anyone in the bedroom was when I went into the bathroom, which was in between the bedroom and the room where the party was, and while I was in there I heard this sort of muffled shouting from the bedroom. I opened the door to see what was going on, and there was this fat Arab guy – Hakim, I think his name was – with his trousers round his ankles, Dina with her dress round her waist, and him trying to drag off her knickers with one hand. He had his other hand over her mouth. She was struggling and kicking, and then suddenly he just fetched her one really hard across the face, and her nose began pouring with blood. It was horrible. So I ran into the room and tried to pull him off, and he began to stumble about, and the next thing I knew one of the other Saudis had come in. He pulled the door shut behind him, so it was just the four of us in there. He saw what was going on, and he was hissing things at Hakim, presumably telling him to pull his trousers up and get out. And I said something like, "Hold on a minute – he was trying to rape her. I saw him." And he just rounded on me, saying things like, "You're all sluts. You deserve what happens. Nothing happened here. You didn't see a thing." And I said, "I most certainly did. What I saw was attempted rape and assault, and I'm going to make sure everyone knows." So I headed for the door, and he followed, trying to grab me, but I made it into the sitting room and – well, I just started shouting about what I'd seen. And the next thing I knew a load of people had gone in and grabbed Hakim, and the other Russian girls were all freaking out, because Dina was just lying on the bed with blood all over her face. It was kind of mayhem.' She stared at her plate, then picked up a piece of Brie rind and nibbled it.

'And then?'

'Then I was just sort of standing in the doorway of the sitting room with all this chaos erupting, and Anthony came out of the poker game and asked what was going on. I told him, and he went through to the bedroom. Then a couple of seconds later the other Saudi guy came out and saw me, and he pushed me into the corridor and grabbed the top of my arm and said something like, "If the police are called, and you say anything, if you say one word about what you saw, I'll make sure you regret it." He sounded so vicious, and I was really scared. And then he asked me if I'd ever seen what a girl looked like after she'd had acid thrown in her face. Because that was what was going to happen to me if I told the police what happened.' Her eyes filled with tears again. 'It sounds so stupid now, but I was a bit drunk, and a bit high, and when Caspar Egan said he was calling the police, I just had to get out of there. I thought if I got away for a week or so, till everything had died down, maybe no one would mention that I'd been there, or that I might have seen something.' She was weeping now, her shoulders shaking. 'I was just so scared. I know it was stupid to run away. I know if the police had been called that it would only have made things worse, but at the time . . .'

Leo laid a hand on her arm. 'Come on. You overreacted, but you were scared.'

'All last night I just lay in the apartment in my sleeping bag, thinking about what would happen if there was a trial, and I had to give evidence. You know, I really believe that man would have carried out his threat.' She gazed at Leo with large, haunted eyes.

'Well, you can forget about that, because it's not going to happen. What you need now is a good night's sleep. We'll talk some more tomorrow. On the way home.'

Later, Gabrielle lay on her bed for a long time, staring at the ceiling of the hotel room, thinking. She picked up her mobile phone from the bedside table and scrolled to Anthony's number. Late as it was, she should call him and tell him where she was, and why. Then she stopped and sighed. It was all so complicated, and she felt so tired. What if Anthony had decided it was over between them, because of Leo? She didn't think she could deal with that. Not tonight. She put the phone back on the table and closed her eyes. Tomorrow. She would find out the worst tomorrow.

CHAPTER TWENTY-FOUR

The next day, Leo and Gabrielle caught the late afternoon flight to London, and talked for the entire journey, mainly about Anthony.

'The difficult part yesterday, talking to Anthony about you, to try to find out where you were, was telling him that you're my daughter.'

'Why? I mean, why was that difficult?'

This stalled Leo. Gabrielle could have no possible inkling about his relationship with Anthony. At last he said, 'Perhaps not difficult, but it was always going to be a bit of a surprise.'

'If you're such close friends, I don't know why you hadn't told him before.' Gabrielle felt a little sorry for Leo, but it irritated her that he seemed unable to utter the truth. One of them was going to have to. It looked like it was going to be her.

'It's complex.' Leo knew it was lame, but it was the best

he could do. Then after a moment he asked, 'Why didn't you tell him? He seemed surprised that my name had come up in conversation between you two, but that you'd never said anything.'

'Oh, Leo . . .' Gabrielle sighed. 'It's because I know there's something going on between the two of you. And I didn't want to have to . . . I don't know . . . confront it. Or mess it up.'

Leo looked away. Then he said, 'I take it Anthony has said something.'

'Nothing. I mean, apart from lighting up when he talks about you. No, it was one night when I was – well, not stalking you, but following you about, trying to summon up courage to speak to you. You and he had come out of the bar in Middle Temple, and you stopped and talked for a bit. And then you kissed him. I mean, properly. It wasn't hard to work out you were more than just good friends.'

'I see.'

There was another long silence. Then Leo turned to Gabrielle and said, 'You knew that, and yet it didn't deter you from starting a relationship with Anthony. I find that odd. Or maybe it was the reason you did.'

'How d'you mean?'

'Some perverted kind of curiosity?' He saw from her face that he had hit a nerve. 'We're not so very unalike.'

At length Gabrielle said, 'How close are you?'

'Close. More so, once upon a time. But Anthony made a deliberate choice. He doesn't want to operate in my strange world. I suppose I'm glad, in the long run. It's not easy.'

'All this – will it make Anthony feel he has to choose between us?'

'It might. I don't know. It shouldn't. I think you'll have to give him time, though. Do you love him?'

'Yes. Yes, I do. If he decided to end our relationship because of this, I'd be desperately miserable. And I would feel hugely guilty.'

'Not quite so guilty as I would, believe me.'

'But I'd get over it. As one does.'

'As one does.' Leo was disconcerted to see his own emotional pragmatism reflected back. 'I can talk to him. He shouldn't feel he has to choose, or give you up, or anything of that kind. What exists between Anthony and myself is very deep, emotionally, but it goes no further.'

She closed her eyes. 'I'm beginning to feel that my coming into your life has caused you nothing but trouble.'

'The trouble is not of your making. It's just luck, fate, call it what you like. And having you in my life makes me very happy, believe me.' She opened her eyes and smiled at him, and he added, 'We're rather a strange pair of people, though, aren't we?'

They arrived at Gatwick a little after seven, and Leo drove them back to West London.

'Holland Park or Kensington?' he asked, as they headed across Battersea Bridge.

'Kensington, please.'

Leo nodded. 'I should think your mother will be very pleased to see you.'

'Maybe. But it's Anthony I intend to see first. I need to find out what he's thinking, whether it's going to make a difference to us.'

'If he loves you, I don't think it should.'

'No – but like you said on the plane, it's complex.'

She got out, waited till Leo had driven out of sight, then walked up the steps and rang the buzzer to Anthony's flat.

'It's me,' she said when he answered.

There was a moment's hesitation, then Anthony said, 'Come on up.'

When she stepped out of the lift, he was waiting for her. He took her in his arms and held her very close for a long moment, and she realised with relief that it was all OK.

'Thank God. I've been so worried.' He kissed her hair. 'Where the hell have you been?'

'In France. At Leo's apartment. He guessed where I was and came and found me.'

'That's mad. Why France?'

'I was hiding. I was frightened.' She sighed. 'Let's go inside and I'll explain.'

While Anthony made tea, she lay on the sofa and kicked off her boots. Then they sat sipping their tea, Gabrielle's feet in Anthony's lap, while she told her story.

'So that's it. Pathetic, no?' she said when she had finished.

'I wish you'd come to me, instead of running away. I was worried. Everyone was.' Anthony massaged her toes through her socks.

She closed her eyes. 'That's lovely. Don't stop. I was going to ring you last night from the hotel, but I was too scared.'

'Scared of what?'

She opened her eyes. 'That after you'd found out that Leo was my father, you wouldn't want to see me any more.'

'How does that work?'

She gazed at him for a long moment. Had he been acting,

he would have looked puzzled. But then, he had no idea that she knew anything about him and Leo. She bit her lip. Who was hiding what from whom? Just as she was trying to decide whether to tell him what she knew, he leant over and took her face in his hands. 'It makes no difference to me that Leo is your father. I don't know why you didn't tell me sooner, or why you think it makes any difference to me now. But if we're going to be together, we have to be entirely honest with each other. About everything.'

Her eyes searched his face, but she could find no clue, nothing to tell her what Leo meant to him. But deep in her heart she thought she knew.

'Agreed?' asked Anthony.

She nodded, and let him kiss her, sealing a bargain she was already failing to keep.

Leo drove to Chelsea, feeling emotionally empty for reasons he could not fathom. Perhaps it was to do with the fact that Gabrielle and Anthony meant so much to one another, and he could now only regard himself as peripheral. The last twenty-four hours had taken it out of him, and the three things he needed now to restore his equilibrium, he decided, were a shower, a change of clothing, and a large Scotch.

When he had accomplished the first two, he came downstairs and poured himself a drink from the remains of the Macallan single malt on which Jamie had made such tremendous inroads at Christmas. Looking at the bottle reminded him of that evening, of lying on the sofa leafing through the book which Sarah had given him, Jamie snoring on the other side of the room, hearing the front door open and close as she came in. *The Lost Railways of North Wales* still lay on a small table near the window. He picked it up and turned it over. What a fool he'd been to let her go. Something had been wrong all the time she'd been staying here, but suddenly he no longer believed it had anything to do with Toby. He should have looked a little deeper.

On impulse, he picked up the phone and rang Sarah's mobile. When she answered, he could hear the clamour of a bar in the background.

'Sarah? It's Leo. You sound like you're busy.'

'A bit. Hold on.' Sarah turned to the young man she was with. 'I won't be a moment.' She slipped out of the noisy wine bar into the chilly street. 'Sorry, that's better. I can hear you now.'

'Look, I won't keep you. It's just I have to see you. Are you free on Friday?'

She had actually been reserving Friday for the man in the wine bar, a fairly interesting new romantic prospect, but decided he could wait. Calls out of the blue from Leo didn't come very often. Weak though it was, she wanted to see him.

'Yes, I think so.'

'You're in Leadenhall Street these days, aren't you? I can come to you, if you like.'

'There's a cocktail bar called Prism, just opposite the Lloyd's Building. We could meet there.'

'Perfect. I'll see you there at six.'

At half five on Friday afternoon reception rang Leo to tell him that Rachel was downstairs, asking to see him.

'Tell her to come up. She knows the way.'

Leo went to the landing to meet her. As soon as he saw

her he could tell, despite her smile, that she was nervous about something.

'Come in,' said Leo. 'This is a bit of a surprise.'

'I had a con with Geoffrey Dempsey, so I thought I'd come and see you.' She sat down, glancing round the room. 'I haven't been here in ages.'

'A special visit means you must be here for a special reason.'

A slight flush touched her pale cheeks. She smoothed down her dark hair with one hand. 'I suppose so.'

'Coffee?'

She shook her head. 'No, I won't stay long. It's something I need to tell you. I thought I'd rather do it face-to-face than over the phone.'

'Is it about Simon?'

She looked momentarily surprised. 'Yes. Yes, it is. Just after Christmas he asked if Oliver and I would like to go away on holiday at half-term. Just the three of us.'

'I have no objection.'

'Well, it's more than that. Simon has been staying off and on at mine for a while now. More on than off. And we've decided it would be a good idea if he moved in. Give up his flat. It makes more sense. And it means life is a bit more settled for Oliver.'

'I see.'

'And if it works out – that is, if we're still together in a few months' time, we plan on finding somewhere of our own. I mean, the house is part of the divorce settlement, and I don't think Simon likes the idea of staying there long-term.'

'That shows a commendable sensitivity.'

'Anyway, I felt you should know before it happens. Oliver is involved, after all.'

'Oliver's really fond of Simon, isn't he?'

'Yes, he is. They get on really well together.' She gazed at him. 'But you're his daddy. There's no question of Simon taking your place. Simon would never try to. And anyway, Oliver worships you.'

Leo got up and strolled to the window and stood staring down at the courtyard for a few moments. Then he turned round and gave her a smile. 'Well, thanks for telling me. I hope it all works out for you. Really I do. I wasn't a great husband. You deserve better. If everything Oliver says about Simon is true, he sounds a first-rate chap.'

'He is. But even though he and I are together, everything to do with Oliver goes on exactly as before. He'll come to you next weekend. Nothing changes.'

Everything changes, thought Leo. Rachel would only take this step if the relationship with Simon was truly serious, and they intended to settle down together. In a few years' time Oliver would probably have a baby brother or sister, maybe more than one. A family dynamic would develop, an ever-growing sphere of influence which would inch Leo further and further to the edge of Oliver's life. It was to be expected.

'I know. I'm sure it will all be fine. I want you and Oliver to be happy.'

Rachel glanced at her watch. 'I have to get back to the office. I just needed to tell you what's going on. I haven't told Oliver yet, but I will have by the time you next see him. Perhaps you could – you know, talk about it with him. If he wants to.'

'Of course. Come on, I'll see you out.'

They went downstairs, and after he had said goodbye to Rachel, Leo wandered into the clerks' room. Liam and Robert were playing an impromptu game of cricket with a ball of paper tied with pink legal tape and a rolled-up copy of the *Law Society Gazette*. Robert whacked the ball towards the door, exclaiming, 'Howzat!'

Henry, coming in, fielded it deftly. 'Enough, children,' he said, tossing the ball into the waste-paper basket. 'Liam, have all those Treasury fee notes been sent out yet? I thought not. Snap to it.' He glanced across at Felicity, who was trying to wedge a very large copy of *Chambers Legal Directory* beneath her computer monitor. 'Felicity, what are you doing?'

'My new monitor's too low. It's driving me nuts.'

'Well, that's no good. What if someone needs to consult the directory? Anyway, there's a thing at the back that slides it up and down. See?'

Michael came in at that moment, holding his umbrella.

'Felicity, I need a plaster. I cut my hand on my umbrella.'

'On your *umbrella*? Honest to God – I don't know how you manage to get through the day, Mr Gibbon, I really don't. Just a minute while I sort this monitor out, then I'll find the first-aid box.'

Henry wandered over to where Leo was standing by his pigeonhole, reading a letter. 'You look a bit grim, Mr D. Everything OK?'

'Here, take a look.' Leo handed the letter to Henry. 'The JAC reckon I'm not High Court Bench material, after all.'

Henry read the contents in disbelief. 'I can't understand it. I thought you were a dead cert. I'm really sorry, Mr D.

I mean, I always said it would have been a huge loss for chambers, but I know it's what you wanted.'

'Well, I did in some ways. But in other ways . . .' Leo glanced around the busy clerks' room and sighed. 'In other ways, I don't much mind. I'd be grateful if you didn't broadcast this, though.'

'Course not. Discretion is my watchword. Still – always next year, sir, eh?'

'Yes, Henry. There's always next year.'

As Leo left the clerks' room, Anthony came hurrying downstairs, pulling on his overcoat.

Leo took him aside. 'I've been meaning to talk to you. How is everything? With Gabrielle, I mean.'

Anthony turned up his coat collar and nodded. 'Good. Everything's good. Lucky you knew where to find her. Listen, I'm meeting my dad, and I'm late as it is—'

'Of course. We can catch up another time.' Those few words of Anthony's, the casual way they had been uttered, told him everything, and told it more clearly than if Anthony had sat down and talked to him for hours on end. His significance in Anthony's life had dwindled in comparison to the importance of Gabrielle. And maybe that was as it should be. It was clear, too, that she had mentioned nothing to Anthony of what she knew, and never would, no doubt hedging her bets that Leo would say nothing either. *Clever girl*, thought Leo.

As he put his foot on the stair, he heard Anthony's voice behind him. 'Leo . . .'

He turned. 'Yes?'

'I forgot to tell you. We got judgment in the Astleigh's casino case.'

'Oh?'

'We lost. Coulson decided that the twelve months the casino gave the Lion King to repay the two million pound debt amounted to illegal credit under the Gaming Act, so Astleigh's claim on the cheque was unenforceable. Still, the upside was that Al-Sarraj's counterclaim was dismissed. Coulson came out with a great line – "This is one of those cases which have everything to do with law, and nothing to do with justice."'

Leo smiled. 'Sounds like every case I've ever been involved in. Still, bad luck.'

Anthony shrugged. 'You win some, you lose some.'

'But you always get paid.'

Anthony smiled. 'Indeed. See you later.'

As he made his way upstairs, Leo suddenly realised that he should have been in the City ten minutes ago, meeting Sarah.

Chay and Anthony had arranged to meet in the bar of the Waldorf Hotel on the Strand. Chay had refused to say over the phone why he wanted to see Anthony, only that it was urgent. When Anthony arrived, Chay was sitting on the far side of the room, a solitary figure hunched in an armchair, still wearing his overcoat. The look of him reminded Anthony of the old Chay, the one who used to huddle cross-legged on the floor of unheated squats in his second-hand army greatcoat, pontificating about art and the excesses of the capitalist system. The only difference was that now the overcoat was cashmere, the granny glasses were expensive tortoiseshell-framed varifocals, and the lank hippy hair was trimmed to fashionable bristle. But Chay's face, latterly serene and self-confident, now wore the morose, disaffected expression of old, and Anthony felt a twinge of alarm as he sat down.

'You OK?' he asked.

'Not really.'

A bartender came over with an enquiring smile. Chay ordered a gin Martini with a twist, and Anthony a vodka and tonic.

'What's up?' asked Anthony.

Chay seemed to sink further into his seat. He stared at the table for a long time. Then he looked up and said, 'You'll have heard in the news about Bernie Madoff?'

Anthony swallowed. Remembering the conversation last time he'd seen his father, he suspected what was coming. 'Yes.'

'Well, he was the financier I met in Palm Beach, the one making investments for me. I'm one of his . . . his . . .' Chay decided to discard the word *client*. 'I'm one of his victims.'

There was a long silence.

'How much?'

Chay cocked his head, as though trying to evaluate, his glance straying round the empty bar.

'Everything. About eight and a half million.'

'Dollars?'

'Pounds.'

'Eight and a half million pounds. Right.'

Neither of them said anything. The waiter brought the drinks on a little silver tray. He laid paper coasters neatly on the table, and set down the chilled cocktails. They looked delicious. A little twist of lemon bobbed in the gin Martini, icy droplets trembled on the side of the vodka glass. Chay and Anthony stared at the drinks in silence. The waiter set down a bowl of nuts and crisps, and went away.

'The thing is,' said Chay, 'I invested Barry's money in that fucking Ponzi scheme.' He took off his glasses and ran a weary hand over his face. 'You were clever enough to see the returns were too good to be true. Your money is still safe and sound in the bank.' He replaced his glasses.

Anthony picked up his drink and drained half of it. 'No, you didn't.'

'I didn't what?'

'You didn't invest Barry's money. You invested mine.'

'What do you mean?'

'I mean . . .' Anthony paused, leaning forward to pick up a few peanuts. 'That you can regard the money in the bank as Barry's, and the hundred grand you lost as mine. Barry has nothing. He needs that money. He's working as a not-very-good stand-up comedian, and I don't think we're ever likely to see him in Forbes rich list.' Anthony popped the peanuts in his mouth and chewed reflectively. 'Mind you, you never know.'

'But you were the one who was sensible, who decided not to let me invest. You were right. Why should you lose out?'

'Because, Dad, if we'd had that conversation in the pub just one month later, I'd have happily told you to invest my money, every last penny. I would have let you gamble it on any old odds you cared to choose. Barry's need is greater than mine.' Anthony sat back. 'I'll always be OK. Do you know, I earned a hundred and twenty grand on a single case last year?'

'Really?' Interest flickered across Chay's features. He picked lemon peel from his Martini, ate it, then drained the glass in two gulps. 'I didn't know you were earning that much.'

'I am, and I intend to go on doing so. That money in the bank is Barry's. OK?'

'OK.' Chay shook his head.

Anthony drank the remains of his vodka and tonic. 'What will you do?'

Chay sighed. 'Oh, it's not the end of the world. I have the houses. I still sell paintings. I'll recover. I just feel such a fool. Such a dupe.' He leant forward suddenly, as though in pain. 'All that money.'

Anthony, who hadn't really felt sorry for his father till this moment, suddenly did. What Chay was regretting was not so much the loss of his wealth, as the loss of his shabby, discarded, idealistic old self. He had become the kind of individual whom he himself would have despised fifteen years ago.

'You're not alone. I've been doing some pretty stupid things myself lately. Mind you, eight and a half million is going it.' Anthony signalled to the waiter for the bill. 'I'll get these.'

Chay nodded. 'You seem to be earning enough. Thanks.'

When he'd paid for the drinks, Anthony stood up. 'Come on, let's go and have something to eat somewhere. I think you and I have a lot to talk about.' He slipped on his coat. 'My treat.'

As Anthony and Chay were leaving one cocktail bar, Leo was arriving at another. He was half an hour late, and was relieved to see Sarah at the far end of the room, sitting on a low sofa, texting on her phone. She looked up and smiled as Leo approached, tucking her phone in her bag.

'I was just about to give up on you.'

'Sorry,' said Leo. He slung his coat on a chair and sat down next to her. 'I got delayed in chambers. And the traffic gets worse every day. I took a taxi as far as Monument, and we sat there so long that I got out and speed-walked. I'm rather out of condition.' He glanced at the two drinks on the table, one of them a whisky. 'This for me?'

'You usually drink Glenfiddich, don't you?'

'Indeed I do.' He took a sip. 'Cheers.'

'Cheers.' Sarah surveyed him critically, thinking he looked a little jaded. 'How are you?'

'So-so. I got a letter from the Judicial Appointments Committee today. Apparently I'm not quite ready for the High Court Bench. Or it isn't ready for me. One of the two.'

'Oh dear. I suppose you'll just have to go on eking out a miserable living as a top QC.'

Leo smiled. 'Thank you. You're very good at putting things in perspective.'

'Seriously – I'm sorry you didn't get it. Any idea why?'

'Who knows? Greg Hind may not have given me his full approval. I can't think of anyone else with a reason to veto me. Your father's on the committee, of course. I hope you haven't been bad-mouthing me.'

Sarah suddenly felt cold inside. Could Leo's chances have been affected by something her father had said to the committee? When she had sought to blame Leo, in her father's eyes, for the break-up with Toby, it hadn't occurred to her that it might have professional repercussions for Leo. In fact, she had forgotten entirely about his application to become a judge.

'Would I do that?' she replied, in a light response to his joke.

'I suppose I shouldn't care as much as I do,' Leo went on. 'It's just—'

'What?'

'It's just that this is the first time since I came to the Bar, that I've felt a sense of rejection.'

'Well, you shouldn't feel that way. You know these things are all about internal politics. There's always next year.'

'Exactly what Henry said. But it rankles.' He shrugged. 'Listen to me. I'll always be the grammar school boy from the valleys, fighting for acceptance.' He glanced at Sarah. 'That's not something I could admit to many people.'

There was silence between them for a moment. Then Sarah asked, 'So, why did you want to see me this evening?'

'If I said, just to see you, would you believe me?'

'No. I might like to, but I wouldn't. I know you, Leo. There's always some agenda.'

'Well, it's the truth.' He swallowed the remains of his drink and placed the glass carefully on the table, hesitating for a moment. 'I've missed you. I've been missing you ever since you left.'

Sarah felt a space open up beneath her heart. She took a sip of her wine, unable to look at him. 'That's sweet. But we didn't exactly see that much of each other while I was living with you.'

'I know. And I've spent a lot of time wondering why that was.'

'You know why it was.'

'I assumed it was because you were regretting Toby, and that you hated me for the part I played in that.'

She looked at him in astonishment. 'Toby? It had nothing to do with him. The reason I kept my distance was because

I didn't like the idea of you stringing me along on the side while you conducted your surreptitious little affair.'

It was Leo's turn to look astonished. 'What affair?'

'Oh, come off it, Leo. Twenty-ish? Dirty blonde hair? About five foot two? Dress sense of a teenager? I know you have strange predilections, but knocking off some Olsen-twin lookalike who's young enough to be your daughter—'

Her words suddenly registered. Leo cut in, 'That's exactly who she is.'

'Who is who?'

'The girl. The one you've just described. She's my daughter. I thought about telling you, but you were being so hands-off, so hard to reach, that I never had the chance.'

'Your *daughter*?'

Leo signalled to a passing waitress. 'I think this calls for another drink.' He told her the whole story, and Sarah listened without interrupting.

When he had finished, she sighed, and said, 'I spent all those weeks thinking you were seeing someone, and not telling me.'

'I spent those weeks thinking you wished you'd never broken off your engagement. I thought you blamed me.'

'Blamed you? You threw me a lifeline.'

There was a long silence. Then Leo said, 'So, would you consider coming back for a while, and seeing how we get on without crossed wires?'

'What? You mean – live with you?'

'That's the general idea. We've done it before, and it was quite amusing, as I recall.'

Sarah gazed at him. She and Leo had been playing games

with one another for years. For her, the games had been a defence mechanism, a way of protecting herself against the truth that she loved him, would always love him. If she was honest with herself, she longed to be wanted and needed by Leo. Other men had always come second best. The trouble was, Leo had never wanted or needed anyone. Except, perhaps, Anthony. So why should she believe that this was any different? Telling her he'd missed her, and asking her to live with him – that had to be the closest he'd ever come to saying he loved her. And she badly wanted to believe he loved her. Maybe this time around they could stop playing games, and just exist for one another. Perhaps that was what he wanted, too. He would be hitting fifty in a couple of months, and playing the field was probably losing its appeal. But if she was wrong, if he finished up hurting her and betraying her, then she didn't think she could bear it. By saying yes, she would be gambling with her happiness.

After a long moment, she nodded. 'OK, why not? We didn't exactly give it a fair shake last time, did we?'

'Far from it. And when I said I missed you, I meant in every possible way.' Leo leant forward and kissed her for several seconds. Then he glanced around. 'I don't think we can stay here and do this for very long. I suggest we take a cab to Chelsea. What do you think?'

Sarah smiled. 'It's the best offer I've had all day.' She drank the remains of her wine. 'Well, almost.'

Later that evening they lay in bed together, talking, caressing one another in an idle, familiar way. Leo had been telling her about Gabrielle's excursion to Antibes, and the reasons behind it.

Suddenly Leo's mobile buzzed on the bedside table. He hesitated, then picked it up. 'I'd better take this. It may be my daughter involved in some new drama.'

Sarah smiled, amused at how he loved using the words 'my daughter'. She watched him pull on his boxers as he answered the phone. He listened for a moment, then signalled to her that he would be back in a second. Sarah nodded and lay back contentedly, making plans for tomorrow, and wondering what she should do about the lease on her flat.

Leo stepped into his study and closed the door. He hadn't realistically expected to hear from Sergei. The recollection of that lithe, slender body, and the promise in those beautiful eyes made his pulse quicken. The conversation was brief, but when it was over, Leo stood for several moments, the phone pressed against his chest, thinking.

He went back to the bedroom. Sarah smiled and stretched lazily. 'Who was that?'

'No one important.' He glanced at Sarah, then at his phone, which was showing Sergei's number. He could either save it, or delete it. He hesitated for only a second before pressing the key.

tB.